W9-BSM-616

EYE CONTACT

EYE CONTACT

STEPHEN COLLINS

BANTAM BOOKS

NEW YORK TORONTO LONDON SYDNEY AUCKLAND

Grateful acknowledgment is made for permission to reprint lyrics from "JUST ONE OF THOSE THINGS" (Cole Porter). © 1935 WARNER BROS. INC. (Renewed). All Rights Reserved. Used By Permission.

EYE CONTACT

A Bantam Book / July 1994

All rights reserved.
Copyright © 1994 by Stephen Collins
Book design by Glen M. Edelstein

Library of Congress Cataloging-in-Publication Data
Collins, Stephen, 1946–
Eye contact / Stephen Collins.
p.   cm.
ISBN 0-553-09585-4
I. Title.
PS3553.047632E97   1994
813'.54—dc20   93-32771
CIP

Published simultaneously in the United States and Canada

Bantam Books are published by Bantam Books, a division of Bantam Doubleday Dell Publishing Group, Inc. Its trademark, consisting of the words "Bantam Books" and the portrayal of a rooster, is Registered in U.S. Patent and Trademark Office and in other countries. Marca Registrada. Bantam Books, 1540 Broadway, New York, New York 10036.

PRINTED IN THE UNITED STATES OF AMERICA

BVG   0 9 8 7 6

For Faye

EYE CONTACT

CHAPTER 1

Making better eye contact with her image in the mirror than she did with most people in life, Nicolette Stallings capped her lipstick, dropped it into her purse, exhaled, and whispered aloud to no one in particular, "Perfect."

She didn't often like the way she looked, but tonight she had to admit that the whole effect was just fine.

Nick Stallings was, in fact, at all times extraordinarily attractive. Not classically beautiful, but with a body that might bring a swimsuit issue to mind, she had, since she was very young, felt herself gawky and horsey looking. She had grown out of any such horsiness long before adolescence, but despite a near lifetime of causing heads to turn, she rated her looks "kind of average" and never let anyone convince her otherwise. Many tried, but the subject was always quickly changed.

On her way to the ladies' room, a handsome Wall Street type moving away from his table had casually overtaken Nick and whispered under his breath, just loudly enough for her to hear, "Great dress." The man had been sitting at a nearby booth with a woman

Nick figured to be his wife. From the look of the gifts exchanged and the champagne opened, Nick was pretty sure they were celebrating an anniversary.

The "great dress" alluded to was a short peachy cashmere. It hugged her hips in a way that might make a leg man reconsider his choices. Her breasts, unbound and all natural, moved against the cashmere in ways that were spoiling the Wall Streeter's dinner.

Nick had observed him trying to lock eyes with her several times. She'd made him crazy by meeting his look for only the briefest of noncommittal seconds. He couldn't be sure if she was returning his gaze or just . . . seeing him. She gave the guy points for the deftness with which he managed this attempted flirtation without tipping off his wife.

Nick had stood up, smoothed her dress, and said to her date she'd be right back, then headed to the ladies' room for an unneeded powder check. She wanted to see if her victim would follow and try to make contact.

She hadn't wholly admitted to herself that she was doing this.

He had followed.

Without acknowledging him, Nick continued around a corner and through the door marked FEMMES. He had said, "Great dress," but Nick had translated like this: "I'm going to the men's room, you're going to the ladies' room—if we time this right, we can exchange phone numbers before we go back to our tables."

She found herself lingering in the ladies' room, running her tongue around the rim of her freshly lipsticked mouth, enjoying the perfumy taste of the Chanel product she couldn't afford. Then she stood back from the mirror with her weight cocked on one hip and ran a hand through thick off-the-shoulder reddish hair.

The color *wasn't* all natural. When asked what her real hair color was, Nick always said she couldn't remember. If pressed, she would have testified that it was a dirty—some might even say mousy— blond. And since more than a few *had* said that, she'd changed it years ago. She'd been practically platinum, then red, and was now a vibrant, utterly convincing, strawberry-blonde.

Washing her hands, she wondered if Wall Street was waiting.

What're you doing? He's attracted. You know that now. Go back to your date, have a lovely dinner, get home early. You have to re-read your script, feed the fish, and get a good night's sleep.

Tomorrow she was meeting the director of an important upcoming film. Her agent had worked for weeks to arrange it. Nick had read the script and was perfect for the part, not the lead, but a solid supporting role, a possible scene-stealer, and one for which the studio didn't need a "name"—all very promising. While Nick had worked fairly steadily, she was a long way from being even remotely bankable. This director had won an Oscar two years before and was seeing only a few New York actresses. It was the kind of project Nick had been holding out for.

As she tossed the linen hand towel into a wicker basket, the ladies' room door opened with a loud creak. It was The Wife.

Nick figured it this way: When she and her date had first been seated, The Wife had spotted her. Everyone had. The cashmere dress always seemed to assure that. The Wife hadn't seen her husband glancing at or speaking to Nick—he'd been careful—but she'd certainly been *aware* of Nick, filing her away in a subconscious danger zone for potential sexual rivals. Noticing that her husband had left their table just after Nick had gone to the powder room, she'd waited a few minutes and then impulsively followed, still relatively secure that there was no cause for alarm. It was their anniversary, after all, and The Wife was quite attractive, probably used to being the most attractive woman around.

Now The Wife, who seemed tipsy, looked closely at Nick, then moved uncertainly toward a stall. Nick smiled a polite, unthreatening smile, and headed out the door.

And there was Wall Street, timing his exit from the men's room just so.

Go on back to your table, Nick thought to herself.

Instead, she raised one foot behind her and glanced back at it, marking time, checking one of her pumps for . . . what? Scuffs?

She wasn't going to speak first.

"What . . . uh . . . do you call that color?" he asked, taking a stab, sounding casual as all get-out.

Nick, making a slight swipe at the imaginary scuff on her not yet paid for Bergdorf fuck-me shoe, pretended to be surprised.

"Color?" she asked with a slight smile. Her heart was beating fast and she was feeling a pleasant hot-cold rush of blood.

"I mean, your dress. What do you call that color?"

"Hmm." She bit her lower lip and shrugged an innocent shrug. "What do *you* call it?"

"Well, let's see," he said, his eyes bright. "Process of elimination . . . it's not pink."

"Nope," Nick said with a grin. "I think we can safely establish that."

He straightened his tie, buying time. He had, at best, a few more seconds to . . . what? Ask her name? Get her number? Just how *much* could he betray his wife in a few passing seconds?

"Well . . . it's an amazing dress," he went on, flustered. "I mean . . . I'm sorry. I just had to say something."

"You're sweet," Nick said, coming to his rescue.

Okay. Back to your table. Now.

But she moved close to him and quietly went on. "Now. Here's what you *wanted* to say: 'My name is . . . Wally Wall Street . . . and I think you're the finest piece of ass I've ever seen, and woe is me because here I am with my wife, and not just *with* my wife, but it's our anniversary, and I don't fool around, but I saw you and . . . I just had to say something because I'd never forgive myself if I let this opportunity go by.' "

There was the slightest of pauses.

"How can I see you again?" asked Wally, doing his best to remain calm.

"Gosh," said Nick. "I don't know. I'm sure you'll think of a way."

"Jesus," said Wally, smiling tightly and trying to look around the corner to where he thought his wife was sitting.

"Here," he said. Slipping his hand into a jacket pocket, he took out a business card and reached to palm it to her. Before Nick could react, the powder room door opened with its loud squeak, both their heads turned toward the sound, and the card floated down onto the marble floor.

The Wife emerged.

Nick swooped down, picked up the card, and handed it to Wally.

"I think you dropped this," she said as though they'd never spoken, and headed straight back to her table.

Now, that's that, she thought as she sat down, smiling a delicious smile at her date, who looked like the happiest man on earth.

★　　★　　★　　★

My date, Nick thought as she put her napkin back onto her lap. *Old . . . what's-his-name.*

He was saying something to her about wine, and she seemed to listen. But she was, in fact, trying to remember his name.

Her heart was still beating from her brush with Wally and The Wife. She wasn't in a panic or anything—she just couldn't remember her incredibly adorable date's name. Well, she'd only met him yesterday. She smiled, nodded. He went on.

"How about a Beaujolais Nouveau? Or maybe something from California . . . ?" She didn't really hear, couldn't have cared less about the wine.

What's his name?

She managed a glance over at Wally's booth. Wally was being especially attentive to The Wife. He had apparently finessed the business-card thing. Nick gave him points for grace under pressure.

In less than the split second that Nick had been checking him out, Wally turned and glanced her way. Nick let him know she was looking this time. Kind of a reward.

"Maybe a white wine first . . . a simple Mâcon," suggested Nameless.

Tom . . . Terry . . . Ted . . . something with a T, thought Nick, her mind racing. *Todd . . .*

Todd!

"Whatever you like is fine with me . . . Todd," said Nick, resting her chin lightly on her raised right hand. "Todd . . . Todd," she repeated dreamily.

"What?" he asked, smiling.

"I just like the sound of it," she said.

"You're something," Todd said. She was looking at him as if he were the only man in the world.

She was pretty sure she'd sleep with Todd sometime. Not as smart as he thinks he is, she thought, but it would be a shame to throw him back. Still, she wasn't sure it would be tonight. Maybe she'd just send him home, change into something a little outrageous, and go dancing.

Or maybe she wouldn't send him home. Maybe they'd neck, and she'd see if she could drive him crazy—see if she drove *herself* crazy. He does have great lips, she thought, and he's in terrific shape. How bad could it be?

No. Not tonight.

"I am something," Nick said, exhaling with a slight pout. "But what?"

"Well, George Haines says you're a good actress, for one thing," Todd offered.

"Oh, pooh on George Haines," said Nick. "What does he know? He's a soap producer."

"He's my producer," Todd replied.

"Are you on that show?" Nick asked, feeling herself turn red.

"Well, what'd you think I was doing there yesterday?"

"I . . . thought you were reading for a part, like I was," Nick answered.

"I've been on *The Gathering Storm* for two years," Todd said, as though revealing he was a spy holding atomic secrets.

"Oh, gosh. I'm sorry. I never watch soaps," said Nick, who did occasionally watch soaps, but not that one.

"Why would you audition for George Haines," asked Todd, "if you don't value his opinion?"

"I thought it might be fun to be on a soap for a few months. I did it once. But I don't think George Haines can tell the difference between a good actress and someone he wants to—how do you say in your language?—fuck."

"You're probably right about that," said Todd, chuckling and making light of it. "Although he's won more daytime Emmys than any producer in the history of television."

"The history of television," said Nick, "is a very short history."

The waiter came conveniently along, and Todd ordered champagne.

She decided to steer clear of anything unpleasant. "So. Are you, like, a heartthrob or something, and I didn't even know it?"

"Well," said Todd modestly. "I get good tables at restaurants. And occasional sidelong glances. Like that woman over there," he said, inclining his head toward The Wife of Wally Wall Street.

This allowed Nick to look at Wally without concealing it from Todd.

As she did, her eyes were met by The Wife's. Nick wondered if The Wife was, indeed, checking out Todd the Soap Star . . . or . . . the redhead who was distracting her husband on their anniversary.

"Well," said Nick, looking back to Todd and brushing his cheek with her finger, "you certainly make my heart throb."

Easy now.

"I'll bet you say that to all the guys," said Todd, trying to seem less pleased than he was.

"Oh, not all the guys," said Nick, mock-demure.

The champagne arrived. Todd motioned for the waiter to let Nick try it. Nick gave him points for that.

"I never met a champagne I didn't like," said Nick. "You could have ordered Gallo." She took a sip and shuddered happily. "Deee-licious. Although very fizzy."

The waiter paused in his pouring.

"Very fizzy is good, though, isn't it?" said Nick as the champagne sizzled down her throat.

"Very fizzy is part of what makes it Dom Perignon," said Todd matter-of-factly, nodding to the waiter, who finished pouring and backed away.

"Expensive is what makes it Dom Perignon," said Nick, smiling a champagne smile. "And you shouldn't have."

"Well, I probably shouldn't have talked to you yesterday," said Todd, leaning toward her a bit. "I shouldn't have looked twice at that T-shirt you were wearing."

It had been a classic Fruit-of-the-Loom men's white tank top, worn tight, with nothing under it.

Not wanting to get jobs because of her body, Nick usually dressed down professionally. But her agent had urged her to go all-out. The T-shirt had felt a little too all-out for Nick in a professional situation. At dinner, or dancing, or somewhere anonymous in one of her moods, the T-shirt would have been perfect. For the meeting she'd thrown a short black jacket over it at the last minute. But when George Haines's secretary had said, "Mr. Haines will see you now," she'd remembered her agent's injunction and tossed off the jacket as she went in—just as Todd had come out of the adjoining office.

He had barely managed a glimpse of her, but it was enough to make him delay his exit. He thumbed through a copy of the next day's script and chatted with George Haines's insufferable secretary in hope of getting a better shot of the T-shirt and the woman in it.

"I certainly shouldn't have waited for you to come out of George's office," Todd went on.

"I'm glad you did," said Nick. She wasn't sure if she was really glad, but it felt good to say it. She took another sip, wishing the champagne were something cheaper and less bubbly.

"You're trouble, you know that?" he said, clearly making it a compliment.

"I'm really not," said Nick, meaning it.

"But then, I couldn't help myself. I just had to see you," said Todd.

"Well—it's a great T-shirt," said Nick, smiling into his eyes.

"I'll bet George liked it," said Todd.

"What's not to like?"

Stop that!

Todd laughed and shook his head. "Do you realize," he went on, "that if you get this job, we'll be working together?"

"Oh. Well, I . . . kind of turned it down."

"You turned it down?"

"Well, not exactly. They called my agent today. . . ."

"Who're you with?" Todd interrupted.

"Linda Blake," said Nick. "Anyway, they want me to come in and do a test, but, I don't know, I just told Linda to forget it."

"The show's a huge success. It could do a lot for you."

"I don't think I want to do a soap again," said Nick. "I promised myself I'd never do anything I wouldn't want to watch."

"What about *Eagle Squadron?*" Todd asked, referring to a short-lived series Nick had done a few years before.

"You know about that? I blush, I blush," said Nick.

"Not exactly *Masterpiece Theatre.*"

"That was before I made the promise to myself. But Linda thought I should meet the much-Emmyed George Haines. And I certainly could use the c-a-s-h."

She'd done a two-month stint on *Loving Days and Nights,* but had hated every minute. She enjoyed soaps as good honest trash. But as an actress, she needed to work slowly. It was the only way she could do her best.

"I mean, I don't know how you tape a whole hour every day. It's too much."

"It's not for everybody, I guess," Todd said, "but it's been awfully good to me."

"Well," said Nick, "it provides lovely champagne and wonderful tables and last-minute reservations at restaurants—so here's to it . . . and you."

The champagne was landing now. And her hands were covertly searching her bag for a pencil or pen.

The waiter returned. "Would you care to order, monsieur?"

"I think so," said Todd. Then, to Nick, "Are we ready?"

"Why don't you order for both of us," answered Nick. "As long as it's not sweetbreads."

From the nether reaches of her bag she came up with an old Bic.

Todd was immersed with the waiter. "Tournedos very rare . . . does the chef understand 'very rare'? . . . and for the lady . . ."

Nick slipped a matchbook off the table, flicked it open in her lap, and wrote quickly: *"Pierre Hotel. Room: name of Nicholas. 1 AM. Tonight."*

Todd ordered on. "That thing he does with oysters . . ."

Nick closed the matchbook, dropped the pen back into her bag, glanced over at Wally's table, and thought to herself . . .

You go too far.

★   ★   ★   ★

Put that matchbook away and behave yourself.

Besides, there was no way to get her matchbook/invitation to Wally. It would require (a) The Wife going back to the ladies' room, or (b) Wally going back to the men's room, and Nick following him.

But The Wife would surely be on to that.

Or—what if (c): The Wife *and* Todd went to their respective rest rooms at more or less the same time?

It'll never happen, Nick thought—but that *would* do it.

If fate is kind enough to hand me (c), I'll go for it.

The first leg of the never-before-attempted Triple.

Too many "ifs," she thought. Getting the matchbook to Wally without Todd and The Wife seeing. That was number one. Then she'd also have to get Todd to leave quickly after taking her home. Well, she thought . . . that shouldn't be much of a problem.

Hold on. I'm getting ahead of myself. What if I'm waiting in an expensive room at the Pierre and Wally doesn't show up?

She looked at Todd, who was well into the story of his life.

Stop it! You're not going to the Pierre. And no more champagne. You know what champagne does to you.

If quizzed on what Todd had been talking about during this reverie, Nick would have flunked, but the waiter kept refilling their glasses. . . .

Okay. Maybe one more . . .

. . . And a tasty little thing arrived with seasoned bread crumbs and oysters, and Nick was nodding, and laughing, and looking rapt. Todd was saying something about who he studied with, and how De Niro and Alec Baldwin had once been on soaps.

You're just going to kiss him good-night—he has such a nice mouth—and send him home. And then you're going to feed the fish, get into bed with that script, re-read it, and get eight hours of sleep. You even have enough time for a quick trip to the gym before your meeting.

The waiter made a move to refill her glass again, but Nick put her hand over it. . . .

No. Absolutely not another drop.

She took her hand off the glass.

"What the heck. Wouldn't want it to go to waste," said Nick. Todd smiled. And the waiter poured.

CHAPTER 2

She really had told Linda Blake to pass on the soap. At her session that afternoon, her shrink had suggested that she was afraid of success.

"Not me," said Nick. "You've got the wrong girl."

"Interesting that you use the word 'girl,' " said Martine, not at all pointedly.

"Oh, give me a break, Martine. I'd be thrilled to have the money. I know I haven't done enough lately to warrant turning down a job like this. But Christ—soaps? I don't know . . . soaps are just not part of The Plan."

The Plan, Martine knew, included success as a film actress, plus a husband, kids, dogs, a house in the country, the works.

"How many successful actresses do you know who have sex in public places?" Martine asked.

"Semi-public, Martine. I've told you. I never get caught."

"Are you saying there's no risk?" asked Martine.

"Of course there's risk—there has to be *some* risk, but, you know . . ."

"The best skiers fall occasionally, Nick."

"This one doesn't," said Nick.

"I wish you were as confident about your work."

"Well, gee whiz, so do I."

"Or your looks."

"Oh, I like my looks all right. I guess."

"You only seem to like your looks when you're doing something you later feel you have to confess to me," said Martine.

"Yeah, well . . ."

"The only time you've reported that you looked good," said Martine, "was when you were on the prowl in some way. Or when you'd had some champagne."

"Oh, yeah—like I'm an alcoholic," snapped Nick.

"I didn't say that," Martine replied carefully. "Although with your family history, you should be cautious."

Nick's mother had quit drinking five years ago. Though she'd never drunk much, a single glass of wine turned her into an outstanding bitch. And she'd had a glass of wine or two every night of Nick's childhood. Nick's father drank excessively as far as Nick was concerned, yet exhibited few, if any, of the traits of an alcoholic.

"I'd like you to think well of how you look without benefit of sex or alcohol," said Martine.

"I look all right sometimes, I guess," said Nick.

"I wish you were in one of my groups. I'd like you to get some feedback about this," said Martine.

"Oh, God, *group* . . . Martine, no," said Nick, laughing and making a cross with her fingers, as if to ward off demons.

"All right, all right," said Martine, looking at her watch and reaching for her weathered little appointment book. "One more question: Isn't it easier to risk getting caught having sex in a semi-public place . . . if you're not a successful actress?"

Nick didn't answer.

Martine stared. "Same time next week?"

Nick stared back. "I'll have to call you."

"Okay. Call me," said Martine cheerfully, standing up and extending her arms for their usual good-bye hug.

"Yeah, yeah," said Nick, somewhat distractedly returning the hug, which always felt better to her than she thought it would.

"And be careful."

"I always am, Martine," Nick said.

"I don't want to sound like a public service announcement, but . . . you know," said Martine.

"I am *so* careful, Martine," Nick said wearily. "God, it was much more fun before you had to be."

"I remember," said Martine.

"Why, Martine, you old harlot, you," laughed Nick as she headed for the door.

"I *beg* your pardon," said Martine, smiling and taking, perhaps, a little offense, but then deciding to enjoy it.

Nick turned at the door.

"Martine . . . ?" She paused.

"What, honey?"

"Same time next week."

★   ★   ★   ★

The matchbook, with its invitation to Wally Wall Street, rested unseen in her lap while she and Todd ate the food and drank the champagne. As the waiter turned the empty bottle over and plunked it into the ice bucket, Todd suggested a second.

"Oh, thank you, no. I'm getting up early . . ."

Good girl.

". . . And I have to keep my girlish figure."

"Not exactly girlish, I'd say," said Todd.

"I keep having to be reminded that I'm not a girl," said Nick almost to herself. Todd, feeling a nice buzz and not wanting to spoil anything, didn't pick up on it.

He seemed to be trying not to stare at her breasts. She smiled and turned her face in profile, as if to say, "It's okay. It's *fine*. Go ahead."

Then Nick saw The Wife get up and head for the powder room. She turned the matchbook in her hand.

Not tonight. The decision has been made.

She was feeling just fine. The Triple was an awfully long shot, she knew. Had she really considered it? Or was it just a nice champagne fantasy to occupy her while Todd talked on?

"Well—dessert?" Todd asked.

The waiter looked expectant.

"I kind of thought we'd have dessert at my place," said Nick.

What?? What're you doing?

"L'addition, s'il vous plâit," said Todd to the waiter, who nodded and slipped away. "Don't tell me you made dessert?" he asked, pleased as punch.

"No, no," Nick laughed. "I'm not much of a cook. But . . ."

Don't.

". . . I have a feeling you could come up with something sweet I'd like. Am I right?" She made the eye contact she'd made in the powder room mirror. "I'll bet I'm right."

Todd tried to look composed. He took a breath and looked away, smiling like a salesman who's just closed a sale he wasn't sure he'd make.

"I'm going to wash my hands," said Todd. . . .

He's getting up. He's going to wash his hands. Have the fates ruled in favor of The Triple?

". . . If the check comes while I'm gone, don't look at it," he continued, grinning and moving away.

Nick just sat there. The Wife would be back soon.

The Triple!

Her heart pumped harder as she turned the matchbook over and over.

If I think about this, I'll never do it.

She pushed back her chair, stood up, and moved to Wally's table.

Never breaking stride, she dropped the matchbook at his elbow. Without looking at him, she walked over to a little tray of mints, took two, and circled back to her chair. She put one mint at Todd's place, and popped the other into her mouth.

★   ★   ★   ★

As the limo headed to Nick's apartment near Gracie Mansion, they were quiet. Todd rolled up the tinted glass that separated the driver from them, and made a move to kiss her. She deducted a few points—she liked to make the first move. She put a hand gently to his chest and whispered, "Wait. Let's just sit and enjoy the ride and feel how good this is."

Todd took it well—she gave him back the points just deducted—and they rode in silence.

After a few minutes, Nick took his hand, opened her coat, and placed his palm on her leg, just above the knee. The short cashmere dress had ridden way, way up when she sat in the car, but she'd covered it with her coat, so Todd hadn't yet noticed the effect. He turned his head to see.

"Just look straight ahead," Nick said quietly. He obeyed.

Now, listen. You're not inviting him in. You're getting eight hours of sleep tonight.

She moved his hand, taking his fingers lightly in hers, gliding them up her thigh. Todd felt the top of her stockings—the kind that simply end, holding themselves up without garters. But Nick kept going. Todd felt skin which was a contradiction of soft and tight. She pulled his fingers up, and inward. When she got them as close to their destination as is possible without touching, she took her hand away, leaving him there.

Just a little something for him to remember me by.

Todd didn't move a muscle in his hand. She knew he could now tell that she wasn't wearing underwear.

After a minute or so, Nick gave him points for not moving. She even thought of telling him so, but decided against it. She'd never told anyone about the Point System.

Feeling Todd's fingers starting to get moist, she thought back to when she'd returned to her seat after dropping the matchbook. She'd waited a few seconds, and then looked over toward Wally's booth.

The Wife had returned and was reaching for a cigarette. A waiter moved to light it for her, but Wally brushed him away, took a match from The Matchbook, and lit the cigarette. The Wife cupped her hand on his match hand, looked into his eyes, and dragged deeply. As The Wife looked away to exhale, Wally had managed a peek at Nick—and, holding her eyes, had shaken the match until it went out.

Wow, thought Nick, giving him points. She took it to be a Yes.

But, back in the car, with Todd's fingers hovering and the tastes of oysters, champagne, and fine beef commingling on her palate—who knew?

What have I done? What if the guy actually shows up at the Pierre? I'll phone them and leave a message.

No. No. He'll never show up. It's fine. I haven't done anything wrong.

Then she felt something like indecision in Todd's fingertips. Without thinking, she crossed her legs, moving his hand away in the process. He looked at her, a little startled.

"We're here," she said pleasantly. The limo pulled up to her building, one of the last pre-wars in the area that hadn't gone co-op.

"Shall I tell him to wait?" asked Todd.

"All depends on how extravagant you're feeling," said Nick in a way that sent no clear signal to Todd.

Men always want to be *sure*, thought Nick.

Todd told the driver to wait. "I, uh, may be a while," he said.

"We're just going to have dessert," Nick said to the driver.

★　★　★　★

As they left the elevator on the sixth floor, Nick took her keys, singled out the Medeco for her top lock (the only one she ever locked), and handed them to Todd. He took them, trying not to look surprised.

The Triple?

No. No! Not tonight.

She reached for the collar of his Italian topcoat and gently pulled it off his shoulders, tugging lightly.

"What are you doing?" said Todd, pleased, not turning around.

"Take off your coat and stay awhile," she said, moving behind him and helping his arms out of the sleeves.

"We're not even inside yet," he said, smiling back at her over his shoulder.

She let his coat drop to the floor, opened hers, and pressed herself up against his back. She raised herself a little onto her toes and eased her hips against the back of his. She put her arms around his neck, marveling at how well they fit together.

Great ass. Major, fine ass.

Todd succeeded with the lock, pushed the heavy door open slowly, and turned around to face her. He leaned against the open door and held her at arm's length.

Okay. One kiss. Nothing that commits you to anything.

She took his hands from her shoulders and placed them at his sides. Then she moved her own hands down to the hem of her dress. . . .

Don't do this. . . .

She slowly pulled the peachy cashmere up. . . .

"Shouldn't we go inside?" Todd asked.

"We probably should," said Nick, but she stood her ground and kept slowly pulling.

The cashmere rose, exposing the tops of her stockings, exposing her upper thighs, exposing the fact that she was *not* wearing underwear. . . .

It feels so good. And I still don't have to do anything.

Todd was transfixed. He glanced at the three other apartment doors in the hallway, then back at Nick.

She pulled the cashmere up over her breasts—there had been no doubt in anyone's mind tonight that Nick wasn't wearing a bra—and kept pulling it over her head, tossing it into the apartment without looking at it.

She ran a hand through her hair and smiled at him as casually as if he were her next-door neighbor.

"Hi," said Nick.

CHAPTER 3

Todd had not yet moved or caught his breath. Nick, relaxed, smiling, and naked but for her garterless stockings and shoes, looked straight into his eyes and repeated softly, "Hi."

"Hi," answered Todd, now leaning in to kiss her. When he got quite close, she turned her head and pulled back.

Send him home. You can do this another night, tomorrow night.

"What makes you think I kiss on the first date?" said Nick with a slight grin as she dropped to her knees, unbuttoned the jacket of Todd's suit, and expertly opened his belt.

Todd stole a look out into the hallway. "Don't you have neighbors?" he asked.

"Sure. Why?" replied Nick.

"Well, I just thought maybe we should, you know . . ."

But she had already reached inside.

No underwear. Oh, my, my, my.

Cupping him gently with one hand, and pulling his fine wool pants down below his knees with her free hand, she stroked him.

"Good *God,*" he said.

"What?" she asked, touching him the way she hoped he liked to be touched.

"That's just so . . ." With a sigh, he didn't finish the sentence.

Very, very pretty. Now put it back where you found it, and send him home. You'll be glad tomorrow.

"You have an astonishing body," said Todd, more sincere than he'd been all evening.

"I bet you say that to all the girls," said Nick, rolling him between her palms.

. . . maybe just a taste.

"You're not a girl," said Todd.

"Oh, sure I am," said Nick, teasing him with flicks of her tongue. "I'm a girl, I'm a woman, I'm a lady, I'm a gal, I'm a dame . . ."

There was the sound of someone coming up the stairs. Todd flinched.

"Don't worry," said Nick. "As long as whoever it is keeps going up the steps, he won't see us."

"But what if it's someone on this floor?" asked Todd, trying not to break the mood.

"People on this floor tend to use the elevator," said Nick, taking him into her mouth and seemingly surrounding him with her tongue.

"Oh, God," said Todd, barely. "Oh my *God.*"

The footsteps were getting closer.

Nick took him out of her mouth and placed him, now slippery, between her breasts. She squeezed her breasts gently together and moved herself up and down. On the down strokes, she met him with her tongue.

The footsteps were less than a flight below them. Nick could feel the effect of Todd's distraction in her mouth.

"It's probably just Mr. Kazura from the eighth floor," Nick whispered. "He's afraid of elevators and always uses the stairs."

"But what if it's *not* Mr. Kazura?" asked Todd, looking down at her lovely breasts and feeling himself ready to explode.

The steps passed, moving on to a higher floor.

"But, you see, it *is* Mr. Kazura—O ye of little faith," said Nick. She called out, "Good-night, Mr. Kazura."

"Good-night," he called back. "Is that you, Nick?" The steps stopped.

"It's me, Mr. Kazura. Sleep tight."

"Everything A-okay down there?" asked Mr. K.

"Jesus," whispered Todd.

"A-okay, Mr. Kazura."

"That's good. That's good," he called. "Nick?"

"Yes, Mr. Kazura?"

"Thank you for the flowers. Thank you . . . for that."

"Oh, Mr. Kazura. You're welcome." Then, to Todd, whispering, "His wife died three weeks ago. They were married fifty-seven years."

"And little May and June?" Mr. Kazura asked. "They're happy?"

"April and Mae, Mr. Kazura," corrected Nick. "Yup. They're dandy, thanks." Then, to Todd, "They're my fish. He gave them to me."

"I hope you all sleep tight," said Mr. Kazura, resuming his climb.

Todd was doing a remarkable job of keeping his composure. Nick gave him points for that.

That's enough. Kiss him good-night. You need your eight hours.

She stood up and moved to him, putting her arms around his neck. She kissed him gently, deeply, making her lips soft. She lingered on the kiss for a full minute, taking him and putting him between her legs—not into her—but just wrapping her legs around him.

"One last request before I die," said Todd. "Let's shut the door and do this right."

"Aren't I doing this right?" asked Nick, sounding disappointed.

"You know what I mean," said Todd.

Nick bent down, picked up her purse, and pulled out a Trojan Sensitive Plus. She held it up.

"Todd." She smiled at him. "Todd, Todd, Todd." She exhaled. "This hurts me more than it does you, but . . ."

Stop! Don't say it. Just kiss him.

". . . But if you want to come in my mouth, I'm going to have to put this around you. . . ."

"I've been tested. I'm fine. . . ."

Oh, fuck the condom. He probably is fine.

She moaned softly. "Oh, I'm sure you are, but, you know—maybe when I know you better."

"Sure, sure. I understand."

"Unless you're happier this way?" she said, returning to her knees and taking him again between her breasts. "Your call."

This is okay. This is fine. I'm right on schedule. No problem.

"I'd ask you in, but I really do have to be up early. Do you forgive me?"

"I . . . absolutely forgive you," said Todd, laughing involuntarily. "And I think I choose . . . your mouth. . . ."

Surprise, surprise.

". . . I just wish I could return the favor."

"Oh, that's so sweet." Nick took him again into her mouth, her fingers working in ways that had never occurred to him.

The adrenaline was back, making her feel strong, right, beautiful, and completely at home.

"Tell me when you're almost ready, and I'll put this on," said Nick, unwrapping the condom.

"Uh. I'm definitely almost ready."

She slipped it on so quickly, he couldn't believe it. Then she stood back a little, admiring him. "You're gorgeous," she said, as though the condom were somehow an added delight.

She stood up again and said quietly, "Feel my lips one more time, so you'll appreciate what I'm doing."

She kissed him with kisses that felt better and tenderer than ninth-grade kisses when you're in love.

She went down again, smiling up at him, and slipped him into her mouth.

After Todd had groaned out the last of many muffled groans, Nick peeled off the condom and dropped it into a little wastebasket just inside the door.

Seven and a half hours of sleep is really just as good as eight.

Lying back on the little sheepskin foyer rug, she pulled his mouth down to her and let him return the favor.

Oh my word. I'm going to sleep so well.

She wanted this expert tongue once more in her mouth. She gently took his thick black hair in her hand and pulled him up to kiss her again. She took complete control of his tongue, swirling it in her mouth, tasting herself everywhere.

She was tempted to invite Todd in for the night.

Discipline! You're going to read that script, get to sleep, and be ready for your meeting tomorrow.

She pushed him back down between her legs, glancing at her watch as his tongue reached inside. It was 12:15. She couldn't help wondering if Wally was on his way to the Pierre.

* * * *

By 12:25, Todd, arguably the happiest man alive, was on his way home.

Nick, still nude but for stockings and shoes, had gone out to press the elevator button for him, holding his hand. She'd stayed there with him until the last possible second when she heard the elevator car approaching. Todd, laughing, pushed her back toward her door. She ducked back into her apartment as the elevator opened, and heard Todd say, "I'll call," as she closed her door.

He'll call. Now look what you've done.

She was still pretty much on schedule though. She'd be in bed in a few minutes, read for an hour, wake at 8:15, take her clothes to the gym, work out till 9:30, and make her meeting at 10:15.

She looked at her answering machine. Only one message, from her mother, and two hangups. She moved to the aquarium near her bed and sprinkled the last of the fish food from a small can.

"Got to go shopping for you gals tomorrow. Anything special you'd like?" They seemed to look at her as they munched bits of food from the surface of the tank.

She felt deliciously wide awake. The buzz from the champagne had not yet peaked, and she was still tingling from aftershocks of Todd's tongue.

She went into the kitchen, and caught sight of herself in a mirror.

What a shame no one can see me.

Her hair was touseled in that way that only sex tousles your hair, she thought.

I wish I were on the beach at St. Barts.

She'd gone to St. Barts last year with her then-boyfriend, Hal. She couldn't believe there was a place where so many beautiful people went completely naked on the beach. She'd gone topless before, in Europe, but this was something else. And here the men were naked too. It had taken her a while to work up her nerve, but hitting the beach after a lovely champagne lunch with another couple they'd met, Nick took the plunge and removed her thong bottom. She had never before been naked in front of more than one person. She found that she thrilled to walking down the beach past admiring, hungry, or envious eyes. That afternoon, nude, she took a long walk by herself way down the beach and back.

Stop thinking about it. Hit the sack.

It was 12:35. She took the script off her coffee table and headed for her bathroom.

Was Wally on his way to the Pierre to ask for a room in the name of Nicholas?

You'll never know.

She slipped out of her stockings and opened her closet to grab her flannel nightgown. Right next to it was a dress she'd bought the day before. Something to go dancing in. It was a loose little retro-60's black-and-white polka dot micro-mini—one of those things she had to have but wondered if she'd ever really wear. It was as short as short can be, and slightly diaphanous. It came with a little teddy to wear under it. She took it off the hanger and held it against herself, looking in another mirror.

Maybe tomorrow night. By myself. If my meeting goes well.

She put it back, threw the flannel nightgown over her head, and went into the bathroom to brush her teeth.

She thought about where he lived. How far would he have to go to get to the Pierre? What had he said to his wife? What kind of excuse could he have made up?

He's probably at home, asleep.

She got into bed, set the alarm for 9:15—she'd skip the gym—and opened the script. A wonderful role, she thought.

Do I really have a shot at this?

Linda Blake had told her that if the meeting with the director went well, she might get a chance to screen-test. It was a good-girl part, but well written and with a sense of humor—and one that was important enough to the plot that it couldn't be cut.

As she read, she moved her hand down between her legs without thinking, and touched herself where Todd had just been. She thought of the Pierre Hotel, and Wally walking up to the desk in—how long?—twenty-five minutes. Her heart beat faster.

You could go to the Pierre, and still be back by, say, three. How late could he stay anyway? You'd get six solid hours of sleep. Come on. You look so good. Don't waste this feeling.

Maybe even a Triple!

No! Not tonight.

But what if you just went to the Pierre and met Wally? (I mean, if he's even there.) It's so outrageous. You could just talk to him for a while and be back in bed by 1:30.

She looked at the little polka dot dress.

No. Discipline.

She closed the script, got out of bed, and pulled the nightgown off. She removed the polka dot dress from its hanger and slipped into it—without the teddy underneath. She looked in the mirror, turning to see it from behind. It was . . . phenomenally short. If she moved too suddenly in it, it rose up . . . too far.

With no teddy underneath, she could just see her breasts—it was ever-so-slightly see-through. The kind of see-through that made people squint to be sure if they were seeing what they thought—hoped—they were seeing.

Put the teddy on.

But all she put on was a tiny black lacy G-string. She slipped on some black pumps, went into the bathroom, brushed her teeth again, and put her toothbrush and some toothpaste into an overnight bag. She grabbed her long fake fur, and, stepping over the cashmere dress which was still lying where she'd tossed it less than an hour before, she walked out the door, letting it slam behind her, and rang for the elevator.

You don't have to do this. You can still go back in and go to bed.

The elevator came. Eric, the old night elevator operator who always looked as if he'd just had two martinis, greeted her. He started at midnight, so he hadn't been on when she'd come up with Todd.

"Evening, Miss Stallings. Cold out there. I imagine you'll want a cab?"

"Yes, thank you, Eric."

He pushed the button that signaled for a taxi on the street below.

As Nick reached the front door, a yellow cab was pulling up. Nick slid into it.

Just tell him you want to go for a little ride, and go on back home.

"Where to?" asked the cabbie.

"Sixtieth and Fifth, please," said Nick. "The Pierre Hotel."

CHAPTER 4

It wasn't a long ride. A few blocks over to Fifth Avenue, then down to Sixtieth.

Tell the driver you forgot something, and turn around and go home.

There was almost no traffic. She saw stars in the clear sky over the park. What with pollution and the glare of city lights, there were seldom many stars to be seen in the New York sky. She made a wish. Nick believed in wishing on stars.

Let me get the part in the film.

No, she thought. Too direct and selfish.

Let me feel good about myself.

But I feel wonderful right now, so I don't have to wish for that.

I wish for Wally not *to be there.*

Well. That tells me something, she thought.

She found a star to wish on, but it was difficult to keep it in focus in the jerkily moving cab.

Squinting up at her star, she started to make her wish, but the cab twisted to the left, and she lost sight of it. She craned her neck to find it again, but couldn't.

Why don't you just go home? You don't need this. He's probably not there anyway.

But now the cab was pulling up to the Pierre, and a uniformed doorman was opening the door for Nick. She paid the driver and let the doorman take her overnight bag.

"Checking in, ma'am?"

No.

"Yes. Yes, I am, thank you," said Nick as he helped her out. "God, what a flight."

"Where are you coming from tonight?"

"The coast. We circled the airport for an hour. I can't imagine why. The sky is so clear."

"Probably something to do with security. All the terrorism," said the doorman, helping her through the front door. "The registration desk is straight down on your left. I'll have your bag brought up to your room."

But I'm not really checking in. I was just seeing how far I could go with a little fantasy . . .

Nick walked up to the desk.

"Good evening, madam," said an officious-looking young clerk, ready to punch up a name on his keyboard. "Reservation in the name of . . . ?" He smiled at Nick with eyebrows raised.

No reservation. I'd just like to use the rest room, if I may.

"Nicholas. Susan Nicholas."

The clerk punched the name into his keyboard. Then did it again. He hit one of the big keys several times, and waited. He looked up.

"I'm sorry, Miss Nicholas. I don't seem to have your reservation. How did you book it?"

Of course you don't have it.

"Oh, God," said Nick slightly impatiently. "I made the call myself from L.A.—yesterday afternoon. I spoke to a Mr.—oh, what's his *name?*"

"It's not a problem, Miss Nicholas. I can't give you a suite, if that's what you wanted, but we do have a very nice room overlooking the park."

Tell him you had your heart set on a suite, turn on your heels, and go.

Nick looked at her watch. It was 12:55.

"Well, I guess I can do without a suite. What kind of bed does it have?"

He punched a few buttons.

"That would be a . . . king-size bed."

Just make an excuse and leave.

"Sounds fine," said Nick.

"Very well. I'm sorry about your reservation, Miss Nicholas. If you'd like, I'll speak to the manager in the morning, and I'm sure we can move you into a suite. How long will you be staying with us?"

I'm not staying. I've changed my mind.

"Just overnight, as it turns out. I have a meeting first thing in the morning, and then it's back to L.A. I'm sure the room will be fine."

"I'm so sorry," said the clerk. "We have a new reservations system, and I guess we haven't worked out all the kinks yet. Now, I'll just need a credit card to make an imprint."

"Oh, of course," said Nick, who'd overlooked this part of her fantasy. Nick opened her purse and wondered which of her poor, tired credit cards stood the best chance of not being refused. She gambled, and flipped him a gold Visa.

As he took it, she realized her real name was on it.

"By the way, my cards are all in my legal name, Stallings. Susan Nicholas is my stage name."

"Of course, Miss . . . Nicholas."

Nick was pleased that he didn't seem suspicious. He turned a registration card around for her, and Nick filled it out, signing in as Susan Nicholas, of 69 Todd Lane, Los Angeles.

Very funny.

"I'd like the room registered under Nicholas." It was the name she'd written on the matchbook.

Fortunately, he took only a credit card imprint, and didn't call it in for a check. Nick didn't want to think about how much the room would cost, or whether she had enough credit to cover it.

"Thank you, Miss Nicholas. That'll be Room 1622. I think you'll find it satisfactory."

"I'm sure I will," said Nick, turning away from the desk.

Last chance. Tell him you changed your mind, you must *have a suite, and have him rip up the credit card thing. Then go home.*

"Right this way, miss," said the bellman, who'd been waiting with her bag. She'd brought the bag so that she'd look like someone who was actually spending the night. Nick had once met a friend at a hotel late at night, and realized to her horror that the desk clerk thought she was a high-priced call girl. It was not a memory she relished.

The bellman walked her to the elevator. The matchbook she'd given Wally had said "1 AM." It was 12:57. At 12:58 they arrived at Room 1622.

The room was beautiful, with a king-size four-poster, a little sitting area, and a fabulous view of Central Park.

"This is the key to your minibar, and if you need anything else at all, call us at once," said the bellman.

Nick slipped him a twenty.

Great. Now you get to ride the subway for a week.

He closed the door, and Nick was alone. It was 12:59.

The champagne buzz was still palpable. She took off her coat and checked herself in the gilt-edged beveled mirror over the couch. The polka dot dress *was* sensational. Slightly backlit, the dress was more see-through than she'd realized in her apartment. She could make out her breasts quite clearly. The filmy material made them look creamy, magnificent.

I should have worn the teddy. This is too much.

Fuck it. You look amazing.

The material was less transparent at the bottom, so there was nothing scandalous there. She turned around in the mirror, checking out the rear view. I'm not sure I could dance in this, thought Nick.

She lifted her arms up and around an imaginary slow-dance partner. The material rose, exposing a bit of G-string. Her heart pumped.

It was 1:01. Nick walked slowly through the room, adjusting the lighting, making it low and flattering. She had the key to the minibar in her hand, so she opened it up to have a look.

Not that you're going to have anything.

There was domestic beer, Mexican beer, Coke, diet Coke, designer waters, three kinds of Scotch, a few Rémy VSOPs, some chocolates, and, oh yes, a split of Moët & Chandon.

No. Absolutely not. Too expensive anyway. Minibars always cost a fortune. Close it up.

The phone rang.

Nick's heart leapt. She reached for the champagne, sat on the bed, and answered.

"Yes?" said Nick.

"Miss Nicholas?"

Oh, my God. It worked. It's him.

"This is the front desk. Is everything all right with the room?"

Shit, shit, shit, shit, shit.

"It's just fine," said Nick. "I mean—it's not a suite, but it's really fine."

"I'm so glad. Enjoy your stay with us."

"Thank you. Good-night."

Nick hung up and looked at the champagne bottle in her hand.

What am I doing here? This is pathetic. I'm being stood up by a man I tried to pick up in a restaurant on his wedding anniversary.

She went to the minibar, put back the champagne, closed the door, and left the key in its lock.

Good. Now go home. There's fantasy, and there's reality. This is reality. You've just spent a couple hundred dollars to make your heart beat a little faster. You're not going to get eight hours of rest. But you can go home now and cut your losses. You get points for having the balls to go this far, but Wally is not going to show up—and even if he does, you'll be on your way home and you'll never know. Call the hotel in the morning. You can check out by phone.

She picked up her coat and watched herself in the mirror as she put it on. As she twisted her arms into the sleeves, the dress rode up, exposing just the slightest peek of her G-string.

What a waste.

She walked over to the window and looked out at the stars. I guess my wish must have gone through, she thought. Martine'll be proud.

And then the phone rang again.

No. Don't answer it.

There was another phone by the window. It rang again, twice-at-a-time in that way that hotel phones do.

You do not have to pick up that phone. There is no law that says you have to pick up that phone.

She picked it up.

Don't speak. Hang up!

"Yes?" Nick heard herself say, as though listening from far away.

"Where were we?" said The Voice of Wally Wall Street on the other end. "We established that the color of your dress isn't pink. So. I think my next guess would have to be . . . peach?"

★   ★   ★   ★

Yes!

"I hope you're not disappointed," said Nick into the phone, "but I changed into something else."

"Hard to imagine you being disappointing," said The Voice.

"Where are you?" asked Nick.

Probably at home, calling to say he's sorry he couldn't make it.

"Downstairs," said The Voice. Nick did not think of him as Wally anymore.

"Oh, my," said Nick.

He laughed. "What room are you in?"

Lie. Tell him the wrong room number and then give him the slip.

"I'm in 1622."

"See you in a minute," said The Voice.

Nick hung up.

Congratulations. You're irresistible. He showed up. Now go home. Walk out the door, take the stairs down a flight, and grab the elevator from there.

Nick picked up her bag, opened the door, and took a step out into the hall.

Keep going . . .

She turned back and closed the door again. She removed her coat, readjusted the lights, and went to the minibar. She took out the split of champagne, opened it, and poured some into a glass on top of the minibar. She took a cool mouthful, swirled it around, and swallowed.

Good old non-vintage champagne.

There was a knock at the door.

She refilled her glass and walked over to the door with it.

There he was, looking even better to Nick than he had in the restaurant. He was about six feet tall, with slightly curly dirty-blond hair and a dimple in his chin. Deep-set eyes. He reminded Nick of a more intelligent Dan Quayle.

"Hi," said Nick in that same simple way. She held out the glass of champagne. "I thought you might need a little of this after your journey." He finished what was in the glass.

"Very thoughtful of you," said the man whose name Nick did not know.

They stood there for a few seconds, looking at each other.

"I hope you don't mind that I changed my clothes," said Nick.

"Well, it was a great dress," said The Man, nodding. "But this one is . . . just fine. I mean, this one is really . . ."

He shook his head and stood back a little, his eyes moving slowly. Nick delighted in the way he took her in, as though he were studying a painting.

"Just something I threw on at the last minute," said Nick, laughing a little, and turning around in the dress. "Why don't you come in?"

"Don't mind if I do," he said, closing the door behind him. Nick drifted back to the champagne and poured another glass, emptying the small bottle.

"Oh, dear," she said after another swallow. "Such a little bottle. Would you like some more?"

"God. I don't know," he said. Then he laughed and shrugged. "Sure. What the hell. Any more in there?"

Nick checked the minibar.

"Nope. That's it."

"Well, let's order down for some," he said, "I mean, when in Rome . . ."

"Is that where we are?" said Nick, picking up the phone and punching in the room service number.

"I'm not really sure where I am," he said. "Or what I'm doing. But . . . I seem to be doing it." He laughed a little and shook his head.

"Hi," said Nick into the phone. "Could you send up a bottle of non-vintage champagne? Moët or something? Great. Thanks." She hung up. "I hope you don't mind, but I prefer cheaper champagne."

"I like that in a woman," he said, settling himself onto the couch, still in his topcoat. "Do you mind if I ask you your first name?"

"Do I mind? No. I just don't think I'll tell you," Nick said pleasantly. "I mean, do you need to know my name?"

He looked at her for a second. With the lamplight behind her, she knew he could see her breasts under the heart-stopping dress.

"I thought I'd made as thorough a study of you as possible at the restaurant. But . . . my projections were off."

"How so?" asked Nick, genuinely curious.

"You, ah—that dress . . . it belongs in the Smithsonian," he said quietly.

"Shucks," said Nick, tilting her glass to her lips to catch the last drops.

"I guess I can do without your first name . . . Miss Nicholas," he said, teasing. "Maybe I'll just call you Miss Nicholas."

This guy is not a slouch. It's good to be alive.

"I like that," said Nick, taking a few steps toward him. "Better to keep it formal, wouldn't you say?"

"Absolutely," he said, flashing a smile.

"Did you have any trouble getting here?" asked Nick, who was dying to know.

He laughed. Then stopped. Then laughed again.

"No, no. No trouble at all. After I got your matchbook, I ordered brandy. We'd already had champagne, and my wife's not much of a drinker. She almost passed out in the car. I carried her in to bed, and she was out like a light." He laughed some more, almost a little out of control. "It was quite easy. I think I ran a couple of lights on the way here, but then, I was inspired."

"Oh, that's so sweet," said Nick. "I *meant* to inspire you, of course, but it's sweet of you to say so. I don't suppose you'll tell me *your* name?"

"Well," he said, enjoying himself, "it's not Wally Wall Street."

"Was I close?"

"I'm an attorney, actually."

"Ah-ha," said Nick. "What kind?"

"Oh, I'm sort of your one-stop-shopping kind of guy. Buy or sell your company, order your trades, even notarize the papers . . ."

"A notary public?" asked Nick, moving herself so that she could see her reflection in a mirror beyond him. She saw what he saw, that the backlighting was rendering her dress virtually see-through. She went on, mock-serious, like a talk show host. "Are there any nota-ries . . . private? I've always wondered."

"Have you?"

"Always."

"You *are* the finest piece of ass I've ever seen," he said, "as you surmised in the restaurant . . ."

"Surmised"? I guess people really talk that way.

"And you were quite right. I *don't* fool around. But I took the chance that you were for real," he went on, "and, lo and behold, you are."

"Lo and behold"? I love it.

"Well, I think you deserve a treat for your troubles," said Nick.

"That's so awfully kind of you, Miss Nicholas," he said, working his dimples.

The champagne was landing, mixing with the Todd champagne, mixing with visions of Todd, and pulling off her cashmere dress, and standing in the hall, waiting for the elevator. Nick felt absolutely on top of the world.

"It's the least I can do," said Nick. "But while we're waiting for the champagne, would you mind if I took a quick shower?" She reached around and undid the little hook at the top of her dress.

"I wouldn't mind at all," said The Man.

She turned and presented the zipper to him.

"Undo me, please?"

He pulled the zipper slowly down to the middle of her back.

She walked toward the bathroom, entering an area of lower light, and let the dress slip off her, stepping out of it with her back toward him. She kept her back that way, walking into the bathroom in her stiletto dancing shoes and G-string. She turned her head back to him, still keeping her breasts hidden, and gave him a little wave as she closed the door.

⋆   ⋆   ⋆   ⋆

The shower felt glorious.

She got out and dried herself with a fluffy towel from a heated metal rack. What a waste of energy, thought Nick, feeling the warmth of the soft cotton on her skin. We fight a war over oil, and this is how we use it.

She heard a knock on the door outside.

"Room service."

Her mind suddenly raced.

Don't you dare. Enough is enough.

"I'll get it," she called.

She threw down the bath towel she'd been using and reached for a smaller one which barely covered her. She made a tuck around her breasts that just held the towel in place, walked back out into the room, and peeked through the eyehole in the door.

The room service waiter outside was male. Her adrenaline returned. She felt . . . perfect.

Go back into the bathroom. Let him deal with the waiter.

She opened the door. The waiter, a sweet-looking boy who couldn't have been more than nineteen or twenty, flinched, but kept his waiterly composure.

"I beg your pardon, madam. Where would you like this?"

"Right over there," said Nick, indicating the coffee table where The Man sat.

The waiter set down the little tray.

"Would you like me to open it, ma'am?"

"No, that's all right, thank you," Nick said, sounding composed, but her heart was pumping hard again.

The waiter took out a pad with the bill on it, and held it out, unsure as to who would be signing it. Nick reached for it. The Man looked up at her, as though offering to take care of it himself.

"No, no," said Nick, taking it.

Don't do it. Don't do it.

As she signed, the motion of her arm tugged enough on her towel to release the tuck Nick had put in it. The towel slid down, revealing her breasts.

With her free elbow, she caught the towel before it slid to the floor, but made no attempt to cover herself. She continued signing, stopping for a moment to figure the tip.

She realized with a thrill that she could have heard a pin drop.

She wrote in a twenty-dollar tip, very casually pulled the towel up to cover herself again, and handed the check back to the waiter, who looked like he'd just seen . . . what he'd just seen.

Nick smiled another of her patented next-door-neighbor smiles and led the waiter to the door. She held it open for him, turning herself in such a way as to block the waiter's eyes from The Man.

If he's offended, you're in trouble. That's indecent exposure.

"Thanks so much," she said, "I hope it wasn't a lot of trouble at this hour."

He looked at her and took a deep breath.

"No trouble *at all,*" he said, not leaving as soon as waiters usually do.

"Well . . . thanks," said Nick, closing the door slowly, as if she didn't want to.

She turned to The Man. She smiled. He smiled.

"I don't think he'll ever forget this night, Miss Nicholas."

"Oh, I hope not," said Nick. She reached for the champagne and let the towel drop to the floor. "I hope you never do either."

She deftly worked off the cork, letting it pop against the wall, and half filled both glasses. He accepted his and stood there, taking her in. She was close enough to touch. Neither spoke. Nick shifted her weight. "What?" she asked innocently.

"I think you dropped something," said The Man.

"Oh, dear," said Nick, not moving and making that eye contact again. "How clumsy of me."

Nothing on earth feels as good as this.

They didn't move—he on the couch and she standing in front of him.

"I'm having an awfully good time," said Nick.

"Me too," he said.

"Are you glad you came?"

"As of this moment, yes. Tomorrow . . . I'm not so sure about."

Tomorrow . . .

"You're going to feel absolutely wonderful tomorrow," Nick said, standing in nothing but black high heels as though it were the most natural thing in the world. "And do you know why?"

"No."

"I'll tell you," she said. Her glass was empty and she moved to the champagne, wiping it off and handing it to him. "Would you, please?" She sat down on the couch, not too close to him, and lay back, opening her legs just enough for him to see a little more.

Although she seemed the picture of calm, she felt her heart thumping.

I live for this.

"You're going to feel wonderful tomorrow," she went on, "because you're going to do things tonight you've never done before. You've already begun. And there's no one better you could have picked to do them with."

"I think I'd have to agree with you there," he said. Summoning all the cool he could muster, he filled both glasses and handed her one. She gave him points for deft champagne-pouring under pressure.

"When was the last time you saw something like this on your anniversary?" asked Nick, taking a long sip.

Please . . . easy with the champagne . . .

"That was a rhetorical question," said Nick before he could answer. "Let me ask a few more. Is that all right?"

"Fine," he said.

"Good," said Nick. "I don't want to do anything that isn't fine with you. This is your anniversary. I want you to have a wonderful time."

He laughed. "Thank you."

"Oh—as you can see, I'm not a natural redhead." She crossed her legs, smiling. "I hope you're not disappointed. But everything else is real—just so you know."

He took a long drink of champagne. So did she.

"Now. Rhetorical question number two: When was the last time you did something like this . . ."

Nick took the glass out of his hand and set it on the coffee table. She placed her index finger under his chin and led his head, like a knife through butter, down to her lap. Nick settled back a little more, parting her thighs still wider, and moved her hand to the back of his head, gently pushing his mouth to her.

". . . When was the last time you did something like this while a total stranger drank champagne and talked to you? These are rhetorical questions, remember, so please don't feel you have to answer."

She felt the moist warmth of his tongue, and took a sudden breath. He stopped, straightened himself, stood up, and moved away.

"Oh, dear," said Nick. "What is it?"

He doesn't like me.

He looked distracted, and began to pace. "I'm sorry. I'm sorry. It's just that . . ." He shook his head violently as if to clear it, then rubbed his eyes and stood still. "Oh, Christ . . ."

He sat on the bed. Nick rose and took a few steps toward him.

Let him go.

"Do you want to leave?" asked Nick, sounding as unpressuring as she could.

"Oh, God," he answered with a halfhearted laugh. Then, sing-song like a school kid, he added, "Yes-no-maybe so-could be-I don't know." He looked out the window. "I'm just . . . I've been going through some . . . never mind, never mind."

"Is it . . . me?" asked Nick.

"God, no. I mean . . . *you,*" he exhaled, and shook his head, "are, in fact, quite the silver lining, Miss Nicholas."

Nick smiled like a nurse. "What can I do to make you more comfortable?"

Just let the guy go home. And then you do the same.

"Would you like me to get dressed?" said Nick.

Please *say no.*

He looked at her standing before him. His shoulders started to shake a little. Was he crying?

"Oh, God, what a day, what a day," he said. "I really sound like such a jerk, don't I? It's just—never mind."

Nick moved to him. She knelt in front of him and took his face in her hands.

Show him to the door.

She gracefully raised herself just enough to kiss him softly on the lips. She searched tentatively, delicately, with her tongue for his.

It's now or never.

He held the kiss, the tenderness of which took him by surprise.

"What do you want?" asked Nick like a mother to a sick child. "I'll do anything you want."

He couldn't help a slight laugh. "Anything?"

"Anything," said Nick.

"I'm sorry," he said. He inhaled deeply and let it all out. "You're a bit . . . overwhelming."

"I don't want to interfere with your life," she went on. "You don't have to worry about me. You'll never hear from me again . . ."

. . . *let him go* . . .

". . . I won't try to find you, or contact you—ever. This is the opposite of *Fatal Attraction*. This is your fantasy, and you can do whatever you want with me."

His face tightened a little. "Where am I?" he said.

"There's only one thing I want from you," Nick said.

"What?"

"I hope you'll understand," she said, as if asking him a terrific favor. "I want you in my mouth. Just for a minute. I won't make you come or anything, and you can leave after that. I'll understand." She made a tentative move with her hands toward his belt, waiting for his permission. He watched her intently, as if this were happening to someone else. Nick took his belt buckle and proceeded carefully, not wanting to go any further without permission. She was slowly pulling down his trousers—keeping her eyes on him as if to say, "Is this okay?" Off went his wing-tip shoes and plain black socks.

She removed his tie and shirt, and placed the shirt neatly around the back of a chair. She picked up his pants and folded them onto the seat of the same chair. She went back to the bed and pulled the covers down, easing him over onto the sheets, fluffing up a pillow for him to lie back on. Never taking his eyes off her, he complied with her nonverbal commands.

"Nice view," he said quietly.

"I was just thinking the same thing," said Nick, going around the bed and getting in on the other side, then moving over to him. She kissed him again.

"Feel my lips," she said between kisses. "Tell me if you like them better up here," she said with another kiss, "or"—she moved down below his waist—"here."

Maintaining eye contact with him all the while, she rounded her lips and slowly took him into her mouth. He wasn't hard, but, as she kept her eyes on his, and smoothly worked him in and out of her mouth, that soon changed. His back tightened and arched a little.

"How do you do that?" he asked, stroking her hair. "Oh, my, my, my—how do you *do* that?"

He noticed the twinkle in her eyes as she took him way in, then locked her lips around him, and without moving her mouth down or up, lathered him with her tongue.

He let his head sink back into the pillow but kept his eyes on hers. She made sure that he felt only the softness of the inside of her mouth.

He didn't think he could hold back any longer. She felt it in him too.

Excuse me . . . remember a little virus called HIV?

Maintaining even pressure with her lips, she pulled her mouth slowly off and nestled between his legs, stroking him with thumb and forefinger in the spot where she knew it felt best.

"Dear God," he said, still looking into her eyes.

"Do you want me to stop?" asked Nick. "I mean, a deal's a deal."

He said nothing. Her thumb and forefinger kept him right on the edge.

"You've given me a bad case of penis envy," said Nick, grinning at him. "I admit it. You're very pretty."

He pulled her to him suddenly and, keeping her on top of him, kissed her, harder than before.

"Wait," she said.

Absolutely not another drop of champagne!

She rolled off the bed, moved deftly across the room, picked up the champagne bottle and a glass, and brought them back, filling the glass. She crawled over to him and sat, straddling his waist. She fed him champagne, holding the back of his head to the glass so as not to spill any. She reached down with her head and gave him another of her tenderest kisses.

"I think you should know," he said, "that . . . I'm safe. I haven't been with another woman in . . . God, fifteen years."

"I'm . . . honored," said Nick.

. . . go home . . . go . . .

"If you'd like protection, I have some," he went on. "I mean, I won't be insulted."

She raised her hips just high enough to catch the tip of him between her legs.

He looked startled but said nothing. Nick found exactly the correct angle, and slowly pushed herself down, taking him up, up into her, until she felt her hips touch down on his thighs.

Her eyes closed and her head dropped back as he filled her.

She moved up and down, up and down. Slowly. Without breaking rhythm, she reached for the champagne glass . . .

. . . no more . . .

. . . and emptied it. She didn't feel drunk in the least. In fact, she felt better than she'd felt in ages. The champagne–adrenaline cocktail was blocking any and all thoughts of tomorrow morning.

Look at his eyes. You're the finest piece of ass he's ever seen. This is who you are!

She arched her back and squeezed on him.

"Is that you?" he asked, unbelieving. He'd never felt muscles work like that around him.

"Uh-huh," said Nick, smiling down at him. She squeezed again.

"Oh, God. You're gonna finish me off," he said, his eyes now on her breasts.

So Nick slowed down a little, then some more, and then pulled herself off, cuddling next to him.

Married fifteen years? You can trust this guy. He's safe.

"Listen," she said, kissing his neck and rolling a leg over him, "I want you in my mouth. It's very selfish of me, but it's so rare these days that a gal finds someone who's safe."

"I really am," he said.

"Well, exactly," said Nick. "So, I'll make you another deal. If you let me have you that way, we'll sip a little more champagne, and for your second one . . ."

. . . second . . . ?

". . . you can have it any way you like."

This was as close as he had ever come to having someone make him an offer he couldn't refuse.

"Do we have a deal, Mr. Attorney?"

"I think we do, Miss Nicholas."

. . . home . . . sleep . . . meeting . . .

Nick made more than good on her end of the agreement. When his time came, he pulled a pillow to his mouth to muffle the cries.

★   ★   ★   ★

They lay for a while without moving, Nick enjoying his now-quiet softness.

She reached over him to a glass on the bedside table and took some more champagne. Some faraway part of her wondered what time it was. It had been around 1:30 when she'd taken off her watch to shower. She'd left it in the bathroom. She made a move to look at his watch, then decided not to think about time anymore tonight. Feeling as powerful as she did, she knew she could make everything all right, and that the morning and her meeting were far, far away . . .

She moved up and kissed him. He held her tight.

"Dee-licious," whispered Nick as they lay nose to nose.

They stayed like that for twenty minutes or more, nuzzling and kissing exactly like two people in love. It thrilled Nick.

"Who *are* you, Miss Nicholas?" he asked, not expecting an answer.

"A girl in a peach cashmere dress."

"I'll always remember you in that dress," he said. "And also out of it. It's difficult to say which way you look better."

Nick couldn't believe how strong she felt. She was timing the champagne just right, maintaining her buzz like a surfer on the crest of a wave.

She stroked him gently, testing to see if there were any signs of life down there yet. To her pleased surprise, he stiffened a little.

"I need a cigarette," said Nick.

"If I'd only known," he said, "I'd have brought some."

"Do you smoke?"

"Gave it up."

"Me too. But—couldn't you kind of go for one now?" asked Nick.

"Now that you mention it, yes."

"I'm going to call down for some. What kind do you like?"

"Oh, I don't know—anything that isn't menthol," he said.

She dialed room service. On the other end, she heard the boy who'd come up before.

Bingo.

"Hi. I'm sorry to bother you. Are you alone down there?"

"Yeah. It's just me at this hour. And the cook."

"If you're not too busy, do you think you could bring up some cigarettes—something filtered that isn't menthol?"

"I think I can find something, sure," he said. "Will that be all?"

"That'll be fine," said Nick, and hung up.

She still held him in her hand. . . . Now he was getting harder. She went down and teased him with her lips to hasten the process.

"I'm afraid I can't seem to get enough of you," he said, rolling over onto her.

"Take all you like," said Nick. "Remember? I said I'll do whatever you want."

He stared at her for a few seconds. "Did you mean that?"

"Absolutely," said Nick, almost daring him.

With a suddenness that took Nick by surprise, he spread her legs and glided himself into her, not quite as gently as before.

"Are you saying, Miss Nicholas, that you'll do . . . anything I ask?" he said in a dark new tone of voice.

Nick stared into his eyes, taking him as far as he could go, feeling dominated for the first time. "Yes. Anything," she said, rising to the challenge.

He looked down at her. The champagne extinguished a faraway flicker of fear in her and turned, for the moment, his indelicate thrusts into something she was now experiencing as pleasure. "What?" she demanded, her heart racing.

"I'm not sure I know you well enough," he went on.

"I said *anything,*" Nick whispered, "and I meant it."

"Well," he said, pinning down her shoulders with his forearms, "watching you with that waiter before gave me an idea. Are you sure . . . ?"

. . . no . . . stop . . .

"I'm sure," said Nick, the champagne still feeding her buzz. "What is it?"

"Well, Miss Nicholas. I would like you . . . to . . . fuck . . . that nice young man when he comes up here with the cigarettes. But I want you to save something for me after he leaves."

The Triple . . . !

Nick felt him swelling inside her as her heart pounded better than it had ever pounded before.

"Are you sure that's what you want?" Nick asked as evenly as she could. "Because I'll do it."

"I'm sure," he said quickly.

"You might not like it."

"I'm a big boy," he said, pushing more. "I want to watch you with someone else. Then I want to have you again. That's . . . what I want."

"Just full of surprises, aren't you?" said Nick, trying to get her breath back.

"You ain't seen nothing yet," he said, pushing faster. Then harder. "Will you do it?"

"Sweet, sweet son of a bitch," gasped Nick, more excited than she'd ever felt in her life. "I told you. I'll do anything."

There was a knock at the door.

"Room service."

CHAPTER 5

In her nightmare, a squad car's siren was screaming, shrieking, as the car bore down on her, huddled naked and shaking in the winter cold against a filthy brick wall in the side alley of the Pierre Hotel. The headlights blinded her and she struggled to cover herself. The siren's ring intensified, its shrill whine everywhere.

Suddenly it was quiet.

Nick felt the smooth plastic of her black Braun alarm clock in her hand. Without opening her eyes, she returned the clock to her bedside table.

She coughed, bringing up acrid mucus that burned her throat with the stale taste of tobacco. She was nauseous. The inside of her mouth tasted like the bottom of a bird cage. She was sore everywhere.

Why on earth did I set the alarm?

She turned over to shield her eyes from the light outside, and her cheek landed on something moist on her pillow. She pulled her face away as she realized that it was her own vomit. She had thrown up in her sleep.

She was still wearing her coat. She had a dim recollection of not being able to take it off when she'd gotten into bed. She looked around her room. The lights were on. The curtains were open and there was a terrific glare from the sun which, Nick noticed with relief, was about to disappear beneath a huge patch of gray clouds.

She tried breathing deeply, but it almost made her sick to her stomach. She looked at the alarm clock. It was 9:15.

My meeting!

Her meeting was at 10:15.

Impossible, thought Nick. No way. I'll have to call Linda and get them to change it to Monday. Or maybe, possibly, late this afternoon.

The script lay on the floor by her bed where she'd tossed it last night.

You slut. You pig.

Nick tried to figure out how much sleep she'd had. She knew she'd set the alarm before she'd passed out on the bed. She tried to remember what time it had been. It was 6:30. She'd had two and three-quarters hours of sleep.

She reached down and grabbed the script, opening it in panic. Linda had said they might want her to read two different scenes. There was a memo from Linda paper-clipped to the cover. Fighting to focus through her headache, Nick saw that the scenes were on pages 11 to 14 and 83 to 84. Good, she thought—fairly short. She flipped the script to page 11. The scene, she now remembered, was solid dialogue for three pages between her character and the hero. She looked at the clock. It was 9:20.

She scanned the pages, unable to focus on anything other than the impossibility of mastering the scenes in the ridiculously short amount of time she had. She'd need a half hour to get ready on a *good* day, and it was a fifteen-minute ride to the meeting. She had maybe ten minutes to spare.

Linda's office opened at ten. She decided to call Linda at ten on the dot and get her to change the meeting time. Linda could do that.

Unable to wait, she dialed Linda at home. A machine answered. Nick spoke, imploring Linda to pick up. She didn't. She must be on her way to the office, thought Nick.

She coughed again, and this one sent her running to the toilet. There was a wet burn at the bottom of her throat. She just made it to the toilet in time, but all she could do was cough up a small amount of noxious phlegm.

She lay down on the bathroom floor, resting against the bowl of the toilet. She hadn't cleaned the bathroom for . . . who knew how long? There was dust and hair around the edge of the toilet. Nick pushed herself up and looked in the mirror.

Oh, sure. Go meet an Oscar-winning director with those circles under your puffy bloodshot eyes.

She turned on the cold water, which ran very cold in winter, and bent over, splashing some around her eyes. She looked up again after several splashes. Her eyes were now puffy, bloodshot, and wet.

She tried to run a wide-toothed comb through her hair, but it snagged. She reached up and felt something which she feared, through a dim recollection, was probably dried semen.

The Triple . . .

It wasn't as if she didn't remember. She hadn't blacked out or anything. But she realized, as another glob of mucus tried to clear itself from her lungs, that she had, indeed, had three men last night. There was a sudden surge in her bowels, and she was glad the toilet was close enough for her to wheel around and sit. She noticed that she wasn't wearing her G-string, which she realized she'd left in the bathroom at the hotel, along with her watch.

As her bowels cleared, she felt a horrid burning.

Oh, no. Did I do something . . . with that part of my body? Oh, God . . .

The room service boy, she remembered, had been more than willing to comply with the attorney's fantasy. Nick remembered that in the throes of her nearly hallucinatory high last night, there was no request she'd turned down. She burned now so badly that she got up and turned on the shower, fearing that the touch of toilet paper would be too painful.

You're going to get AIDS.

She remembered, too, that any fear of AIDS had been pushed away by her champagne-certainty at the time that everything and anything she did would be all right. She had felt omnipotent. She had told herself that the attorney had been, after all, married for fifteen years and had been faithful.

What if he was lying?

She had told herself that the boy was probably too young and inexperienced to carry any dangerous disease.

What made you think that?

Nick turned the hot water up higher than usual to fight off a sudden chill, and, letting her coat and polka dot dress drop to the floor, she stepped into the shower.

She wanted to cry, but couldn't contact any kind of release. Her nausea had eased a little since she'd relieved herself, but Nick knew from the amount of champagne she'd drunk that it would return. She figured she had a grace period of five or ten minutes.

She reached for one of her several shampoos and washed her knotted hair. Holding her head under the nozzle, she let the suds glide down her. Normally, this was a sensation she loved, but right now she couldn't imagine ever again having a pleasing physical sensation.

There was a burning pain in her upper thigh. It had been there since she woke up, but had been upstaged by the goings-on in her stomach. She looked down and saw a red spot, not quite a second-degree burn. She remembered that she had invited the attorney to touch his lighted cigarette to her thigh sometime after room service had left and she had opened his sexual Pandora's box.

You're sick . . .

She remembered that he had done everything in his power before she left the hotel to get her phone number or address. She had refused, and he'd tried to grab her purse from her before she left the room, in order to find some kind of ID. She had stopped him.

She'd thought, as her cab brought her home in the reddish early morning light, that he was following her. She thought she'd seen a car staying close behind, but she'd been so near to throwing up that she hadn't been able to turn around in the cab to check if it was him.

He knows where I live.

An accurate sense of time was not her strong suit on the best of days. She had no idea how long she'd been in the shower as she dried off.

My meeting . . .

She peered into the bedroom and saw that it was almost 9:45. She wondered if she should try to choose an outfit. No, don't be ridiculous, she thought. There'll be no meeting for me this morning.

She picked up her robe, which had fallen off its hook on the back of her bathroom door, and which smelled musty. She realized that she hadn't done laundry for over a week.

She decided to call Linda, go back to sleep for a couple of hours, drop off the laundry, come back and re-read the script, have some soup when her stomach cleared up, get to bed early, and start all over again tomorrow. This made her feel a little better.

She walked into the kitchen, automatically opening the refrigerator before remembering that there was nothing in it she'd be able to keep down. She was a terrible shopper and usually ate out or ordered in. There were a few Diet Cokes, some ancient goat cheese, and a quart of milk she'd never opened, the carton now bulbous.

Where's the Pepto-Bismol?

She went back to the bathroom to look for it. There was only one pink tablet left in the box in her medicine cabinet. She pulled open the cellophane with her teeth and chewed it down.

It was getting close enough to ten to try Linda Blake.

She took the phone, punched Linda's number, then sat in a leather chair that had been very expensive and attractive in the showroom but which she'd always found, since its delivery, irritatingly uncomfortable.

"Linda Blake," said Linda's voice. Her assistant was obviously not in yet.

"Oh, you *are* there. Great."

"Is that you, Nick?"

"It's me. Hi."

"You sound terrible."

"I am."

"Well, are you still going to make your appointment?" asked Linda, concerned. She'd worked hard for this one.

"That's just it, Linda. That's why I'm calling. I hate to do this, but —do you think you could get them to see me on Monday, or later this afternoon? I think I've got the flu."

"Oh, I know, I just got over it. But look . . . they won't be here Monday, I already know that. Sidney only came in for one day."

It infuriated Nick that directors from L.A. came to New York for only a day or two, seeing dozens of actors in meetings that were insultingly brief. In L.A., it always seemed that directors took weeks to meet actors. Everything there was *mañana.*

"Oh, God," said Nick. "What about later this afternoon, then? I just don't think I should meet him feeling like this."

"Well, okay, sure. Let me try. I really want this to work. Are you home?"

"Yeah."

"Let me call over there and I'll get right back to you. But listen, just in case they can't change it—are you ready? I mean, the meeting's in less than twenty minutes."

"Oh, sure. I got ready and everything," lied Nick, "but I just really feel awful, and, you know, Linda . . . I want to do this one right."

"Let me see what I can do, sweetie. I'll call you right back."

Nick sat on the chair and looked out the window. Her view was mostly of a building across the street. The sun had mercifully stayed behind the clouds, which were thickening and taking over the sky, or what she could see of the sky.

The nausea began to return in full force. Nick put her head in her lap and scanned the floor for a wastebasket to throw up in. The nearest one was in the hallway, dead ahead. Still slumped over at the waist, she made her way to it, picking it up just in time. She steadied it under her, and saw the used condom from her foray with Todd. She threw up, cursing herself for not putting some kind of plastic liner in the wastebasket.

The phone rang.

Thank God . . .

Feeling a little stronger with more of the poison out of her, Nick pounced on the phone.

"Yeah . . . ?" was how she answered.

"Yeah? *Yeah?* That's a nice way to answer the phone. Did I teach you that?" said someone who was not Linda Blake.

"Mom. Uh . . . hi. Look . . ."

"I know, I know, it's a bad time."

"It really is, Mom. I'm sorry, but I'm expecting a very important call. . . ."

"So isn't that why you have that call-waiting thing? I just have to ask you a question."

Nick's mother had a way of calling only when Nick was running out the door late for an appointment, or preparing for an audition, or entertaining gentlemen callers. It was uncanny.

Why don't you tell her about what you did last night?

"What, Mom? What's the question?" asked Nick, trying to sound patient, and failing.

"Well, it's about Easter. Remember, I invited you and your beau. . . ."

Nick had run into her mother two weeks before at the Museum of Modern Art. Her mother went there often, and Nick had been on a first date, a lunch date, with someone who'd seemed promising but who had turned out not to be. When she'd introduced him to her mother, it was during the promising part. Nick had her arm on his, and her mother had assumed it must be something serious, and had actually invited both of them to Easter supper.

"Mom, do you think I could call you back a little later? I'm in an awful hurry here."

"I just need a yes or no. There'll be your father, myself, you, your young man—I'm sorry I don't remember his name—and Jeanne Shea and her niece, who's at Princeton."

"Mom. It's December. Can we just take care of Christmas and New Year's and Martin Luther King's birthday and Valentine's Day and Groundhog Day. I mean, *Easter*?"

Two call-waiting beeps sounded.

"Mom, I'll call you back."

"When?"

Two more beeps.

"Later." She knew she'd need to sleep all day. "Around five."

"All right, because if you aren't coming, I really need to invite someone else. . . ."

Get a life!

"Okay, Mom. Bye." She tapped the thingy on the phone to activate call waiting. "Yes, hello?"

"Nick. It's me. Look, I talked to Sally Cashmore. You have to go this morning." Sally Cashmore was the casting agent for the studio. "They're booked solid all day, and there's nowhere else they can fit you in. Sidney has to leave by three to make his flight."

By three?? The jerk flies to New York to meet actors for less than a whole day??

Nick started to cry, holding the receiver away so Linda wouldn't hear. She managed to say, "Thanks for trying, Linda."

Linda went on. "Sorry, sweetie. You better get right over there. And look, here's the good news. Sally says you're her first choice for the part. Isn't that terrific? Go get 'em!"

★   ★   ★   ★

Nick hung up, and only now remembered to put down the waste-basket. She ran into the bathroom and pulled out her hair dryer. She didn't even notice that she'd stopped crying.

She opened the medicine cabinet with her free hand and took out a Chanel base, some powder, a little rouge, and mascara. She let them all fall into the sink, ran into her bedroom, and opened the closet. She threw on some underpants, hesitated for a second . . .

Yes. Wear a bra.

. . . grabbed one, and snapped it on. She ripped the dry cleaning plastic off a perfect faded-blue work shirt in her closet and buttoned it most of the way up. Then she thought about the character in the script, and buttoned one more button. She found her non-clingy jeans and jumped into them, chose a brown leather belt with a simple silver buckle, and finished with ankle-high brown tie shoes over cashmere argyle socks.

She ran back into the bathroom with her big brown shoulder bag and scooped the makeup out of the sink into the bag. There was no time to brush her teeth, so she gargled with some Listerine, the taste of which almost made her faint.

Nick, who could easily take an hour getting ready for a date or an appointment, had accomplished all this in six minutes.

She grabbed the script and a long camel-hair coat, and headed for the door.

My wallet . . .

She had no idea where she'd thrown her bag when she got home. It must be in the bedroom, she thought, and headed back. It was lying at the foot of her bed. She thrust her hand into it, but came up with only a five- and a ten-dollar bill. She pulled the bag open with both hands, dropping the script and her coat. She peered into it.

There was nothing. She now remembered that she'd also left her toothbrush and toothpaste in the hotel bathroom.

Then she realized that she'd left her wallet in the cab.

She'd been close to throwing up, and had put her wallet down on the seat after extracting a twenty from it to pay the driver. She had tried to compute a sensible tip, but had found it too difficult to concentrate. She had wanted only to get up to her apartment before she got sick. She'd told the driver to take an even five dollars, and he had put the change into her hand. She had pushed open the car door and moved in a blur to her building and into her place.

In her mind, she could now clearly see her wallet on the seat of that cab. There was no doubt. Her wallet also contained her checkbook. She'd have to notify the bank and the credit card companies, but there was no time. It was 10:08. She picked up her coat and the script and went out the door. Fifteen dollars would be enough for a cab ride to the meeting, and, if traffic wasn't bad, back home.

There was a little sign taped near the buttons for the elevator. Nick had seen it before and knew what it said.

OUR ELEVATORS ARE IN NEED OF SERVICE. WE APOLOGIZE FOR THE INCONVENIENCE. PLEASE USE THE STAIRS.

She cursed her building, ran down the stairs, out into the street and the now-gray day.

Nick had inordinately good luck with cabs, and, to her surprise, today was no exception. She got in and told the driver to take her to the Time-Warner building.

She would be about five minutes late—an utter miracle, she thought, under the circumstances. She opened the script onto her lap, found the first scene, and began reading, applying makeup with both hands.

You have five minutes. Breathe. Relax. You can do this. In an hour, it'll be over and you'll be back home in bed. The character isn't glamorous. It's okay that you don't look your best.

She was sweating. Would her perspiration show through the light blue work shirt? She hadn't put on deodorant.

You probably stink. And what you did last night is written all over your face.

She read the scene once. It was a part she had an intuitive handle on. She was very right for it—an outdoorsy, independent Southern woman making a life for herself after the Civil War. The cab headed into the side streets of Rockefeller Center.

I can do this. Besides, Linda said they might not even ask me to read.

Many meetings for films, she knew from experience, didn't require auditioning. It puzzled Nick. In the theater, you always went out onto an empty stage before meeting anyone. You'd read the scene. Then, if the director liked it, you might talk. But movies were usually just the reverse. Nick liked auditioning for plays better—she never knew what to say in a meeting.

The cab swerved over in front of the Time-Warner building, and Nick paid the fare, $6.25. With a tip, it came to $7.50. If traffic were no worse, she'd be able get home on what she had left.

She saw herself in the rearview mirror as the driver changed her ten-dollar bill. She berated herself for not bringing Visine. The makeup had helped, but her eyes were still awfully puffy. She got out of the cab. She wasn't quite steady on her feet, and she seemed to burn everywhere below her waist.

She took the elevator to the ninth floor, as directed in Linda Blake's memo, and walked toward a reception area.

Before she could speak, the receptionist looked up, "Nicolette Stallings?"

"Yes," said Nick, pleased that the receptionist knew her name. She looked down and saw the list of appointments with Nick's name second on the list.

"Go right in, they're waiting for you. Do you know you're five minutes late?"

"Yes, yes," Nick said, horrified that there was no time for a quick check in the ladies' room. "I'm so sorry, but the *traffic* . . ."

I'm a liar. Can you see that I'm a liar?

"Welcome to New York," said the woman dryly. "Please. Go right in. Mr. Halpern is waiting."

Nick could see on the list of appointments that there was another at 10:30. It was now 10:21. She felt moisture in her palms and under her arms. She wondered if she should take off her coat. She left it on. She wiped a bit of perspiration from her upper lip and looked to the door. She prayed that it would be only the director, and not a room full of producer types. She was far better one on one.

As she moved through the open door, she saw four men and one woman. There was no sign of Sally Cashmore, her ally. One of the men was talking animatedly. He glanced up at Nick with a trace of annoyance, because, Nick realized, he was about to deliver the punch line of a joke, and her entrance had come right on top of it. She hoped it wasn't Sidney Halpern.

"Lady," he said, holding a hand up to Nick to indicate that she should wait just a second while he finished, "I shit in your purse, I fucked your dog—I'm outta here!"

The four others exploded with laughter. They howled. One of the men stomped his foot, and the woman took off her dark glasses and shook her head. The joke teller looked at them, pleased, then over to Nick, then down to his list.

"Hi . . . Nicolette," he said, still chuckling, "I'm Sidney Halpern. God, what a way to meet. Excuse us, excuse us—it's a very funny joke."

The man who'd stomped his foot suddenly did it again, and doubled over with an aftershock of laughter.

"Hey, hey," said Sidney Halpern, suppressing a grin. "We got work to do here." Then to Nick: "Please. Come in."

"Thanks," said Nick, hoping no one would ask her to remove her coat.

"This is Marvin Deitch, Howard Pangburn, our writer, Steve Cruikshank, and Natalie LeVine, from the studio."

How do you do? I'm a worthless piece of shit. I committed adultery last night. I'm an exhibitionist, a voyeur, a masochist . . .

Marvin Deitch was still laughing at the joke. Natalie LeVine (pronounced le-*vine,* not le-veen) looked disappointed and hostile. Nick had no idea who Steve Cruikshank was, and was pretty sure he didn't either. Sidney Halpern was still trading knowing glances with Marvin Deitch over the joke. Only Howard Pangburn, the writer, seemed interested in meeting Nick.

"Here, why don't you sit down," said Sidney Halpern. "Which scene are you gonna read for us?"

Oh, shit.

"Can I take your coat?" said Steve Cruikshank, making himself useful.

I'm sweating. I smell. Do I have sweat stains?

"Thank you," said Nick, letting him take her coat and looking down at her armpits surreptitiously as she sat. She couldn't get a good look without being really obvious, so she decided just to keep her arms fairly tight by her side.

There was a moment of silence. Nick couldn't think of anything to say, so she smiled. Sidney Halpern smiled, as did Steve Cruikshank, Marvin Deitch, and Howard Pangburn. Natalie LeVine snuck a look at a copy of *The New York Times* that was on the couch next to her.

Make small talk . . .

All of Nick's small-talk circuits were shorted.

There was a pause.

"Well?" said Sidney Halpern.

"Well . . . what?" said Nick, a little bewildered.

"Which scene would you like to read?"

Oh . . . I was in Nicky Stallings Land.

Nick's ex-boyfriend, Hal, referred to Nick's more than occasional reveries as "going to Nicky Stallings Land." At those times, Nick would simply . . . go away for a few seconds . . . lost in thought.

Today she wasn't so much lost in thought as simply lost. She laughed, covering, and did her fairly good Jack Benny imitation.

"I'm *thinking,* I'm *thinking!*" said Nick/Jack Benny.

No one smiled. Natalie LeVine looked up from her *Times.*

Nick explained. "You know the joke where the mugger asks Jack Benny, 'Your money or your life?' "

"I beg your pardon?" asked Sidney Halpern, smiling, looking to the others for help.

"Sure," said Howard Pangburn, nodding, and still seeming friendly.

"So then what does Jack Benny say?" asked Sidney Halpern, feeling a little left out. "Oh, I see—he says . . ."

Nick and Sidney spoke in unison: "I'm *thinking*. I'm *thinking*."

"Right. *Right,*" Sidney Halpern went on. There was another small silence. "So—which scene would you like to do?"

Nick, who usually learned her lines for auditions, felt drops of sweat pop out around her hairline. "Well," she said, feeling as though she were choosing between lethal injection and hanging, "I guess . . . the first scene."

"Let's try the second scene," said Sidney Halpern. He turned to Howard Pangburn. "I've heard so many actresses read that first scene. I just don't want to hear it again."

Nick hadn't even had time to look at the second scene.

Natalie LeVine spoke up. "Weren't you in *The Prized Possession* at Second Stage?" she asked without looking at Nick.

The Prized Possession had been a slight triumph for Nick a few months back. She'd played a small but important part and received good reviews, including more than passing praise from the *Times*. It had made it a little easier for Linda Blake to get Nick important meetings, like this one. Nick was proud of her work in the play.

"Yes, I was," said Nick. She noticed that Sidney Halpern was looking at his watch.

"I didn't like it," said Natalie LeVine, finally looking in Nick's direction. "I know I'm in the minority there. I mean, I know the *Times* liked it and all, but . . . I gotta tell you, I didn't get it—at all."

"A lot of people felt that way," said Nick, at once wondering why she was accommodating this woman.

"Did you see it, Sidney?" asked the Vine, as Nick now thought of her.

"No. No, I didn't," said Sidney Halpern with a little shake of his head.

"But *you* were good," declared the Vine.

"Oh. Well, thank you," said Nick.

"Very good," the Vine went on, turning to the others. "She had this intensely funny scene with a mime . . ." She started to laugh at the recollection.

"No," said Nick. "That was the other woman. I played the niece."

Natalie LeVine narrowed her eyes. "The niece. The niece? I don't remember a niece."

Sidney Halpern was looking at his watch again.

"I had a scene with the landlord," said Nick, helping her out, "toward the end of the play."

"After the intermission?" asked the Vine.

"Yes. Almost right at the very end," said Nick.

Natalie LeVine thought for a moment. Then she solved it. "You know what? I didn't see the second act. We left." She turned to Sidney Halpern. "I was with Stan Bondy . . ."

Sidney Halpern nodded as though this made everything clear.

She turned back to Nick. "So—who played that scene with the mime?"

"That was Becky Sheehan," said Nick.

"Becky Sheehan," said the Vine thoughtfully. "Well, *she* was hilarious."

"She was," agreed Nick. There was another pause. "I'm sorry you didn't see the end."

"Well, I would have stayed," said the Vine, "but . . . I mean, you know Stan Bondy."

Nick didn't, and it must have showed on her face.

Steve Cruikshank made a little snorting sound, as though to say to Nick, "Well, if you *did* know Stan Bondy, it would be utterly clear."

"So," said Sidney Halpern. "The second scene. Yes?"

I'm dead.

"Sure," said Nick, turning the pages in her script. "That was page . . . ?"

"Eighty-three," said Sidney Halpern, Steve Cruikshank, Howard Pangburn, and Marvin Deitch, almost simultaneously. Nick went past page 83, then thumbed back, searching for it, before realizing that pages 83 and 84 were reversed in her script. The office boys who did the copying in Linda Blake's office had struck again. She ripped the two pages out of her script. Howard Pangburn looked a little startled, as though he might have just been injured by voodoo.

"Now," said Sidney Halpern, setting the scene, "the war's over, and you've just been through the whole thing with your attorney . . ."

The word "attorney" stirred more than a faint recollection in Nick, but not the one Sidney Halpern had in mind. She fought off thoughts of last night and focused on the director.

". . . and you're happy, *really* happy for the first time in months. You're just radiant."

Nick tried to summon forth radiance. On a normal day, it wasn't that difficult.

"I'm going to read with you," said Sidney Halpern. "So just go ahead and start when you want to."

Nick hated it when a director read with her. How could he keep his eyes on his script and still have any idea what she was doing?

She fought off her panic about being unprepared and not having had any sleep. Here was an Oscar-winning director. You didn't, Nick knew, show up unprepared for a meeting with such a man.

All eyes, except Natalie LeVine's, were on her.

Radiant. I'm radiant . . .

"Well, Jeff Johnson," read Nick, "as I live and breathe!"

"Hillary?" read Sidney Halpern, his eyes glued to his script. "My God—is that really you?"

"Of course it's me. Have I changed all that much?"

"I don't remember you being so . . . so . . ."

"So . . . *what*? My, my. I don't remember you ever being at a loss for words, Jeffrey Johnson."

Nick tried to read a stage direction, which said something about Hillary looking coquettish.

"I don't remember you being so . . . grown-up," read Sidney Halpern, his face in the page.

"Well, when was the last time you looked, Mr. Jeffrey T. Big-Shot War-Hero Johnson?"

"You were always . . . one of the kids, Hillary."

"Doesn't feel like anybody's a kid anymore, Jeffrey."

"It's . . . awful good to see you."

Sidney Halpern had not looked up once. He was getting into his performance. Nick went on.

"I hear you did some wonderful things at Shiloh and Vicksburg."

"Not wonderful enough."

Here Nick took a moment, as the script indicated, and looked into his eyes. Sidney Halpern looked up. Nick hoped she was projecting the right feeling. She chose adoration.

"You're back, Jeff Johnson. *That's* wonderful enough."

That was the scene.

Sidney Halpern studied her for a second. She felt very looked at. *What does he see?*

He looked around the room. "Howard? Anything you want to add?"

Howard Pangburn, the writer, who'd been glad to see Nick a few minutes before, now looked as if he were trying to forgive her for something. He shook his head.

"Guys?" asked Sidney Halpern. "Natalie?"

Marvin Deitch was looking at Nick's breasts, which were well concealed beneath her modest shirt. Steve Cruikshank was scanning his copy of the appointment list. He looked up brightly, with a little forced smile, and said, "No." Natalie LeVine was flipping through a Rolodex. She looked up and shook her head at Sidney.

"Would you like me to read it again?" offered Nick.

Sidney Halpern tried to look as thoughtful as possible. He appeared to be giving Nick's suggestion every consideration—but for the fact that he was getting up and clearly ending the meeting.

"No . . . no, thank you, Lisa. Thank you, but that won't be necessary."

Lisa?

She extended her hand to Sidney Halpern and he took it. Even his handshake seemed distracted. "Thanks for coming in," he said, smiling and nodding his head. He was standing near the door.

No one had said anything about the meeting being over. But it was over. Nick now had to make her exit, always her least favorite part of any meeting.

"Well," said Nick, "thank *you*. And thank you all too," she said to the others. They each nodded or raised a hand in a slight wave.

Just leave. Don't shake everybody's hand.

Nick went to each of them and shook each one's hand. No one spoke except Nick.

"Good-bye. Thanks. Bye. Nice to meet you." She made her way to the doorway.

Just turn around—and leave.

She stood there for a few seconds and smiled. She took a breath and raised her eyebrows hopefully.

"Well," she said, and looked at Sidney Halpern as earnestly as she could, "Thanks."

"Thank *you*," said Sidney Halpern.

"No, no, no," said Nick, making a joke, "thank *you*." She waited for him to continue the joke with another "No, no, no, thank *you*." But he didn't.

"Okay. Bye," said Nick, finally forcing her body to turn around and leave the room.

As she walked past the receptionist, she saw a gorgeous woman reading the script, waiting. The woman was dressed in a plain blue work shirt and jeans. She was radiant.

As Nick waited for the elevator, she heard Sidney Halpern's voice on the receptionist's intercom.

"Miss Hays," said the voice, "see if you can find out who represents Becky Sheehan, and try to get her in here before 2:30."

"But, Mr. Halpern, there's no extra time. You're booked straight through until three, and you absolutely have to leave by then to make your flight."

"Well—cancel someone, then. I have to see this girl."

★   ★   ★   ★

On her way down, Nick's ailments rallied back to the surface. She craved Pepto-Bismol but realized she couldn't afford any right now.

Oh, Christ. I have to call American Express, Visa, Citibank . . .

Of course she had chosen the easiest number in the history of the world to activate her cash card. Not good at remembering figures, she'd picked 1-2-3-4. She felt sure now that it would be the first combination attempted by whoever had found her wallet.

She tried to recall the cab driver. Had he been a trusty sort? All she could summon up was that he'd had the worst B.O. in her collection of taxi-driver–B.O. memories. She had no sense of whether he might be the wallet-returning type.

The Listerine seemed to have worn off, and the fetid taste of cigarettes returned with a burp for which Nick felt otherwise grateful.

As she got about a block away from the Time-Warner building, it started to rain. Nick had been walking with no sense of where she was going. She now realized she'd gone in the wrong direction. A slight detour to Nicky Stallings Land. She had no umbrella, no hat, no wallet.

She was fairly close to her parents' apartment. I could go there, Nick thought, get some TLC, make my calls, maybe take a nap. Mom'll take pity on me and make soup.

Are you out of your mind? Today?

She looked for a taxi. What with the cold, hard rain, they were all taken. She saw a man get out of one halfway down the block and ran toward it, arriving just behind a very pregnant woman who appeared out of nowhere.

"Where did you come from?" asked Nick in frustrated amazement, but deferring to her pregnancy.

"I just had ultrasound," the woman beamed as she opened the door of the cab and got in. "It's a girl!" she said to Nick as though they were old friends. She got in and closed the door, leaving Nick on the wet sidewalk.

Nick looked around, then down at her soggy camel-hair coat. She had to get off her feet and she had to find a phone.

She noticed that her legs, as if on automatic pilot, were taking her in the direction of her parents' building, a few blocks crosstown at Beekman Place.

What the hell . . .

They'd been ensconced in the suburbs, in Dobbs Ferry, but had moved into the city around the time that Nick, the younger of two daughters, graduated from high school. Nick's father was embroiled in the aftermath of Watergate. A vice president of an airline that gave illegal campaign funds to Nixon, Nick's father, while not guilty himself, was held partially responsible for the company's involvement. To avoid indictment, he'd had to hire the best legal counsel, and the costs had forced them to sell their house and take a small co-op in the city. Nick's father, in his new kicked-upstairs post-Watergate job, found that he loved not having to commute. A Nixon fan, he often joked that Watergate had been bad for everyone but him.

And there were her mother's soups, which she made often, delivering them herself to Nick's building. Mom, Nick had to admit, had an uncanny knack for making soup at the right time. It matched her knack for phoning at the wrong time.

As she made her way east across Park, Lexington, and Third avenues, Nick, ever wetter, hoped that today was a soup day. Maybe, she thought, after a nap on my old bed—they had moved it from the Dobbs Ferry home to the guest room of their apartment—I'll be able to keep down some soup.

She walked into the staid brick building at Beekman Place, where Nick usually felt underdressed. In this neighborhood women wore Chanel suits to walk their dogs.

The doorman, whose name Nick never remembered but who always remembered Nick, had trouble recognizing her.

"Is that you, Miss Stallings?" asked . . . Phil? Robbie? Paul?

"It's me," said Nick, whose hair was pasted down to her head, and whose coat looked like a wet sponge. "Is my mom home?" Her father would be at work.

"I think Mrs. Stallings is in, yes," said the doorman, picking up the intercom and pressing a buzzer. He waited a moment. "I seen an old movie of yours on TV the other night."

"Really? What was it?" asked Nick.

"Something with you and, I think it was George Peppard."

Nick had never worked with George Peppard. It had to have been some TV show episode she'd done years before. With cable, nothing ever went away.

"Oh, yeah," said Nick, not having the strength to figure out what it might actually have been.

"I only saw a couple minutes of it. The wife made me turn it off. It was like two, three A.M. Anyways, you looked great."

As opposed to now.

He got no reply on the intercom.

"I guess she went out," he said, bewildered. "I was downstairs for a few minutes with a delivery. Maybe I missed her."

Nick knew with utter certainty that she could not now make it home alive.

"Do you think it would be possible to let me in, so I can get dry and make a few phone calls? I lost my wallet, and I need to call the bank."

"You weren't mugged, were you, Miss Stallings?" asked the doorman, concerned.

"No, no. I left it in a cab. Do you believe that?" Nick tried to look as helpless as possible, which wasn't too difficult.

"I'm not supposed to let anyone into an apartment who don't live here, Miss Stallings. . . ."

She tried to squeeze his name out of the back of her brain. *Jerry!*

"Jerry . . . I really, *really* need to lie down. I'm sure my folks wouldn't mind."

Jerry made an executive decision. "Here's the extra key, Miss Stallings. If I can't trust you, who can I trust?"

Nick had no desire to hazard a guess. She took the key gratefully. "Jerry, you're an angel."

"My wife always says I have too much of the devil in me, Miss Stallings, so I'll tell her you said that," said Jerry with a wink. Nick attempted to muster a return wink, but found she couldn't close one eye without the other drooping as well.

★   ★   ★   ★

As she opened her parents' door, Nick smelled that wonderful smell. The smell, if she'd ever named it, would have been called My Life, or My House. It was the same smell Nick had breathed every day of her life as she was growing up, whenever she entered the house in Dobbs Ferry. It seemed miraculous that this smell could have made the trip to Manhattan from Westchester, arriving intact at Beekman Place. It was the delicious, comforting, composite aroma of her parents: their furniture, their clothes, their stuff, themselves. It was a balm to Nick.

Everything was in perfect order, as always. It wasn't a huge apartment, but it was well laid out. Her mother was oppressively fastidious, and yet the result, minus her mother, was soothing and orderly.

Nick realized that she'd never before been in this apartment when her mother wasn't there. Since her mother talked more or less constantly, and always loudly enough to be heard throughout the place, it was almost eerily quiet.

This is what it'll feel like, thought Nick, when I walk in here after they've died.

Nick removed her spongy coat. At home, she would have let it fall to the floor, then picked it up hours or days later, rumpled and smelling of mildew. But here, she carefully hung it on a rounded wood hanger from the hall closet, moving the other coats aside so they wouldn't catch its wetness. She took her answering machine beeper from her bag, removed her shoes, and pulled off the soggy socks. She carried them down the hallway to the guest bathroom and slung the socks over the shower curtain pole, leaving her shoes on the ledge of the tub.

Nick felt completely at home. But she was too at home to notice.

She went into the guest room—her room, on those rare occasions that she stayed there—and looked at the bed. It was the bed she'd grown up in, and the sight of it brought Nick's blood pressure almost down to normal.

It was warm in her room, and dry. She peeled off her jeans and pulled down the covers, feeling the clean sheets. She had a sudden urge to get to a toilet. The burning was still there, not quite as bad as before. But the soreness between her legs was worse, and her stomach was still under siege. She reached around without looking and opened the medicine cabinet, finding some milk of magnesia. Not having the strength to go to the kitchen for a spoon, she opened the bottle and took a hearty swig.

She made her way back to the bed. Then she remembered she still had to make her calls. There was no phone in the guest room, so Nick went into her parents' bedroom and sat on their king-size bed. She picked up the rotary Princess phone by the bed. She had never been able to persuade her parents, who lived in a world free of cordless machines and Sprint access numbers, to get a Touch-tone.

She called the credit card companies. During the endless periods on hold, Nick dozed on her parents' bed with the phone at her ear. She was assured that she'd have new cards within three business days. The bank was more difficult. For a moment, she couldn't remember her social security number, and this caused the robot-woman on the other end to become suspicious. Nick finally coaxed the nine digits from the far reaches of her brain and was told she'd have new checks, a new card, and a new account number within the week.

She mustered one last bit of energy and called her machine at home. It was an automatic thing with her. She called her machine the way a smoker reaches for a cigarette.

There were, as usual, a few hangups. Also a message from her dearest friend, Meg, who lived in L.A. but was calling, inexplicably, from Aspen. There was nothing from Linda Blake. It was too soon, Nick figured, to have heard anything. Then this:

"Hi. It's, ah . . . Todd," said his voice dreamily. "I thought I was going to die happy last night, but I seem to still be here, and I thought I'd call and say . . . what? . . . that I'm glad to be alive, and that I can, uh . . . still . . . taste you. I can't talk like this to a machine—what am I doing? I just wanted to hear your voice. Why don't you call me when you get back from wherever you are. You're not still out in the hall, are you? I'll stop talking now. I'm definitely talking too much, but, unlike most people, I *love* machines. Makes me feel like I'm talking to you, since I know you'll be hearing this . . . whenever you . . . hear it. Wow. Uhh . . . yeah. I'll sign off, and . . . talk to you later, I guess." There was a pause. "Oh, 847-3826."

Nick felt as if she'd seen Todd about twenty years ago.

There was one more message. Nick's heart beat fast for the first time since last night.

"Hi. It's Sam. I've been meaning to call, but it's been crazy here. I'm probably gonna be pretty hard to reach, but you can try me at

456-0604. That's 818, not 213. You were great in the play, by the way. Did I tell you that?"

He hadn't. Sam was an actor she'd worked with last week at a one-time-only workshop play reading at the Manhattan Theater Club. He was well known, not exactly a household word, but respected by other actors. Nick had accepted the workshop partly because he was in it.

He was, Nick figured, about ten years older than she. They'd lingered in the dank hallway outside the reading room and talked for over an hour after everyone else had left. He was quick and funny, and for that hour, Nick had felt curious, attractive, and vulnerable. He'd been terrific in the play, while Nick was sure she'd seemed self-conscious and over her head. He'd been on his way out to L.A. for a month of re-shoots on a movie, and had asked for her number.

He'd left for the coast over a week ago. Nick had been checking her machine a bit more fervently since then.

She liked the sound of his voice. She put the phone back on its cradle, and, smelling her mother in the now-warm pillow, she buried her face in it and went to sleep.

★   ★   ★   ★

In the steamy afternoon sun of St. Barts, a still-frosty champagne glass in her hand, Nick fanned herself with the dessert menu.

She was just finishing lunch with her mother and several of her mother's friends, all of whom were wearing shoes on their heads and Burberry raincoats. Nick was covered up—by St. Barts standards—in a relatively modest bikini with a nicely pressed, perfectly faded blue work shirt, tied at the bottom.

A yellow New York cab drove by on the beach, and the driver asked people at an adjoining table if anyone had lost a wallet. Nick tried to speak, but no sound came out of her mouth. The cab drove into the water, became a speedboat, and sped away.

Lunch had been nothing but talk of Easter plans, and Nick was restless. Way down the beach, where it curved into another bay, she saw a group of people swimming, sunning, body-surfing. It was difficult to tell, but they seemed young, athletic, and, in the tradition of St. Barts, nude. There were fifteen or twenty of them, all men.

"I think I need to walk off this wonderful lunch," said Nick, hoping that no one would want to join her.

"Good idea," said her mother. "Be careful crossing the street, dear, you have no shoes on. And remember, we're meeting that nice young . . . what's his *name*? . . . Todd . . . for dinner. Such a nice young man. He told me all about what you did to him last night. Really! It must have been an *awfully* good restaurant. Will you be bringing him for Easter supper, or that other nice young man?"

"All of them, Mother. I'm bringing all the nice young men."

"That'll be fine. Shall we say supper at three o'clock?"

"Supper at three o'clock," said the women with shoes on their heads as Nick started away.

"Unless 3:30 would be better . . . ?"

"Sure," said Nick, her eyes on the men down the beach. As she moved toward them, she could feel adrenaline flowing. She took a sip of champagne, delighting in the decadence of the cool liquid on the hot nude beach. She looked over her shoulder. Her mother and their party were beginning to be almost far enough away.

Air raid sirens rang and a male voice on loudspeakers from her mother's direction called out, "Nicolette Stallings! Long distance call for Miss Stallings!"

She kept walking, just along the ocean's edge.

"Miss Stallings!" the voice called after her. "It's your agent! About Sidney Halpern. Urgent! And please call the concierge for the results of your HIV tests."

She kept walking and the voice faded. She looked back. Her mother was now a speck in the distance. A tiny wave lapped her feet as Nick untied her work shirt and unbuttoned it.

She looked at the group she was approaching. They were tan all over, and there was one in particular who looked so good to Nick that it gave her chills. She dropped her work shirt to the sand, walking on. As she got closer to the man, she could see that he was watching her.

One hand went behind her back to unclasp her top. It snagged, and Nick couldn't release it. His eyes were on her. She wanted desperately to remove her top for him in a beautiful way, but the clasp was hopelessly stuck. She gave it a violent tug. It wouldn't give. The others in the group were now watching her too.

Nick was almost upon them. The man was smiling, inviting. He said something to her in French. Nick smiled, as though she understood, and toasted him with her glass. She poured the last bit of champagne slowly over her shoulders and down her top, feeling the fizz on her warm skin. All eyes now on her, she reached for her bikini bottom and pulled down. Before she could move it, she heard something, and looked up.

CHAPTER 6

Her mother stood over her, a mug in her outstretched hand.

"Well, someone's had a good long nap! I tried twice before, but I couldn't wake you," said Nick's mother. "Have some soup. I just made it. Delicious, if I say so myself—and I do."

Where am I?

"Mom," said Nick, reflexively taking the soup. "Hi."

"Remember when you used to make soup with me?" her mother asked wistfully.

"Yes," said Nick, although her recollection wasn't as nostalgic as her mother's. When Nick was a kid and her mother had too much to drink, her temper became, to young Nick, frighteningly mercurial. Nick had often found the best defense was to become Mommy's kitchen helper. It kept the anger and flashes of disapproval to a minimum.

"Terry said he'd let you in and that you lost your wallet."

Oh, God. It's not Jerry it's Terry.

She sipped from the mug. Her stomach seemed to be vaguely

receptive to the soup, for which she was grateful. She looked up again at her mother. "How do you always know when to make soup?"

"Mothers know these things. Someday you'll know too. Now, what about your wallet? You weren't attacked, were you?"

"No. Stupider than that. I left it in a cab."

"Doris Erman was attacked last week. . . ."

"Oh, God," said Nick, not wanting to hear about another mugging.

"*Attacked!*" said her mother. "What is the world coming to? Do you want to stay for dinner? Your father's in St. Maarten." They had a condominium there, and her father was head of the condo association. "He had to go down for an association meeting, but he seems to have been caught in a hurricane. He called right before it hit, and they'd closed the airport. He's afraid we might lose our roof, poor thing. Just think. But life goes on, and I am going to commence a meat loaf. Doris says she believes in putting *anything* into meat loaf. Anything, she says! So I'm going to do an experiment."

"What time is it?" asked Nick.

"About 4:30."

"Jesus," said Nick, still trying to focus.

"How do you like that *soup*?"

"It's . . . wonderful. Just what the doctor ordered."

"Good. Now tell me all about whatever happened."

"Oh, God," said Nick, her brain working to censor the activities of the past twenty hours in such a way as to explain her appearance in her mother's bed. "I drank too much last night, I'm afraid. . . ."

"Oh, dear," said Mother-the-recovering-alcoholic. Nick noted an almost irritating lack of judgment to her tone. "And how did you lose your wallet?" With her finger, Nick's mother wiped a speck of soup from Nick's mug, cleaned the finger with a Kleenex from the bedside table, then balled up the tissue and made it disappear into her apron—all in an unobtrusive nanosecond.

"It's a long story, Mom," said Nick, thinking, thinking. "I guess I just left it on the seat while I was paying the—"

"Don't you want to hear about my experiment?" asked Nick's mother.

"What experiment?" said Nick.

"With the meat loaf."

"Oh. Sure," said Nick. Her mother's interruptions were usually infuriating. She would typically profess to want to hear all about Nick's life, only to cut her off after thirty seconds or so with a non sequitur.

But today Nick was pleased not to have to go on. She smiled, grateful for the soup and the mothering. "By all means—tell me about the experiment."

"Rice Krispies. And dried figs," said her mother, as though she were revealing the location of buried treasure, furrowing her brow as if she didn't believe it herself.

The soup was going down surprisingly well, though the thought of figs and Rice Krispies was not a tonic to Nick. She persevered in what she knew her mother always needed most: listening.

"Doris Erman swears that she dumped half a bowl of leftover Rice Krispies into her last meat loaf. Also some rather tired dried figs. Doris never throws anything away. She said it was delicious."

"And you believed her?"

"She's always right about food. Precious little else, poor dear, but I've never known her to be wrong about a recipe."

Nick wondered if her life would ever include recipes for meat loaf.

"Now, you mustn't tell your father about the experiment. I'm putting some in the freezer for when he gets back, and if he knows, he won't eat it."

"I won't say a word," promised Nick.

"I confess I would love to add a half a cup of red wine. But no. My AA sponsor tells me I shouldn't even cook with it. Oh, la." She studied Nick's face for a few seconds. "I suppose this means that you're now doomed to journey into the bowels of Manhattan to the dreaded Bureau of Motor Vehicles."

"Oh, God," said Nick, who'd forgotten about her driver's license.

Her now ex-license was from California, acquired during a three-month stay in L.A. several years before. She so seldom used a car in Manhattan that she'd let her license lapse, but in Los Angeles she needed one. She mourned the loss of her California license with the wonderful picture of her on it.

In the California license photo, taken after a weekend in Malibu doing things you don't tell your mother about, Nick looked happy, tan, and sun-streaked. Whenever a new boyfriend flipped through her wallet for the first time, Nick relished it. She'd thought seriously of trying to have it blown up to use for her eight-by-ten. Her resumé pictures, in which she'd always been too hair-sprayed or made up, had never been half as good. The little photo machine at the DMV had caught her off guard and unselfconscious.

The thought of resumés reminded her of Linda Blake. She reached for her beeper to check her machine again. Without interrupting her mother, who was now discussing finer points of meat loaf, Nick, all the while seemingly attentive, dialed the phone and retrieved her messages.

There was one from her mother, a few hours before, obviously from a pay phone, imploring Nick to call about Easter.

Mother Stereo.

She berated herself for not having a newer answering machine so she could fast-forward. She kept nodding to her actual mother, while listening to her voice on the machine prattling on about Easter plans.

A few thoughts of last night returned.

You're a pathetic slut and all the mother's soup in the world isn't going to save you from dying a miserable, well-deserved death from AIDS.

Her mother's message on the machine finally ended, and there followed one from Linda Blake.

"This is Patrick in Linda Blake's office," said the voice of another of Linda's revolving door of euphemistically titled assistants. "Linda would like you to call her when you get a moment."

Not a great sign, thought Nick. She makes the call herself when it's good news.

Her mother went on. ". . . they say the winds hit a hundred miles an hour twenty miles off St. Maarten last night. Your poor father. I should have gone with him, but it sounded like such a bore, and we have ballet tickets . . ."

Nick pressed the appropriate button on her beeper, and hung up.

"Mom, I need to make a call in private."

Her mother was a bit taken aback, but nonetheless started to leave.

"More soup?" she asked at the door.

"No thanks, Mom, but that was—"

"I made it specially because Terry said you weren't feeling well."

"It was great, Mom, but I don't think I can keep any more down . . . I must be coming down with the flu or something."

"Are you staying for dinner?"

"I don't think so, Mom. But thanks."

"Doris Erman's meat loaf," said her mother, eyebrows raised, intentionally silly, as though dangling the Hope diamond before Nick.

Sure. And I can tell you all about the Triple. . . .

"I have plans tonight, Mom," said Nick, looking apologetic. "And I really have to make this call. I'm sorry."

"I don't think you should be going out if you have the flu, but suit yourself," said her mother, moving toward the kitchen. "I'm giving you some soup to take with you."

Nick dialed Linda Blake. Patrick the New answered in his officious, just-out-of-the-mailroom tone.

"Hi, Patrick. It's Nicolette." Only good friends called her Nick.

"I'm sorry," said Patrick, "that's Nicolette . . . ?" He paused, searching for her last name.

"Just tell her it's Nick, returning her call."

Linda came on. Nick knew that in the time-honored tradition of agent-training, Patrick was listening in to this and every call. "Tell Patrick to do his homework," said Nick.

"He's new," said Linda, laughing, and no doubt, thought Nick, winking at Patrick. Linda didn't go on.

"So . . . ?"

"Oh, sweetie, I'm sorry. Sidney's going to go with someone else."

It irritated Nick that Linda referred to the director by his first name. What were they, ex-lovers?

"I don't believe it," said Nick, believing it all too well. "I'm so perfect for that part."

"You really are, sweetie. And they were so high on you too. Sally Cashmore said she had a really good feeling about it. . . ."

"Is it over?" asked Nick. "I mean—is that it?"

"I'm afraid so, sweetie. Sally loved you for the part, but she said Sidney just, you know, decided to go another way."

"Well, what did they say about the meeting?" asked Nick, prolonging the agony.

"Just that, you know, it didn't . . . click. I mean, they *liked* you, but they just didn't—"

"—get off," said Nick. "They just didn't get off. Shit." No one spoke for a few seconds.

"Do you have some kind of history with Natalie LeVine?" asked Linda.

"No. Why?"

"I don't know. Sally seemed to think that Natalie might have been the problem. Sidney was leaning toward testing you, but Natalie evidently turned him down."

"But he's the goddamn director, for Christ's sake," said Nick.

"She's the studio. And Sidney's last picture didn't do that well. . . ."

"He won an Oscar . . ."

"But the one after that didn't make a penny." There was a long silence. Nick heard her mother wrapping the soup in the kitchen.

"I'm sorry, sweetie."

Say good-bye and hang up.

"Do you know who got it?" Nick asked.

"Well, they have an offer out to someone, but it hasn't been accepted yet. Who knows, maybe if it doesn't work, they'll come back to us."

Don't ask.

"Who is it? Do you know?" asked Nick.

"Well, yes. Because she's a client of the office," said Linda Blake a tad hesitantly. "It's . . ."

. . . Becky Sheehan . . .

". . . Becky Sheehan."

May you die a long, slow, painful death.

"When did you guys sign Becky Sheehan?" asked Nick.

"About a month ago."

After you saw us both in The Prized Possession. *You signed her to hedge your bets.*

"I never thought of you two as being right for the same kinds of parts," Linda Blake went on. "I didn't even submit her for this, sweetie. But they *asked* for her."

Nick fought off simultaneous urges to scream, curse, and cry.

"Okay," said Nick. "Thanks, Linda."

Thanks?? What the hell are you thanking her for?

"Onward and upward, sweetie. Let's have lunch next week."

"Sure," said Nick lamely. "When?"

"Why don't I call you the first of the week?"

"Sure. Call me Monday."

"Actually, I may be out of the office on Monday. You know what? The week after would be better."

"Great," said Nick flatly.

"Bye, sweetie."

"Bye, Linda," said Nick. "You too, Patrick."

She sat up and caught a glimpse of herself in her mother's mirror. She looked as though she'd spent several nights in these clothes. Her hair was pushed in on one side of her head. Even through the soup, she still tasted cigarettes.

You're in your mother's bed. Pathetic.

She rose to her feet and went to the hall closet. Her coat wasn't there. Her mother appeared with some soup in a large, ungainly plastic container, and found Nick whipping through the closet.

"Oh," said her mother, "I hung your poor coat up in the maid's bathroom. You're not staying?" She went to retrieve the coat.

Why don't you just accept a little comforting?

"No, Mom. I really gotta go."

"I really *have* to go," said her mother, returning with the coat and correcting her.

"Oh, lighten up," said Nick, moving to her for a hug. Her mother accepted hugs, but wasn't much at returning them. Her arms tended to stay by her sides while she vaguely leaned in the general direction of the hugger. "And thank you for the wonderful soup," Nick added, meaning it.

"I'm so sorry your poor father wasn't here. He *never* gets to see you."

Nick had seen her father for lunch less than a week before. After his usual anaesthetizing martini, they had slipped into their long-established rhythm of small talk and evasions, punctuated by arid silences. She had always felt provided for by her father, but had seldom found comfort in his company. He found all vivid emotions difficult.

"Tell Dad I love him," said Nick. "Tell yourself the same thing. When will he be back?"

"Monday or Tuesday, depending on the damage. Here's your soup."

"Thanks, Mom—for the port in the storm." Nick was out the door, pressing for the elevator in the hallway.

"I always want you to feel free to come here. Always. In fact—" Her mother disappeared for a few seconds as Nick heard the elevator approaching. She returned, brandishing a key for Nick to take.

"Now you won't have to talk the doorman into letting you in. This is your home too, you know."

The elevator arrived. Nick took the key. "You're so great, Mom."

"Am I?" her mother asked, shedding fifty-odd years and sounding suddenly like a little girl.

"You are," said Nick conclusively. The doors started to close.

"Oh, dear," Nick heard her mother call as the elevator started moving down. "You still haven't told me about Easter."

*   *   *   *

In the elevator, Nick realized she hadn't asked her mother for any money. She'd certainly need some cash to see herself through the weekend. It was Friday afternoon, the banks had closed, and without a bank card or checkbook Nick had no way of getting money until Monday. She thought about going back up, but she didn't have the strength for another leave-taking—not to mention the embarrassment of borrowing money from her mother. No, she thought, I'll gut this one out.

As she headed toward the exit, the doorman was holding the intercom phone out to her.

"Your mother wanted to catch you before you left."

Nick took the phone. "Mom. It's been so long. How *are* you?"

"It occurred to me that without a wallet you might need a little cash. Do you have any money?"

Nick's mother was always inquiring about Nick's finances in ways that made it clear she thought Nick was broke. She found her mother's assumptions insulting, but endured them rather than discuss money with her.

But now she *was*—at least until Monday—broke. Not actually broke, and yet, in a practical, irritating, and tangible way . . . broke.

How are you going to get through the weekend on $7.50? You can't even order out for food. Go back up and borrow fifty bucks.

"I'm fine, Mom. Thanks."

"Okay. Just wanted to make sure. Get some sleep. Oh, and what do you think about Easter?"

"Well, Mom, I always had a little trouble grasping the Resurrection—literally anyway. But I think it's a lovely holiday. Gotta go. Thanks for the soup. I love you, Mom."

"Cab?" asked Jerry or Terry. Terry. It was Terry. Yes.

"No thanks," she said, not using his name, unwilling to trust any impulse today. She had to call Martine before she went any further. There was a phone on the corner.

"It wasn't George Peppard," called the doorman as Nick went through the door. "It was James Woods."

Nick stopped in her tracks. "No one has ever before, in the history of the planet, confused George Peppard and James Woods," she said.

"I was switching channels. You know. *Breakfast at Tiffany's* was on, and then that thing with you and James Woods. You had just the one scene, right?"

"Right."

"I kept clicking around, you know, during the commercials. I love that *Breakfast at Tiffany's*. My granddaughter's name is Tiffany."

"Audrey Hepburn in her glory days," mused Nick. "Not too shabby."

"I rest my case," he said. And Nick was released into the street.

The rain had let up a little. Nick's coat had dried considerably. She looked at the sky. It was no longer the kind of rain that instantly gets you wet. It had slowed to that more friendly rain which somehow, quite miraculously, *doesn't* get you wet. As she made a beeline for the pay phone, Nick, fortified by her mother's soup, felt she had a chance of making it home without passing out.

Dialing Martine, Nick realized she couldn't remember her calling card number. Weeks often went by without her using it. She hung up. The number was, of course, written down in her lost wallet, which meant she'd now have to use a quarter from her dwindling cash reserve. She put the container of soup down on the phone booth's little shelf, reached into her pocket, and found, to her surprise, a bonus dime she hadn't known was there.

Eureka.

She longed for everything about the time in her life when pay phones only cost a dime. She finally fingered one of her two quarters and dialed.

Please be there.

She got, as usual, Martine's answering machine. Nick was pretty sure that if she talked to the machine in a needy enough voice, Martine would pick up. Martine's machine was even more antiquated than Nick's, and she waited through the longish message which, in all the time that Nick had known her, hadn't changed.

It had a kind of waterfally New Age musical background, with Martine speaking slowly in a voice that sounded as if she were talking to a crazy person who needed calming down. It had put Nick off at first, because the voice didn't sound real. But over a few years of listening to this same message, Nick now found that she *was,* in fact, calmed by Martine's soothing voice on the machine. This—today—made Nick wonder if she was crazy.

"Martine. It's Nick. Can you pick up?" She waited a few seconds. "I, uh, really need to talk to you."

"Hi, babe," said Martine, the only woman Nick knew who called people babe. "What's up?"

"Do you have any time left today, or tonight, or—any time—over the weekend?"

"Are you all right?"

"Uh. No."

"Okay. Let me see." Nick heard her shuffling through her diary. "I'm booked for the rest of today, and . . . I have a dinner I can't cancel, and then I have a phone session when I get home. Can this wait till tomorrow?"

No.

"Oh, God, sure, I guess."

"You guess?"

"No, I mean . . . what time tomorrow are we talking about?" Nick was increasingly unsure how much of the weekend she could get through without seeing Martine.

"How about one o'clock? I just had a cancellation."

I can't make it that long.

"One would be great," said Nick.

"Okay, babe. I'll see you then."

Nick had envisioned Martine telling her to come right over. In addition to her emergency session, she'd figured she might borrow a few bucks to tide her over for the weekend. After the phone call, her treasury was down to $7.25—$7.35 with her new-found dime.

It was Friday rush hour, and it was raining, and all around her the traffic was starting to gridlock. Her only choice was a bus. A cab would get held up in traffic, its meter eventually demanding more than she had. The bus, at least, would leave her with about six bucks for the weekend. She couldn't face the subway. She loathed buses too, but today she had no choice.

At the bus stop around the corner, Nick found herself amid a clump of weary nine-to-fivers in various states of wetness elbowing each other for a space under the little roofed shelter. A man in front of her who smelled musty and noxious repeatedly turned around to leer at her, making no bones about checking her out. She pretended he didn't exist, but it didn't discourage him.

She suddenly swung around and lurched toward a small bank of three pay phones a block up First Avenue. One was in use. She picked up one of the others. It was dead. She grabbed for the middle one, just managing to beat a harried-looking woman with an enormous open address book. "Shit! Shit, shit shit!" said the woman, trying to wipe the rain off a vulnerable Filofax page. The woman proceeded to the nonworking phone, and, after verifying its deadness, asked Nick brusquely, "You gonna be long?"

"Five minutes, maybe."

"Shit. Shit, shit!" she said, looking up the block at the gathering gridlock, then glaring at Nick.

Making a pay phone call in New York, thought Nick, had become a kind of musical chairs—the city was always one pay phone shy of the number needed at any given moment.

She punched 411. A recorded voice came on.

"Directory assistance requires a deposit of 45 cents. Please deposit 45 cents or stay on the line for a NYTel operator."

Nick realized that she was on one of those treacherous, post-deregulation pay phones that don't give free information. The Filofax woman was pacing very close to Nick, and Nick made a point of avoiding her eyes. After an interminable number of clicking sounds, an operator came on, sounding extravagantly uninterested.

"NYTel at your service," said the woman, who was anything but.

"Yes," said Nick. "I need the number of Allied Limousine." Nick had an account with them. It was a brilliant idea, she thought—have a car pick her up and take her home, and she'd sign for it.

"That's 45 cents please," replied the NYTel woman.

"I don't have 45 cents in change, operator. Can I charge it to my home phone number?"

"Oh, *Christ,*" said Filofax.

"NYTel cannot make charges to a third party. Please deposit 45 cents."

"I don't have 45 cents," said Nick, trying to remain calm. "Can't you please help me?"

"NYTel cannot accept third-party billing."

"Oh, sure it can," said Nick, making a pathetic stab at charming the NYTel woman. Without thinking, she looked back at Filofax, who was glaring. Filofax had almost-jet-black, sprayed hair, and, despite hard features, looked like she might be pretty in a better mood. Her suit, jacket, and ankle bracelet seemed a little cheesy to Nick, who also thought that her heels were awfully high for daytime.

"It's 805-9100," said Filofax, looking right through Nick.

"What?" said Nick, not sure she'd been spoken to.

"Eight-oh-five mother-fucking nine one hundred," said Filofax. She was pointing at a crinkled page in her book. "The number for Allied Limo. You want *me* to dial it?"

"Oh. God. Great!" said Nick, recovering. "I don't know what's wrong with me. I never forget anything, but it's just been one of those—"

"Eight-oh-five," said Filofax, biting off each digit. "Nine one hundred."

Nick put the quarter into the phone. It dropped straight through, falling into the coin return slot.

"Try my quarter," said Filofax. Nick took it and deposited it—with the same result.

"Let me use the goddamn phone," said Filofax, practically pushing Nick aside. In possession of no further game plan, Nick just stood there. Filofax tried another quarter, and another. She slammed the phone on all sides with the flat of her hand.

"Moth-erfucker!" she said. Her Queens accent made it: "Muthuhfucka." She slammed the receiver against the phone. Then, doing something Nick thought happened only in movies, Filofax ripped the receiver from its cord and rather calmly hung it up.

"Come on," said Filofax as she walked away from the phone. Nick didn't move, her brain not quite having caught up. Filofax stopped and turned back to her.

"Don't you have any money?" asked Filo, looking Nick up and down.

"Well, I have a little. But not enough to get me home. I'll just . . . take the bus."

"The bus? Forget the muthuhfucking bus. You're sick. It's obvious. Where you goin'?" demanded Filofax, a woman in a hurry.

"Oh. Uh . . . York and Eighty-fourth."

"We'll ride with Frankie. Come on." She was heading toward an indigo Cadillac Seville that was double-parked at the corner. A man was in the driver's seat. "I was gonna ditch the crown prince here and go visit my friend Irene, but the fucking phones in this city . . . come on, we'll drop you."

"That's very kind," said Nick, following halfheartedly. "I can walk."

"Don't be stupid. You're not a well person. Come on."

With a choice between walking, a relentlessly stop-and-go bus ride through the worst of rush-hour traffic, and riding with Filo and Frankie, Nick followed. Growing up in Dobbs Ferry, Nick had acquired a fondness for New Yorkers with thick accents. They usually proved more colorful and real than the Westchester types she'd grown up with. This woman, thought Nick, is a pistol, but she seems kind.

As she and Filo reached the back doors of the Cadillac, Nick's stomach churned. It felt as if it were filled with used antifreeze. The soup was not bonding well with her hangover fluids.

Filo rapped on the back window. The driver looked up and the doors snapped unlocked with an electronic thump. Filo took the shotgun seat, motioning Nick into the back. Nick realized with mixed feelings that she'd left her mother's container of soup at the first pay phone. She hoped that someone hungry would find it.

"We're going to Eighty-fourth and York, Frankie, and I swear to God, if you say one word to me . . ."

"Who's this?" said Frankie with a look at Nick, who thought immediately that if anyone was still holding Fabian look-alike contests, Frankie was their man.

"Just drive the fucking car, Frankie. I'm not talking to you. Okay? Eighty-fourth and York."

"You know something, Joanne?" said Frankie. "Fuck you."

"Oh, nice. Just drive the fucking car."

"What am I, Joanne? Your fucking driver here?" Frankie slammed on the brakes and whipped the gearshift up into park. A Volkswagen beetle following too closely in the dense traffic rear-ended them, as gently as anyone could hope. Frankie opened his door and got out of the car to examine his bumper for damage. The driver of the beetle, a thin, earnest-looking city prepster, was opening his wallet as he got out of his car, eager to do the right thing. Frankie stared at the Cadillac's rear bumper. Then he spit on the street, slapped the side of his car, and yelled to the heavens, "Fuck!"

"Sorry," said the kid, "but you stopped so suddenly."

"Hey, if you'd been any closer, I'd hafta be tested for AIDS."

"I can just get out and walk," said Nick, who didn't want to add back-seat vomit to Frankie's woes.

"Relax," said Joanne. "He's insured."

Frankie was looking at his Cadillac's rear end as though someone had just pronounced it dead. Cars were honking mercilessly.

Joanne turned to Nick. "So what happened to you anyway? I'm Joanne DeLessio."

"Susan Nicholas," said Nick, automatically using a fake name. "I'm just . . . hung over."

Joanne looked back at Frankie, who was berating the kid. "He's really a good driver. He just has bad luck. You think I should marry him?" This last question was asked in earnest.

"He's very cute," said Nick. "If, as you say, he's insured—then yes. You should marry him."

"He's such a palooka, but you know what? And this is where I'm stuck. I don't want anybody else. I swear to God in heaven, I'm in love. Do you believe it? Me?"

Frankie was getting back into the car. Nick had barely noticed the cacophony of car horns imploring the Cadillac to move. Frankie closed his door.

"Where to, ladies?" he said in a way that charmed Nick.

"Oh, now you're Mr. Nice Guy," said Joanne, smiling and tossing her hair at nothing in particular.

"I don't believe I've had the pleasure," said Frankie, extending his hand toward Nick.

"You behave yourself, Mr. Smarty Pants. This is Susan," said Joanne, "and she thinks we should get married."

"Hiya, Susan," said Frankie, smiling. He seemed to be unaware that every car in the city of New York was honking at him. "Whatta you? Some long-lost friend of Joanne's?"

"Susan is hung over and we have to get her to Eighty-fourth and York." She looked at Nick. "What, your limo didn't show up?"

Nick started to explain, then just shook her head no. The car moved about fifteen feet before having to stop again. Nick looked past Frankie's broad shoulders up First Avenue. The traffic was unending.

"Frankie used to drive for Allied, didn't you, Frankie?" she said. Frankie nodded. Joanne smiled. "Can you believe what a small fucking world this is?"

Frankie idly sang the Disneyland "Small, Small World" song off-key.

Joanne whispered to Nick. "I'm not thinking about marrying him for his voice. Just tell me to shut up if you want. I'm trying to pass the time so you don't think about puking."

"That's OK," said Nick. "I think the worst may have passed."

Frankie, obliviously continuing his mumbled torture of "Small, Small World" and adding the word *fucking* in a way that Mr. Disney would not have approved, whipped the Cadillac into a right turn at Sixty-second Street.

"Francis!" yelled Joanne, trying to keep her balance and throwing her arm in front of Nick to steady her too. "What in the name of Jesus are you doing?"

"I'm goin' up York. It's gotta be better than this," said Frankie.

"We got a woman with a bad stomach back here," said Joanne. "Drive like a goddamn gentleman or the wedding is off."

"I didn't know it was on," said Frankie, breaking into another grin. "Is that, like, a yes?"

"That's, like, a you-just-goddamn-well-behave-yourself-and-we'll-see," said Joanne, winking at Nick.

It occurred to Nick that nobody knew where she was at this moment. She was . . . unreachable. It calmed her. Her nausea seemed to be fading.

The car turned left onto York. It was every bit as tied up as First Avenue had been.

"Sorry, Susan," said Frankie, indicating the traffic.

"I could probably walk if you two have somewhere to go," said Nick. "Like to the altar or something."

"I should live so long," said Frankie.

"Okay, Mr. Smarty Q. Hotpants," said Joanne. *"Yes."*

"Yes, what?" challenged Frankie.

"Yes, I'll marry you."

"Don't pull my chain about this, Joanne," said Frankie.

"When I pull your chain, you'll know it. Stop the motherfucking car if you don't want to marry me."

"What is this?" said Frankie, as though he were the victim of a stickup.

Nick thought she saw Joanne wipe away a tear. "What *is* this? This is yes. Let's get married." They hit another red light. Frankie turned and faced her.

"When?" he asked.

Joanne threw open her door, got out, ran around, and rapped on Frankie's window. The window slid down. "Right now. I'll marry you right now," said Joanne. She stuck her head in, grabbed his with both her hands, and kissed him until the light turned green and horns started up again.

"Hey, Frankie," she yelled, breaking the kiss and laughing,

"they're playing our song." And she kissed him again, practically pulling him out of the car.

A burly man in a sky-blue Pontiac Firebird behind them got out of his car and took a step toward the happy couple.

"Move your fucking car, Romeo," said Firebird.

"Watch your mouth around my future wife," said Frankie.

"Oh," said the burly man. "I figured she was some hooker you found on the corner. Would you get going now, please?"

Nick got out of the car suddenly and turned to Firebird. "You apologize to this woman at once!"

Nick's appearance took him by surprise. There was something so cleanly adamant in her tone that he involuntarily replied, "Hey, lady, look—I'm sorry, I just want to get home." But Frankie was now three feet away from him, staring.

"I'm sorry, fella, okay?" Firebird went on. "Look, I had a long day, okay?"

Frankie grabbed the man's head with both hands and pulled him close.

"Lucky for you I'm so happy," said Frankie, who suddenly released Firebird, went back to the Cadillac, calmly opened the door chauffeur-style for Nick, and did the same for his fiancée. The tires squealed as they zoomed forward. No one spoke. Joanne played with the hair on the back of Frankie's head.

"Hey, Susan," said Frankie to Nick in the mirror, "I'm a lover, not a fighter. You know what I mean?"

"I know what you mean, Frankie," said Nick, who wasn't sure she knew exactly what Frankie meant about anything.

They managed two more blocks before the next red light.

"I got a favor to ask," Joanne said to Nick. "You can say no. I mean, it's Friday night. You got a hot date?"

"Not tonight," said Nick, who felt no desire for another hot date as long as she lived.

"I can't believe you don't have a date on Friday night. You're very attractive. Isn't she attractive, Frankie?"

"Very," said Frankie simply.

"You're not supposed to notice another woman when you're with your wife," said Joanne.

"Hey. When you're my wife, I won't."

"That settles it, Mr. Smarty L. Pants. Turn left."

Frankie looked surprised. Joanne grabbed the wheel and started a left turn.

"What are you doing?" asked Frankie.

"We're going to your uncle Edward's," said Joanne. "He's gonna marry us. If he's home."

They picked up speed across Sixty-seventh.

She turned around and explained to Nick, "Frankie's uncle is a judge. You're gonna be our witness. Okay?"

"Don't you need a blood test?" asked Nick.

Frankie reached over, opened the glove compartment, removed an envelope, and handed it to Joanne.

"Our blood test," said Frankie. Then, to Nick, "We almost did it last week. We went down and got the tests and everything."

"Then we had this mondo fight," said Joanne, beaming. "We're talking *mondo*. And the wedding was off."

Frankie looked at Joanne. "I kept it, just in case."

She shook her head happily. "Drive to Third and Seventy-sixth before I change my mind. Okay with you, Susan?"

"Don't you have someone else you'd rather call?" asked Nick. "I mean—family?"

"Oh, sure," said Joanne. "We'll call my motha." This broke them both up. "No, Susan. You're perfect. You sure you don't mind?"

Nick shrugged, hoping that Uncle Edward didn't ask her for identification and find out she'd lied about her name. Then she realized she didn't have her wallet anyway.

Joanne looked out the window as if from a Learjet flying over the Riviera. They reached a new high rise at Third and Seventy-sixth. In an effort to give it stature which it otherwise lacked, someone had dubbed it the Worthington Somerset. Frankie steered down the ramp of its indoor parking lot. An attendant gave him a receipt, and they walked up a few steps and through the rear entrance of the lobby. They approached a doorman behind a podium. "Edward Costantino," said Frankie.

"Who shall I tell him is calling?" asked the doorman.

"His nephew Francis," said Frankie, who looked a little apprehensive.

They waited a second. Nick wasn't sure if she wanted Uncle Edward to be home or not. The doorman spoke again.

"Judge," said the doorman, "it's your nephew Francis to see you." He listened for a few seconds, nodded, and looked at Frankie. "He says he doesn't want to see you. He's very busy."

Frankie didn't seem surprised. "Tell him I've come to introduce him to my wife." Joanne smiled.

"He says he's come to introduce you to his wife," repeated the doorman, who then listened for a moment. He nodded, put down the phone, and said to Frankie, "Go on up. 17F."

"Thanks," said Joanne, taking Frankie by the arm and gesturing for Nick to follow. Nick eyed some marigolds that were holding on for dear life in a little vase on the podium. "Mind if I take one of these?" she asked.

"Take 'em all," said the doorman. "You'd be doing me a favor. "I'm allergic."

Nick swept up the little bunch of flowers and followed Frankie and Joanne to the elevator.

As they sped up to the seventeenth floor, Joanne did a dum-dum-da-dum version of "Here's Comes the Bride." The doors opened and Joanne said to Nick, "Bet you didn't plan on being a maid of honor when you got up today."

"Maid of honor," said Nick quietly, almost to herself. "What a concept."

Frankie pressed the buzzer at 17F. Nick heard the shuffle of what sounded like leather slippers. A small man in an old plaid bathrobe opened the door. His face was taut, and his eyes, despite his seeming to be at least eighty years old, were clear. It was impossible to read his mood.

"Which one is your wife, Francis?" said Uncle Edward. "Seems to me either one is more than you deserve."

"This is Joanne, Uncle Edward. You met her last Christmas, remember?"

"Hello, Uncle Edward," said Joanne, as if they'd just arrived for dinner.

"When did you get married?"

"Well. That's just it, Uncle Edward," said Frankie. "See—we're not. Yet. We just said that so you'd let us up. We would like for you to marry us."

"When?" asked Uncle Edward.

"Uh. Now," said Frankie.

He looked at them both, back and forth, back and forth. "Just like that?"

"We've thought about it a lot, Uncle Edward," said Joanne. "I love your nephew. Would you please do us the honor?" No one spoke. Joanne bravely went on. "We have our blood test and everything."

"That's nice," said Uncle Edward, "but you don't need blood tests in this state anymore."

"We don't?" said Frankie.

"Nope," said Uncle Edward. "What about a license?"

Frankie looked sheepish. "We were kinda hoping like maybe you could help us out there, Uncle Edward."

"I see. And who is this young woman?" asked Uncle Edward, referring to Nick.

"This is a friend of mine: Susan . . ."

". . . Nicholas," said Nick before Joanne had to dig for it. "I'm to be the witness."

"With this one," said Uncle Edward, referring to Frankie, "you may need witness *protection*." Nick smiled. Joanne's face had a kind of breathless anticipation that seemed completely appropriate and flattering.

There was an awkward silence. Then Uncle Edward looked at Frankie. "I know how much it would have pleased my sister to see you married. I'll take care of the license."

"You can do that?" asked Joanne, brightening.

"I'm a judge," said Uncle Edward with a shrug. "I can do anything. Come in, come in."

Frankie held up a backward open palm, waist-high, and Joanne quietly low-fived him. Nick hadn't noticed yet, but her headache was gone.

"Look at this, look at this," said Uncle Edward, motioning them into the small living room and pointing to a computer on a crowded but tidy desk. Nick looked around, calmed by the total absence of clutter in the apartment.

"Where's Aunt Marie?" asked Frankie.

"She's sleeping," said Uncle Edward. "Don't anybody make noise."

"Yes, sir," said Frankie automatically.

The old man flipped a switch on the back of the computer and it booted up with the aid of a few clicks of something Nick was pretty sure was called a mouse. Uncle Edward seemed as at home with the machine as a kid with Nintendo.

"I love this thing," said Uncle Edward. "It plays casino with me. Always wins. But last week I beat it at chess, and I have a little program here—" He clicked the mouse a few times, and something came on the screen that looked to Nick like a diploma. "It makes certificates. Look at this." He started typing as Nick, Joanne, and Frankie crowded around him.

"You are something, Uncle Edward," said Joanne, holding Frankie's hand.

"Yes," said Uncle Edward, who typed like lightning. The certificate on screen was, indeed, beginning to look like a rather official document.

Typing all the while and adding horizontal lines for signatures, Uncle Edward went on. "My sister—Francis's mother," he said, "gave me this. She wanted me to write. She'd be very happy to see the kind of writing I'm doing on it." He clicked the mouse a few more times. "What's your last name, dear?" he asked Joanne.

"DeLessio," Joanne said, looking at the screen. She didn't spell it; he didn't ask how to spell it. He had apparently gotten it right the first time.

He clicked some more, then hit a switch on a printer that was next to the computer. In an instant it spat out an authentic-looking marriage license.

"If you had called me first," said Uncle Edward, glaring a little at Frankie, "I could have done better."

"Is that, like, legal?" asked Joanne.

"It's not only *like* legal," said Uncle Edward, "it *is* legal. If I sign it. Which I can't do until I perform the ceremony." He pulled a Bible down from an orderly bookcase. He turned it over in his hand.

"Your mother gave me this too," he said to Frankie. "For my confirmation. My, my. She's all over the place tonight." He stood still for a moment with a distant look. Then he picked up a picture on the desk and turned it to face them, the way a child might position a favorite stuffed animal so it, too, can watch what's going on.

"This," Uncle Edward explained to Joanne, "is your mother-in-law, whom you will not have the experience of being mother-in-lawed by. Which is too bad for you."

Then he looked at Nick. "Susan, you stand there, next to . . . I'm sorry, dear. What's your name?"

"Joanne," said Joanne and Frankie together.

"Forgive me," he said with a look of genuine regret. "I shan't forget your name again. And, come to think of it, I shan't say 'shan't' again either. It just isn't often a fella gets the chance. Now: We are gathered today to join this man and this woman . . ."

Nick fought back tears as Uncle Edward led them through a brief, plain-wrap marriage service.

"Joanne, do you take Francis . . . ?"

"I do," said Joanne, who looked tense, determined.

". . . And do you, Francis . . . ?"

Joanne stared up at Frankie while Uncle Edward administered the vows. Nick wondered if she'd ever have a look like that in her own eyes while words like these were spoken to her.

"If there is anyone present who feels that these two should not be joined in matrimony, let that person come forward now or forever hold their peace."

Nick couldn't muster the slightest objection.

"Francis?" said Uncle Edward.

"Sir?"

"Don't screw this up. . . ."

"Yes, sir."

"I now pronounce you man and wife."

Joanne looked as if she'd just won the lottery. Nick felt a tear squeeze through. Frankie seemed dazed.

"If I were you, Francis," said Uncle Edward, "I would kiss the bride. You've skimped enough on the rest of the service, and it would be a shame for Susan and me to miss that."

Frankie kissed her, and Joanne pulled herself to him. They suddenly seemed glued together, kissing as if in the back of a parked car. Uncle Edward reached for the picture of Frankie's mother and turned it away, smiling at Nick. The kiss still unbroken, he made a show of looking at his watch. Nick laughed, cried, and finally Frankie and Joanne came up for air—man and wife.

Joanne turned around and took Nick into her arms as though they'd been best friends all their lives.

"Oh, Susan," said Joanne, "I don't have a bouquet to throw you. Or are you already married?"

"Me? No. No . . ."

"Well, here," said Joanne, and she mimed throwing a bouquet to Nick. Nick "caught" it.

First time you ever caught the bouquet, and it isn't even there.

Uncle Edward shook Frankie's hand and turned to Joanne. "Do I get to kiss the bride?"

"Of course," said Joanne.

"Go easy," said Uncle Edward, moving in for the kiss. "I have a very jealous wife." Joanne blushed and kissed him on both cheeks.

At that moment a small, feisty woman with hair in large curlers and a robe that matched Uncle Edward's emerged from behind what had been a closed door. She watched as Joanne planted the second kiss on Uncle Edward's cheek.

"Hey!" she shouted. "You wake me up, and then I find you kissing a young girl in your pajamas. Hello, Francis. Go home. Let me get some sleep. You," she said, pointing at Uncle Edward, "get in here and give me a little of that action." And she disappeared behind the door again.

"You'll have to excuse me, ladies and gentlemen of the wedding party," said Uncle Edward, "but you heard the boss." With that, he grabbed an old-fashioned fountain pen, signed his computer-generated license with a flourish, and handed it to Nick.

"Susan, sign at the bottom there."

Nick took the pen, frozen for a moment. Unable to confess, she wrote "Susan Nicholas." Joanne and Frankie quickly signed too, and then the wedding party was ushered to the door.

"Uncle Edward," said Joanne, pulling on her coat. "I'll never forget this."

"No, I don't imagine you will."

Heading down on the elevator, the happy couple necked mercilessly. The rush-hour traffic had thinned and they were able to scoot back over to York and up to Nick's place at Eighty-fourth in comparatively no time. Joanne and Frankie talked, argued, shouted, and cooed just as they had before the ceremony. Nick realized that she still believed that marriage was like having a magic wand waved over you, and that everything would be different and somehow perfect afterward.

"So, Susan," Joanne said, turning around to Nick as they pulled up to the building, "I'm, like, extremely glad you couldn't get hold of Allied Limo."

"Me too," said Nick. "I think we should all get together every year on this day for an anniversary party."

"Hey, absolutely," said Frankie. He handed Nick a scrap of paper and a stubby pencil. "Write down your number. We'll call you. Seriously. Right, Joanne?"

"Abso-fuckin'-lootly," said the bride. As Nick took the pencil and began writing, she was again at odds with herself. Should she give them her real number? She actually might want to see them again. They'd been an oasis today.

And yet she doubted this feeling between them could ever be recaptured. She decided simply to write a wrong digit in her phone number, substituting an "8" for a "3". This was what she did whenever a guy she didn't like asked for her number. It spared her the saying no.

She handed the paper back to Joanne. Frankie bounced out of the car and made a grand show of opening the door for Nick. As she emerged onto the sidewalk, she found herself looking directly into the eyes of last night's attorney from the Pierre Hotel, the former Wally Wall Street, who was leaning against her building, waiting.

CHAPTER 7

H is face was strained, and he didn't see Nick right away, but he seemed to be trying to appear casual. Nick hoped that somehow Frankie and Joanne would disappear before Wally saw her.

She also realized that she didn't know Wally's name—and that neither he, Frankie, nor Joanne knew Nick's real name.

Please, God, don't make me do introductions.

Nick turned away from Wally's direction—he was Wally again in her mind—trying to come up with a plan. But before she could form one, Wally arrived at the curb.

"Hello, Miss Nicholas," he said as though he'd been expected.

"Oh, hello. Hello," Nick said, vamping and coming up with nothing. She decided to go with the truth, or at least a piece of it.

"These are my friends, Frankie and Joanne . . ." She didn't know Frankie's last name, so she let it drop. "They just got married." Frankie beamed and nodded, and reached to shake Wally's hand.

"Did you?" said Wally, returning the handshake. "How nice for you." He looked at Nick. "I was wondering if I could talk to you for a minute?"

"Oh, gosh, uh, do you think maybe I could take a raincheck?" asked Nick, who wondered how long Wally had been waiting. So he *had* followed her this morning.

"It'll just take a minute," said Wally, who was doing a pretty good job of sounding natural but who looked to Nick as though he'd had as tough a day as she. He made a move to usher her away from Frankie's Cadillac and into the building. "Nice meeting you both," he said as if in a hurry. "Mazel tov."

"Susan?" said Joanne with a trace of concern in her voice. Nick stopped and turned around. "Are you, like, okay?"

How does this woman know me so well?

"I'm . . . fine, Joanne. Thanks for the ride. Uh, call me."

At that moment Fernando, the evening doorman, appeared, opening the door for Nick.

"Evening, Miss Stallings," he said automatically. Wally looked surprised, not having heard that name before. Nick, unsure if Joanne and Frankie had caught it, scooted into the building with an expression on her face that said to them "I'd like to explain, but this isn't the time or place."

"What are you doing here?" said Nick to Wally as soon as they were inside. She could see Frankie's car pulling away. She wasn't sure if that made her feel better or not.

"Miss *Stallings*?" said Wally. "I thought it was Miss Nicholas." He looked angry now that they were alone.

"Oh, I changed my name today," said Nick, attempting an inane joke. "Yeah. That's it. I phoned ahead from the name-changing agency and told the doorman to use only my new name. Amazing, huh? And look," she said, pulling him over to the mail area, "they even changed the label on my mailbox. Terrific building, huh?"

"What else did you lie to me about?" he asked, genuinely offended.

"Look," said Nick, pressing the elevator button, "I've had a rough day. A very rough day. I'm not blaming it on you, but you did have a little something to do with it. . . ."

"Why wouldn't you just give me your number?" he demanded.

"Because last night was last night. It was . . . one of those things. Not exactly a trip to the moon on gossamer wings, but, well, you know what I mean." He wasn't amused. "Or maybe you don't."

"One of those things?" he said. "Well, another one of those things is that my wife was waiting up for me when I got home this morning. I'm afraid I didn't lie very well. I'm afraid I was a little too drunk, and I'm afraid my car was a little too dented in front from where I had a little too much of a collision on the way home. She threw me out. In front of the kids. I have nowhere to sleep tonight."

"God," said Nick. Fernando the doorman was watching discreetly. Nick had an urge to call out to him, but decided it would be too dramatic.

"Look," he said, grabbing her by the shoulders. "Something happened last night."

"I remember . . . a good deal of it," said Nick, not meeting his eyes.

"Maybe it meant nothing to you, but I can't believe that."

"I'm very tired," said Nick, "and I don't feel well. I'm really sorry about what happened on your way home." The elevator arrived, empty. It was only manned after midnight. "But . . . you didn't *have* to meet me last night. I think you're very frazzled, and—"

"*Frazzled?* My attorney called this afternoon and told me my wife is initiating divorce proceedings."

"Oh, God. I'm sorry," said Nick, who was starting to feel dizzy. "But . . . what exactly do you want me to do about this?"

His voice started to rise. "I want you to—" He stopped and tried another tack. "Look. You're right. I am frazzled. I just had to see you. I had to get a look at you. I guess . . . I don't know . . . I wanted to see if it had all been worth it."

What occurred to Nick at that instant was that she certainly didn't look her best, and that he must be disappointed. What occurred to him was to push Nick into the elevator and press the CLOSE DOOR button.

"What're you doing?" said Nick, attempting to stay in control.

"I'm sorry. I'm sorry. I have to be alone with you. What floor are you on?"

Nick had told so many lies in the past twenty-four hours that she didn't have another one at the ready. She said nothing. He pushed the button for every floor.

"Oh, that's cute," said Nick. "They have closed circuit TV downstairs, you know."

I wish.

She went on. "If I yell, they'll send cops up here."

"Oh, please don't," he pleaded. "I beg you." Nick looked into his eyes. They were an awful blur of red and gray with a slightly yellow tinge that made Nick wonder if he wasn't ill on top of everything. The door opened on the second floor.

"Look," said Nick, a plan emerging. "Why don't we just get out on this floor, walk downstairs, go across the street, and have a cup of coffee?" She had her hand in the door. He pushed her away from it and back into the elevator.

"What floor are you on?" he demanded. Nick's mind rushed. "I know what you're thinking," he continued. "Why not yell for help? Let me give you one good reason. I'm a lawyer. If you call for help, someone might conceivably decide to press some kind of charge against me. I've lost my family today because of you. I'm not going to risk a police record and get disbarred too. I can make you look awfully bad if you try anything like that, and you can be quite sure I have the friends and the connections to do it. So why don't we just go to your apartment on the . . . what floor?"

Make him feel safe.

"I have a roommate," said Nick, taking one last stab.

"Well," he said, "If she—or is it *he* . . . ?"

Say he.

"She," said Nick.

"Well, if she's home, we can, as you say, go across the street and have coffee. But I'm afraid, you see, that my wife may have people following me already, and I'd rather not be seen anywhere with you in public. I'd rather just stay indoors."

Make him relax.

"I'm on the sixth floor," said Nick. They were now on the fifth. He let the door open and then close again. Nick thought about pressing the alarm, and then remembered that the tenants had been advised last week that the alarm didn't work.

The door opened on the sixth floor. It had been less than twenty-four hours since she and Todd had emerged from the elevator. As she put her key into the top lock, Nick decided to make a pretense of having a roommate. She called out, "Nick? Nick, are you home?"

"I thought you said your roommate was a woman," said Wally.

"It's short for Nicolette," said Nick, who couldn't believe that she hadn't been able to come up with a name other than her own.

"And you are Susan . . . Stallings?"

"Yes. I'm . . . I'm sorry," she said, trying to sound genuinely so. "I just thought it would be more fun and . . . mysterious to, you know, check into the hotel under a fake name. Are you awfully mad at me?" They were now alone in the apartment. Nick closed the door, seemingly unconcerned.

He's not dangerous. He's just wired.

"So," he said. "We're alone?"

"I guess so," said Nick. "Funny. She's usually home by now."

"What's that smell?" he asked.

It was her morning vomit in the foyer wastebasket. Being careful not to breathe through her nose, she picked up the wastebasket and casually went into the kitchen to empty and rinse it out.

"My roommate," Nick said, forcing a little laugh, "is not exactly the best housekeeper." She ran cold water into the wastebasket. A whiff of it hit her and she fought back a dry heave. He followed her into the kitchen.

"You know, you never told me *your* name," Nick said as friendly as could be, wiping out the wastebasket with a paper towel.

"Jeffrey," he said as if it were a clue that would make something clearer. "Jeff, if you like."

"Which do *you* like?" asked Nick.

"The better people get to know me, the more they call me Jeffrey."

Just make him relax and get him out of here.

"Well . . . Jeffrey," said Nick. "I guess in some ways I know you well."

"In some ways, yes. In some ways, you know me better than myself."

"Oh, I doubt that."

"Look," he said, "I've never had sex like that. I didn't think it was possible. I was . . . I was almost relieved when my wife threw me out this morning. I don't know how I could ever go to bed with her again without thinking of you."

Oh, Jesus . . .

"That's so sweet," she said. "But you know, when you and your wife—what's her name?" Nick wanted to make his wife real to him.

"Barbara."

"Barbara," said Nick. "Great name." She was trying to sound sisterly. "When you and Barbara sort all this out—and you will—I have a feeling you'll put some of those things . . . you never knew before . . . into practice."

"You don't know Barbara," said Jeffrey, sliding onto the couch. "Sex isn't . . . it just isn't something she ever seems to really enjoy."

Nick didn't know what to say. She saw him look at something on the floor between the living room and foyer. It was Nick's peach cashmere dress, in a rumpled pile where she'd tossed it down so long ago. Jeffrey got up and walked over to it. He bent over, picked it up, and held it out as if it were something he was thinking of buying. He looked at it and shook his head. Then, to Nick's alarm, he spoke to it.

"You. You are the cause of all my troubles," said Jeffrey, smoothing out the wrinkles. "Just a piece of cloth. But on her," he said, indicating Nick, "you're a home wrecker." He laughed and shook his head. "Oh, Jesus." He gave Nick a goofy look, a look that seemed to proclaim himself a poor schmuck with a sense of humor about the whole thing. Nick relaxed a little.

"Put it on," he said.

"What?" said Nick.

He was holding the dress out to her. "Put it on. I really want to see you in it again. I want to remember why I threw my life away this morning."

"Have you had any sleep?" asked Nick in as pacifying a tone as she could. "You could take a nap here on the couch."

"I've had no sleep. No. But I can get along without sleep. I do it all the time when there's a big case coming up. I'm great at all-nighters. I just wing it the next day on coffee, and I'm fine. Really." He was smiling as if he had nothing whatsoever to hide.

Get him out of here.

"Well, *I'm* exhausted," said Nick. "Here. Let me give you my number. You can even see from the phone that it's my real number, and we'll—I don't know, we'll have dinner. Say, tomorrow?" She tried to look as if she didn't have a care in the world. "Is tomorrow good for you?"

"Tomorrow, tomorrow," he sang quietly, grinning at her. "No. To-morrow I'll . . . be out of town. No. Please. Put this on." He dan-gled the dress, and then walked across the room to hand it to her.

"It's just that I'm so tired, and I've been hung over all day," said Nick, not wanting to rock the boat. "I doubt it'll have the desired effect."

"I'll be the judge of that," said Jeffrey. "Please." He handed her the dress. Nick didn't know what else to do.

"I guess I'll . . . go in the bedroom and change, and I'll, you know, comb my hair."

"Great," he said. "Thank you. It would just make me feel so much better."

"Hey," said Nick, moving into her room. "We aim to please."

"And I doubt," he called after her, "that you ever miss."

Nick pulled off her shoes and jeans and tossed her now-wrinkled work shirt onto the bed. She hesitated, then unhooked her bra, moved out of her underpants, and put on the cashmere dress. She looked in the mirror. It's not last night, she thought. She ached for sleep. She was also scared.

She decided to pick up the phone and call . . . who? She dialed her parents' number. As she put the phone to her ear, though, she heard none of the sounds of a call going through. Instead, Jeffrey's voice came, over the dial tone.

"Just come out here, Susan."

She hung up. She wondered if she could calm him by seducing him again. But sex was inconceivable right now. She still burned between her legs from last night. She felt as if she'd never desired sex in her life. She made a cursory attempt to comb out her hair, and walked back out into the living room.

He was standing near the living room windows, tall ones that extended almost to the floor and opened like doors. Her apartment had originally been built as a studio for painters. He had drawn the blinds. He was naked. And he was smoking a cigarette.

He looked up as she entered. Nick didn't flinch.

"I've been smoking all day," he said. "Can you believe it?"

"Well," said Nick simply, "I guess it's been that kind of day."

"How's your leg?" he asked, taking a drag on the cigarette. In the less-flattering, sober light of her apartment, Nick now observed his skin's pastiness, which she'd been willing to overlook last night.

"My leg?" she asked.

"Well, your thigh, I mean. Is it all right?"

No. It burns.

"It's okay."

"I guess I got a little carried away," he said. Nick tried to shrug it off. She wondered if he thought his penis looked attractive right now. She could not, at this moment, understand what anyone had ever found attractive about any penis.

"Want to join me?" he said. Nick didn't know if he meant in a cigarette or in the nude. Her answer covered both bases.

"No, thanks. But you go ahead."

He took another deep drag, and motioned for her to join him by the window. She walked over, stopping a few feet away, trying like crazy not to appear wary.

"This is great," he said. "You look, well, just as I remembered you."

"It hasn't been that long," said Nick, making light. "I'm glad you're not disappointed."

You are *glad he's not disappointed. You're pathetic.*

The intercom buzzed. Nick made a move toward the door to answer it.

"Don't get that," said Jeffrey, trying not to sound as though he was giving orders. Nick stopped. The intercom buzzed again.

"I don't want Fernando to worry," she said. "He knows we're up here. Let me just see who it is?"

"Okay, sure. Just get rid of them."

Nick answered the phone and murmured a couple of noncommittal uh-huhs. While talking, she unbolted the lock. She turned around to Jeffrey and said, "Wow. I forgot to lock the door. Do you believe that?" Jeffrey seemed unconcerned.

"Sit down. Sit down," he said. "I've been counting the hours. I want to do something. And I want you to watch. Please. Sit."

Nick moved to the couch.

"I want you to watch this, Miss Nicholas," he said in a tone that eerily reminded Nick of last night. He took another drag of his cigarette so that the end glowed. Nick thought she noticed a slight stiffening in him as he brought the cigarette down to the same place on *his* upper thigh where he had dared her, in her champagne-adrenaline high of five A.M., to burn herself.

"This is for you, Susan," he said.

As the cigarette was about to meet his flesh, the front door burst open and slammed against the wall of the foyer with a tremendous clang. It was Frankie.

*   *   *   *

Joanne was right behind him as they swept into the room like a very small SWAT team.

"Susan!" said Frankie. "You okay?"

"Jesus, Mary, and Joseph," said Joanne.

"Jeffrey—this is Joanne and Frankie," said Nick. "I believe you've already met."

Jeffrey froze. As Nick looked at him, she was suddenly terribly embarrassed that she'd indicated to Joanne and Frankie that they should come up. Jeffrey now seemed so helpless.

Nobody spoke for a second or two. Jeffrey took another drag of his cigarette, and then, unable to find an ashtray, laid it on the windowsill next to him. He reached over to the arm of the couch where he'd piled up his clothes.

"I guess I'll be going," he said, looking at Nick as if to say it wasn't over yet. He put on his shirt first.

"You couldn't have started with, like, your pants?" asked Joanne.

"You don't have to watch," said Jeffrey, not covering himself.

"My wedding night," said Joanne, "and the first dick I see is small, limp, and not my husband's. Go figure."

"Susan," said Frankie. "What the hell's going on?"

It occurred to Nick that if Jeffrey had a gun, they'd probably all be dead. Jeffrey picked up his cigarette, took another drag, opened the window, and flicked the butt into the night.

"You want me to call the cops?" asked Joanne.

"No. No," said Nick. "There's no need to do that. Is there, Jeffrey?"

Jeffrey, who was now doing up his belt, said very softly, "There's no need for anything now."

Frankie moved over to Nick. "Whatta you want me to do?"

"I'm not sure," said Nick. "I think you'd better go home, Jeffrey."

"Home," said Jeffrey as if it were a word he'd just heard for the first time. "Yes." He walked over to Nick and Frankie. Frankie's back straightened.

"I really . . . need . . . to talk to you, Susan," said Jeffrey, glassy-eyed and seemingly about to cry. In spite of herself, Nick felt sorry for him.

"Whatever you want to say, you can say in front of my friends," said Nick.

"Oh, please," he begged, shaking his head. "Be fair. I'm sorry, but I can't say what I want to say in front of your friends." He looked at Nick in an attempt to block out Frankie and Joanne.

Nick stared at him.

"Please," he said, wiping away a tear that was sliding down his cheek. "Can't I speak to you alone? Just for a minute? Then I'll leave." He looked over to Frankie. "Really. I promise." Frankie and Joanne turned to Nick.

"Why don't you guys go sit in the bedroom for a minute," Nick said to the newlyweds. Then she looked at Jeffrey. "Okay? Then you've got to go home and let me get some sleep."

"Of course, of course," said Jeffrey, hugely relieved. Then, to Joanne and Frankie, he added, "I'm so sorry."

"Come on, husband," said Joanne, looking toward the bedroom door.

"It's really a mess in there," said Nick. "I was in kind of a hurry this morning."

"Mess?" said Joanne as she moved into the room with Frankie. "You don't know the meaning of the word. I'm leaving the door open, Susan. Just yell if this twerp tries anything."

"Believe me, I won't," said Jeffrey.

"Oh, well," said Joanne. "That just makes me feel a whole lot better." She and Frankie disappeared behind the still-open door to Nick's bedroom.

Jeffrey looked pathetic and contrite. He picked up his shoes and walked back to the window, sitting on the low sill. He pulled on his socks.

"What is it, Jeffrey?" said Nick, trying not to sound impatient. He laced up his shoes and didn't answer right away. Then he looked into her eyes.

"I want to . . . say things to you."

"Okay," she nodded. "Sure. Go ahead."

"Come here," he said, patting the spot next to him on the sill.

"I'm fine here."

"I want to . . . *say* things to you. Up close. Please."

"No. Whatever it is, please just say it."

"You know what it is, don't you?" he said forlornly. "I want to know . . . when we can be together again."

"Oh," said Nick. "That's just not going to happen." She bit a cuticle from her left forefinger. "I'm sorry."

Jeffrey looked at her like a sheepdog who's just been put out by its master. "Is that final?"

"I'm not good at things like this, Jeffrey, but you're not giving me any choice." She inhaled deeply. "Last night was last night. If I'd wanted to see you again, I would have given you my number."

"I see," he said, nodding slowly. "I see. Well. I'm sorry too." He turned, threw open the window as wide as he could, and jumped out.

CHAPTER 8

She heard a thunk below. She didn't realize she had screamed. Joanne and Frankie were back in the room in a split second.

"What? *What?*" said Joanne, rushing to Nick's side.

Nick nodded toward the window. "He . . . jumped."

"Jesus God almighty," said Frankie. He and Joanne ran and looked down.

He's dead.

Nick didn't run, perhaps because she'd remembered that there was a terrace below the window, one flight down. She'd almost taken that apartment, but the extra cost of the terrace—one of only three in the building—had been prohibitive. Joanne followed Frankie to the window. Nick was afraid to look.

"Holy shit," said Joanne, turning back to Nick. "He's, like, splayed out on the barbecue down there."

"He's moving," said Frankie.

Nick numbly made her way to the window as though she were sleepwalking.

"Hey! Are you okay?" called Frankie.

Nick heard Jeffrey's voice. "I think I broke something. Oh, God. It hurts. My arm. And my neck."

"I'm going down there," said Frankie, pushing away from the sill.

Nick felt as if she were watching all this in one of her dreams. She looked at Joanne. She couldn't think of anything to do. Joanne yelled down, "Don't move. I used to be a nurse. Don't move."

"You're a nurse?" asked Nick.

"Well, I did some classes," said Joanne, heading for the door right behind Frankie. "But the money and the hours suck the big one. I'm going down there. You just stay put."

"No, I'll go with you," said Nick, and they headed out the door. She grabbed Jeffrey's coat.

As they moved down the hall steps, Joanne noticed Nick's wrinkled peach cashmere dress. "You oughta sue your dry cleaners."

Frankie was outside the door to 5F, ringing the bell and pounding on the door. He turned as Nick and Joanne joined him.

"Oh, God," said Nick. "The Claytons are out of town."

She tried to think. It occurred to her that Jeffrey might continue his plunge if no one came to his aid. "Joanne. Run downstairs and get Fernando, the doorman. Tell him *not* to call the police. Make it sound like no big deal."

"You got any pointers," asked Joanne, "on not making it sound like a big deal?"

"Just go!" said Frankie.

"Right. Right," said Joanne, and rang for the elevator.

"Take the stairs," said Nick. "It's faster." She headed back up the steps to her floor, calling to Frankie, "Stay there. I want to make sure he knows that help is on the way. I'm sorry about this."

"Hey," said Frankie, waving her off, "it's only my wedding night."

Nick tore into her apartment, ran to the window, and looked down. Jeffrey had somehow rolled himself off the barbecue and was bent over the balcony, looking at the street below.

"Just stay still," Nick called. "Joanne went for the doorman. Are you all right?"

Jeffrey turned his whole body around painfully slowly, so as not to move his neck. He looked up at her. "Alone at last," he said.

Nick didn't answer.

His cheek was badly scraped. It looked as if he'd landed face down on the rusty barbecue grill. "I think my arm is broken. They say you know when you've broken a bone. This must be the real thing." He made an extra effort to focus on her. "It hurts."

"Are you all right?" Nick repeated lamely, not knowing what else to say. Jeffrey's shoulders heaved, causing a movement in his neck that made him cry out in pain.

"Am I all *right*? Jesus. Are you sure someone is coming?"

"Yes. You're not thinking of jumping again, are you?"

Oh, sure. Remind him.

"Well, now that you mention it," he said, and made a move to lift his leg over the rail.

"Don't do that!" Nick called out involuntarily.

"Will you have dinner with me?" he asked, pausing in his move.

"What? Well . . . of course," said Nick.

"When?"

"Well," said Nick, "I don't think tonight is a good idea." This made him smile.

"Who *are* you?" he asked.

Good question.

She heard the sound of voices entering the Clayton apartment. Frankie, Joanne, and Fernando rushed onto the balcony. Nick hurried back down again to join them. When she arrived, Frankie was helping Jeffrey to his feet.

"Are you all right?" asked Frankie.

"Don't move," said Joanne. "You really mustn't move."

"I call ambulance," said Fernando.

"No," said Jeffrey. "I'm . . . all right."

"You gotta have that looked at," said Joanne. "Seriously."

"What happen?" asked Fernando.

"It's nothing, Fernando," said Nick, making her way to them. "Thank you for coming up, but we're really fine." She looked at Jeffrey. "Aren't we?"

"I'm okay," said Jeffrey to Fernando. Nick realized that Fernando might have trouble accepting this at face value, since they weren't in Nick's apartment and since Jeffrey's face was pretty cut up. She moved past Fernando to where the other three were huddled. Fernando took a few steps back toward the door.

"We really should call an ambulance," said Nick quietly.

"No!" said Jeffrey. "I'm fine."

"And I'm queen of all the Russias," said Joanne.

Nick saw a phone, went to it, and dialed 911.

"Please don't call anyone," said Jeffrey, trying to sound for Fernando as if it wasn't all that important.

"It's not the police," said Nick, waiting for an answer on the other end. "It's just 911 for an ambulance."

Nick handed Jeffrey's coat to Joanne, who offered it to Jeffrey. He turned and let her drape it around his shoulders. "We'll be fine, Fernando," Nick said, still waiting for an answer on the phone.

"What happen?" demanded Fernando.

"She pushed me out the window," said Jeffrey simply, looking at Nick.

"I call police?" asked Fernando, looking at Nick. No one spoke for what felt like forever.

"I'm kidding," said Jeffrey to Fernando. "I had a bit too much to drink, and I'm afraid I leaned out to look at the stars, and . . . over I went. But I'm fine, you see." Nick wondered if Fernando had noticed that there were no stars tonight. She wanted desperately to tip him a huge sum to keep him quiet, but remembered that she had only seven dollars and change.

"Frankie," she whispered. "Do you have any cash?"

"Sure," said Frankie. "How much?"

"Slip him . . . fifty? If you can," said Nick. "I'll pay you back."

Frankie greased Fernando as if he were the headwaiter at the Copa. Nick finally got through to 911. She reported that a man had fallen down, appeared to be in pain, and might have broken his arm. They took the address and Nick gave them the Claytons' number, reading it off their phone. She wasn't thrilled about this, but they'd demanded a phone number.

"They said it was pretty slow for a Friday, and that it wouldn't take too long," said Nick, hanging up.

She realized that they'd have to wait there in the Clayton apartment. Aware that she was being absurd, she nonetheless wiped her fingerprints from the phone as she hung up.

Fernando said, "I tell Mr. and Mrs. Clayton when they come back?"

"Oh, I'll take care of that, Fernando," Nick said. "Thanks."

"I don't know . . ." said Fernando, shrugging.

Nick raised her eyes at Frankie again. He slipped Fernando more cash.

Fernando turned and headed out. "I wait downstairs?"

"That would be great," said Nick. Fernando gave a look around the apartment the way cops do on television, and left.

"Oh, God, it hurts," said Jeffrey, walking in a little circle.

"You shouldn't move, you know," said Joanne. Jeffrey stopped.

"I'm sorry, you guys," said Nick. "You must be dying to get home."

"Yeah," said Frankie, "but what if Bozo here decides to do another trick?"

"I won't," said Jeffrey soberly.

"Begging your asshole pardon," said Joanne, "but your credibility isn't exactly at an all-time high around here. Anyway, it's better if we're all here to tell them the same story."

"Which is?" asked Nick. They looked to Jeffrey.

"Just . . . what I told the doorman," said Jeffrey.

"Except there are no stars out tonight," said Nick.

"I'll say I was looking for some, then." Everyone nodded.

They stood around for several minutes, Frankie and Joanne hugging loosely and murmuring to each other, Jeffrey and Nick standing a few feet from each other like two people who had never met. Nick imagined headlines. . . .

Lawyer Leaps from Actress's Love Nest

Never during this wait did it viscerally come back to her that she had, in the early hours of this same day, made wild love to the sad man next to her. She didn't know how to comfort him, or even if she wanted to. She felt that she should go with him to the emergency room, but had no desire whatsoever to do so.

In about ten minutes, Fernando arrived with two EMS guys. To Nick's horror, there was also a cop. Jeffrey looked dismayed too, but they all did their best to seem friendly and normal. Fernando posted himself at the door outside. Nick wondered how much money she owed Frankie for what had obviously been a swell tip.

"Which one is the injured party?" asked the cop, a fellow in his late thirties with the gut of a woman three or four months pregnant. To Nick's relief, he seemed weary and bored, as if he wanted to get this over with quickly.

"It's me," said Jeffrey, whose bloody face made him quite clearly the one. One of the EMS guys moved to Jeffrey.

"What happened?" continued the cop.

Jeffrey paused and looked mischievously at Nick for a second as though he might claim again that she'd pushed him. She held her breath, but when he spoke, he gave the agreed-upon version. He sounded almost charming. She realized that he *was* charming, but probably only when he wanted to get out of trouble or into sex.

"Okay," said the cop, making notes and apparently satisfied.

The second EMS guy never spoke, while the first dabbed at Jeffrey's facial cuts and asked if he was allergic to any medication. The cop asked for Jeffrey's name. It was Jeffrey White. One EMS guy put a cervical collar around Jeffrey's neck and strapped a back plate around his torso, while the other prepared a stretcher.

"I need the name of one o' you," said the cop, looking around the room. "In case there's any further questions or insurance problems."

"There won't be," said Jeffrey, who didn't seem to relish the idea of having his insurance company inquire into this. Nick didn't feel it was fair to Frankie and Joanne to ask one of them to be the witness, so she raised her hand and motioned the cop over to a semi-private place. She quietly gave him her real name and phone number.

"This is your apartment?" he asked Nick.

Shit.

"No. I live upstairs."

"Is this your place?" the guy asked Frankie and Joanne.

"Isn't it great?" said Joanne. Nick gave her major points for finessing the question without actually lying.

"Okay, we're gonna take you in for observation," said the first EMS guy loudly, as though Jeffrey had a hearing problem. "I'm afraid we don't have room in the van for anyone else, so as soon as we get to the hospital, someone'll call."

Thank you, God.

"Which hospital?" asked Jeffrey.

"Well," he said, "it's Friday night. Probably Lenox Hill. That's where we usually go." He and his partner readied the stretcher. "I want you to get on here now."

"I can walk," said Jeffrey.

"No can do," said the cop. "It's procedure."

"Ah, well," sighed Jeffrey, setting himself carefully onto the stretcher. "I'm sorry," he said to Frankie and Joanne, "that I can't dance at your wedding."

"Lovely meeting you," said Joanne.

"That's the nicest thing anyone's said to me all day," said Jeffrey, smiling, and looking as reasonable as when he'd shown up at the Pierre last night.

"Okay," said the cop to Nick. "Somebody'll call from the hospital. Don't worry." And he and the EMS team ushered Jeffrey out to the elevator as Frankie held the door for them. Jeffrey did not look back.

Nick wished there were stars in the sky.

I'd wish never to see that face again.

When the elevator doors had closed, Nick followed Frankie and Joanne into the hallway. Joanne paused, looking around.

"Hey, hubby," she said, "how about a quickie right here?"

"Joanne," said Frankie. "Would you do me a favor, please? Get real?"

"He used to have a sense of adventure," said Joanne as Nick closed the Claytons' door.

"How can I thank you guys?" said Nick.

"Well, you could tell us what was going on when we arrived at your place," said Joanne.

"Hey," said Frankie, cutting her off.

"Okay, okay," agreed Joanne. She turned Nick aside. "I'll call. You'll explain."

"Well, um, okay," said Nick, feeling sheepish and disoriented. The elevator arrived. Frankie and Joanne got in.

"You are something, Susan," said Joanne, almost admiringly. "You really take the cake."

Nick suddenly blurted out, "My number . . . is 846-3120." It was her real number. "I think I wrote it down wrong."

Frankie searched for the scrap of paper.

"I think I may have written 8-1-2-0," said Nick. "I just had it changed," she lied, "and I keep mixing it up. But it's 3-1-2-0."

The door was starting to close. Nick jammed her arm into it and stopped it. "Do you have the marriage license on you?" asked Nick.

"I plan to have it never leave my person," said Joanne. "Why?"

"Give it to me," said Nick. "And a pen."

Joanne took out the license and handed it to Nick. The elevator door made repeated little ramming attempts to close itself. Nick held it at bay with her leg, took the pen, put a line through her signature on the license, and signed Nicolette Stallings.

"My name isn't Susan Nicholas," said Nick. "It's Nicolette Stallings."

Frankie and Joanne didn't speak for a second. They looked at each other, then back at Nick. Frankie said, "We knew that."

Nick blinked.

"He recognized you," said Joanne. "You were on that series—"

"*Eagle Squadron?*" asked Nick, feeling her face flush.

"I loved that show," said Frankie squarely. "That was a great show. How come they take all the great shows off? You were *great* on that show."

"He never forgets a face, this one," said Joanne, nudging him. "He told me after you got out of the car. He was like, all starstruck."

"How do you think we knew what name to ask for when we called from downstairs?" said Frankie.

It hadn't occurred to Nick.

"Look," said Nick, "if I have to go back to Uncle Edward's and sign a new license, I'll do it."

"Does this mean we're not married?" asked Frankie.

"We're married," said Joanne flatly.

"I was there," said Nick. "If anybody is married, it's you two."

"I got an idea," said Frankie to Nick. "Initial it."

"What?" said Nick.

"Initial your signature where you crossed out the other one. Like on a check."

"Listen to you," said Joanne admiringly. "Mr. John Q. Smartypants."

Nick initialed. "Susan," said Joanne, "—and I will probably always call you Susan—I want to get this palooka into the sack, so we're gonna, like, arrivaderci Roma."

"Y'know, Joanne," said Frankie, "I hate to disappoint you, but I didn't exactly plan on a wedding tonight. I gotta get up early and help my brother with the deliveries. . . ."

"This is our wedding night, schmuck, and you are gonna make a delivery—to me."

Nick was still holding the elevator open. "Call me," she said, letting the door close. As it descended, Joanne laughed loudly at something.

She decided to take the stairs back up to her apartment. On her way, she met Mr. Kazura, plodding down at a snail's pace.

"Nick?" he asked, pausing in his descent. "Is the elevator out again?"

"No, no, just . . . getting a little exercise, Mr. K. You?"

"Going out for a walk. Can't sleep."

"Be careful out there, Mr. Kazura. Make sure Fernando keeps an eye on you."

"Don't let the bedbugs bite, Nick."

"I won't."

"They're biting something fierce tonight."

"Okay."

"They bite when you're lonely. How about some night I let you beat me again at hearts?"

"Anytime, Mr. Kazura. Don't walk too far."

"Hugs and kisses to May and June." Nick was too tired to correct the fish names.

She entered her apartment, closed and double-locked the door, slipped out of the dress, and folded it neatly into a pile for the cleaners. She moved about, methodically straightening up. She threw the old milk carton out of the refrigerator. She got a sponge and wiped up around the toilet. She picked up clothes and either hung them up, placed them in a hamper, or added them to the cleaning pile. She wiped the ash from Jeffrey's cigarette off the windowsill and threw out the empty fish food can. Unable to brush her teeth for want of a toothbrush, she gargled with hot water and salt.

She made her bed, took a shower, and slipped into the flannel night-gown which had eluded her last night. She tossed the script for Sidney Halpern's movie into the kitchen garbage, burying it a little so she wouldn't see it the next time she dropped something in. She drank a glass of cold water, turned off all the lights, and let the dull glow of the city illuminate the apartment.

She pulled down the sheets on her bed, got in, and reached over and hit the rewind button on her answering machine. Because it was such an old one, she hadn't been able to erase her messages when she'd called from her mother's. In the near dark, she ran the tape back a little, and then forward and then back, until she found what she wanted.

Hi, it's Sam. I've been meaning to call, but it's been crazy here. I'm probably gonna be pretty hard to reach, but you can try me at 456-0604. That's 818, not 213. You were great in the play, by the way. Did I tell you that?

She got into bed and nestled under the covers. She dialed the number Sam had left. It rang twice, then three times.

Hang up.

On the sixth ring, someone answered.

"Hello?"

"Is . . . Sam there?"

"Speaking."

"Oh, hi."

"Who is this?"

"I'm sorry. It's Nicolette Stallings."

"Well." He didn't sound unhappy. "Hi."

"I hope it's not too late to call."

"I don't think of 6:15 as particularly late."

You jerk. It's three hours earlier there.

"I got your message," said Nick.

"Oh. Yeah. Good. What're you doing?"

Well, so far today I had group sex, got burned, lost my wallet and a big job. But enough about me . . .

"Thanks for what you said on my machine . . . about the reading," she said.

"Well . . . I meant it."

"Thanks. *You* were just . . . amazing. I thought."

"It's a great part," said Sam. "When the writing's that good, all you have to do is get on and ride it."

Say something clever.

"So . . . how's it going out there?"

"Oh, it's torture, you know: L.A."

"I always kind of liked it out there," said Nick. "Is that tremendously uncool of me to say?"

"Kind of refreshing, actually. But you'll have to explain to me what it is you like."

"Okay. I guess it's the—"

"Uh, look," he said, "I'm kind of running late for something, and I should, ah, get going."

He has a date.

"Oh. Sure," said Nick.

"Listen . . . I'll call you."

"Okay."

"It's just that I'm really late."

"Right, right. Go ahead."

"Okay. Well. Good night."

"Good night."

She hung up, sure that Sam was up to his ears in L.A. honeys.

The phone rang.

It's Sam.

She picked it up.

"Hi," said the dejected voice of Jeffrey.

Nick remembered that she'd given him her number.

"Hello," she said, trying to keep her distance without sounding patronizing. "So . . . ?"

"So. It's a broken navicular bone on my wrist, a sprained thumb, and a strained neck. I have a cast on my left wrist and I'm supposed to wear this silly neck brace for a while. And a couple of stitches in my cheek."

"God," said Nick, wanting desperately to get off the phone but trying to sound concerned. She *was* concerned. She just didn't want to lead him on in any way. "I guess it could be worse."

"I could be dead. Would that be better or worse?"

"Don't say that," said Nick.

"You don't know. You just don't . . . know." Then, with an attempt to sound upbeat, he said, "Would you mind if I slept on your couch tonight? I won't try anything. I promise. But, ah . . . I don't think I can handle a hotel tonight."

"Maybe that's not such a good idea," said Nick.

"No, no. Of course," he said meekly. "Just thought I'd ask."

"Did they give you pain killers?" asked Nick.

"Demerol. It's like the pain is renting a room somewhere far away in my body. It's kind of nice. Maybe I'll take a whole lot of it."

"Don't do that," said Nick.

"Okay. If you say so," he said, his voice brightening. Nick realized to her dismay that it took almost nothing to encourage him.

"Listen," she said. "Don't you have any other family or friends you could call?"

"Go to sleep," he said, suddenly sounding fine. "I just wanted you to know that I'm okay."

"I'm glad," said Nick, who felt guilty that she wasn't.

"I'm not dead, so—I'll call you," he said.

I'm going to have to change my number.

"Okay," said Nick, trying to sound like she meant it. "Do that."

"We're still on for dinner tomorrow, right?"

"Oh. Yeah. Sure."

"Okay. Good. And . . . Miss Stallings?"

"Yes?"

"Remember: I know where you live."

Nick didn't reply.

"Just kidding," he said in a way that failed to reassure her. "Good night."

"Good night," said Nick.

"Sleep well. Call me when I wake up."

"I . . . beg your pardon?"

"Sorry," he said. "That's just something . . . my daughter always used to say when she—" His voice cracked a little. "Never mind. Never mind."

Nick, who wanted to scream, just said, "Okay. Good night." She hung up carefully, as if the receiver might explode if she put it down too hard.

She set her alarm for noon so as not to miss her appointment with Martine, and lay down. She usually fell asleep on contact with her pillow, but she lay for a long time, studying the shadows on the ceiling, not moving, not sleeping.

CHAPTER 9

Nick was on the beach again at St. Barts. A perfect St. Barts day. She was sprawled luxuriously on a beach towel, nude, alone, enjoying the quiet rhythm of the waves lapping near her, and absorbing the hot, hot rays as if they were vitamin injections. Everything felt fine.

She rose a little on one elbow to re-apply some suntan lotion. Down the beach, a man was walking toward her. The sun seemed to shine more brightly on him, as though he were in a spotlight. It was Sam. Amid the naked bodies all around, he was wearing old-fashioned men's bathing trunks. He didn't have a tan, but he looked healthy. He didn't yet see Nick.

She watched as he kept moving in her direction. He seemed absorbed in the easy serenity of the place. As he came close enough to recognize Nick, she had an urge to cover herself, and she slipped into her one-piece bathing suit.

She greeted him with a friendly wave. He returned it, seemingly unsurprised to see her. But he kept walking, passing her and continuing down the beach. She heard a muffled squawking, as if angry birds were flying far overhead.

She reached over to silence the alarm clock.

Even before opening her eyes, Nick could tell that things were looking up. Her sleep had been restless, but her stomach was calm. As she sat up in bed, taking in the clear blue sky of late morning, she felt light-years away from the night and day before.

She moved into the bathroom, and it occurred to her that maybe she should consider not drinking anymore. She had been noticing lately a connection between the times she drank and the times she . . .

But I like to drink.

I don't drink often, she told herself, sometimes not for weeks on end, and never when I'm working.

She toweled off, feeling like a new person. The burn on her thigh no longer bothered her. Most of the soreness was gone too.

Her phone rang. She had left the machine's volume up when she went to bed, hoping Sam might call when he got home from his . . . date? Almost late for her appointment with Martine, Nick let the machine pick up.

"Hi, it's me. . . ."

There was a pause. Due to the rustling of the clothes Nick was taking out of her closet, she wasn't sure, but it sounded like Todd again. She groaned. Todd hadn't yet earned the right, Nick felt, to say "it's me."

"I guess you're not there. I was just calling 'cause it's such a beautiful Saturday, and . . . I don't know . . . I thought maybe we'd go to the park, or a movie, or just take a walk. Are you sleeping? No, you're not sleeping." He paused again.

Nick said sweetly to the machine, "Hang up now, please."

"I'll try back again. If you're not in later . . . I hope you're having a great time wherever you are . . . but not *too* great a time, 'cause . . . I'd like to be with you. Call me. 847-3826. Bye."

She chose an outdoorsy outfit, not unlike what she'd worn to the meeting with Sidney Halpern. Yesterday, though, she'd felt like a fake. Putting on the jeans and work shirt after the cashmere dress and polka dot outfit—and what had gone on in them—she'd felt as if she were hiding something. But this morning, with a similar outfit—a tighter pair of jeans and a flannel men's shirt—she felt at home, and herself.

Maybe I should cancel Martine and go for a walk with Todd or something.

No, she thought, it's a good idea to see Martine.

I know there are things I have to deal with. But why was I in such a panic? It's amazing what lack of sleep does to me.

Maybe, she thought, it isn't a question of not drinking, but more that I need to be sure to get enough sleep.

I know I should have taken it easy with the champagne, but that doesn't mean I couldn't have stopped. I could have. I just wasn't being disciplined.

Discipline, she thought, *that's* what I should talk to Martine about.

She toweled off and glanced at the mirror. She looked so much better that the thought of yesterday, and the meeting, made her laugh at herself.

How could I have been so . . . disabled?

She was determined not to wallow in guilt. After all, in some secret part of herself she'd fantasized The Triple for a long time. If she could only figure out a way to get out of this dinner with Jeffrey, everything would be fine.

She found an English muffin in the bowels of her refrigerator, toasted it, and ate it plain since there was no butter. She grabbed a light winter jacket—it looked so warm outside—and headed out.

It was a glorious, temperate winter day. The sunshine and lack of wind made it feel almost like April. Nick hailed a cab, got in, and headed for Martine's office in the Village. The cabbie was young, and, Nick thought, attractive in an off-beat way.

Don't flirt.

"Ninth Street between Fifth and Sixth, please."

"You got it."

Nick rolled down the window and gulped in the fresh, bracing air. She loved taking taxis on weekends, when a car could really move through Manhattan. She saw in the rearview mirror that the cabbie was checking her out.

Don't flirt.

"God," she said. "A day like this makes me almost feel like going to the beach."

"Hey," he said, grinning, "You wanna go to the beach? I'll take you to the beach."

"Ooh," said Nick, shaking her head. "It's almost tempting."

Stop it.

"I hear today it'll be up in the high sixties, maybe even low seventies in the sun," he said. "Can you believe it?"

"Just my luck," said Nick. "I have an appointment."

"Cancel it. It's Saturday. Surf's up!"

"I've never been to the beach this time of year. I'll bet it's beautiful," she said.

"Seriously?" he asked. "I love to go out there this time of year. Nobody there. You have the whole place to yourself."

"It's tempting," said Nick. "I wish I could."

"There's a telephone," he said, pointing to a pay phone on an approaching corner. "You're a big girl. You can do whatever you want."

"Oh. Do I have your permission?" asked Nick, smiling at him in the mirror.

"Tell you what," he offered. "You cancel your appointment, I'll take the rest of the day off."

Nick just smiled and looked out the window as they headed downtown on Second Avenue.

"So . . . don't you think it's a little cold . . . for the beach?" Nick asked.

"I got blankets in the trunk. Anyways, under the sun at midday on a day like this, it's really warm."

*I'm going to my shrink. I have an emergency appointment with my
shrink.*

"Gee," said Nick. "If I had a bathing suit, I just might go for it."
She thought he might take that bait. Her pulse quickened.

"Hey, you don't need a suit on a day like this. There's nobody
there."

Martine is waiting . . .

"Turn off the meter," said Nick.

"Huh?"

"Well, I don't think I should pay for us to go all the way out to
the beach together," said Nick. "It hardly seems fair."

He reached over and cut off the meter. "That," he said, referring
to the $4.25 fare Nick had already accrued, "is on the house." This
was a good thing, because Nick had forgotten that she still had only
$7.35. She had hailed a cab automatically, forgetting her financial
plight.

"That's sweet of you."

"Hey," he said with an extravagant sweep of his arm, "I love this
job. I love this city. Where else would something like this happen?"
He turned left sharply into the Midtown Tunnel. There was almost
no traffic. Nick had never gone so fast through the tunnel's narrow
lanes.

They shot back into the daylight and up to the toll booths. Nick
had once done a commercial in a studio in Long Island City, just
beyond the tolls. She knew where they could find a phone and get
back onto the highway easily.

"Take a right here," she said, pointing to the exit. "I just have to
make a call." Martine had a very liberal policy about canceling appointments. As long as you called before the actual time, she'd cancel
it without charge. They turned and headed down the barren, ware-
house-lined streets, which usually reminded Nick of the end of the
world, but which today, under the clear blue sky, seemed like a place
that humans might actually inhabit.

She looked at his hack's license next to the meter. There was somebody else's picture, and the name on it was Daslamir Massid.

"You don't look like a Daslamir to me," said Nick, scanning the street for a pay phone.

"A friend," said the cabbie. "He lets me use the car on weekends."

"Naughty, naughty," said Nick.

"Yeah, well," he said. "It pays for acting classes."

"You're an actor?" asked Nick, masking her disappointment.

Why does every cute guy in New York and Los Angeles have to be an actor or a model? Why couldn't you just be a cab driver?

"Well," he said, "I'm studying to be one."

"Tough business," said Nick, as though she were in another line of work.

"Yeah. It is. But I'm working with this teacher—Don McElvoy—right now, and he's great. I think I'm really ready to go to work."

Don McElvoy??

Nick studied with Don McElvoy.

She and Daslamir's friend were in different classes, but now, looking closer at him, she remembered seeing him at a scene night a few months ago. The different classes produced scene nights from time to time, and all students were invited to look in. Daslamir's friend here was in a beginner's class, Nick in the advanced. She had seen him in a scene that was supposed to be funny but had failed to get a single laugh.

She spotted a phone.

"There's one," she called out, and Daslamir's friend pulled over.

"Don't be long," he said cheerfully. "Sun's a-wastin'."

Nick's mind was flooding. She made it a practice not to do things like this with anyone who was actually *in* her life, particularly in her professional life. Her episodes were always anonymous. Todd had been a little too close for comfort—now she might have to go out with him a few times just to somehow legitimize what she'd done.

Nick liked to be a mystery woman when she was in one of her moods, and she was careful not to be recognized.

On the other hand, she didn't have to *do* anything with Daslamir's friend. She could just, say, take her clothes off and make him a little crazy. Maybe walk around nude and put her feet in the water if there were a few people just close enough to make it interesting.

She got out of the cab, walked slowly to the phone, deposited one of the quarters, and dialed Martine's number. It was ten minutes past one. She was already late.

Martine's machine answered, and Nick waited through the New Age waterfally music. When the beep finally came, Nick spoke. "Martine, it's me, Nick." Martine picked up.

"Hi, babe. Where are you?"

"I'm running late. I'm *so* sorry."

"When can you be here? Are you all right? You didn't sound good last night."

Nick knew that it would take at least fifteen minutes to make it through the tunnel and down to Martine's.

Let Martine make the decision. I can't make decisions.

"It'll take me about twenty minutes," said Nick, stretching it.

"I don't have another meeting till three. If you're here in twenty minutes, it'll be fine."

I want to go to the beach. I want to see the look on this man's face when I take off my clothes for him.

"Okay," said Nick. "I'll get there as soon as I can."

"Great," said Martine.

Nick hung up and got in the cab.

"All clear?" asked Daslamir's friend.

"You're not gonna believe this," said Nick, "but I have to go back."

"Oh—come on."

"Yeah, yeah," said Nick, making as little of it as possible. "I'm *so* sorry, but it turns out my friend is ill, and she really needs me." She looked at him sadly but definitely.

"Oh, man," he said.

"She's . . . she's got cancer, you see," said Nick. "Her husband just told me she doesn't have much time, and . . . you know."

"You mean you didn't *know* she had cancer?" he asked.

"Oh, I knew. But I guess last night she took a turn for the worse. I can't believe it. This is so upsetting," she said, acting as bravely upset as she could.

"I knew it was too good to be true," he said wistfully, turning around and heading back to the toll booths to re-enter Manhattan.

"Well, maybe another time. We'll arrange to forget our suits again," said Nick. "I have some wonderful bathing suits I could forget to bring."

"Oh, God," he said, shaking his head. "What's your favorite?"

"Favorite? Let me see." They were almost through the tunnel now, back in Manhattan. "Well, I have one I got from Brazil . . ."

"Oh, God . . ."

"Yeah," said Nick. "It's just a bottom. Not much of a bottom at that."

"Not much of a bottom, huh?" said Daslamir's friend.

Her heart was still racing. "Well," said Nick. "It's just a string in the back, and it's cut . . . very low in front." Nick had worn it on St. Barts prior to going nude for the first time. In some ways it had been better than being naked.

"She's really, like, dying of cancer, your friend, huh?"

"I can't talk about it," said Nick.

They rode in silence out of the tunnel, down Second Avenue, and onto Ninth Street.

"You're a good friend," he said. "If it was me, I'd probably be a pig and go to the beach."

They pulled up to Martine's building.

"What do I owe you?" asked Nick.

"Just a phone number."

"It's 846-8120," said Nick, giving him the eight instead of the three. "Thanks for being so understanding."

"That's me," he said, writing down the number Nick gave him. "Hey. I don't even know your name."

"You don't need my name," said Nick, who had stepped out and away from the cab. "You have my number. In more ways than one."

"Boy," he said. "I can only imagine what you'd look like . . . on the beach."

"Well," said Nick with a sad smile and a wave, "imagine away." She turned around, walked over to Martine's door, and pressed the buzzer. Martine answered on the intercom.

"Yes?"

"It's Nick."

"Come right in," said Martine, buzzing the buzzer.

As Nick walked through the door and closed it behind her, she had the feeling that she'd just finished an unfamiliar race of some kind. She didn't feel she'd won the race. But she'd finished.

"So?" said Martine, directing Nick to the big stuffed chair.

★   ★   ★   ★

"Sorry," said Nick, settling into the chair after throwing off her coat. "I was caught in the most horrendous traffic."

"On Saturday?" asked Martine. "Is there some kind of parade today?"

Nick thought for a second. She started to create the details of a fictitious parade. Martine was waiting, eager, nonjudgmental, as always. Nick couldn't conjure up a parade quickly enough.

"I wasn't caught in traffic," she said.

"Oh?"

"I was on my way out to the beach."

"The *beach*? In this weather?"

"It's pretty warm," Nick said a little defensively.

"Sure—if you're in one of those polar bear clubs," said Martine. "Why were you on your way to the beach?"

"That's what I started to ask myself," said Nick. "So I came back."

"I don't follow," said Martine.

"Oh, God," said Nick. "The cab driver was . . . sort of cute, and I . . . I got into this fantasy about . . . I don't know, taking off my clothes at the beach. Next thing I know we're in the Midtown Tunnel. I was thinking about canceling the appointment anyway—I didn't feel so desperate this morning. But then I figured it was more important to talk to you than . . . you know."

"What?" asked Martine.

"I figured I meant business when I called you yesterday, and that I should honor that."

"Why?"

"Because—I just did," she said almost angrily. "I don't know. I would've felt guilty lying to you."

"Guilty? Really?"

"Well, lying to you, and then going out and . . . doing something."

"You know," said Martine, *"I* don't mind if you take your clothes off in front of a man. And I have a feeling that very few men ever mind. So—who do you think minds?"

Nick didn't have to answer. She nodded.

"It isn't the things you do," said Martine. "It's how you feel about them."

"Why can't I just do whatever I want? No one else has to know. Why do I torture myself with all this guilt?"

"I'm not sure it's guilt," said Martine.

Nick went on. She told Martine about Todd, Jeffrey, and the disastrous meeting with Sidney Halpern. She left out the room service boy, The Triple, and the burn on her thigh. She wasn't lying, she told herself—simply omitting a few details.

"What would it have taken for you to have been prepared for the meeting?" asked Martine.

"I wouldn't have gotten that part anyway. Natalie LeVine had it in for me. She hated me on sight."

"Don't you think it's possible that she was picking up on how you felt about yourself?"

"No. I don't think so. It was—" Nick paused. "I left out some stuff."

"Oh?"

"I've had this recurring fantasy about . . . oh, God . . . I'm such a slut . . . about being with three men." She looked at Martine for signs of parental disapproval. There were none. She went on.

"So . . . we, uh . . . oh, God. I was really drunk—do you think maybe I should stop drinking? I want to talk about that. Anyway. Jeffrey had this idea that he wanted to . . . God, this is really embarrassing . . . he wanted to, you know, watch me?"

"Yes," said Martine.

"So, there had been this pretty cute room service boy who'd been up to the room earlier. I had . . . flashed him a little. . . ."

"A little?"

"Well, just . . . really quickly . . . it was a perfect opportunity. . . ."

"What if he had reported you to the hotel?"

"This guy would not have done that. You have to trust me, Martine. I'm really good at picking the right people."

"You'll tell yourself anything when the urge hits you."

"No. I can really tell. . . ."

"Junkies lie to themselves when they need a fix. Be careful."

"That's a little extreme," said Nick.

"Is it?"

"*Junkie?*"

"It's junkie behavior," said Martine. "It doesn't matter what the fix is. Go on."

"That just sounds so extreme."

"Why do you think people take heroin?"

"This isn't heroin. This isn't injecting poison into your body. . . ."

"You better hope not. Did you use protection?"

"Of course," Nick lied.

"Good," said Martine, "because if you want to talk about putting poison into your body . . ."

"You think I'm that stupid?" erupted Nick.

"It isn't a question of stupid, it's a question of whether you need a fix," said Martine.

"Okay. Okay. I *didn't* use protection. . . ."

"Oh, boy," said Martine.

"I just felt . . . safe. Oh, God. I don't know." She exhaled slowly. "I'm sure I have AIDS now. I can't believe it. I've always been careful. I just, I wanted it to be beautiful . . ."

"I got news for you," said Martine.

"I know! I know! But it's . . . intoxicating. I wanted them to never forget me."

"How about making an audience never forget you?"

"What do you mean?" asked Nick.

"If you're an exhibitionist onstage, it's appropriate behavior. If an audience never forgets you, that's good. You think you're the only woman in the world who's done outrageous things? It isn't that you did it. It's how it made you feel."

"I forgive myself," said Nick.

"I'm not hearing that," said Martine.

"I'm just so tired of this."

"Of what?"

"Is it so terrible to want a husband and, you know . . . The Plan?"

"Wouldn't you have to stop doing things like this if you had a husband and a house and The Plan?"

"Of course. Part of the reason I think I give in to my . . . urges so often is that once I have a husband and a family, I'll . . . well, I know I'll have to stop.

"You think you won't still be a junkie?"

"I wish you wouldn't call it that," said Nick.

"I know you do. Look. Junkie behavior is junkie behavior. Drinking, cocaine, heroin, sex, food. Doesn't matter. Well—it does matter. And I want you to *own* it."

"Own it?"

"Don't try to gloss over it so you can give yourself permission to go out and do it again. Unless it's what you really want. In which case you have to ask yourself how much it's going to cost you."

"Own it," repeated Nick. "Own that I'm . . . a junkie?"

"Yup."

"How do I do that?"

"We'll talk about it next time," said Martine, reaching for her appointment book. "Meanwhile, there's something you can do to set your mind at ease—but you'll have to wait a while."

"Good. What is it?"

"Get tested."

★　★　★　★

As she began walking away from Martine's office and up Sixth Avenue, she realized she wasn't about to waltz into an HIV testing clinic and risk anyone—*anyone*—recognizing her. She'd never work again.

She'd been tested once, three years earlier, when, after a few glasses of cheap champagne she'd had unprotected oral sex with a beautiful young Cuban boy in a men's room at the Palladium. He had danced with her for an hour. Shortly after he'd pulled his sweat-soaked shirt off during a furious fast number, she'd led him to the lavatory, checked to see if it was empty, and pushed him into one of the stalls. Without so much as a kiss, he'd slid down and had her with his mouth. She came in seconds, stood him up, and, whipping his pants down, found him too beautiful and herself too drunk to give any thought to a condom. She drank him in, thrilling to the lack of latex. Months later, she'd gone to a clinic and taken the test. She'd dressed in semi-disguise and used a fake name. When the result came with the good news, she'd felt as if she'd had a death sentence commuted.

So how would she get tested now? She didn't trust the secretaries in her doctor's office not to gossip, and it was getting harder to disguise herself. She'd done the soap, the short-lived series, a few plays, and enough small parts in films over the past few years that people recognized her more and more. Not that they walked up to her all the time and said, "Aren't you Nicolette Stallings, the actress?" She'd get uncertain looks of recognition, followed by questions like "Don't I know you?" or "Did we go to school together?" or "Haven't we met?"

On one hand, it was great to be recognized. But she'd come to dread the inevitable "What have I seen you in?" She usually felt obliged to offer a likely choice, and would end up going through her resumé until she hit on the right one. It was humiliating.

Several times, and to her great relief, she'd read that it was truly difficult to contract the AIDS virus during a single sexual act. That is, if no blood was involved. No tearing of the skin. But blood *had* been involved at the Pierre Hotel, and skin had, indeed, been torn.

It would be comforting to talk to a friend, she thought. Nick had very few, if any, of the kind of friend she could call at a moment like this. Most of the past few years had been spent on her career or in cultivating relationships (of one sort or another) with men. Nick liked women, needed friends, but seldom applied herself in that direction. She would hit it off with a woman she was working with, and there would be a time of bonding and acting like real girlfriends, but Nick would inevitably meet someone ("I met a guy"), and become totally involved with him. Friends, unconsciously ignored, would drop away. The closest she'd come recently was with Hal. They'd had a genuine coterie of people they saw regularly, people she might have grown old with had Hal been The One. But Hal had found out about one of her infidelities, and it had shattered his image of her. With their breakup, Nick had lost a couple of girlfriends who had sided with Hal.

She'd been so caught up in her session that she'd forgotten to ask Martine if she could borrow some money to get through the weekend. She turned and started walking back. But after a few steps, she changed her mind and headed once again up Sixth.

I'll walk. It'll make me a better human being.

It was a long way, but it was a perfect day for it. She decided to stay on Sixth Avenue.

She paused, checking out some shoes in a store window, and heard a voice.

"Don't I know you?"

Nick turned with a slight start. It was an overweight woman with an open, friendly face.

"Yes. Yes. I'm sure we've met," the woman continued.

Here we go.

"I don't think so," said Nick.

"Are you . . . an actress?"

Lie. Say no.

"Yes, I am."

"Weren't you in . . . *The Prized Possession* at Second Stage?"

Nick brightened a little. "Yes. I was."

"You were *terrific*. I don't want to bother you," she said, starting away. "I just had to tell you."

"No, no. That's okay. You're not bothering me. In fact—"

The woman paused. "In fact—what?" she asked in a friendly way.

"No. It's only that I was just thinking about . . . never mind. Thank you for stopping and saying that."

"You're very good. We expect great things from you."

"We?" said Nick.

The woman raised her arms, indicating everyone around them, the whole city, the entire world. "All of us," she said.

"Well," said Nick, laughing. "I'll try."

"Forgive me for saying this, but don't try," said the woman. *"Do."*

Nick had an absurd idea. "I wonder if I might ask you a favor?"

"I'll do what I can," said the woman.

"Okay," said Nick with a nervous laugh. "This is really crazy, but I . . . uh . . . lost my wallet yesterday and I . . . need some money to get through the weekend. If you could lend me, say, twenty dollars, I'll take your address and mail it back to you on Monday. Or I could have it delivered to you, or FedExed, or whatever."

"FedExed?" said the woman.

"Federal Express," said Nick.

"When it absolutely, positively, has to get there overnight!" said the woman with a fierce wink.

"Right," said Nick.

"Only one problem," said the woman. "I don't have an address."

"Oh?"

"I'm homeless," she said, smiling. "Sorry."

"Oh. *I'm* sorry," said Nick.

"Well, on a day like this, it's not half bad."

"How is it that you saw *The Prized Possession,* if you don't mind my asking?" said Nick.

"I have my priorities," said the woman. "Food. Shelter. The theater."

"I see," said Nick, who didn't know what else to say.

"I hope you have your priorities," said the woman. "You should. You're good."

"Thank you," said Nick, staring into the woman's face. "Thank you very much."

"I do have about eleven dollars here," said the woman, going through a small purse.

"Oh, no. I couldn't," said Nick.

"Why?" said the woman, her voice suddenly rising. "Because I'm homeless? Take it!"

"Really," said Nick. "You keep it. I only have to walk home. You need a place to sleep."

"Take it!"

"No, really . . ."

"Go fuck yourself, then! Go on. Fuck yourself. Go on!" She was screaming. "Go on. Fuck yourself. *Actress!* Get out of my sight."

The woman walked away, muttering loudly, leaving Nick amid a small group of passersby who had stopped at the sound of screaming.

One of them approached her and said amiably, "Don't I know you?" Nick walked away as quickly as she could, and didn't break stride until she was home.

When she got to her building the front door was locked. It was the doorman's dinner hour. Automatically looking both ways for muggers, Nick unlocked it, breezed through the lobby invigorated by her walk, and headed up on the elevator, which, she was pleased to notice, was working.

At her door she plunged her Medeco into the top lock, but the pressure of her hand on the key pushed the door open before the bolt had turned. It had already been unlocked.

C H A P T E R   1 0

Had she left it unlocked? She did that occasionally. She couldn't remember. She stood for a moment, not moving, a shot of distinctly nonsexual adrenaline surging through her.

It's Hal. He has a set of keys.

But Nick had recently heard he had a new girlfriend and was finally settling down.

"Hal?" she called out, almost happy at the possibility of seeing him.

She didn't hear anything, so she inched slowly in. If the place had been broken into, the robber would have left by way of the bedroom fire escape. It had happened before.

It's just healthy New York paranoia. You left the door unlocked.

"Close the door," said a voice from right behind her. Nick jumped and turned as Jeffrey moved out from the winter early-twilight shadows and smiled at Nick.

"Close the door, Miss Nicholas. I do hope you don't mind my calling you Miss Nicholas." His speech was slurred, and he seemed wobbly on his feet. "Close the door."

She did. He moved behind her, double-locked it, and made a gesture for her to go into the living room.

As he followed her in, Jeffrey did an imitation of a narrator in a suspense film. "How, she asked herself, trembling with fear at the deranged man with the gun, did he get in?"

He stopped near the window from which he'd recently jumped and turned her around to face him. "He stole a set of keys, you see." He held up Nick's spare set. "Yesterday, when you obliged me by changing back into your gorgeous cashmere dress, I became a thief for the first time in my life. I saw a set of keys. I thought at that moment, 'I'm going to want those. I'm going to need those keys sometime.' Just like I wanted and needed your address, and your phone number, and you, and all the loveliness that you've managed to bring into my life in just a matter of days." He held up a small revolver.

"I was going to use this to scare you into doing whatever I want you to do, but I don't think we need it, do we? I feel so silly having brought it." He sounded normal now. "It's not real. It's a starter gun I use when I referee my son's track meets." He laughed an unmerry laugh. "If my wife has anything to say about it, I won't be seeing my children soon, let alone refereeing any track meets."

"Jeffrey . . ."

"Be quiet, Miss Nicholas. Miss Stallings. Miss Fuck. That should be your name. Miss Fuck. There should be a picture of you in the dictionary next to the word *fuck*. Also next to . . . let's see . . . oh, yes, *fellatio*. Oh, yes, yes: *fellatio*."

"What do you want, Jeffrey?"

"You'll see, you'll see. I won't leave your home without it."

Make him relax. Do whatever it takes. Get to a phone.

"Do you mind if I go to the bathroom?" asked Nick.

"Only if I can watch," said Jeffrey.

"Please."

"Is there a phone in the bathroom?" asked Jeffrey. Then, grabbing

Nick's wrist and pulling her toward the hallway, he said, "Let's see."
He found the bathroom. There was no phone.

"Go ahead," said Jeffrey, releasing her. Nick closed the door and
pretended to go to the bathroom.

Give him what he wants.

She came out and he was waiting by the door.

"Jeffrey, please tell me what you want."

"Oh, well, let me see. Hmm. I know this may seem like old hat,
but I must see you in that cashmere dress once more before I—
Would you be so kind?" He sounded almost pleasant.

"I'm afraid it's all balled up in the hamper," said Nick.

"No matter, no matter," said Jeffrey almost gaily. "It's a tradition
now."

He was definitely drunk, or on something. There was a cast on his
left wrist almost up to the elbow and a bandage on one cheek. He
had discarded the neck brace. But he was also six feet tall and in
fairly good shape. Nick could not hope to get any sort of physical
advantage over him. She would simply have to get him to leave.

"Do you want me to call the police, Jeffrey?"

He mimicked her. "Do you want me to jump out the window,
Miss Nicholas?" He stuck out his tongue like a four-year-old. "The
dress, the dress."

"It's in the bedroom."

"I'll go with you!" he said, mock-happy, and followed her in. She
dug the dress out from the middle of the hamper and held it up to
him with an expression that suggested he couldn't possibly want to
see her in it.

"Yes, yes," said Jeffrey.

He suddenly looked dazed, as though he'd been hit in the face.
He shook his head, fighting something off.

"Jeffrey. What's the matter? What do you want? Please. Let's go
out and get a cup of coffee. We'll talk."

"There'll be no more coffee!" screamed Jeffrey. "Ever!"

"Jeffrey . . ."

"Put it on."

He didn't move, and Nick realized that he wasn't going to avert his eyes, so she removed her boots and jeans, keeping herself covered as much as possible with her shirt while stepping into the dress. She managed to remove the shirt and get herself into the dress without exposing her breasts.

"So modest. So modest," laughed Jeffrey, applauding. "Such a modest young maiden." He looked at her, now re-clad in The Dress.

"Oh, yes, yes. Oh, dear me, yes, yes," he said, admiring her. He jerked his head to indicate that she should head back toward the living room. He followed her.

"What is it, Jeffrey?" said Nick, trying not to sound frightened.

"What is it?" repeated Jeffrey. "What. Is. It? Oh, dear me, so many things. Oh, God." He had that just-punched look again.

"Do you need something, Jeffrey? Can I get you something?"

"Can you take me back in time two days—to before I'd ever seen you? Could you do that, dear Miss Nicholas? Could you be Rod Serling, and just Twilight-Zone me back there? It would save us both so much trouble." His right leg buckled, and he caught himself just before he fell over.

"Are you hurt, Jeffrey? From your fall?"

"It wasn't a fall. I jumped! I knew. So I jumped. You don't know my wife. Of course you don't. You *may.*" He looked deep into her eyes as though just struck by a new thought. "Yes, yes. You may, indeed. Well—you'll see. I must say she always warned me. She always said she'd be ruthless if I fucked up. But then to fuck up—like this—and I'm such a horse's ass, I *told her,* I confessed all about you and me. I was so drunk when I got in. She sat there sweetly and listened, and I thought she was taking it all in, forgiving me!" He laughed. "*Wrong!* And when I've *just* been fired. Yes, yes. I'm one of the many, let's just call this spade a spade—yuppies—who've lost jobs in these parts recently. I can't hold on to my house. There's absolutely no way—I was stretched to the limit as it was. My wife doesn't work, I never wanted her to and now she's lost the desire. My kids go to the best—the very best—private schools. And I have no job. I was going to tell my wife the day after our anniversary. I couldn't let it ruin our anniversary, could I? And then . . . there was you. And I was so happy for a time." He chuckled. "You seemed to be almost a reward for my trials. An antidote. I felt I . . . deserved you. And, oh, dear me," he laughed an eerie laugh, "I guess I did."

He stumbled again. "Whoops." He looked behind him, as though someone had tried to trip him. Then he raised the index finger of his right hand into the air. "It's the Demerol. They gave me Demerol because I'm such a wimp. I begged them for it at the hospital. And I've taken a lot, you see. A very, very lot. I can't feel much of anything in the way of pain right at this particular moment. I'm just watching myself in a movie, and, if I do say so, I'm doing a heck of a job. And I have no doubt that I can carry off the whole thing. Now. This knife—" He produced a long, thin boning knife which Nick recognized from her kitchen.

"This knife is going to make your life as miserable as you have made mine. You see, I figure that the last couple of days have already determined that I'm going to hell, so I'm going to go in a very unforgiving way, my dear Miss Nicholas, since that's how I feel."

Nick looked as though she were about to speak. She didn't have any idea what to say, but she thought that if she set the right muscles into motion, something would come out.

"No, no. Don't speak. Watch, Miss Nicholas. Carefully." He ripped open his shirt, pulled it up, and, with an almost balletic deftness, aimed the knife toward himself, pointing its tip upward, and plunged it into his upper stomach.

Nick didn't move right away because her brain hadn't yet processed what was happening. She might have screamed, she wasn't sure.

"It's cool," said Jeffrey with an amazed narrowing of his eyes. "It feels . . . cool. And it doesn't hurt." He wildly jerked the knife to

one side, making a cut several inches long. He twisted the knife—
and pulled it out.

"I want . . . to look . . . like . . . struggle." The words spewed
out, and so did volumes of blood and matter. Spitting red, he made a
strangled effort to twist his body as though he were trying to jump
into the air. He barely left the ground.

Then he doubled over, making a small crying sound, and stopped
moving. "Oh, God," he said. "Oh, dear God. It does hurt. Oh,
God. Help me. Oh, God, no. Miss Nicho—" He stopped.

Nick tried to move toward him. She couldn't.

He was spilling, dropping, bleeding everywhere. Nick didn't
know if it took two seconds or two minutes before he fell to the
floor. His expression was frozen bewildered astonishment. It had not,
apparently, occurred to him that he would feel so much pain.

She moved to his side. He made a sudden jerk which Nick feared
was an attempt to stab her. She backed away and watched for—a few
seconds?—a minute? He was groaning and moving a little. Nick
wasn't sure if she was in danger, but she knew that she had to do
something to help him. He was half curled up on his side, turned
away from her. She made another move, kneeling by his back, and
saw a rivulet of blood and ooze running out of his other side.

Nick had never had any training whatsoever in first aid. Trying
not to look at the blood, she fixed her eyes on his face for any sign
that he might strike out further, and extended her fingers toward the
knife. She reached it, taking it with surprising ease from his hand,
not realizing until it was too late that her fresh prints were now on
the handle.

C H A P T E R   1 1

As a child, and then as a pre-teen, Nick had been an okay dancer, not much of an athlete, and a slightly better than average student. With an invisible but ferocious lack of self-confidence, she had truly excelled at nothing.

Her colossal self-doubt was her secret. No one suspected her of it. She was always in the right crowd and teachers liked her, but there was nothing at which she stood out.

The first thing in her life, in fact, that she'd been good at was looking good.

Years later, she would tell Martine that she'd felt like the ugly duckling. She'd worn the worst sort of braces throughout fifth and sixth grades, and sported thick glasses from kindergarten through second grade before her eye doctor had found that her faulty vision in one eye wasn't correctable with lenses. Her earliest school memories were of being ridiculed for her Coke-bottle glasses. She had dreaded each day of first grade. The friends to whom she gravitated were the shy, more awkward ones. Aggressive, competitive kids scared her. Her glasses, followed by the braces, had made for a solid one-two punch. Her natural shyness became dominant. In her mind, she was a nerd.

This was paralleled by an almost total lack of confidence in sports. She eventually tried tennis, softball, a little field hockey, and suffered through gymnastics. It was always the same. She'd be fine in practice, moved well enough, and had a certain natural grace. But in a game, when it counted, she would never come through. A voice from within told her she couldn't do it. Again and again she made those inner prophecies come true. In a team game, if sides were chosen by a group that hadn't seen her compete before, she'd be picked early. She *looked* like an athlete. But if the team leaders were familiar with her, she'd be chosen almost dead last.

When she was twelve, her parents, who belonged to a country club, enrolled her for tennis lessons as automatically as they themselves had been enrolled as children. Nick soon found that she couldn't beat friends less good than she. No matter how far ahead, she'd find a way to lose. She gave it up. As long as she didn't play, she didn't have to have those feelings.

Her father, an awkward athlete himself, had no tools to help her with sports. And her mother, too self-absorbed to notice, wanted her to play tennis only because it was the sort of thing she liked to imagine her daughters doing. Nick's parents were providers, not supporters, and neither of them spent much time with the kids. And Nick, raised to be polite and to please, never learned to ask for help. She drifted away from sports as she drifted away from anything at which she didn't immediately excel.

And then, in seventh grade, came what felt like a gift from above: looks.

Her older sister Martha started having parties. Little sister was allowed to hang around and watch, light-years separating the twelve-year-old from Martha's ninth grade friends. But the boys . . . ever so subtly, were paying attention. She was tall, but not intimidatingly so, and her curves arrived early, even before Martha's, which was a source of discomfort to them both.

Nick blossomed into a genuine looker, and while she was never as popular as Martha, she was always far more datable, which strained the closeness they'd enjoyed as kids. By the time she hit eighth grade, Nick knew—and everyone else did too—that she was one of the desirable ones. Boys—the right boys—wanted her. Socially, she was at the top.

And she hadn't had to do anything. It had been bestowed on her. It was astonishing how much easier it made everything. Boys, girls, parents, and teachers paid attention. The shyness, nurtured by braces, glasses, and self-doubt, taken together with her new looks, gave her a real and engaging modesty. She hadn't expected to be pretty.

At dancing school in seventh grade she became the envy of the other girls as boys raced across the room asking her to dance. Almost no one noticed that she was a mediocre dancer. Throughout high school, even in the company of the coolest boys, her reserve on the dance floor increased. The lack of confidence that shadowed her in sports followed her there. Fast dancing, all joy and self-expression, was not her forte. She felt that all eyes were on her, everyone expecting her to be as good a dancer as her image promised. She sat them out.

For the slow dances, though, the touching and holding and romance, she was right at the center of the floor.

During her emerging swanhood, she discovered a power previously unimagined. She experienced the effect of removing her clothes in front of the opposite sex. It became her deepest secret.

It started early in seventh grade. She'd been walked home from school one day by Dave, who was emerging as one of the most popular boys. Their first school dance was coming up. None of her friends was dating yet, but everyone knew that boys would be taking girls to the seventh grade dance. All her friends were talking and worrying, trying to figure out how to handle it. Dave was definitely the one Nick hoped would ask her. One afternoon a few weeks before the dance, he offered to walk her home. She was thrilled.

They lived in roughly the same part of town, but her house was just enough out of his way to make it special.

Everyone saw them leave the school yard together, which heightened the thrill. It was a bright fall day, neither hot nor cold. She was wearing a white blouse, open navy cardigan, knee-length kilt, knee socks, and Top Siders. As they walked through the town's quiet, hilly streets, Dave made what she felt was a perfect, smooth move to take her books without actually asking. She surrendered them easily. The point system was born as she awarded several to Dave.

When they reached her house, Martha wasn't home. She would be at field hockey practice for at least another hour. Her father was still at work in the city. Her mother, she remembered, was also out, playing golf at the club. Her parents hadn't yet laid out rules about having boys over, so she wasn't breaking any by asking Dave in for a while. He accepted.

They made small talk about their new teachers and classes. She served iced tea. They were on the sofa, a few feet apart. It occurred to her that she would probably let Dave kiss her if he tried.

She had a sudden and overpowering desire to get up—she wasn't sure why. Her heart beat faster. She found herself saying that she was too warm and wanted to change clothes. She noticed how completely she had his attention as she removed her sweater. In the middle of a sentence about this weekend's football game, she rose, still talking, and headed for the stairs as she began unbuttoning her blouse. As soon as the blouse started to fall open, she turned her back to him and headed up the stairs, saying she'd be right down.

Once in her room, she had no idea what to change into. Then it hit her. She found a one-piece tennis dress, recently relegated to the back of her closet with her decision to give up the game that so frustrated her. It was cotton knit, all white, and very short, worn with tight matching undershorts. She removed her blouse and new brassiere, stripping down to her underpants, and pulled on the dress. From the front, the little dress just barely covered her, but from the rear, she saw as she twisted herself around, an inch or so of her underpants showed. If she bent over at all, a good deal more was exposed. She removed the underpants and started to put on the matching undershorts, but suddenly changed her mind, tossing them away as well. She turned to check the effect in the mirror, and saw a pleasing curve of rounded skin uncovered by the dress. Her heart started to race, and there was a stirring between her legs. She felt euphoric.

A voice inside her told her that she absolutely must not go downstairs like this.

The thrill of it was beyond any ability she had to control herself. Before the voice could get through to her, she was moving down the steps and back into the living room.

"That's better," she said, sitting on the couch. He had only seen her from the front. Her thoughts were frenzied. She sat with her legs crossed. She saw Dave try mightily not to look at her thighs. She knew he'd never seen a skirt as short as this. He was talking and she was listening, but she could barely hear a word through the sounds in her head. They were shouting at her to go back upstairs.

She had never felt so strong. She wanted to touch herself. The thought crossed her mind. The slightest touch, she knew, would bring those wonderful sensations she had recently discovered. But the voices overruled her. They told her to change her clothes back. They screamed at her.

And as they screamed, she nodded at whatever Dave was saying, and then glided off the couch and down onto the rug in a move designed to make it look as though she were merely trying to get more comfortable. She reached the thick carpet, rolled easily over onto her stomach, and placed her chin in her hands, still seemingly taking in everything Dave was saying. But the little tennis skirt was now riding way up, exposing virtually her entire rear end to him.

She saw him struggle to remain cool—struggle, unsuccessfully, not to glance at what she had come to know was lovely flesh. She went on talking, now completely in control. She knew that Dave wasn't going anywhere.

It wasn't her intention to have sex with him. She wouldn't have known what to do. *This* was the experience she wanted.

She felt frighteningly fulfilled. She wanted it to last forever. She asked him innocently if he'd like another iced tea. He declined. She knew he didn't want her to move. They talked, and Nick never made the slightest effort to cover herself, nor did she acknowledge in any way that she was uncovered. She felt whole.

Finally, she caught him glancing down there, and she flicked a gentle smile, as though to grant permission. He then looked as often as he wanted, and as he did, talking on, she moved herself almost imperceptibly against the soft carpeting until, locked in eye contact with Dave, but unbeknownst to him, she felt wave after wave of rolling pleasure between her legs. It seemed to last forever.

Almost immediately after the tingling left her, the voices returned, reviling her for what she'd just done. The voices now had her undivided attention. She was horrified. She had just done something, she knew, that good girls don't do. She went to her room and put on the matching undershorts. When she got back downstairs, she could tell he was disappointed. Neither of them acknowledged the addition of the undershorts, or anything that had happened. She behaved like the picture of a nice girl until she sent Dave home a half hour later. She then changed back into her school clothes.

Dave did ask her to the dance, and they dated a little, but she found to her surprise that she didn't really want him as a boyfriend. For relationships, for kissing and sex, she chose other boys. But occasionally, and throughout high school, she'd ask Dave to walk her home. There were myriad variations on the tennis dress.

It never felt good afterward.

Months and months, sometimes as much as a year, went by without a repeat. But occasionally the timing and their mutual compulsion would coincide and they'd suddenly find themselves walking home. Nick knew—and this was absolutely essential—that Dave wouldn't risk losing a good thing by telling anyone. She had to be altogether sure that it would remain their secret.

They never had sex together, even after they'd both ventured into it with others. She wanted him for what she experienced naked in his presence.

Over the years she occasionally found other Daves, non-boyfriends to whom she could display herself. Her family went away each July. Most summers there were new boys, and she seldom had trouble enticing one to a remote beach or other private place.

She began to expend an enormous amount of energy in seeming to be a person who absolutely would not do such things. She had a good instinct for the kind of boys who were not braggers. That was essential. And while either or both of them might experience an orgasm, they had no sexual contact. That was reserved for her boyfriends.

By keeping her romantic and her compulsive lives separate in school, she accomplished two things. She could act on what she didn't yet acknowledge or understand was a forceful compulsion, while telling herself that she was true to her boyfriends.

She didn't know that she was also feeding and nurturing her shame, which became an inconspicuous but constant companion.

★   ★   ★   ★

Suspended in shock, Nick looked at the knife, then put it down.

She knew she wasn't thinking clearly, and she knew she must change that, and hold her panic down. The blood, she noticed, was a color different from what she'd seen in movies. It looked less alive.

Think. Think.

Knowing nothing of emergency medical procedures, she started for the phone.

No! He'll die in the time you make the call.

She reached for his wrist and felt nothing. She tried his temple.

Nothing. He'd fallen in such a way that his wound was covered by his body. She didn't think she could stand to see it, but she turned him over enough to place her hand near his heart. She found no pulse.

He's dead.

Another sort of survival instinct told her not to get blood on herself. Massive amounts of it had poured out of him, seeping into her old beige wall-to-wall carpet. The red was working its way upward, in seeming defiance of gravity, into the ruffle of her chintz sofa, turning the couch's predominant yellow a vibrant pink.

Phone call.

She got up. Her hands were bloody. She made her way to the kitchen sink, washed, dried, and picked up the phone.

Nine one one.

She dialed Martine. The waterfally music played, and Nick waited forever for the message to get to the beep.

"Martine? It's Nick. Please, pick up."

Nothing.

"Martine? It's Nick. It's ten after four. Please pick up. . . ."

Martine must have gone home early, or else turned down the volume on her machine the way she did when something intense and breakthrough-like was happening with a client. Someone, Nick thought, is having a breakthrough while I fall out of the sky.

"Martine. Whenever you get this . . . *whenever* . . . please call me. No matter what time it is. Okay? Any time is okay."

She disengaged with one finger and held the receiver to her breast. As long as she didn't leave or call the police, life would remain the same. She flashed on a documentary she'd seen on TV about the last days and hours of a man on death row. She remembered how he spoke on the phone during his final minutes, conscious and utterly aware that he was about to die. People can do that, she'd seen. They can do normal things even when they know they're about to die. She couldn't *not* call the police. And yet she couldn't call them either, and have her life.

She dialed 911. It rang three times.

Hang up . . .

It rang again, and again.

They can't help him . . .

Someone answered. "Please state the address from which you are calling."

Nick held the phone for an instant. "There's . . . a man . . ."

"Your address please . . ."

She started to answer, but didn't. Noise inside her head mingled with a thumping silence. She told herself she was innocent of any wrongdoing.

. . . he did this to himself . . .

To quiet the raging inside her and to maintain her denial, she hung up the phone, grabbed her coat and bag and walked out into the hallway. She was quite sure to lock the door.

When she reached the lobby, Fernando the doorman was back from dinner. Had Jeffrey watched the building and waited until Fernando's dinner hour, so that he could get upstairs unannounced? Or had he somehow talked his way up? Did Fernando know he was upstairs? Somewhere in her brain's cyclone she was hearing words like "witness" and "alibi." She thought she'd better know. She started to speak but couldn't find her voice. She cleared her throat.

"Has anyone been by to see me, Fernando?"

"No, Miss Stallings. Not since I've been on. Are you expecting someone?"

"Oh, no. I just . . . thought there might be a script arriving. I guess it'll come on Monday."

"Okay, Miss Stallings. Have a good evening."

There's a dead man in my apartment.

"Thanks, Fernando."

He seemed more attentive and willing to help than usual. Frankie's tip last night had apparently put Fernando squarely in her corner. As she opened the door, she was mentally hailing a cab and trying to figure out where that cab might take her. One drove by immediately, her cab karma running true to form. It stopped and Nick got in. The driver, tired and angry-looking, had a noxious odor that made its way through the plastic divider separating the front seat from the rear. Nick almost got out.

"Thirty Beekman Place," she said, the decision having spontaneously been made to go to her parents' apartment.

Let them be parents.

The cab pulled up to the red light at the next corner, and Nick saw a phone booth. She decided to make sure someone was home. "Could you pull over, please? For just a second? I need to make a call." There was some kind of time meter running on her options now, and she didn't want to get to Beekman Place and find no one home.

"You make phone call?" asked the driver, astonished, in a thick Middle-Eastern accent.

"Yes. I'm sorry. It'll only take a second."

"Can't wait. No, no," he warned, wagging a finger at this most cardinal of New York sins: asking a taxi driver to wait—for anything. Their bosses, Nick knew from exhaustive experience, have drilled into all cabbies' heads the dictum that they must turn over the meter. They must never, ever, wait—another invisible erosion of the quality of life in the city.

Nick, who normally would have argued with him, got out of the car, leaving her door open so that he wouldn't suddenly drive away. She saw a man hurrying toward the same pay phone, so she picked up her pace and got to it first. He hadn't sized her up as a potential phone adversary, so when she grabbed the receiver he stopped suddenly, threw an imaginary punch at the air, and yelled, "Damn!" He then placed himself a little too close to Nick, as if in line behind her, to make sure she understood that he was there, waiting. She dialed her parents' number, turned to him, and manically hummed a bar or two of the musical opening of "New York, New York." He backed off a few feet.

Her parents' machine was apparently not hooked up properly—

they had recently bought their first answering machine. It simply beeped at Nick without delivering any message.

"Mom? Anybody home? It's Nick. Pick up. Hello, hello? Hello, hello, hello, hello? Are you at the movies?" She often took in a movie on Saturday afternoons. "Oh, well. Never mind. Never mind." She laughed involuntarily. "Uhhh. You should read the directions for this answering machine, Dad. Are you back? There's no message. From you, that is. I don't know if this is recording or not. Oh, well. Talk to you later."

She got back in the cab. The driver was staring at her as though she'd just pulled a rude fast one on him. She shut the door, and he sped on. It took Nick a couple of blocks to realize that Beekman Place was no longer her destination.

"Oh—wait a second. Wait a second," said Nick. "Change of plans."

He glared at her in the rearview mirror and hit the brakes.

"Where we go, then?" he asked impatiently.

"Just a second, just a second."

"Where we go to, lady?" his voice rose a bit.

Nick put her hand to her forehead, trying to squeeze out an address. "I'm not sure. Let me think for a minute."

"You no *sure*? You no sure, you please to get out. Please." He indicated the door for her, as though he were being extremely polite.

"Just a second, just a second," said Nick, assembling a map of the city out of the whirling ooze of her mind.

"No. No, lady. You please go. Take another taxi. Thank you, thank you . . ."

Nick roared. It was a roar from somewhere far down in a hitherto untapped place. Had she tried to affect such a sound ever before in her life, she would have done lasting damage to her vocal cords.

"SHUT THE FUCK UP! I'm thinking! Just shut up. Shut up." He was quiet, stunned. "I've almost got it," she said. "Yes. Third and Seventy-sixth. I think. The Washington . . . Something. It's a big high-rise."

"Third and Seven-six?" asked the driver politely.

"Yes. Thank you," said Nick, feigning composure.

Frankie's uncle Edward. She prayed he was home. Actually prayed.

CHAPTER 12

The cab ride brought an eerie sense of normalcy. Nick looked out the window and saw people walking dogs, holding hands with children, hurrying on errands.

It was still difficult to breathe, to digest any of this. Wally Wall Street, who'd slipped Nick his calling card less than two days ago, was cut open and dead at her apartment.

She didn't have a lawyer. She'd never been in legal trouble. Her career hadn't yet involved the kind of deals that required attorneys. Nor, she struggled to think, was she absolutely sure she needed one. She hadn't done anything wrong. She hadn't had anything directly to do with Jeffrey's death.

My fingerprints are on the knife.

Had Jeffrey succeeded in making it look like there'd been a struggle? Nick had no idea, but the thought of his intention brought a new dose of nausea that made what she'd experienced yesterday seem minor league.

As the cab turned onto Third Avenue, Nick saw Uncle Edward's building, the Worthington Somerset.

"This one here?" asked the driver.

"That's it," said Nick, feeling something that was a distant relative to hope.

"Not Washington, lady. *Worthington*. You sure . . . ?"

"I'm sure, I'm sure," said Nick, fumbling for her purse, then remembering that she was down to her last $7.50. The meter read $3.75. She gave him the five-dollar bill, bit her lip, and asked for a dollar back—indicating a 25-cent tip. He handed her a dollar and a quarter, rejecting the tip. Nick had the melodramatic thought that she might need the quarter to make her one phone call from the police station.

He sped away and Nick approached the Worthington Somerset's front door by way of the building's showy circular driveway. The temperature was doing a midwinter sudden free-fall, and the wind cracked Nick's cheeks.

The doorman she'd seen last night was on duty. She greeted him with her best smile, a far cry from her usual. The doorman, she felt sure, must be asking himself who this desperate woman is.

As she started to speak, Nick realized that she couldn't remember Uncle Edward's last name. She was pretty sure he was in 17F, however. That had somehow stuck.

"How are your allergies today," she asked as though they discussed them daily. He looked at her and seemed to remember her taking the flowers from him last night.

"Better. Better. Couldn't've been any worse. What can I do for you?"

"Oh, I'm just on my way up to see Uncle Edward. . . ."

"I *think* Mr. Costantino is in. I haven't seen him leave." He reached for the intercom phone and hesitated for a split second, looking to his list.

"It's 17F," said Nick. The man winked his agreement.

"Whom shall I say is calling?"

"Nicolette Stallings," she said without thinking. Then she remembered that she'd signed Uncle Edward's computer certificate as Susan Nicholas.

"Mr. Costantino?" said the doorman into the phone.

Nick blurted out, "Tell him it's Susan Nicholas." She looked at the doorman, a little wide-eyed. He seemed puzzled.

"It's an old joke," said Nick. "He'll know what I mean."

"There's a Susan Nicholas to see you." He listened. Then, to Nick, "He says he doesn't know a Susan Nicholas."

"Tell him . . . I was the witness for Frankie—Francis—and Jo-anne last night."

"She was the witness for Francis—" Uncle Edward apparently cut him off. The doorman grinned. "The judge said, 'Why didn't you say so?' Go on up."

Nick wondered how long it had been since she'd left her apartment. It felt as though time was suspended—time out!—but she knew better. She envisioned her whole couch a fresh, bursting blood-red, having absorbed everything on the floor.

She couldn't remember which direction to go as she got off the elevator, but then she heard Uncle Edward's voice to her right. "This way, Miss Witness-Maid-of-Honor." She found him holding the door ajar, still in his robe, to which he had added one item of clothing: earmuffs.

He made no mention of the earmuffs. Nick decided it would be best to ignore them too.

"What can I do for you, young lady, and why is it I wish that you had married my nephew instead of that other woman?"

"Your nephew did well," said Nick. "You'll see."

Don't chat.

"I hope you're right. Still, if it had been up to me . . ." His eyes twinkled. He was flirting, but not at all lasciviously. "What brings you my way?" asked Uncle Edward.

"I'm in trouble, Mr. Costantino—"

"Uncle Edward," he corrected her. "Please."

"Okay. Uncle Edward—I'm in . . . trouble and I don't have a lawyer. I need some legal advice. Fast." She hadn't decided yet how much to tell him.

"Would you like to come in? I'm just making some hot chocolate. Sugar-free."

"Thank you," said Nick. "But I don't have time. Someone is . . . waiting for me, and I have to be there pretty soon." She tried to sound as levelheaded as possible. Uncle Edward stepped inside, motioned her to do the same, and sank onto the arm of a chair.

"Could you speak up a little bit, my dear," said Uncle Edward impatiently. "I've never had any trouble with my hearing, but today, I don't know what it is . . . could you just speak up a bit?"

"Uncle Edward," Nick said, taking a deep breath. With her finger she made a circular motion around one of her ears.

Uncle Edward watched thoughtfully. Then he smiled, reached up, and removed the earmuffs. "There's a draft by my desk and—never mind. Never mind." He put the earmuffs on the seat of the chair. "So. What's up, Miss . . . ?"

"Stallings. My name is Nicolette Stallings." The words rushed out. "I signed the wedding certificate with another name last night, Uncle Edward, because I'd never met your nephew or Joanne before, and I don't know why, I guess I was . . . I don't know. I don't know why I lied to them, and to you. I don't know why I did that. They were so kind to me." Nick started to cry. "Oh, dear God," she said. "I don't know what's happening."

"What's the proverbial bottom line here, Miss Stallings? Why did you come see me? Don't you have family?"

"I couldn't reach my parents. I don't have a lawyer, but someone is hurt. No. He's . . . he's dead. He's dead, Uncle Edward." She looked into his eyes and saw that he was listening without a trace of judgment. "He committed suicide. He . . . slept with me and his wife found out and—I don't know, I don't know . . . he'd just lost his job . . ."

"Miss Stallings, Miss Stallings," said Uncle Edward firmly, raising his hand to stop her. "Have you called the police?"

"No. I . . . I guess I panicked. No, I haven't."

"Well, dear. You have to do that. Right away. Right now."

"I know. Of course. But . . . I was afraid. I think he tried to make it look like I did it. . . ."

Uncle Edward looked at her very hard. She was crying silently and staring back.

"You must call the police. And you'll need a lawyer." He turned away and headed for his desk.

"I'm just very scared, Uncle Edward. I'm not trying to hide anything."

He thumbed through an address book. "I can recommend several lawyers. Good ones."

"I'm so sorry," said Nick, now crying harder. "Please forgive me . . ."

"No, no," said Uncle Edward, who seemed distracted that he couldn't find the numbers he was looking for. He searched through a pile on the desk. "You're a lovely young woman and we were . . . fellow wedding guests. Also, I like the way you handled the earmuffs."

Nick wept, and Uncle Edward moved to her and reached out his arm, placing it awkwardly but firmly around her shoulders to indicate support.

The bedroom door opened, and Mrs. Costantino emerged. She took in the scene.

"You better talk fast," she said to her husband, making her way to the kitchen and never breaking stride. She opened the refrigerator and took out a jar of pickles. "I knew you were trouble when I saw you the other night, sweetie. Edward, is there something I should know about here?"

Nick started to speak, but Uncle Edward managed to get in the first word.

"My dear, this is Miss Stallings, Francis's friend. She's in some trouble."

"She certainly is. I may scratch her eyes out," said Mrs. Costantino, crunching down on a gherkin.

"My wife knows that I am utterly true-blue, Miss Stallings, but she always goes through the motions of jealousy, for which I am somehow grateful. Tell Miss Stallings that you are not, in fact, jealous, my dear. Are you?"

"Only because I'm allowing for your age, and this young girl's looks. I have to figure you'd be smarter than to do it right under my nose. Pickle?" She raised the jar.

"No thanks," Nick somehow managed to say.

"My dear," said Uncle Edward, "do you think you could find Albert Pearson's phone number for me? And Ferris Fanning."

"Albie Pearson?" said Mrs. Costantino. "You must really be in trouble, young lady."

"Just look them up, please," said Uncle Edward as his wife instantly produced another phone book from the bowels of the desk. She looked up the numbers, wrote them down on a Post-It, and handed it to Uncle Edward.

"I'm going back and finishing my movie," said Mrs. Costantino. "You're very pretty, young lady, and I'm sorry for your troubles, but if I find you here when I come out again, I'm shooting first and asking questions later. Understood?" Then she smiled.

"Thank you, Mrs. Costantino," Nick said.

"Albie Pearson," said Mrs. C., drifting back through the bedroom door, pickle jar in hand. "My, my, my. Good luck, my dear."

"Would you mind giving me Frankie's phone number too?" asked Nick. She didn't quite know why, but she wanted it.

"Not at all," said Uncle Edward, writing Frankie's number from memory. "But now you must call the police. Then get in touch with Mr. Pearson or Mr. Ferris Fanning." He was writing. "It's Saturday, so you might have some trouble finding either one. It's only ethical for me to give you at least two names. You can say that I referred you. It may or may not help you get through."

"Are you sure I need a lawyer, Uncle Edward?"

"Yes. I'm sure. And these are both good men. I've seen them work. But you have to call the police. Since you'll have to tell the police everything—and that includes your coming here—you might as well make the call from here. I'll have to talk to them too, eventually."

"Oh, God," said Nick, now sobbing. "I'm so sorry."

"Hey," said Uncle Edward with a shrug. "We do our best. Here." He handed her the phone. "You lied to me and Francis about who you are. I don't know why you did that. I'm not asking. But you have something in your favor. My sister liked you. She talks to me. You can laugh. She's dead, she's just a picture on my desk . . . but she talks to me." Nick was about to dial. "Don't call 911. It's too late. Call the Nineteenth Precinct." He looked up and squinted, as though reading a phone number from the air. "It's 452-0600."

Nick dialed.

"Nineteenth."

Her heart pounded. She felt incredibly alert. "I want to report a . . . there's a man, dead."

There was the slightest of pauses.

"Where are you, ma'am?"

"Oh. I'm . . . I'm not there," said Nick a little absently.

"Where is the body, ma'am? And where are you calling from?"

"510 East 84th Street. Apartment 6F. I mean, that's where I live. That's where the body is. I'm . . . somewhere else."

"200 East 76th," said Uncle Edward.

"I'm at 200 East 76th Street."

"And your name please?"

"Nicolette Stallings. S-t-a-l-l-i-n-g-s."

"I've got that. Are you certain that there's a dead person, ma'am?"

"Yes. I am. I was there. . . ." She was seized with a sense that she'd just confessed to something.

"Miss Stallings. I'm going to have to ask you to hold on for just a second. Okay? I'll be right back. I have to ask someone a question. Okay? Just hold on, and don't hang up. Is that clear?"

"Yes," said Nick, who was relieved to be following someone else's directions. "I'll hold."

Uncle Edward looked at Nick. "You're on hold?" Nick nodded.

Uncle Edward shook his head disapprovingly. A man's voice came on the line.

"Miss Stallings? Are you there?"

"Yes."

"This is Detective Kerrigan, Miss Stallings. You're calling from 200 East 76th Street?"

"That's right."

"Is there an apartment number?"

"Apartment number?" Nick looked at Uncle Edward as if to apologize. He shrugged that it was okay. "17F," she said.

"Miss Stallings. Did you by any chance make a 911 call from your apartment?"

She felt with some certainty that she should talk to a lawyer before she answered that. But she thought that to insist on a lawyer right now would only make everything sound worse. "Yes. Well, no. That is—yes. I called, but I hung up . . . I was scared."

"I understand, Miss Stallings. Believe me. It's understandable. Excuse me just a second." She heard Detective Kerrigan say to someone, "I think this is that 911 hangup, Paulie. Okay—Miss Stallings?"

Nick cleared her throat. "Yes?"

"I want you to just sit tight, all right? We're gonna send a car over to pick you up and take you back to your building. It'll be there in two, three minutes. Can you just sit tight, Miss Stallings?" He was trying hard not to sound patronizing. He was succeeding.

"That's fine. Okay."

"Okay. Great. Now, if you don't mind, I'm just going to talk to you until the car comes. All right, Miss Stallings?"

Nick had to clear her throat again. "I'm not going anywhere, Detective."

"Would you mind giving me the number you're calling from?"

Nick put her hand over the receiver. "He wants this number," she whispered to Uncle Edward. "Is it okay?"

"Sure, sure," said Uncle Edward wearily.

Nick read the number from the phone.

"That's just in case we get disconnected, Miss Stallings. Okay? Now: 510 East 84th Street is your legal residence?"

"That's right."

"Thank you." There was an endless pause. "Are you all right, Miss Stallings? There's gonna be someone there in just a minute or two."

Nick nodded distractedly before realizing that he couldn't see her. She quickly said, "Fine. Fine. I'm . . . do you want any . . . other information right now?"

"No, no. You're doing great, Miss Stallings."

The intercom buzzer sounded. Uncle Edward picked up, listened, and murmured, "Right. Okay." He hung up and looked at Nick. She was reminded again of the documentary about the condemned man. Uncle Edward was looking at her the way the guard looked when he came to take the prisoner to the electric chair.

"They're on their way up," said Uncle Edward.

"Detective?" said Nick into the phone. "They're downstairs. What do I do now?"

"Just go with them. I'm going to meet you at your apartment."

With Jeffrey there?

"By the way, you don't have to go into your apartment if you don't want to, Miss Stallings. I certainly understand if you don't want to. We can talk outside, or in the lobby, or the car. But—I'm sure you understand—we need you to verify the scene." She didn't like the word "scene."

"I understand," she said, trying to sound cooperative. Uncle Edward's doorbell rang. He answered it, revealing two uniformed policemen who looked out of breath. Nick was in their immediate line of sight.

"Miss Stallings?" said the taller of the two, who had red hair poking out of both sides of his too-small hat.

Nick raised her hand a little. "Yes," she said quietly.

"I'm Officer . . ." He said his name, but Nick, who was trying too hard to concentrate, didn't catch it. "Would you please come with us, ma'am?" Nick half expected to be handcuffed, but they were both very polite.

She said into the phone, "They're here, Detective."

"Okay. Listen. Just relax. I'll see you in a few minutes."

"Thank you," said Nick as she hung up.

Thank you?

"What's your name, sir?" the redhead asked Uncle Edward.

"Edward Costantino. Cos-tan-tino," he said. The redhead's partner made a note.

"This is your residence, Mr. Costantino?" asked non-Red.

"It is," said Uncle Edward.

"Do you mind my asking how long Miss Stallings has been here, Mr. Costantino?" asked Red.

"Maybe fifteen minutes," said Uncle Edward, looking toward Nick. "Wouldn't you say so?"

Nick had no idea if it had been five minutes or an hour. "Uh, yes. I suppose . . . yes," she said, nodding. Then she was afraid she might sound evasive. "Fifteen minutes. Yes."

"Thank you, Mr. Costantino," said Red. "Do you have any plans to go out of town in the next few days?"

Uncle Edward almost laughed. "Not this fella."

"Okay." Red nodded. "Would you come along with us, please, Miss Stallings?"

Nick wanted to hug Uncle Edward, but felt that any affection shown between them might, in some unknowable way, compromise him. When she was almost out the door, he stopped her, took her by the shoulders, and gave her a wink. Nick could tell that he didn't know exactly what to say.

"You're very kind, Uncle Edward," said Nick, who immediately wished she had called him Mr. Costantino.

"Well," said Uncle Edward. "It's . . . all right. You just . . ." He nodded a few times, uncertainly. "You're okay?"

"I'm okay," said Nick.

"My sister's a good judge of character," he whispered to her. Nick felt the corners of her mouth pull slightly upward. "Just tell them everything."

"Right. Thank you. Bye," she said as Red and non-Red herded her down the hall.

CHAPTER 13

Some weeks before her incident with Dave and the tennis dress, there was a sexual event which had thrilled, mortified, and shaped her. It accompanied her first orgasm.

Alone in her house one afternoon after school while her mother was at the A&P, she wandered into her parents' room and explored their bureaus. At first she was drawn to her mother's things, as she had been in different ways since she'd been little. She browsed through lingerie, held a too-large bra up against her blouse, contemplated the intracacies of a girdle with its many snaps for holding up stockings.

But she'd seen it all before, and so today she ventured into new and unexplored territory: her father's bureau. He had long ago declared it strictly out of bounds, on account, she assumed, of his overreaching penchant for neatness.

Two top drawers, holding underwear and socks, held little interest. But a third contained items she'd never explored before. There were cuff links and shirt studs, collar stays, his college ring, some apparently French coins, and, tucked in the back, an old black-and-white, small, worn photo. Nick's breath shortened when she turned the photo over and saw that it was a nude young woman walking on a rocky shoreline. To her astonishment, she realized that it was her mother, at the age of perhaps twenty. Her mom, she saw, had been possessed of a beautiful shape. She tried to imagine the circumstances under which the picture had been taken. It seemed unfathomable to her that her mother had ever run naked, anywhere. She slipped the picture back into the drawer, in what she hoped was the same position in which she'd found it. Next to it, Nick found a small balled-up piece of red fabric. She pulled it out. It was a tiny red man's bikini.

Nick remembered a surprise birthday party for her father the year before last, and how he had opened a present and pulled out, amid squeals and catcalls, the bathing suit. He'd held it up between forefinger and thumb, while everyone whooped and whistled. It had been a gag gift from one of her parents' racier friends, a sexy woman named Sybil, who had dared her father to wear it on a forthcoming trip to the Caribbean. Nick had suspected her father of having an affair with Sybil—he flirted with her nonverbally when Nick's mother wasn't looking. As long as Nick could remember, her father had never worn anything but a long, droopy navy blue bathing suit he'd had since college. As he held up the tiny red thing and laughed, he also blushed. Nick had always assumed he'd thrown the suit away. But here it was.

Did he wear it, secretly? No—it still had a store tag on it, attached by a piece of plastic filament. It was brief and almost indistinguishable from a woman's suit. She tossed it on the bed.

The next drawer contained shirts, stiffly laundered, button-down, mostly Brooks Brothers oxford cloth, mostly white. Their starchy scent was pleasantly, familiarly Daddy. She pulled one out from the bottom, a yellow one she hadn't seen him wear for ages. With the care of a safecracker, she slipped off its paper belt and pulled the cardboard out, taking pains to damage neither. She placed the shirt on the bed next to the bikini and watched herself in the mirror as she slid out of her skirt, blouse, and underwear. She studied her newly forming breasts, which were the unexpressed envy of her girlfriends, and which had been causing a stir among the boys.

There was a sound she thought might be her mother's car door opening. She stood breathlessly still. It was the next door neighbor's station wagon. She stared into the long mirror on her father's closet. Her excitement frightened her. A voice said strongly, *no*.

She picked up the bikini and put it on. It was apparently of the one-size-fits-all variety, and she hiked it up in back, creating a kind of thong effect, exposing most of her rear end. Then she added the shirt. It was loose. She closed it like a robe, tying a knot in front. She had recently come across a spread about St. Tropez in one of her mother's old *Vogues*, replete with topless models on glorious sands, and now, as she checked herself out again in the full-length mirror, her father's shirt became a daring beach coverup. Were there really women in France who dressed this way on beaches? In front of men? In public? She tied the front tails in a knot and pulled it open on top so that her breasts were uncovered. The knot caused the shirttails to ride up high in back, showing most of her rear.

Watching herself closely in the mirror, she slowly unbuttoned the shirt and removed it. She felt sensations below her waist that made her heart beat faster. She sank to the soft carpeting, rolling on her side so she could study her reflection as she touched herself. She imagined, as she made eye contact in the glass, that she was returning the gaze of a beautiful boy far down the St. Tropez beach. As he watched her, she turned over onto the shirt, which now became a beach towel. She held the imaginary boy's eyes in the mirror, taking in the familiar aroma of her father's shirt as she rolled her pelvis slowly on it. An incomprehensible pleasure approached. Voices told her to stop. She couldn't. The climax slowly worked its way toward the surface and, as it overcame her, she pulled the bikini tighter, touching herself through the cloth.

The thrill was followed by the full-blooded certainty that what she'd just done was wrong.

She moved off the shirt and tried to refold it. It was wrinkled more than it should have been, though the starch had held some-what. She removed the bathing suit and discovered to her alarm that it was moist, and that it smelled of her. She carefully rinsed the moist part with a washcloth from her parents' bathroom. Methodically, she started to dry it with her mother's hair dryer, when, from the win-dow, she saw their Plymouth Fury back into the driveway. She turned off the dryer and started to roll up the still-moist garment, but in her rush she pulled off the store tag, which had apparently been partially removed when she had rolled around on it. She hur-riedly folded the tag inside the rolled-up suit and placed it next to the old photo of her mother in the drawer. She folded the shirt as best she could, re-wrapped the paper belt around it, re-inserted the cardboard, and slid it back into the bottom of its drawer. She grabbed her clothes and ran to her room to get dressed.

She was certain that her father would come home that evening and check his drawer, find the bathing suit, moist and without its tag. Or perhaps he'd decide to change into his long-neglected shirt, only to find it wrinkled. The inevitable inquisition would follow. She prayed to God for an opportunity to iron the shirt and properly wash the bikini. The deal she offered God was that she'd never do such a thing again, or even imagine it.

After school the next day she found a note from her mother that she was next door playing bridge. Nick rinsed and dried the bathing suit, and managed to staple the tag back onto the plastic filament. She ironed the shirt—once again replacing it in its cleaners' wrap-pings.

She held her breath every day for weeks when he got dressed. How good a detective was he?

One morning a month later he came down to breakfast wearing the yellow shirt with a blue suit. Her mother remarked that he wore the shirt too rarely, and that she was glad to see him in it. He winked at Nick.

She held her breath, unsure as to the meaning of the wink. Had he, in the past couple of weeks, noticed the stapled tag or seen a change in the way the bikini was rolled up? Did grown-ups—or at least *this* grown-up—keep track of such things? Did he know, and was he forgiving her? Or was it simply a wink? She never asked. The threat passed.

Her guilt was matched only by her desire for a repeat performance. After reviewing the picture of her mother and then of the perfect topless models, she waited again until no one was home, and repeated the event. This time her voices told her what she was doing was premeditated, sick. The orgasm lasted longer. The shame did too.

She hadn't yet heard the word *transvestite,* but she knew that this wasn't something she could ever tell anyone.

One summer night a few weeks later when her father was away on business, her mother, after her usual cocktail and two glasses of wine at dinner, suggested impulsively to the girls that they go to the movies. The theater in town was doing a Hitchcock retrospective, and Mom had an itch to get out of the house. They bundled into the Plymouth, the girls, as always, nervous about their mother's driving. She wasn't smashed, but she wasn't sober. Whenever her mother had been drinking, Martha sat in the back seat, but Nick, not wanting to seem as though they were accusing their mother of driving drunk, rode shotgun, her feet up on the dashboard in case of sudden stops.

The movie that night was *Psycho.* She was twelve. She watched in ever-increasing horror as the story unfolded of a man who stabbed people to death when dressed in a woman's clothes.

She was transfixed. The redness in her face from blushing was so constant that she was sure her mother or sister must have seen it, even in the dark of the theater. On the way home she was paralyzed by her pre-adolescent distillation of the story. The film's message to her was clear: People who dress in the clothes of the opposite sex are insane—killers. Her voices had new ammunition.

She felt that she must certainly be *some* kind of criminal. To her increasing self-loathing, it didn't stop the thrill of repeat forays into her father's bureau.

She was mortified that her first orgasm had been produced in this manner. She became convinced, deep down, that she was sick. She learned soon that there were laws, too, about indecent exposure. What was sexy in the South of France was illegal in her part of the world.

In the court of her worst fears, she convicted herself. The sources of her first and most heightened sexual experiences were not merely frowned upon, but illegal and sick. Feeling every inch a criminal, she covered the evidence, created alibis, and appeared in all other aspects of her life to be guileless and innocent, so that no suspicion would ever be thrown her way.

In school she went out of her way to be respectable, steering away from sexy clothes and behavior. She began to secretly envy the so-called bad girls, who were open in their sexuality, not seeming to mind who knew it. She worked to make her reputation so secure that if anyone—like Dave—ever slipped and spilled the beans about her, it would seem that *he* must be lying.

She became the fresh-faced, nice, proper girl-next-door—an old-fashioned girl. She came to think of herself as a liar and a criminal. She came to think of Dave and the others as victims.

She expended a huge amount of teenage time and energy looking over her shoulder, fearful of being exposed, wondering what she'd do if and when she was found out.

But when she landed in a situation where she could dally nude before a new victim, she could not deny herself the pleasure, a pleasure the likes of which she found nowhere else. A cycle began: anticipation; wild, secret gratification; a relapse into self-loathing and denial.

With no one she could talk to about it, her sense of herself as purely *bad* intensified. Since she couldn't control her compulsion, it became a matter of survival to make sure that *no one* ever knew the truth. She became a good liar. She became an actress.

★   ★   ★   ★

In the squad car, her escorts behaved as if they were chauffeurs. No one said a word. Nick was grateful that she'd had at least a little sleep last night. She was starting to be able to think. The ride up Third Avenue felt like another time-out. She was relieved that no one was speaking.

She tried to imagine the sort of questioning she was about to face. She remembered a session a few months before with Martine. Nick had been relating her guilt over a recent sexual escapade in which she'd cheated, again, on Hal.

"And you couldn't help yourself?" Martine had asked, a little incredulous.

"Well—that's just a figure of speech," said Nick. She'd been away for a night and day of antiquing in Bucks County with her girlfriend Meg, who was in from Colorado.

"Go on," said Martine.

"Well, we were at this little bed-and-breakfast we found. We were about to go out to dinner, and I wanted to take a shower. None of the rooms have private baths. There's just a big bathroom in the hallway with a tub, and a shower with a glass door. Meg was taking a nap. I put on a robe and I was heading to the bathroom at the same time as this quite attractive man we'd seen a few hours before when we checked in. He was alone.

"Now, I swear to God, I didn't plan this or anything. I didn't even think about the guy until this moment. It was just . . . a perfect little setup. He sort of motioned like why didn't I go ahead and go first, and he started to turn around and head back to his room, and I couldn't let the opportunity slip by. I said, 'Look, I'm just going to take a shower, if you want to shave or something, you won't be in my way.' He took it completely in stride—which is always a turn-on to me—and we both went in. He started to shave. I took off my robe and got in the shower. I knew he could see me as I got in. I mean, I hung up my robe, and I took my time—like we lived together or something. I just behaved like it was the most natural thing in the world. That's what I always do. He was great. He didn't flinch. I knew he was checking me out. The shower had that slightly smoky glass that you can see through, and it went up to about my shoulders, and we could look at each other in the mirror he was shaving in. I just kind of shamelessly made eye contact with him, and he smiled and shaved and I knew he could see me through the glass —I was letting him see—turning my body and . . . oh, shit, Martine. God help me. It's such a rush. Finally, I caught his eye again, and I just said—like we'd known each other for years—'You wouldn't happen to have a condom in that travel kit of yours, would you?' He fished around in it and said, 'Why, yes, I do.' So I said, humdrum as could be, 'Why don't you come on in here when you're done shaving?' And he did.

"We made love, all wet and standing up, and it was just . . . perfect. It felt so good. And that was all. I saw him the next day when Meg and I checked out, and he just smiled a little, but not so anybody'd know, and . . . that was that.

"Why are you telling me this, then?" asked Martine. "If it was so perfect and it felt so good?"

"Because when I got home and saw Hal, all of a sudden I felt guilty. My mind started screaming at me. We didn't fight or anything. I know Hal didn't suspect anything. I just . . . I know he trusts me, and he loves me, and . . . goddammit. I just, you know . . . it was like when they stole the Red Cross box at school. . . ."

"You never told me about that."

"I didn't?"

"I'd remember," said Martine.

"Oh, God. When I was in fifth or sixth grade—it happened more than once—there'd be a Red Cross collection box in every classroom, and we'd put in our change from lunch—pennies and nickels. One day the teacher came in and closed the door and said, 'Class.

Someone has stolen the Red Cross box. I'm not going to ask who did it. I'm just going to leave this door open for an hour after school, and I hope that whoever took it will have the good grace to bring it back. There'll be no one here, and there'll be no questions asked.' Now, I didn't take that goddamn Red Cross box, but I felt the blood rushing to my face. I felt myself blushing, red hot. I was horrified. I prayed that no one would look at me. I was petrified that someone might *think* I took the box. A couple of my friends saw me blushing, and I could tell they thought I was the one. Just this free-floating guilt."

"Guilt is an appropriate response—to doing something that you think was wrong," said Martine. "You felt guilt about the guy in the shower. What you're describing is more like shame. It's a feeling of just being . . . innately bad, or wrong. Is that it?"

"Yes," said Nick eagerly. "Like—I didn't steal the Red Cross box, but I'm so bad I might as well have."

"Yeah," said Martine quietly.

"I always thought I'd fail a lie detector test if it was important, because I'd just be so afraid that I'd—" She searched for a word.

"You'd manifest the behavior of the guilty person?" finished Martine.

"Exactly," said Nick.

CHAPTER 14

The police car headed east on Eighty-fourth Street, passed
York Avenue, and pulled up to Nick's building. She saw
two other squad cars double-parked, one with its light
flashing and revolving, and a group of five or six people
who had gathered to see what was going on. Red and non-Red
politely helped her out of the sedan. Two other men, not in uni-
form, approached. Red and non-Red immediately deferred, handing Nick off. One of the plainclothesmen, a little shorter than
average, tightly built with a no-nonsense but pale, boyish face said,
"Miss Stallings, I'm Detective Kerrigan." Nick felt sure he was an
ex–altar boy. "This is Sergeant Whelan."

She wanted to get inside. As they walked toward the front door,
she saw someone in the little crowd raise a tiny home video camera.
She reflexively did what she immediately wished she hadn't: She put
one hand to her face and fended him off with the open palm of her
other. He stepped back a few steps but didn't lower the camera, and
Nick saw a little red light glowing on the side of it. She tried to force
a relaxed expression to her face.

They passed quickly inside, Nick unable to make out clearly what anyone was saying. Once in the lobby, Nick saw Fernando, and John, the building's usually pleasant super, waiting with two more policemen. The cops were holding rolls of yellow tape with black letters on it.

"Now, Miss Stallings," said Kerrigan, "we're gonna need you to come up and let us in. Okay?"

"Oh, God," said Nick. "Okay. Sure."

"You don't have to go in yourself. I'm sorry to put you through any of this. We'll make it as easy on you as we can." He held his arm across the elevator door, indicating that she should get in. They squeezed into the smallish elevator with Whelan, Red, and non-Red. Everyone's eyes moved to the floor indicator above the door, which changed, too slowly for all of them, until finally the light glowed with a faint, red 6, and the doors opened. They moved toward her apartment and gathered at the door, facing her. Nick wondered what would happen next. Then she realized that they were all waiting for her. They wanted the keys. She reached into her coat pocket and handed them to Kerrigan, with the Medeco out, in much the same way she'd offered her keys the other night to Todd. Kerrigan handed them to Whelan, who, Nick now saw, had a face that looked as if it had been punched a lot.

"Why don't you stay out here and make sure Miss Stallings is okay," Kerrigan said to non-Red. "This'll take a few minutes, Miss Stallings. You wanna maybe go downstairs and wait?"

Once again she was staring at them and they at her.

"So . . . you wanna wait downstairs, Miss Stallings?" repeated Kerrigan. "Or up here? Either way is fine."

Nick was able to make out a corner of the rug in her foyer, a snatch of her couch beyond. She knew that Jeffrey was there too, just out of her line of sight.

"I guess I'll . . . I'll wait downstairs," she said, heading back to the elevator as if on automatic pilot. Kerrigan, with a nod, assigned non-Red to accompany her.

"We'll be with you in a few minutes," said Kerrigan, heading inside. While Nick and non-Red were waiting for the elevator to come back, the others disappeared into her apartment. Nick was tempted to follow them in. She had an eerie thought that the body had somehow been moved, or perhaps wasn't even there. Maybe none of this had happened. The elevator arrived, and non-Red let her in first. In the delay before the doors closed, she heard Kerrigan say to Whelan and Red in a wholly different tone from the restrained politeness she'd thus far heard, "Guys, come on. Don't just stand around holding your dicks. We got work to do."

When they reached the lobby, Nick absently made her way to a couch and chairs in the middle hallway, between the building's two banks of elevators. She had never sat in this area before, nor had she seen anyone else sit there. She settled onto the couch, looking away from non-Red, who never took his eyes from her. John, the super, was now gone, but Fernando was at the door. He seemed to be pretending she didn't exist. She craved a cigarette, but, not wanting to appear nervous, didn't ask non-Red for one. She sat, thinking about whom, if anyone, to call. She longed to talk to Martine.

She stood up after a few minutes to ask Fernando if she could use the doorman's phone to call her machine and check messages. Then she realized that she'd left the volume on her machine up, and that Kerrigan and the others would be able to hear the messages being played back. She returned to the couch. She didn't want them to hear what might be, for instance, another message from Todd about how she tasted. She wondered if Sam had called. She wondered if she'd ever see him again.

She didn't know how long she'd been in Nicky Stallings Land when she saw Kerrigan pulling up one of the chairs next to her as Whelan stood at a discreet distance with non-Red.

"Can we just sit here for a minute, Miss Stallings?" said Kerrigan. He saw Nick's eyes drawn toward two new cops coming in the door and talking to Red. "I gotta ask you a couple of questions. Okay? We've called in the M.E., Miss Stallings." Nick looked blank. "The medical examiner. He has to make a determination. It's all strictly routine, but there'll be a few people coming in and out. Sorry about all this."

"Does *he* know what's going on?" asked Nick, referring to Fernando. She had an irrational wish that this could somehow be over without the people in her building knowing about it.

"One of my guys had to use the phone down here to call the M.E., so, yeah, I'm afraid he knows there's a body up there. We didn't tell him anything else."

"You could've used my phone," said Nick.

"Well, thank you. Actually, we can't disturb the scene until the M.E. is done, so we don't want to, you know, move or touch things up there."

Nick could tell that he was doing everything possible to keep her relaxed. But somewhere in him, she knew, he was being thorough and allowing for the possibility—however slight—of foul play.

"Okay. Now, Miss Stallings, I've gotta ask you a few questions. I wish I didn't have to. Let me just say how sorry I am about this. I don't want to make it any more difficult for you, but I, you know, I gotta do my job. I'm sure you understand."

"Yes. Yes."

"And, look. You're not in custody here. Nobody is accusing you of anything. You understand what I'm sayin'?"

"Yes."

"Okay. I just need a little information about this man." He glanced at Whelan, who took out a small pad. "What was his name?"

Was . . .

"Jeffrey . . . White."

"And your relationship to him?"

Such a simple question, thought Nick. And as soon as I answer it, everything changes.

"We . . . knew each other. Not well. Just for a couple of days, actually."

"You met him . . . when?"

"It was"—she thought for a second—"Thursday evening."

Whelan kept making notes while Kerrigan went on. "Lovers?" he asked. Nick looked stricken. "I'm sorry, Miss Stallings," he said with a polite shrug, "but, hey . . ."

Nick hesitated. Then nodded.

"Miss Stallings, why don't you just tell me what happened?"

She felt hysterical, unable to concentrate. She was surprised she wasn't screaming.

"Miss Stallings?" Nick, who had been looking at him but not seeing anything, suddenly refocused. "Are you up to answering some questions now? It would really be a help if you could. Otherwise, you know, we could have you come down to the station later, but, hey, believe me, I hate to ask you to do that."

"You want to know what happened," said Nick, repeating the question in the form of a statement. She was trying to pin down her thoughts, which were screeching obscenities at her. "Yes. Okay. I want to know too," she said.

"I beg your pardon?" said Kerrigan, trying to be patient. "I don't understand. Don't you know?"

The elevator door opened, and a small, grayish man stepped out, so stooped over it was a wonder his hat stayed on. He saw Nick.

"Hiya, Nick," he said, brightening.

"Hello, Mr. Kazura," said Nick. "You okay? I'm not used to seeing you on the elevator."

"Gotta live dangerously from time to time, Nick," he said, making a move as if to tip his hat. "May and June okay?"

"April and Mae, Mr. Kazura. They're . . . fine. Everything's . . . under control, Mr. Kazura. Thanks," said Nick, nodding a lot and wishing him away.

"Did I thank you for those wonderful flowers?" he asked.

"Yes," said Nick, nodding. "Yes, you did, Mr. Kazura."

"So . . . thoughtful," he said, continuing out the door as though the cops weren't there.

"April and Mae are my fish," said Nick to Kerrigan. "He gave them to me."

"Miss Stallings," said Kerrigan. "Could you please tell me what happened?"

Nick didn't feel she could speak at any length without falling apart. She tried to compose herself. She couldn't get over how normal this all appeared, as though these policemen might simply be asking her to move her car out of a tow-away zone.

"Yes," said Nick. "Of course. I'm just . . . trying to find the right words. I'm not sure I can quite . . . *put* this into words, is all. Okay. Okay. I know I have to—so, I will. I just . . . will." Her right knee started to shake.

"Let me say it again, Miss Stallings, you're not in custody here, or under suspicion, or anything like that." His tone was reassuring. "I'm just trying to do my job. I've been up there. I have to ask you about it. That's all. Okay, Miss Stallings?"

Nick was looking at him. She was making an effort, but no words were coming.

"It might be a little easier if you hadn'ta left the scene, Miss Stallings." The word "scene" got her attention. As in "crime scene," she thought.

"I didn't think of it as a crime, Detective."

"No, no. Hey. Nobody's sayin' it's a crime. That's just the problem." He smiled affably. "Nobody's sayin' anything."

"I . . . wasn't thinking. I just couldn't stay in there. I was hysterical. I couldn't think. I still can't. I'm sorry I left, but I just couldn't be there with—"

"Okay, okay. Let's back up, Miss Stallings. Would you like a glass of water or something?"

"No. Well—yes. That would be great, actually."

"Somebody bring Miss Stallings some water?" Kerrigan asked, glancing back at Whelan and the others. Two of them shuffled away.

"Okay, so, we just have absolutely no idea what happened here,

Miss Stallings. And you do. So let's work together here." Nick could
see that he was doing his best not to show anger. His anger gave his
boyish, well-groomed visage a sudden and unexpected aspect of danger.

"What happened," said Nick, hoping she could get the words out
before her shaking overtook her, "is that he took a knife from my
kitchen and stabbed himself." Her teeth were chattering despite the
overheated lobby in which they sat. "I was standing there, in my
living room—oh . . . you know that—and he just . . ." Nick did a
vague mime of the thrust of Jeffrey's knife. She looked at Kerrigan as
though to say "please don't make me find words for this."

"Okay, wait a second, wait a second," said Kerrigan. "Back up.
Did you two have a fight, a quarrel? What was he doing in your
apartment?"

She focused hard on Kerrigan's eyes and spoke quietly in a rush.

"We met the other night. We went to a hotel and . . . he followed me home to find out where I live. He came over the next
afternoon, and I let him up, and he was just . . . he was a real mess.
He said he'd gotten home so late and so drunk that he'd just admitted everything to his wife, and that she threw him out and, oh, God,
began divorce proceedings, like, that day. She didn't even know he'd
lost his job. He was just . . . wired, really crazy, when he came back
to see me."

She didn't mention Jeffrey's jump. There wasn't time to think it
through. Wouldn't the fact that he had jumped out her window lend
credence to the notion of his eventual suicide? But there had been
no other witnesses to it—Joanne and Frankie hadn't actually seen
Jeffrey jump.

Would he think I pushed him?

"How'd he get in?"

"He had stolen a set of keys, and let himself in—I think during
the doorman's dinner hour. He was there when I came in."

"Where had you been?" asked Kerrigan.

"I'd been," said Nick, embarrassed, ". . . to my therapist."

She could tell that Kerrigan thought therapy was a waste of time. "Did you ask him to leave?"

"I didn't have a chance. It happened very quickly."

"Go ahead."

"He said he was going to make my life miserable, and then he just, I don't know when he picked it up, but he had this knife—"

"We saw the knife, yes."

"And he just . . . did it. . . ."

"I'm sorry, Miss Stallings, but I need you to tell me exactly what he did."

"He . . . pushed it in . . . in the . . . right here," said Nick, pointing to the center of her stomach right below her ribs. She knew she had to get through it. "He just . . . cut himself open. He was incredibly doped up. I forgot to say that. He said he'd had lots of Demerol. I think he was telling the truth. Because, he—" She started to cough, and felt sobs invading her throat, constricting her voice box. "This knife from my kitchen. It's very sharp. It's . . . very sharp. And he . . . and he . . . he said he didn't think he'd feel any pain and he said he was going to hell and he . . . oh, God, I just stood there, Detective, I just stood there. I didn't know what to do . . . he just . . . pushed it in—fast—and then he turned it, and then he said . . . oh, dear God, he said he wanted it to look like a struggle. So he tried to jump—"

Kerrigan didn't speak.

"—and then he said, 'It hurts' . . . and I could see that it did and —he fell. AND I JUST STOOD THERE. I was afraid he'd stab me. But I thought, 'No. Do something. Get the knife away from him. Help him.' So I went over to him, and I turned him a little, and I took it out of his hand. I wanted to help him, but I wanted to make sure he wouldn't hurt me. But he was already . . . he was . . . you know." She shook her head.

Nick had not noticed the elevator doors open and the return of some cops who'd been upstairs. She looked up and saw them, held at bay by the left arm of Whelan, who was now seated and taking notes with his other hand.

"Is that when you called 911?" asked Kerrigan.

Nick looked up, seeing the cops standing and waiting. "Yes," she said. "But he was dead. There was nothing anybody could do. And I was terrified. So . . . I hung up."

"How long since he'd stabbed himself?"

"I'm sorry. I'm not sure. I wasn't very . . . a minute? Maybe two. I'm not sure." Whelan kept writing.

"There's a difference, Miss Stallings, between a minute and two minutes here. Like, maybe life and death."

"I just had no sense of time . . . it was . . ."

"I understand," he said not particularly understandingly. "You couldn't help him because you were afraid he might stab you. Is that what you mean?"

"I thought he'd lash out at me if I got too close. Yes. He was . . . full of hate. I was just . . . frozen. And then he was dead."

"You're absolutely sure of that, Miss Stallings?"

"Yes."

"Are you a nurse?"

"I'm not a nurse, but . . . I'm sure. Yes. I couldn't think—maybe I was in shock. I probably still am. I just hung up the phone and walked out. I know that sounds terrible, but I had to get out of there."

Kerrigan took a long look at her. He looked neither accusatory nor sympathetic. He turned around and saw the cops waiting. "Everything okay?"

"Yup," said Red. "What about down here?"

"Make a path so's people can get to the elevator." He called to Fernando, "No one goes upstairs who's not a resident of the building. No one goes to the sixth floor without being escorted by one of the boys here, okay?"

Nick looked at Fernando. He was staring at her, but she couldn't tell what he was thinking. She wondered if it would be a good thing to tell Kerrigan about Jeffrey's jump.

No witnesses.

And hadn't she unlawfully entered another person's apartment? Should she mention it or not? She could read nothing in Fernando's eyes. At least he wasn't speaking up—she couldn't handle that complication. She needed to talk to a lawyer.

"Miss Stallings," said Kerrigan. "I'm sorry. I'm very sorry. Believe me, it's a terrible thing to have to ask questions at a time like this, but it's my job. I won't keep you any longer. I just have one more question. Okay?"

Oh, sure. Like I have a choice.

"Okay."

"When you called 911, and then you hung up, what exactly were you afraid of?"

Nick looked into his eyes. "Is that just, like, curiosity, Detective? I mean, am I being questioned here, or not?"

"Gee. I thought I was clear—but let me just say it again. Okay? Yes, you *are* being questioned, Miss Stallings. But you're not under suspicion. You're free to go at any time. Okay?"

"Okay. I'm sorry. I'm sorry. I'm just so—"

"Hey. I understand," said Kerrigan as though he were suddenly her best friend. "So what were you afraid of, that you called 911 and hung up, and left your apartment?"

"I guess I was afraid it would look . . . like he had succeeded."

"Succeeded in . . . ?"

Nick knew Kerrigan wasn't stupid. He just wants me to say it, she thought. It was the truth, so she went on.

"In making it look as though we *had* struggled. As though . . . maybe . . ." She wanted to stop. This was not a good idea. But it was too late. "Like maybe I *had* done it to him. Like it wasn't a suicide."

"Uh-huh."

"And I was afraid."

"Listen—I don't blame you. Where'd you go?"

"I went to the apartment of a friend. And he told me—of course —that I had to call the police . . . which of course I knew."

She kept waiting for Kerrigan to say something comforting about how he believed that Jeffrey had indeed committed suicide. But he was disturbingly noncommittal.

"Who was this friend?"

"His name is Edward Costantino."

"Edward Costantino?"

"Yes."

"The judge?"

"Yes."

"He's a friend?"

"Yes."

Kerrigan rubbed his ear. "We have his address, right, Joey?" Whelan nodded. "So—then you called us?"

"Yes. I mean, I was never *not* going to call. I just panicked. I needed to talk to someone."

"I understand," said Kerrigan, still noncommittal. "Now, Miss Stallings, some people from the medical examiner's office are going to be here shortly—I hope." He looked at his watch. "They're gonna have to take pictures and remove the body and examine it. Do an autopsy. It's all procedure. You understand. So as soon as we have the results, assuming that it's all like you described—and I have no reason to think otherwise—then this is over. The M.E. makes a ruling that it's a suicide, I do a little paperwork, toss it onto my lieutenant's desk, and we're done. So if you can just bear with us, we're gonna have the body removed as soon as we can, and then we'll have to seal off the apartment. I'm sorry about all this. Is there somewhere you'd like us to take you, Miss Stallings? Somewhere you'd be more comfortable?"

She wished she could call Hal. But he'd been so angered by his revelation that she'd slept with someone else that he'd vowed never to speak to her again. She didn't want to call her parents. She wished they weren't so close by—she felt guilty *not* calling them. But they'd be berserk if she called now. Nick didn't think she could handle her mother. And Dad—assuming he'd even made it back—would be furious she'd gotten herself into such a mess. He'd never been much comfort in a crisis.

"Mr. Kerrigan"—she cleared her throat—"what if the autopsy doesn't . . . turn out that way?"

Shut up . . .

"What do you mean?" He tried to look as though the thought had never occurred to him. "If it shows that you two—what?—that the wound wasn't self-inflicted?"

"Yes."

"Well. Hey. I wouldn't worry about that, Miss Stallings. These people are experts."

"He *wanted* to make it look like I did it. Do you understand that . . . ?"

Shut up . . .

"I doubt—very much—that he could have succeeded," said Kerrigan.

"That's why he doped himself up. So he could inflict that much pain on himself."

"I understand, Miss Stallings. Look. Why don't you call someone and we'll give you a lift to wherever it is, and you can relax. Is there anything you need from your apartment?"

Nick knew that there was no way she could set foot in there. She wondered if she ever would again. She also realized that under her coat she was still in her wrinkled cashmere dress. She wanted desperately to remove it and bathe. She also wanted to keep her emotions in check until she could get away from the police.

"Well, maybe if someone could . . . go upstairs and get a few things for me?"

"Of course," said Kerrigan. "Jocko?" Her red-headed driver appeared. "Miss Stallings needs a few things from upstairs."

"I just want my bathrobe—it's hanging on the bathroom door.

It's white. And the sneakers, and jeans and shirt that are on my bed —the sneakers are on the floor next to the bed." She could not bring herself to say "bra" or "brassiere" out loud. She looked up to Fernando. "Fernando?" He turned immediately. "May I use the phone?" The phone at the doorman's station was reserved for house business and was usually off limits to tenants.

"Of course, Miss Stallings." Fernando now seemed attentive and polite. Perhaps he was still in her corner.

She looked at Kerrigan, as if for permission to make the call. He smiled.

"We're pretty much finished, Miss Stallings. For now."

For now . . .

As Nick went to the phone, trying to decide whom to call, she saw an ambulance-type van pull up with a red light swirling and watched as two men in white uniforms, and a pale young man in a wrinkled suit and light raincoat—too light for this weather, thought Nick—entered the building. The pale man approached the cops and said, "Medical examiner. Where's the scene?"

"Six F," said Whelan. "I'll go with you." Whelan, the M.E., the men in white, and Jocko got aboard the elevator and headed up. Nick dialed her parents. She wasn't sure whether she wanted them to answer or not. She hung up after one ring, dug the Post-It out of her coat pocket, and called Joanne.

She absentmindedly tried to undo the tangle of knots in the grimy phone cord. Outside, cars were honking, no doubt due to the extra pileup of vehicles. The line kept ringing. Nick was about to hang up when a machine answered.

"Hey there," said Joanne in a dreamy voice. "We can't pick up the phone right now 'cause we're up here on cloud nine—yes, yes, the rumors are all true—but leave your number, and either me or the little man'll get back to you. If you're calling for Frankie and you're of the female persuasion, you better have an awfully good reason, and I mean that in the nicest possible way." The machine beeped.

"Joanne. It's Susan. Only it's . . . it's Nicolette. But, anyway, it's me . . . and I really would like to talk to you guys, but of course you're not—"

Joanne's voice broke through. "Susan? Hey! We were gonna call you!"

"Oh, God. I'm so glad you picked up. Listen, is this a terrible time . . . ?"

"I wish. I still haven't been able to get Mr. Prince Q. Charming into the sack. He's been on, like, a double shift. Hey—should I be calling you Nicolette?"

"Well, you know . . . Susan is fine."

"Uncle Edward called. What can I do, Susan?"

She checked to make sure she was out of earshot of Kerrigan and the others. "I don't know why I'm calling you. I just didn't know who else to call . . ." Her voice was cracking.

"I'm, like, honored, okay? I'm honored anybody would call me in a pinch. It means . . . I don't exactly know *what* it means, but I take it as a compliment is what I'm trying to say."

"Did Uncle Edward explain anything?"

"Just that you left his place with a police escort and that you were pretty upset. He said you asked for our number, so he figured we'd be hearing from you. He doesn't really like me, so it's hard for me to read him. What's goin' on?"

"Jeffrey killed himself."

"Oh, Jesus, Susan. Oh, Jesus. I'm . . . like . . . Jesus. Are you okay?"

"He did it in my apartment . . ."

"Oh, *Jesus* . . ."

". . . and they're up there now, the police, and the medical examiner, and they're going to remove the . . . body, and then I have to wait for an autopsy so they can rule that it really was a suicide. And it *was,* Joanne. He stabbed himself. It was just . . . oh, God. I can't talk about this anymore. I feel like I'm choking all the time. I just feel like I'm going to blow up or something."

"Jesus. What can we do?"

"This is so ridiculous," said Nick. "But I need somewhere to spend the night. I just . . . I mean, they're going to seal my apartment."

"Come on over," said Joanne.

"Oh, God," said Nick through new tears. "Really?"

"Hey, I read enough Shirley MacLaine to know everything happens for a reason," said Joanne. "Without you, Frankie and I wouldn't be married—I mean, I would have had to grab a witness off the street, and I wouldn't've, you know? The moment would have passed. If we hadn't run into you—who knows? I owe you."

"Oh, God, Joanne. You really don't owe me. But if you could just . . ."

"Hey—it's done. You're here. Got a pencil?"

Nick found an old ball-point and a little pad on which Fernando and the other doormen had made innumerable scrawls. She found a clean sheet. "Shoot."

"We're at 373 East 22nd Street—apartment 10A. Got that?"

"Got it," said Nick. "Is it really okay?"

"Hey, Susan. We're not exactly lifelong friends, but I think you know me well enough to notice I don't say things I don't mean. Get your ass over here. You want Frankie to pick you up? He gets off in a few minutes."

"No thanks, I have a ride."

"Are you hungry?"

"I don't know if I can eat."

"Well, there's some pretty fabulous linguini primavera if you feel like it. Oh, God, listen to me. Just come on over."

"Apartment 10A?"

"You got it. And, hey, Susan. Forgive me, but it's the maid's day off, if you know what I mean. It's, like, the maid's *month* off. It's like—there's no maid. And I don't do housework, so . . . you get the picture."

"Joanne . . . ?"

"Am I talking too much?"

"Thank you."

"Hey, that's what friends are for."

"Yeah," said Nick. She was touched and wanted to say something more, but she just repeated, "Yeah."

"So. We'll see you in a little while."

"Okay."

Nick hung up. She already was starting to feel as if she were separating herself from this building. She wondered if she'd ever go back to the sixth floor. She checked in her purse to see if she had the beeper for her answering machine. It was there. Eventually, she'd want to change her message or check to see who'd called. She turned around and went over to Kerrigan.

"I guess I'll take you up on that offer of a ride."

"You got it," said Kerrigan. "Where're you headed?"

"East 22nd Street, if that's okay."

"Oh, sure." He called out to non-Red. "Billy. You want to take Miss Stallings down to Twenty-second Street?" Billy blinked for a second, as though Twenty-second Street were possibly some obscure police destination with which he was unfamiliar. Kerrigan spoke slowly and distinctly to him. "Just drop her off down there, okay? And head back up here."

Jocko emerged from the elevator with Nick's clothing. Nick immediately wished she'd told him to bring more stuff, but didn't have the heart or stomach to ask him to make another trip. She wanted to get away. "Thank you," she said to Jocko as he handed her the clothes, wrapped loosely in her white bathrobe.

"Miss Stallings," said Kerrigan, "I want to thank *you*. I'm so sorry to have had to put you through anything like this now, but—you know. Look, if there's anything that comes to mind that you think might be useful for me to know, here's my card." He crossed out all the phone numbers on the card and wrote one in. "They move me around a lot," he explained. Nick read the card further. His name was Thomas.

"Now. We may need to get in touch with you. I mean, we'll be in touch irregardless, you know, with the autopsy results, but, just in case you're not home, you got a number where we can reach you?"

Nick reluctantly gave Kerrigan Joanne and Frankie's number. "I'll call *you*, Detective," she said, "if you tell me when would be a good time to do it."

"Well, that's just it," said Kerrigan. "I don't know. It's the weekend. It could take till Monday, but we might know something tomorrow. Is there a machine at this number?"

"Yes. And there's one in my apartment too. I'll check in."

"Okay, I'll be in touch. Just go relax. Thank you very much for your time, Miss Stallings. I know this hasn't been easy."

"Well," said Nick, who didn't know how to take leave of him. "I guess . . . we'll talk soon." She looked at Billy as though to say she was ready to leave.

"So, I'll just double back here then, okay?" Billy asked his boss.

"I think we'll still be here," said Kerrigan. Then to Nick he added, "I gotta go up and take another look now, Miss Stallings. Thanks again." He did not sound thankful.

Nick let Billy open the front door for her, and he trotted ahead to do the same with the car door. As she moved in the direction of the squad car, she was stopped by a voice right behind her.

"Hi. I'm Connie Cuevas, Channel 5 Action News. Can you tell us what happened inside, miss?"

C H A P T E R   1 5

Alight snapped on in her face as Nick turned. She was looking into a news camera. Connie Cuevas, over-coiffed black hair, bright lipstick, and petite in a man's trench coat, held a microphone to her face. Nick was completely disoriented. She saw Billy holding the car door open for her, but he was making no move to fend off Connie, whose name and nasal, drone-like tonality Nick remembered from numerous local news reports. Nick blinked and searched for the right words. Connie Cuevas waited a few seconds and went on.

"We were cruising the neighborhood and saw the medical examiner's van. We understand that there's been a murder. Do you have any information . . . ?"

"It wasn't a murder," Nick said, correcting her, and immediately regretting having established herself as a source. She started to move slowly toward Billy and the open door. "That's . . . all I can say."

"Do you live in the building, miss?"

"Uh, yes. But I can't really—" She was walking and they were walking with her, the light still in her face. She didn't want to act evasive but she didn't want to talk.

"She's that actress," called a voice from the dark behind the news camera. Nick squinted and saw that it was the guy who'd videoed her on her way in. "She's the one the cops were waiting for."

"Were the police, in fact, waiting to speak to you, miss?" asked Connie Cuevas almost politely.

It didn't occur to her to clam up and simply get in the car. She wanted, as she always did, to make things all right. And the fact that she was now getting into a police car made it difficult to evade the question.

"I really don't have anything to say," said Nick, bending to get in but not wanting to look as though she were rushing. She wished that Billy would strong-arm them a bit. Instead, he was watching all this with a schoolboy-rapt expression on his face.

"Her name is Nicole Stallings. She's been on TV," said the voice from behind the camera, adding insult to injury by getting Nick's name wrong. Connie Cuevas picked up the ball. She smoothly placed herself between Nick and the car door so that Billy couldn't close it—not that it seemed to occur to Billy to do anything other than watch.

The medical examiner came out through the front of the building followed by the body of Jeffrey White, now bagged and carried by two helpers.

"Miss Stallings, why were the police questioning you?" asked Connie Cuevas.

Nick saw the body bag, and her eyes went dead. She looked back to Connie Cuevas. "I'm sure they just . . . they're questioning everybody in the building, I think," said Nick, who then looked at Billy. "I'd really like to go now, Officer," she said to him, trying to keep an edge out of her voice. Billy suddenly snapped to, as if he'd been asleep.

"Sure, sure," he said, trying to ease Connie Cuevas out of the way. "I'm afraid that'll be all, Miss Cuevas."

Connie Cuevas looked at Billy with deference. "Of course," she said. "Just one more question." Billy, to Nick's astonishment, stepped aside, granting the request. "Miss Stallings. Is there a reason you don't want to talk to us?"

"I'm very tired," said Nick. "And very upset. Please. That's all I have to say."

"Did you know the deceased?"

"Officer? Can we go? Please?" said Nick, who saw that the camera was still on. "Please. I have nothing to say," she said, making an effort to hold back tears. Every word that passed out of her mouth, she knew, was the wrong one. But Connie Cuevas seemed, finally, to be backing away. The light was switched off, and Nick saw her and her cameraman turn around as someone in Cuevas's crew called, "It's the medical examiner. Come on!"

"Sorry about that," said Billy as though there were nothing he could have done about it. Their car pulled away. "If you try to make them stop, it just gets worse. Now, where are we going?"

Nick was furious, but afraid to show it. "373 East 22nd Street."

"You're an actress, right?" asked Billy, who, Nick now realized, was vitally lacking in perspective.

"Yes. Yes, I'm an actress. That's right," said Nick as rudely as she could, in hope he wouldn't pursue it. He didn't speak for a minute or so.

"I *know* I seen you in something. I know it. Don't tell me. Do you do soaps?"

"Look," said Nick. "I really don't want to talk about what I do for a living. Okay? I'm just . . . not in the mood right now. Okay? Please?"

"Jeez. Sure, sure. I'm sorry. Of course. I guess you're . . . jeez. I'm sorry." Nick could tell that he was attracted to her and was stumbling all over himself. At another time it might have struck her as cute. But right now she didn't want another man to be attracted to her as long as she lived. She caught sight of him in the mirror. He was staring at her as much as possible while driving. She was pretty sure he wasn't even aware of it. She decided not to look at the mirror again.

She wondered if Connie Cuevas had enough for a story. It would probably depend on how much she could find out from the police or the medical examiner. Nick had often seen Action News vans around the city, trawling for stories. If she was on TV tonight . . . She blocked out further thoughts on the subject. She'd have to call her parents. And she was going to need one of the lawyers Uncle Edward had suggested, although perhaps her father would know someone even better.

But then, maybe it would all blow over with the medical examiner's report. As long as there was nothing on TV, Nick decided she'd wait for the report, and then tell her parents, after the ruling.

She tried to close her eyes. Her body ached for sleep. She rubbed the base of her neck and made herself focus on what had happened. She wondered if she deserved this. Was it somehow, punishment, self-inflicted, for her sexual acting-out? Was this her way of finally putting a stop to it? Was it God's way of putting a stop to it?

Does God bother with things like this, with people like me?

Nick prayed whenever she was in a crisis. At those times she had always promised herself, and God, that she'd get into the habit of praying all the time, not just when she needed immediate help. But when the crisis passed, she'd forget her resolution—until the next crisis.

Closing her eyes, she tried to formulate a prayer worthy of God's attention.

Dear God, I'm in trouble. I'm not sure what I've done wrong. That's not true. I know what I did. I committed adultery with a married man. And my adultery, which happened purely for pleasure, and probably because I was drunk, has resulted, somehow, in a man killing himself. Oh, Lord, I had no idea how troubled this man was when I met him. I was . . . I was looking to have fun. And now this man is dead, and I'm afraid I can't live with the fact that it was my having sex with him that led to his death. I almost feel like I did kill him. I feel like if I had just left him alone, he'd probably be alive right now. I'm scared. I don't know how I can live with myself, God. I can't stand hearing "murderer" and "whore" and all the things my mind won't stop yelling at me. Please let me rest a little, God, and please guide me, and please let me have a little peace. Please.

She kept her eyes closed. It was the best she could do.

★   ★   ★   ★

Everything was quiet. The car had stopped. She opened her eyes, and there was Billy, turned around, looking at her. She had no idea how long it had been since the car stopped.

"What is it?" she asked him.

"We're here," said Billy, who looked as though he regretted that they were.

Oh, please don't look at me that way.

He couldn't have been more than twenty-five, she thought. She felt as though she should warn Billy against herself. But there was really no need. In another life, perhaps, she'd get to know Billy better. But it seemed to Nick that there would be no more such episodes in this life. No more "victims."

"Are you going to . . . need a ride later or anything, Miss Stallings? I mean—" He looked away, out the window. "Are you okay?"

"I'm fine, Billy. I don't think a ride later is such a good idea."

"Um. I could come by after I get off," he suggested as casually as he could.

It occurred to Nick that she could use this somehow against the police. Couldn't she make it look like sexual harassment? She had no desire to pursue such thoughts. She wished there were a switch she could use to turn off her sexuality. She felt dirty for not being able to block it.

"I'm going to pretend I didn't hear that, Billy," said Nick, getting out of the car.

"I wasn't trying to . . . you just look so . . . unhappy, and, I don't know . . . you're right. I just thought you might need company. I'm way out of line. Jeez. I'm sorry. I didn't mean any disrespect."

"I know you didn't," said Nick. "Thanks for the lift." She looked up at Joanne's building, a modest postwar high-rise of white brick and aluminum.

★   ★   ★   ★

"Ten A please. Say that it's Susan." Nick still didn't know Frankie's last name, or Joanne's.

You met these people less than two days ago. You don't even know their last names. God almighty. Call your parents.

"A 'Susan' here to see you," said the doorman into the intercom.

Nick heard Joanne's voice booming through, "Send her up, send her up." The doorman pulled the receiver away from his ear and signaled Nick to the elevator. A man who had just entered the building walked briskly by, and the doorman nodded at him. He entered the elevator first, pushed his button, and impatiently held the door open for Nick.

Everywhere Nick had gone in the few hours since Jeffrey's death, she'd noticed how insistently and cruelly life continued around her. Nothing and no one had stopped to mark her predicament. This man on the elevator with me, she thought, is filled with thoughts of the problems and crises and good and bad things in his life. He's in a hurry. He's the absolute center of his universe. He doesn't have the slightest idea that this woman he's eyeing so subtly has been careening around this city with visions of death and guilt and shame and the end of her life as she knows it. He has no idea, she thought. He just seems to like the way I look.

I look like hell. . . .

At the tenth floor she followed a sign which read A–J and soon

found herself at their door, which was slightly ajar. She knocked and
it opened farther.

Joanne was there in an instant, her arms open to Nick. "Oh, Jesus,
Susan. Jesus. How *are* you . . . ? Dumb question, don't answer it.
We just . . . God." Nick rested in Joanne's arms, and saw Frankie
coming from another room. He was tucking in his shirt.

"Hey," he said. Unsure what name to use addressing Nick, he
chose neither. "How you doing?"

"Don't ask her that, for chrissake, Frankie. She's . . . how do
you *think* she's doing? Let me take your coat, Susan." She started to
help Nick out of it before Nick remembered that she was wearing
the short peach dress. She pulled back and closed her coat.

"Do you mind if I change my clothes? I brought some stuff," she
said, holding up the bathrobe.

"Sure. Sure," said Joanne. "You want to borrow something of
mine?" Nick could see that they weren't far apart in size.

"Maybe," Nick said. "Maybe to sleep in. I didn't bring over any
pajamas or anything." She felt herself crumbling. "Oh, God. Is it
really all right for me to stay here? I don't have to. I can go to my
parents'."

"Hey," said Joanne. She took Nick's face in her hands. "You got
a bed here as long as you want one." She let go of Nick's face.
"Frankie's gonna sleep on the couch, and you'll sleep with me.
Okay? It's a king-size, you'll never know I'm there—unless you
thrash a lot." She covered her own face now. "Oh, Jesus, I'm sorry.
It's not like I meant you'd be thrashing around *tonight* particularly,
just, you know, I meant—in general." Nick was shaking her head
quickly to indicate that she understood. "I'm such a palooka-head. It
comes from hanging out with this one," she said, tousling Frankie's
hair. "Come on. You can change in the bedroom. Make yourself
comfortable. *Mi casa,* and all like that." She led Nick down a short
hallway to a bedroom.

It wasn't that the place was dirty. It was simply the most cluttered
apartment Nick had ever seen. Clothes and magazines, socks, panty

hose, and towels were everywhere. Surveying the room, Nick was able to reassemble, as if parts of a puzzle, the outfits that both Joanne and Frankie had been wearing the night they'd all met.

Last night. It was last night.

Joanne didn't seem at all self-conscious about the way the place looked. She was behaving like a proper hostess showing her apartment to a house guest. Having apologized for the mess on the phone with Nick, Joanne obviously felt no need to do so now.

"G'head and change. I'll leave you alone. The bathroom's over there, and just . . . whatever." She backed out, closing the door.

"Joanne," said Nick, stopping her. "I can't tell you how much—"

"Hey," said Joanne. "I'm glad you're here." She started to close the door again, then opened it again a crack. "Do I look married?" she asked Nick with a secretive smile.

"You look . . . yes . . . you look—" Nick couldn't finish. Her affection for Joanne, added to everything else, overcame her. She ran over and threw her arms around her, holding on for dear life. For the first time since Jeffrey produced the knife, she made no attempt to keep her feelings down. "Oh, God, Joanne," she sobbed. "It was . . ." She struggled to speak. Joanne stroked her head and held her tight.

"Okay," Joanne whispered. "It's okay."

"No, it's not!" said Nick louder than she meant to, her words coming like waves between sobs. "It's not . . . okay. He has a wife . . . and kids, and—"

"Listen, Susan," Joanne said quietly but firmly. "He was nuts. It couldn't have been your fault."

"Yes . . . yes . . ."

"Hey. This guy wanted to die, Susan. You just happened to step into his life at the wrong time."

"I didn't just step into his life, Joanne. Oh, God, you're so sweet, but you don't know me. No. He could have handled his life if he hadn't met me. You have no idea." She quieted down a little. "I'm afraid. I think maybe they think I did it."

"The cops?" Joanne looked confused. "What are you talking about?"

"He was all doped up, Joanne. He cut himself with a knife. He didn't think he'd feel the pain. He cut himself, and jumped around and twisted the knife . . ."

She started to wail, a small, almost distant cry. Joanne held her and rocked her, still standing up.

"There's an autopsy, and who knows . . . oh, God. I just want this to be over, please God. Please God. I didn't know how to help him. I was afraid he'd stab me, Joanne. And then . . . it was so fast. The life was just out of him . . ."

"Shh. Shush," said Joanne, cradling her.

"What time is it?" asked Nick, suddenly alert.

"About nine," said Joanne. "Why?"

"The news. We have to watch the news."

"Oh, Susan. Don't make yourself crazy."

"No, you don't understand," said Nick, pulling away slightly from Joanne and unconsciously looking around for a Kleenex. Joanne reached behind her, pulled one seemingly from thin air, and handed it to Nick. "One of those Channel 5 news vans was outside my building. They interviewed me."

"Oh, Jesus," said Joanne. "You didn't actually talk to them, did you?"

"They kind of ambushed me," said Nick. "I really don't know what I said. I don't think I said much of anything, but that little bitch used the word 'murder.' She just shoved a microphone in my face and asked me if I knew anything about 'the murder.' "

"So? You didn't give her anything, did you?"

"I don't think so. I think I said a lot of very noncommittal things. I just tried to play the whole thing down, like it was nothing. But somebody who was hanging out there gave her my name, and said I was an actress, and, oh, Jesus, Joanne . . . I'm just so tired." She blew her nose into the tissue, and Joanne immediately handed her another.

"You want to sleep?" asked Joanne. "Maybe that would be best. Forgive me, Susan—I mean, I really don't know you that well, but you really look like shit."

"Oh, great," said Nick, blowing again. "In addition to all this, I'll probably be on the news, really looking like shit."

"Hey. It probably won't even be on. I watched the six o'clock news. There's like, a huge fire out of control on Staten Island, and there's that date-rape thing, and somebody high-jacked a sub-way . . . I don't think there's any room for you in there. Just be glad he wasn't black."

Nick looked bewildered. "Why?"

"If he'd been black, or you were black and he was white, now, *then* you could be pretty sure some local TV news would pick it up. Anything they can do to inflame racial tension in this city, it's like, I swear to Christ, it's their motherfucking First Amendment obliga-tion."

"Oh, God. Oh, God," said Nick, who felt as though she were catching her breath for the first time in hours. She shook her head and looked upward. "Please, God. Just keep it off TV."

"You want a cup of coffee?" asked Joanne. Then, quickly, she said to herself, *"Hello. Hello?* What am I saying? You need to sleep. You want a Valium? These things, I swear to God, konk me right out. They're like—*mañana* Rio. Whatta you think? You want maybe I should just shut my trap for one motherfucking *second?"* She slapped her own forehead. "Jesus, Susan. I'm sorry. It's like it's all happening to me too. It's like, I don't know, we've known each other all our lives. I'm sorry, sweetie. I just feel bad for you."

Nick looked at Joanne. She was glad she'd come here. "Thank you," she said simply.

"For what? Not having a fucking clue what to do or say? Hey, it's a breeze."

"Just for . . . not judging me."

"We're family. We're making you an honorary Triziani. We don't judge family around here."

"Well, at least I've got you and Frankie's mother in my court."

"Frankie's mother?"

"Uncle Edward says she talks to him," said Nick. "Did you see him turn her picture around last night so she could 'watch' your wedding?"

Joanne smiled sadly. "I wish he liked me. He just . . . doesn't. It's hard. Frankie's parents are both gone, and Uncle Edward . . . I don't know what it is. Probably this mouth I got on me. I wish he liked me better." She started to sniff. "Listen to me. This is *your* party and *you* can cry if you want to. I'm sorry. It's this whole weekend, with the wedding and all."

"Oh, God," said Nick. "I should go. This is your honeymoon."

"Can I tell you something? Every night is a honeymoon with Frankie."

"That's so sweet."

"Yeah, and I'm queen of all the Russias," added Joanne. "Listen, we can have a honeymoon . . . whenever. So, what can I get for you?"

Nick was still in her coat. "I just want to take a shower, and maybe lie down for a few minutes."

"The shower's right in here," said Joanne, turning on a fluorescent light that lit up a pink bathroom highlighted by black and silver wallpaper. Some apparently well-used towels were jammed indecorously into a pink and black towel rack. "Lemme get you some clean linens. I swear to God, Susan. Don't smell those towels. Your condition is delicate enough." She yanked them all away and trotted off to get fresh ones. Nick looked in the mirror, something she'd managed to avoid for several hours. Her face was puffy, her eyes red, and her cheeks blotched by tears and wiping. She was grateful that her hair was short. It merely looked dirty. Her dress appeared to have been slept in for weeks. She stared at her face. Had it been just two days since she'd eyed herself in the ladies' room prior to meeting Jeffrey?

Somewhere in her study of her own face she was able to see a person. And this was unusual, because all she usually saw were hair, lips, eyes—a canvas for makeup or self-hatred. She wanted to know this woman in the mirror, and what could be done to help her.

Joanne returned with fresh towels of a vibrant royal blue. She handed them to Nick. "Here. The hot water takes forever to come on, and it goes hot suddenly and burns you whenever somebody on this side of the building flushes their toilet, but the pressure's pretty good if you want to wash your hair."

"Hint, hint?" said Nick.

"Well, hey, you'll feel better. Take your time. Try to relax. You sure I can't get you anything?"

"Joanne Triziani," said Nick, looking far into her friend's eyes. "Good name." She nodded. "Thanks. I'm fine."

"Really, Susan, don't run it too hot or you'll get scalded like a motherfucker when somebody flushes. I kid you not."

Nick pulled the dress over her head. She had a brief flash of Todd. *Todd.* Her troubles would probably serve to keep him at a distance. Or was he, if her situation worsened, the kind who'd want to go out with her for the publicity? She wasn't sure. She barely knew him. She had emblazoned herself on his sexual consciousness and he was poised to pursue her, but she barely knew him. She had a sudden paranoia that Todd might recognize Jeffrey's picture if it was flashed on TV and remember him from the restaurant. No, she told herself. He hadn't been aware of Jeffrey at all. She was building a case for herself, trying to see herself in the most innocent possible light. But her mind kept sending her stray bits of what felt like incriminating evidence.

Her eyes went to her breasts. Her skin appeared greenish-pink from the fluorescents. She had never quite liked her breasts. They were breasts that dozens—hundreds?—of men had admired. She had made more than a few of them rush to orgasm by merely exposing them at the right moment. But she had also been wondering recently if she should have them worked on. No, she thought now. This is my body. My body.

She sank to the toilet. She'd been too distracted to notice that her bladder was full, and, as she emptied it, was relieved that there was almost no burning now. She kicked the dress off her feet, turned on the shower, and parted the shower curtain, a clear vinyl see-through with an abstract design in pink and black. She got in and let the hard spray fall on her back. She washed every inch of her body, and her hair twice, choosing from an array of shampoos, all of which she'd seen advertised for years on TV. The brand names were a comfort to her. Jhirmack, Prell, Tegrin, Head & Shoulders. She was soothed by their familiarity.

Sure enough, someone upstairs must have flushed a toilet. Suddenly, she was twisting her body away from the surge of hot water. It was over in a second, but it had ruined whatever tonic effect had been achieved by the shower. Choosing not to play more Russian roulette with the plumbing, she turned off the water and dried herself with the bright blue towels. She took the peach dress, balled it up again, and walked back into the bedroom, unrolling her clothes from her white robe. She sat on the bed, suddenly feeling she didn't have the strength to get dressed, or dry her hair. Falling back onto the quilt, her feet still touching the floor, she closed her eyes.

CHAPTER 16

She was naked in court, attempting to cover herself with something while trying to figure out where to sit. All the seats were taken. Connie Cuevas followed her everywhere, asking over and over, "Where did you get your breasts done?" Nick, searching for a seat, finally told Connie Cuevas that her breasts were her own. Connie Cuevas shouted, "Liar!" and everyone looked over at them. At the defense table were Fernando and John, the super. Nick saw them and they immediately looked away, as though they wished she were not there. Billy the cop ushered Connie Cuevas away from Nick, then came back, turned Nick to him, and kissed her passionately. They kissed and kissed, and Nick decided that she would kiss him until everyone in the courtroom went home. Then a door in the back opened, and Sam walked in. He called her name. She broke the kiss with Billy and looked at Sam. He seemed disappointed, turned on his heel, and went back out the door. Billy walked away, leaving her, and she stood in the center of the room. She put her hands to her side and stared back at everyone. "They're real," she said simply. "And I'm innocent." Everyone turned around, and the trial went on as if she were not involved. Nick wasn't even sure it was her trial.

"Susan! Susan. Wake up," said Joanne, whispering loudly, rousing Nick. "I'm sorry, but I think you're gonna be on TV."

She took Nick's hand and pulled her gently but firmly. Nick's hair had made a big wet spot on the quilt. She was partially covered by the towels, and she struggled into her white robe.

"Jeez," said Joanne admiringly. "Wrap that robe tight, Susan. Frankie's a happy man, but I don't want to push my luck. Come on, come on. They said it was gonna be right after the commercial."

"Is it Channel 5?" said Nick as they made their way into the living room.

"Yeah, they said Connie Cuevas is coming on after the break," said Frankie, sitting on a white Naugahyde couch with the remote control in his hand. Channel 5's news came on at ten, an hour earlier than most of the other stations. Their newsroom was stripped down, no frills, as if to emphasize a dedication to unvarnished truth.

Joanne pushed Frankie over. "Hey, Mr. Chivalry-Is-Dead? How about making room for our guest?"

"Sorry, sorry," said Frankie as he moved over on the couch. His glance fell for a fraction of a second on Nick's robe. He was completely gentlemanly, but Joanne caught it.

"Keep your eyes to yourself, Mr. Just-Got-Married," said Joanne, smiling and elbowing him. Frankie took it in stride, intent on the television screen.

"Here it is, here it is," he said. Nick looked. There was an overly groomed, mustachioed anchorman, and behind him on a screen inset was a blow-up of an old eight by ten photo of Nick taken four years before, when a lousy acting coach had convinced her of the need to look "commercial." The picture had always been too starlet-like for Nick's taste, and she'd replaced it soon after. But it had still crossed many a casting director's desk, and now here it was again, presenting her to the world like a hair-sprayed prime-time wanna-be. Nick felt dizzy. She took hold of Joanne's hand.

"We'll have more on Hurricane Frank, which is making its way north, right after this. Something hot is just breaking on Manhattan's fashionable Upper East Side tonight, and Action News's Connie Cuevas was on the scene to get the story for you," said the anchorman, moving to Connie's desk. "This is an example of Action News at its best. We sent Connie uptown tonight to cover a celebrity-studded benefit for animal rights, but she was steered to this story when she alertly sighted some flashing red lights on her way to the benefit. Is that right, Connie?"

"That's right, Art. I'm afraid the animal rights story—important as it is—will just have to wait," she said.

"All yours, Connie."

"Well, Art," said Connie Cuevas, seated at her cubicle and looking straight into the camera as it tightened onto her face, "a beautiful woman, a corpse—and no charges. That's what we have tonight on the Upper East Side, where actress Nicolette Stallings was questioned earlier this evening in the death of Jeffrey White, an attorney from Hastings-on-Hudson. We pieced this story together with the help of neighbors who saw Stallings enter her building accompanied by police."

The screen filled with a somewhat blurry image of Nick being led into her building by Kerrigan and Whelan. Their faces were lit by the flashing red light of a squad car. "This footage of Stallings and two police officers was shot by a neighbor who saw squad cars pull up and ran to the scene with his video camera." Nick saw herself, slightly out of focus, look angrily into the lens and then thrust her hand up to block it.

The TV then came back to a tight shot of Connie Cuevas, all business. "Stallings left the building a short while later in a police car. Jeffrey White, we learned from a source close to the scene, was found dead tonight in Stallings's apartment. Action News arrived on the scene as members of the medical examiner's office left the East

Eighties high-rise. Police were careful not to point any fingers. They say they are making no charges at the present moment, and not ruling out the possibility that Mr. White's fatal stab wound may have been self-inflicted. We tried to question Miss Stallings about what went on in her apartment."

They cut to footage of Nick coming out of the building. There she was, looking furtive, pursued by Connie Cuevas. It was difficult not to get the impression that Nick was running away from something. On the couch, Nick squeezed Joanne's hand and they watched as Connie Cuevas asked on-screen, "Were the police, in fact, waiting to speak to you, miss?" And there was Nick's elusive reply: "I really don't have anything to say."

Then Nick realized that they had edited out several questions. The footage jumped to Connie asking, "Miss Stallings, is there a reason you don't want to talk to us?" Joanne glanced at Nick then looked back at the screen. "I'm very tired," said Nick on TV, "and very upset. Please. That's all I have to say." It cut back to Connie: "Did you know the deceased?" Then back to Nick: "Please. I have nothing to say."

Connie Cuevas's face filled the screen again. "You may remember Nicolette Stallings from a stint a couple of years ago on this station's short-lived *Eagle Squadron.*" They flashed a shot of an old *Eagle Squadron* still photo that showed Nick in a lowcut sweater, toting an automatic gun and staring straight out with a tough look on her face. Then back to Connie again: "The medical examiner's report is expected by tomorrow or Monday, and we'll be updating this story as it breaks. Art?" The shot widened to include the anchorman again.

He raised his eyebrows and said soberly, "Thanks, Connie. Nice work."

Frankie zapped the set off, and they all sat there for a moment, staring at the blank screen.

"Sons of bitches," said Joanne under her breath. "Motherfucking sons of motherfucking bitches."

"Well," said Nick, stretching her arms and feigning matter-of-factness, "my life is over."

"Jesus," said Frankie, unable to take his eyes from the now-dormant screen.

"You want a drink or something, Susan?" said Joanne.

"I don't think I'm ever going to drink again as long as I live. But thanks," said Nick, patting Joanne's leg. "I'm serious, by the way. If you ever see me ask for a drink, just shoot me, okay?"

Joanne rose, full of nervous energy, and moved to the kitchen area, which was separated from the living room by a counter. "Frankie? Lord of the manor? Can I get you something?"

"Nothing."

Nick looked at Frankie and said, "Boy, I'll bet you two are glad we all met last night." Joanne and Frankie did their best to smile. "Jesus, I can't believe how they edited that stuff. They managed to make it look even worse than it was. I wonder when my parents will get wind of this. I should check my machine. Not that they watch the ten o'clock news, but I wonder how long it will take before one of their friends calls them."

"Maybe you should call them first," said Joanne. "I mean, I don't know what kind of terms you're on with your mother. Me, I talk to my mom twice a day. We're, like, sisters, always have been. I mean . . . *listen to me!* Sorry, Susan. I'm, like, motor mouth here. It's just nerves."

"I keep thinking about my apartment. I can't go home. I have no home." Her shoulders started to heave. She didn't feel there was enough moisture in her body to produce tears.

"Get some sleep," said Frankie. "Check your machine in the morning. Does anybody know you're here?"

"I gave the police this number. I'm sorry, but they wanted to know where they could reach me when they know something."

"Who's your lawyer?" asked Joanne.

"I don't have one yet. . . ."

"Are you kidding? You gotta call a lawyer," said Joanne.

"Saturday night at 10:25?" said Nick.

"Yeah, yeah," said Joanne. "You got one?"

"Uncle Edward gave me a couple of names," Nick said. "But I don't know. Maybe I should talk to my father. This is up his alley. I mean, he knows lawyers."

"Believe me, so does Uncle Edward," said Joanne, "but, hey, suit yourself." She bit a nail. "I can't stand it. Can I make you some hot chocolate or something?"

"You know what I'd like?" said Nick, feeling a faint appetite. "Do you have any cereal?"

"Like what? Oatmeal, granola?"

"Like *cereal* cereal. Rice Krispies, or grape nuts . . ."

Joanne was scanning her shelves. "Cheerios," she said, uncovering a box in one of the cupboards. "I don't know when these were opened, possibly before Christ, but"—she sniffed the contents— "smells okay."

"Perfect," said Nick. Joanne emptied some into a bowl. Nick went to the refrigerator as if it were her own and found some milk. She poured it on and Joanne handed her a spoon. She'd always found a bowl of cereal to be a comfort, no matter what the hour. She crunched a large bite, savoring the familiar, satisfying sweetness.

"Do you guys mind if I go into the bedroom and make a call or two? Do you need to go to sleep?"

"Nah. We'll be in here necking our guts out," said Joanne. "Sorry, Susan, but we got a little overdue celebrating to reckon with here. Frankie's been working practically since we saw you. You go on in. I may just sleep on top of the palooka here, or else I'll climb in with you later."

Nick could see that part of Frankie's quietness and distraction had been due to his need to be alone with Joanne. "Okay," she said, heading for the bedroom. She stopped after a step or two and turned back to them. "I was your maid of honor, wasn't I?" she asked rhetorically.

Joanne gave her a long look, nodded, and said, "Yeah. You were great."

"Good night, Frankie," said Nick.

"Hey, I don't care what anybody says," said Frankie, "they shoulda left that *Eagle Squadron* on the air. That had 'hit' written all over it."

This almost made Nick smile. She went back to the bedroom, sat on the bed, and felt the spot where her hair had wet the quilt. It was still damp. She searched in her pocketbook for the Post-It Uncle Edward had given her, got under the covers, and pulled the phone to her. She decided she should try her parents first, started to dial, but aborted before the final digit. Instead, she found herself dialing Sam's number in L.A., aware for the first time that she'd memorized it. She was almost afraid he would pick up. Maybe it would be better, she thought, to get his machine.

"Yeah?" said a sleepy voice she knew was Sam's.

"Oh, God, I woke you. I'm sorry. It's Nick Stallings."

"Hey. Hi. Wait a second." Nick heard some shifting around of pillows. "I guess I fell asleep. What time is it?"

"There or here?"

"Just give me a hint," said Sam.

"It's about eleven here."

"Wow. I was really out." There was a tiny pause. "So. Hi."

"Hi."

"Do people call you Nicolette, or Nick?"

"Nick, usually."

There was a silence.

"Um. Sam?"

"What is it? Are you okay?"

Nick was starting to cry.

"What is it?" She didn't answer. "Nick? What's wrong?"

"I wanted to see you. When you got back. And now I'm afraid I won't."

"Why not? Look. I want to see you too. I was going to say

something right after the reading, but I didn't want to hit you with . . . all my baggage. I'm in kind of an excess-baggage period in my life, and I just . . . what's wrong?"

"You want baggage," said Nick. "I'll give you baggage . . ."

"I really don't know what you're talking about. This is hard. I wish I could *see* you."

"Having a great time, wish you were here," said Nick absently. She was pretty sure he could hear her sniffing. She sort of wanted him to.

"What's going on?"

"Would you please call me when you get back, Sam? Would you do that? You may hear some stuff, and when you hear it, you may not want to call me—and that's all right. It's just that you've been making some surprise appearances in my dreams, and—"

"Really? I think I'm kind of glad to hear it."

"Oh, God. This is all wrong. Erase this. I mean—forget this. I wanted to have this conversation on our fourth or fifth date, by a fireplace or something. I, uh, I have to go now, Sam. I just wanted to see you in the clear, and now I'm afraid there won't *be* any clear."

"Are you in some kind of trouble?"

"You could say that."

"Can you tell me about it?"

Her head was spinning in a way it had done before only when she was wildly drunk.

"Um. No. I don't think I can right now. Thanks for asking. Please call me when you get back if you're still so inclined, which I have a feeling you won't be, unless I'm just paranoid, which I'm afraid I'm probably not. I just wish I could have shown you who I am."

She started to sob.

"I . . . feel kind of helpless here," he said. "What can I do?"

Come back. Right now.

"I have to go, Sam. Are you really this nice? I mean, are you a nice guy?"

"Nice. I don't know. Does anyone aspire to nice?"

"Are you? Are you, Sam?"

"I wish I could see your face."

"Well. I'll see you in my dreams, Sam. Clothed."

"What?"

"Nothing. I'm sorry. Oh, damn, I'm really sorry. This conversation didn't happen, okay? Go back to sleep. I gotta go." She hung up.

She dialed her parents. After it rang, once, twice, she had an intense urge to hang up. But then her mother answered, sounding sleepy.

"Hello?"

"Mom?"

"Oh. Is that you, dear?"

"Yeah. Hi, Mom."

"What is it? What's the matter?"

"How do you know something's the matter?"

"Don't be silly—you don't sound right. What is it?"

"I think I need to talk to Dad. Is he there?"

"He's still in St. Maarten."

"Oh, God. I forgot. Can you give me the number down there?"

"What is it, dear? Can I help you?"

"Mom, I just really would like to ask Dad something. How do I call down there?" They'd had their St. Maarten condominium for years, but it was only recently that you could dial direct.

"Well, first you dial 011. That's very important, that's the overseas code . . ."

"Right, right . . ."

"Then it's 599-5-22898 . . . oh—what am I saying? You can't call him."

"What do you mean?"

"The phones are out. The hurricane. I just tried about an hour ago. Shall I try again?"

"That's okay, Mom. I'll do it."

"You're being awfully mysterious. Will you let me know if you get through? I want to talk to him. I'm dying to see if we still have a roof."

"If I get him, I'll tell him to call you. Okay?"

"Are you sure you're all right, dear?"

"Mom," said Nick. "Sometimes I'm not all right, but there's nothing you can do about it. You know what I mean?"

There was silence.

"Have I done something wrong—that you want to shut me out like this?"

"Mom," said Nick. "I love you. I adore you, in fact. But if I tell you my problems now, it'll somehow—don't ask me how, because I don't know how you do it—but it'll end up being about you. It's a kind of magic you do, Mom."

"I see. So you're going to talk to your father instead?"

"I'm just going to ask his advice about something."

"What is it?"

"Mom. I love you. But I'm going to call Dad now, and if I *do* get through, I'll have him call you."

"All right."

She wanted to warn her mother of the rumors she'd probably hear at any minute. But Nick also knew there was no way to tell her without an ensuing longer conversation for which she didn't have the strength. This had always been the way with her mother. If she told her her deepest problems, she felt frustrated at her mother's inability to merely listen and support her. If she *didn't* confide in her, she felt guilty for shutting her own mother out.

"Mom. I'll call you tomorrow. Because there's some stuff we'll need to talk about. I just . . . can't do it tonight, Mom . . ."

Mommy, Mommy . . . make it go away . . .

". . . but I'll call you soon and explain. Okay?" There was silence. "Okay, Mom?"

"I love you, Susan."

Nick took a deep breath. "I love you, Mom."

Nick hung up. She had an urge to run to Joanne to explain that her real name was, indeed, Susan, that Nicolette was a stage name she'd chosen years ago to jazz up what she felt was her too-ordinary name. Her mother, a little insulted and never able to bring herself to say Nicolette, had always resorted to "dear." To her father she was Susie. When she was on the prowl, when she needed an alias, she'd always resorted to her real name. "Nicolette" had proved a little embarrassing, a little too frou-frou for her present taste and had lost its uniqueness when Nicollette Sheridan of *Knots Landing* became well-known—hence her cultivation of "Nick." But she'd used Nicolette enough now professionally that it was too late to change back. As an actress, she was known, to the extent that she was known, as Nicolette Stallings.

But then, she thought, Joanne's intuition is so good, she *already* calls me Susan.

She pictured her father in St. Maarten.

Please, God. Make Daddy safe.

It had been on a trip to St. Maarten that she'd first found her way to St. Barts. Her parents had offered for years to let Nick use their condo for a vacation. Finally, she and Hal had taken them up on it, to save the cost of a hotel. The condo, nice enough in itself, was in the bland, drab, Dutch part of St. Maarten. They'd found an undercurrent of racial tension there, the quiet hostility of island natives whose livelihood consisted almost solely of waiting on tourists. To Nick, the Dutch influence didn't mix well with the Caribbean culture. It seemed to impose something incongruously tight and restrictive on this otherwise bright and free place. Nick and Hal fought a lot.

After several days they'd taken a day sail to nearby St. Barts, and were instantly struck by the serenity and the lack of racial stress. And the sexy, topless French beach culture was just what Nick and Hal had been looking for without knowing it. They spent the rest of their vacation there, a perfect five days. It was then that Nick had ventured nude onto the beach. They had five days of sun, sex, and good food, returning to St. Maarten only to pick up their things and fly back to New York. The beaches of St. Barts appeared again and again in Nick's dreams as sources of pleasure or frustration, depending on the lesson of any particular dream. But she'd never felt as at home with her sexuality as when she'd been on St. Barts.

Nick's parents had been disappointed. They loved St. Maarten, and had hoped that Nick would use their place there often. Like so many things they had offered her, she'd used it as a stepping-stone in somehow distancing herself from them.

There was a lot of static on the line. After several series of clicks, an overseas operator came on.

"How can I help you?"

"I'm trying to reach St. Maarten, operator."

"I'm sorry. Most of the lines there have been knocked out by Hurricane Frank. Try again later, please."

"When? How soon before they fix it?"

"Usually it takes two or three days. It could be a week, ma'am. You'll just have to keep trying."

Nick hung up and read Uncle Edward's Post-It. There were phone numbers for Albert Pearson and Ferris Fanning. Recalling Mrs. Costantino's tone of respect when she'd spoken Pearson's name, Nick dialed him. It was almost eleven P.M.

"Law offices," said a youngish-sounding male voice.

"I'm calling for Mr. Pearson," said Nick.

"This is the service, ma'am. May I take a message?"

"Is there any way of getting one to him right now?" asked Nick.

"Are you a client?"

Nick thought about lying, but figured it might not be the best way of starting a relationship with a much-needed attorney. "No," she said, "I'm not. But I very much need to speak with Mr. Pearson at his earliest possible convenience."

"I understand. Who shall I say is calling?"

"Nicolette Stallings." She spelled her last name and added

Frankie's and Joanne's number. "Let me give you another number, in case I'm not at this one." As she gave her home number, she imagined her answering machine overflowing with messages, like a bathtub. "Would you also please tell Mr. Pearson that Judge Edward Costantino referred me? Have you got that?"

"Yes, ma'am. Anything else?"

"I guess not. Do you have any idea when I might expect his call?"

"Well, ma'am. It's Saturday night."

"I'm aware of that."

"Okay. Well, I don't know. I would expect probably on Monday, wouldn't you?"

"I'm asking *you,*" said Nick.

"Well, I'm new here, ma'am, so I'm just taking a shot. I'll pass this along to his secretary though. She checks in a lot. You sit tight. Is there anything else I can do for you tonight?"

"Yeah," said Nick. "I'd like a chateaubriand, very rare, with the blue plate special, maybe a bottle of Margaux '85—unless you think it needs more time to age. I mean, I don't really know that much about wine. I prefer cheap champagne."

There was a pause at the other end. "So. One chateaubriand. Very rare, did you say, or just medium?"

Without really meaning to, she'd hooked one. "Does your chef understand the difference between medium rare and rare?"

"Hey, lady. *I'm* the chef."

Nick started to laugh. She couldn't stop.

"We get pretty punchy around here too," said the guy. "I'm just finishing a double shift."

Nick's instinct would normally have been to flirt, get a sense of what the guy looked like, make him crazy, and then maybe, if she was in a mood, meet him somewhere. She'd once done that at a hotel in Louisville during a brief tour of *The Merchant of Venice* with a fledgling Shakespeare company. She'd been a decent enough Portia, but the tour had been a bust, closing prematurely after only three weeks. Back in her room after a couple of margaritas at a makeshift farewell cast party, she'd struck up an innocent enough two A.M. conversation with a male hotel operator while ordering a wake-up call. She liked the sound of his voice and they talked for a while. He was just about to finish his shift, and she ended up inviting him to her room. In the glow of her tequila buzz, she'd checked him out through the peephole in her door when he knocked, opening it to him in very low light, dressed only in a V-neck cashmere black sweater. He'd been remarkably cool, and they smoked a few cigarettes and drank most of the bottle of wine before Nick asked him to lie down on his back. Then, standing over him, she'd lowered herself onto his mouth. Turning herself around with his tongue inside of her, she undid his belt and peeled off his trousers. Then she turned around again, moved her thighs until they were over him, and slid slowly down on top of him. So excited by herself that she started to climax almost at once, she slowly pulled her sweater off. The sight of her above him, now naked and arching her back as she came, caused him to join her in what had been a long, flowing mutual climax. She sent him on his way and fell asleep less than an hour after she'd made the wake-up call. She left town the next day.

Now, talking to Albert Pearson's answering service, she couldn't believe that she felt excited. It shocked her, and, had it not felt so good, it would have disgusted her. But like the cereal she'd just eaten, sexual fantasy was a comfort, a place of refuge. She knew that there was no room for such sanctuary now, but that didn't stop the reflexive yearning for it. She even went so far as to assure herself that if she did something with this guy, he'd never be able to tell anyone because he'd lose his job. So it was safe, wasn't it? Why not? After all, if she'd just gone with that cab driver to the beach and spent the rest of the afternoon with him, she might have avoided the whole thing with Jeffrey.

"You have a sense of humor," Nick said into the phone. "Thank you."

"Hey, thank *you*," said the guy. "So, where do I deliver all this food?"

"Just . . . give Mr. Pearson the message," said Nick. "And thanks for making me laugh."

"We aim to please," said the guy. He didn't seem to want to say good-bye. Two days ago, thought Nick, this would have been a perfect setup.

"Thanks," she said, and hung up. She then dialed Ferris Fanning. She got a machine.

"You have reached the law office of Roberts, Fanning, McQuade, and Streich. Office hours are Monday through Friday, from nine until six, eastern time. Please leave a message here after the tone. Speak clearly, and have a good weekend." It beeped.

Nick, who had been about to hang up, thought better of it and said, "My name is Nicolette Stallings. It's Saturday night, late. I'd very much like to speak to Mr. Fanning, on the recommendation of Judge Edward Costantino. Please have Mr. Fanning call me as soon as possible, even over the weekend if you get this message that soon, at 358-3304 or at 846-3120. It's all right to call any-time."

She put the phone on a plastic doily on the bedside table, lay down, and looked up. Her mind flashed to the Madeline books she'd grown up with, and she searched the ceiling for a crack that looked like a rabbit. She heard recurring muffled sounds from the living room. Frankie and Joanne were making love. As tired as she was, there wasn't enough calm in her to sleep. She could tell that Frankie and Joanne were doing their best to be quiet.

Unable to keep appropriate thoughts in her head, she fantasized disrobing, going out to the living room, and joining them. She remembered a time right before her friend Meg had moved to Los Angeles. Nick's place had just been painted, and she couldn't stay in it that night because the fumes were so bad. She'd slept at Meg's. Meg had been out on a late date—a mercy date, as she'd put it—with a boyfriend with whom she'd told Nick she was bored. The guy, a model for JCPenney catalogues, had made it clear on several

occasions that he found Nick attractive. Meg had even encouraged
Nick to date him, but Nick, like Meg, found him dull. They'd
awakened Nick when they came in, and Nick had heard them having sex. She put a pillow over her head and tried to will herself back
to sleep. She turned on the light and began reading, but after several
pages she hadn't retained any of the novel she'd begun. In a sudden
fit of daring she closed her book, removed her nightgown, and
walked into their room. Meg had fallen asleep. The guy, whose
name Nick could not now remember, was coming out of the bathroom. Seeing Nick, he quite clearly didn't know what had hit him.
She took his hand, quietly led him to her room, and treated him to a
memorable send-off. She later confessed to Meg, who hadn't
minded in the least.

The sexual fantasies, usually so comfortingly distracting to Nick,
were short-circuiting and fizzling. Frankie and Joanne, she realized,
were not merely making love. No doubt they had done that countless times before. They were now, officially and literally, consum-
mating their marriage. The situation with Meg and the boyfriend,
she knew now, had been a once-in-a-lifetime setup. It was an episode from a stage in her life she realized she was moving away
from. Or was she? Was it just the fear and brutality of the moment? If Jeffrey White were alive and well and she was, say, simply
spending the night at Joanne's and Frankie's—would she try something?

You'll never know.

She listened to the sounds they were trying—sweetly, Nick
thought—to suppress. There were colors to these sounds. She heard
humor, impatience, need, joy.

They were making *love,* she thought.

She heard them making, fashioning, one kind of love out of another. She heard them turn their feelings, anxieties, fears, respect,
and chemistry into a sculpture snapshot of themselves. She listened
closely, not precisely eavesdropping. The hotness between her legs

cooled, her fantasies quieted. She was not ashamed to listen, was not using it in any way to turn herself on. The sounds of their sexually expressed trust and faith and joy in each other seemed to quell Nick's fears, dispelling the images of blood and death that had so dogged her senses for the past few hours. She fell asleep.

CHAPTER 17

She couldn't get to St. Barts. The hurricane had prevented anyone from landing there, but the pilot decided to try to put in on St. Maarten. The plane was a winged police car. Nick's father met her on the tarmac, and he opened his arms wide to her as she disembarked. She ran to him and let him hold her for a long time, and then her mother appeared from nowhere, carrying a large, steaming meat loaf. The three of them held each other tightly.

"Mind the meat loaf," warned Nick's mother. Nick broke the hug.

"I'm in a lot of trouble," she said to them.

"I could use a pot holder," said Nick's mother.

"We believe in you completely, Susie," said her dad. "What can we do to help?"

"Just believe me, and stay by me, and don't make me wrong," Nick said. "That's all I've ever really needed from you."

"That's easy, dear," said her mother. "Ask for something harder. A car? Do you want to go to law school? Your father will send you to law school, dear. You don't have to be an actress."

"But that's all I really want, Mom."

"Who'll join me in a martini?" demanded her father pleasantly.

"I will," said her mother.

"Mom, you don't drink anymore. I really need you two not to drink right now."

"Well, then maybe just a nice meat loaf on the rocks. Doris Erman is coming by to join us, dear. Is that all right?"

"I thought it could be just the three of us," said Nick.

"Susie," said her father. "Don't whine."

"But I'm in trouble."

"We'll have some nice meat loaf, and we'll forget all about *that*," said her mother. They got on board the plane, and on the cockpit's movie screen they saw a disembodied face, vague and misshapen amid swirls of smoke. The face spoke.

"I am Ferris Fanning. What is your bidding?"

"Two no-trump!" said Nick's mother, clapping her hands. "I love it—video bridge!"

Nick jumped out the window.

"Write when you get work," said her father, gaily waving.

She fell down, down, until she saw Joanne and Frankie's Cadillac drive by through the clouds. "Susan!" Joanne called. "You're falling. You want a lift—you should pardon the expression?"

"I can't believe you're punning in my dream," said Nick.

"Susan. Susan," said Joanne, whispering. "Telephone."

★   ★   ★   ★

She opened her eyes. Joanne was lying in bed beside her, holding out the phone.

"What time is it?" asked Nick quietly.

"Almost nine," said Joanne. "Here."

"Who is it?" asked Nick.

"A Detective Kerrigan," said Joanne conspiratorially. "I wanted to let you sleep, you were so out of it, but then I figured . . . You want me to say something to him?"

Nick took the phone. Joanne got out of bed wearing a lacy satin-green teddy with almost no back, and slipped out of the bedroom to give Nick some privacy.

"Hello," said Nick a little tentatively. She felt her heart beating hard.

"Sorry to wake you, Miss Stallings."

"No, no. That's okay."

"Jeez, I'm really sorry. Listen, I hate to bother you, but I wonder if you wouldn't mind coming down to the station this morning."

"This morning?"

"I really hate to ask you, but do you think you could make it?"

"What's wrong?"

"No, no. Nothing. I got this pain-in-the-ass kid medical examiner, you know what I mean? Pardon my French. He's fresh out of school. Thinks he's Barnaby Jones or Quincy—I don't know—and we just have, you know, a few questions."

"But I don't understand. Did he make a ruling?"

"Well, see, his report isn't completely conclusive, Miss Stallings. I'm sorry. I was hoping to have it all wrapped up for you, but . . . what time do you think you might be able to get down here?"

"Well . . . I don't . . . tell me something. Should I have a lawyer present?"

"*Should* you? Hey. Up to you. Nobody's making any accusations, Miss Stallings. You're not under suspicion. I'd just like to clear this whole thing up once and for all and I just need to ask you a couple of questions. Really. It'll only take a few minutes."

"I have calls in to . . . my lawyer, but I made them late last night. I don't know when he'll call back, or even if he will, you know, before tomorrow."

"Well," said Kerrigan, "it's Sunday."

"I want—" She struggled to catch her breath. "I want to cooperate in any way I can. What should I do?"

"To tell you the truth, Miss Stallings, I think you might feel a lot better if you just took care of this." He sounded warm and caring. "We could finish this up and, you know, you'd probably sleep better tonight, and maybe save yourself a lot of money. But, hey, it's *totally* up to you."

"He committed suicide. I mean, I explained—" Nick could not find words.

"I know, Miss Stallings. Look. I'm sorry. But this medical examiner has some questions, and these guys, I'm telling you, some of these new guys"—he laughed in what Nick felt was a friendly way —"they can really be a pain in the butt. So I'm sorry, but I gotta get these questions answered."

"Can you tell me what they are?"

"Look. I can only imagine how difficult this must be. I want to make it go away. And I think we can do that in a very few minutes, if you could just help us out."

Nick was desperate not to appear to be hiding anything. "I want to cooperate in any way I can," she repeated.

"I *really* appreciate that, Miss Stallings. Listen. It's 233 East 67th. Okay? Just ask for Detective Kerrigan. When do you think you might be here?"

"What time is it now?"

"Nine forty-five."

"I guess . . . I don't know, ten forty-five? Eleven? Is that okay?"

"Of course. Just ask for me at the desk. All right?"

"Okay."

"Hang in there. I know this has been an ordeal, and I really appreciate your helping us out. So—I'll see you when you get here. Take your time. I mean, you know, don't kill yourself. Have a cup of coffee. Whatever."

"Okay. Thanks."

You keep thanking this guy . . .

"Hey. You're welcome."

"Bye," said Nick. She hung up and ran to the bathroom. Her bowels emptied in an instant. She struggled to slow down and think. She must do a few things. Yes. She must brush her teeth. But how? She had no toothbrush. She must go into the living room and ask Joanne if she or Frankie had an extra toothbrush. Yes. Then she'd brush her teeth. One step at a time. During the night she'd been too warm and she'd discarded her robe. Naked, she picked it up from where it lay by the side of the bed. She pulled it on, knotted the belt, and headed for the kitchen.

Joanne had a sweatshirt on over her teddy, and Frankie was gone. "He went to see if there was anything in the papers." Nick looked sick. "I'm sorry, Susan, but we thought you'd want to know. So?" Joanne said. "What? Good news?"

"I don't know. They're not sure. Do you have an extra toothbrush, Joanne? I'm so sorry. I don't have a toothbrush. I left mine—" She started to block it, but found she couldn't. "I left mine at the Pierre Hotel. We had . . . room service . . . and then I went home, slept a little, blew a big movie meeting, met you guys, then Jeffrey jumped out the window, I saw my shrink, almost slept with a cab driver, went home, and Jeffrey killed himself. So I don't have a toothbrush. Can you lend me one?"

Joanne moved toward Nick, turned her around, and steered her through the bedroom and into the bathroom.

"I don't have another toothbrush, Susan, but, here, use mine. You have the worst breath I've ever experienced on a human being. Forgive me, but I'll never bullshit you." She rinsed off an incredibly streamlined purple toothbrush, put some striped toothpaste on it, and handed it to Nick. "Don't talk for a second. You're upset. Just, you know, brush." Nick brushed. "Good," said Joanne. "Get the back teeth, get the gums, get your tongue, that really makes a difference. I can take it if you're a little crazy, Susan, I don't blame you— but I could never handle bad breath." Nick finished. She held the brush out for Joanne, who took it, rinsed it, and replaced it in a pink and black toothbrush holder. "Now," said Joanne, "what did the medical examiner *say*?"

"It's . . . uncertain," said Nick. "They have a few questions. I'm going down to the station. I don't know. He said it would just be a few questions, and this'll be all over. I've been thinking I should call Jeffrey White's wife and tell her."

"Tell her what?"

"That I didn't do it."

"That's not such a hot idea, Susan."

"I saw her, Joanne."

"You saw her?"

"His wife. In the restaurant. She seemed—" She broke off.

"What? She seemed what?"

"She *exists*," said Nick. "She's real. She looked at me. I can see her eyes."

Joanne turned on the shower, helped Nick out of her robe, adjusted the water temperature, and nudged Nick in.

"G'head," said Joanne. "You'll feel better." She closed the curtain around Nick. "What about a lawyer? What are you gonna do?"

"I'm gonna pray that one of these guys calls. I don't think I want to bring in Jacoby and Myers, you know what I mean? You say Uncle Edward has good taste in lawyers?"

"I would think so, yeah." Suddenly, Joanne's tone changed. "Susan! Step forward—now!" Nick did so, barely escaping a sudden blast of hot water.

"How did you know?" asked Nick in amazement.

"You live in this apartment, you get so you can hear a toilet flush within half a mile. It's either that, or take a permanent room in the burn ward."

"Can't they do something about it?" said Nick, easing herself back under the spray.

"I'm sure they'll get to it. Soon as they take care of homelessness and crime in the streets. Wait a minute, Susan, the phone's ringing."

"Oh, God, Joanne. Get it. Get it, would you?"

Having soaped up, Nick rinsed off in case she had to make a quick exit from the shower. Joanne was back in an instant.

"Susan. It's somebody called Ferris Fanning. I swear to God, that's what he said his name was." Nick threw open the shower curtain, and Joanne handed her another of the fresh royal blue towels. Nick rubbed herself furiously.

"Susan. I know this isn't the time or the place, but I swear to God if you don't have the tits of *life*. Jesus. Are they—no, never mind . . . Jesus Christ, they're like, real, aren't they?" Nick nodded. "I will not envy my new friend. I will not envy my new friend. I will not . . ." chanted Joanne as Nick made her way into the bedroom. Joanne closed herself into the bathroom. "I'm gonna take a shower myself, Susan. Go ahead. I'm not listening."

Nick sat on the edge of the bed, stared at the floor for a few seconds, and picked up the phone. "Hello?"

"Is this Miss Stallings?" asked a voice with a southern twang.

"Yes."

"Ferris Fanning here. I understand you called . . ."

"Yes."

"And you're a friend of Ed Costantino's?"

"Uh. Yes. I am. He suggested I call you. I need some advice."

"Well, Miss Stallings, I could see you first thing tomorrow morning."

"Oh. I was hoping . . . I know this is incredibly inconvenient, but I was hoping you might be available today. I think it's pretty urgent, you see, and I—"

"Miss Stallings, I'm afraid my son and I are about to engage in a father-son ice sailboat race from which I cannot, on pain of death, extricate myself. Weekends are rather sacrosanct in the Fanning clan, Miss Stallings. We're only a few minutes from the start of this race, Miss Stallings, and this is something my son and I have looked forward to for an awfully long time. I'm sure you understand."

"Dad," Nick heard a young voice near Fanning imploring him. "You *promised*. No calls."

Fanning went on abruptly. "Are you free tomorrow morning, say, ten o'clock?"

"Well. I don't . . . I guess . . . ten o'clock? Okay."

"I look forward to it."

"Dad!"

"Where's your office?" Nick asked.

"Park at 52nd Street, 350." He was clearly trying to get off.

"Okay. Okay. Thanks for calling."

"My pleasure, Miss Stallings. See you in the morning."

Nick hung up. She sat naked on the bed, having let the royal blue towel fall to the sheets during her conversation with Ferris Fanning. She heard Joanne in the shower. She was singing the Four Seasons' "Sherry," and was, apparently, attempting all four vocals simultaneously at the top of her lungs.

Nick sat in the half-light of the room. The blinds were still drawn, but a glow came in through the open door to the living room. Staring out at the entry hallway from which the light was coming, she made a short trip to Nicky Stallings Land which was interrupted by the front door opening and Frankie entering. There was a split second in which Nick realized that if she didn't move, Frankie's eyes would be on her. It would look like an accident, and he would see her sitting bare-breasted and only slightly covered by a towel below the waist. In that split second, variations of which she had played out throughout her life, there were choices to make. She could fumble for the towel and stand up, naked. They'd see each other, he might apologize and perhaps look the other way. But the point was that she could bare herself to him and no one would appear to be out of line. It would seem a natural little accident. And Joanne was safely in the shower.

Before Frankie had time to turn in her direction, Nick had pulled the towel up around her and moved to the bathroom door and out of his eye line.

She couldn't remember ever before having passed up such an

opportunity. It felt odd. Frustrating. She didn't feel particularly good about it. All she knew, with certainty, was that shame had already taken all the available space in her body. There were no vacancies at the moment.

She didn't feel better, but she didn't feel worse.

As she opened the door to the bathroom though, she noticed with unfamiliar relief the absence of secrets between her and Joanne. Many were the times that she had displayed herself to the likes of Frankie, making, for sport, someone's boyfriend or husband lust after her . . . making her victim obsess about her and seek out repeat, private, usually fleeting times together. Later Nick felt a barrier, a betrayal, between her and a friend.

Such episodes had not been for sex per se, but rather stolen, necessary, unconscious affirmations for Nick that the most forbidden men around—mates of best friends—wanted her.

Today, at least, she couldn't do it.

As she went into the bathroom and heard Frankie taking off his coat in the hallway, she realized, to her disgust, that with every bone in her body she still wanted to turn around and create some kind of pseudo-accidental revealing of herself to him.

She had but an instant to consider it. Perhaps she could pretend she hadn't heard Frankie come in and wander out into the hallway nude.

She forced herself through the muck of this second-thought temptation, and continued into the bathroom, closing the door.

Maybe it never goes away, she thought, the need to be seen and hungered after. There was no time to consider it further.

"Joanne," she said, "I'm going to need to borrow some clothes."

"No problem," said Joanne, turning off the shower. "What's going on?"

"Well, this Fanning guy can't see me till tomorrow morning."

"Shit. Why not?"

"He's going ice-boating with his son."

"*Ice*-boating? Motherfucking lawyers." Joanne offered a tattered pink silk robe to Nick, who put it on. "Who else did you try?"

Nick looked at the Post-It. "Somebody named Albert Pearson. I got his service."

Joanne, wrapping herself in a bath towel, looked nonplussed. "Albie Pearson? How'd you get his number?"

"Uncle Edward. Why? Do you know him?"

"He's good, very good, but he'll never return your call." Joanne appeared to be making a decision. "I wasn't sure if I should say anything before, but you gotta call Ernie Moran."

"Who's Ernie Moran?"

"Just an asshole I used to work for. One of the best there is."

"You *worked* for him . . . ?"

For a couple of seconds Joanne seemed miles away. Then she snapped to. "It's a long story, Susan. What did Pearson's service say?"

"Just that they'd give him the message."

"I got Ernie's home number, if the jerk hasn't moved." Before Nick could ask her another question, Joanne ran out of the room. She was back in a matter of seconds, flipping through her Filofax. She grabbed the phone and dialed. Someone apparently answered, and she listened for a few seconds. "Shit!" she muttered, hanging up. "He moved, the rat bastard," she said, and then added, mimicking the operator's recording, *"And there is no new number."*

Frankie walked in. "Everybody decent?"

"Yes," said Nick. "What's going on, Joanne?"

"Ernie's the best, Susan. Just the goddamned best. Shit. Where would he be?"

"Ernie Moran?" said Frankie. "The Wizard of Ern?"

"What did you say to that cop?" Joanne asked Nick.

"I told him I'd come right over."

"Okay. Okay. Then you should go. But listen to me, Susan, don't give him anything. You should have a lawyer present."

"Are *you* a lawyer?"

Joanne laughed. "Oh, sure. And queen of all the Russias. No, I was a secretary in his firm . . . in another life. Long story."

"Well, look," said Nick, trying to steady her nerves, "I'm just going to go down and talk to this detective and answer his questions. I mean, all I have to do is tell the truth. Right?"

"Listen, Susan," said Joanne, taking Nick by the shoulders and looking right into her eyes. "Answer his questions, but don't answer his questions. I'm gonna see if I can't hunt up Ernie."

"On a Sunday?" asked Nick.

"He owes me. If I find him, I'll bring him over there and meet you, but I wouldn't count on it. Just act all nice and cooperating, but if anything tough comes up, tell him you have to have your lawyer present. It's your constitutional right."

"Won't it make me seem guilty?"

"Not if you don't *act* guilty. Act frightened and a little apologetic. You're a beautiful woman, for chrissakes. Just stonewall him, but don't *seem* like you're stonewalling."

"Oh, God, Joanne. I'm sorry. This is your honeymoon."

"If this is my honeymoon, Susan, I might as well slit my wrists. You should get going. If you're late, it'll seem like you're avoiding something. I'll keep trying to reach Ernie."

"How do you know so much?" said Nick almost admiringly.

"You hang around Ernie Moran for a while, you pick up a few things. I used to sit in sometimes when he briefed clients. I'm not overly fond of the guy, but he's, like, great in a pinch. Which this is."

"The Wizard of Ern," echoed Frankie thoughtfully.

"Oh, God," said Nick, glancing around the room. "What can I wear that wouldn't put you out?"

"Frankie," said Joanne. "Put on some coffee, would ya?" Frankie headed to the kitchen. Joanne yanked open her closet, stood to one side, and with a sweep of her arm said, "Mi closet, su closet."

Nick looked at the clothes, jammed every which way. "I don't think I'm up to choosing an outfit. Maybe I'll just go like this," she said, indicating the robe.

Joanne started rummaging through the racks. "I think we want something very definitely, you know, *un*–cherchez-la-femme, if you know what I'm saying. How about this?" It was a black suit of slightly shiny material. Joanne glanced at it and immediately rejected it before Nick had the chance. "Nah. On me it might be low key. On you it's, like, forget about it. Shit. What we need is something . . . loose. Long. Lemme see." She whisked a few more hangers around. "Bonzai! Yes. I don't think I've worn this since, like, 1978." She pulled out a long, simple, off-white cotton summer dress, and held it up. Nick walked over, felt the material, and put her hand under it to make sure it wasn't at all diaphanous. It wasn't.

"It's, like, whattayoucallit—muslin? I don't know," said Joanne. "Whatta you think?"

Nick could see that she'd look baggy and modest and relatively asexual in it. She dropped her towel and pulled the dress over her head.

"You need a bra," said Joanne. "I'm not sure I can help you there, but let's just see." She rummaged through a bureau drawer. For all of Joanne's compliments to Nick, Nick had noticed that Joanne was possessed of quite a figure herself. Not perhaps as well-proportioned as Nick, Joanne was nonetheless nicely built. She tossed a bra to Nick, who adjusted it and found that it wasn't a bad fit.

"Maybe a slip?" suggested Joanne. Nick nodded. Joanne searched for one. "I don't know about you, Susan, but I hate underpants. Just hate the motherfuckers. And yet," she continued, working through another drawer, "today is a definite panty day. I mean, they won't know, but *you'll* know—right? I'm looking for something kinda Sears, Roebuck here. I mean, they're not gonna, like, strip-search you, but whatta you think?"

Nick was looking at her but not hearing. She snapped to. "What? Oh. Yes. Yes. If you have something really simple. And the slip is great." She pulled off the dress, tried on the slip and some plain white underpants that looked like they hadn't been worn in years.

"Those are pre-Frankie," said Joanne as Nick pulled them on. "Now: hose. Here." She tossed some over. Nick, who could never stand to wear other women's clothes, found it soothing to be dressed this morning by her new friend. She pulled on the panty hose, but then realized she had only last night's heels and the sneakers she'd brought from her apartment. She rolled off the panty hose, and she and Joanne said, almost simultaneously, "White socks." Joanne found a pair and tossed them to Nick, but they had little ruffles at the top that made them kind of sexy, and Joanne saw Nick balk.

"Wait a second. Here's some really plain ones," said Joanne, lobbing over another pair.

"I can't believe I'm dressing up—or down—for the police."

"You want a cup of coffee, Susan? Maybe some toast, or a muffin? I think there might be a muffin, if the Prince of Hearts in there didn't eat the last one."

"Just a little coffee maybe," said Nick, who had opened her purse and headed into the bathroom to apply some base. Then she decided she'd go without makeup. Better not to look too composed, she thought. She told herself not to worry about looking innocent. I *am* innocent, she thought.

Liar.

She walked out of the bedroom and into the kitchen. Frankie had brought home the *News* and the *Times,* and was rapidly flipping through *Newsday*.

"Nothing," he said, snapping the pages. "There's nothing in the papers. These're all early editions though," he added. "You're lucky there's no Sunday *Post,* and these all go to press around the same time the news was on last night, so I guess they just missed it."

Joanne handed her a mug of coffee. Nick felt something in the middle of her stomach that she associated with the end of summer and the words "back to school."

"Susan's going up to the police."

"Yeah?" said Frankie.

"They just asked me to come in and answer a few questions. I want to get this whole thing over with."

"Maybe I'll go to mass," said Frankie. "I'll light you a candle. Did any of those lawyers call?"

"One did. I'm seeing him tomorrow morning."

"You want a lift?" asked Frankie.

"You wait with me," Joanne said to him. "In case I find Ernie."

"I can take a cab," said Nick.

"What about after?" asked Joanne. "You want to come back here? You can stay, like, forever if you need to." Nick managed a smile and shrugged uncertainly as she gulped some coffee. She was grateful Joanne had added milk. Nick couldn't have stomached it black, her usual preference. The digital clock on the microwave said 10:23.

"I don't want to be late," said Nick, draining the mug.

"Have a piece of toast," said Joanne, buttering it like a short-order cook as it popped out of the toaster. She put it on a pink and black plate and slid it to Nick. Nick munched, and they stood in silence. Nick looked at the headline in the *News*—"Batten Down the Hatches." And, in smaller letters, "Hurricane Heads North." She wondered if her father was all right. Joanne tore at the other piece of toast that had popped up with Nick's, and looked thoughtfully out the window. There was no view, just the dulled white brick of a building across the street that seemed to Nick—like most buildings in New York—too close. The sky was overcast. It made for a depressing vista.

"I'm gonna go," she said suddenly, wiping her hand on a paper towel she ripped from a rack by the sink. "Oh, Jesus. Could you spare a few dollars for cabs? I don't have a cent on me, and I lost my bank card." Frankie pulled a fifty out of an envelope from a drawer next to the utensils and handed the bill to Nick.

"I don't have any small bills, Susan. Sorry. Joanne: We need more cash in petty cash."

"I'll go to the machine later," said Joanne. "I liked it better when you didn't have to go shopping for money every couple of days, like milk."

"This city eats cash," said Frankie. "Munches it from your hand all day long." There was another silence.

"Where'd you put my coat?" asked Nick. Joanne disappeared into the hallway.

"You really don't need one," said Frankie. "It's like, almost hot out there. I swear to God."

"Still," said Nick. "I think I'd like to wear it." Joanne was already holding it open for Nick to put her arms through.

"Button up your overcoat," said Joanne. "Take good care of yourself and all that."

"How can I thank you two?" said Nick, her mind already on her impending interrogation. Joanne gave Nick an enveloping hug.

"We'll see you," said Joanne. "Don't answer any questions they don't ask. You know? I mean, just—" She stopped herself. "You don't need my advice. See ya."

When she hit the street, Nick felt that Frankie must be even more hot-blooded than he seemed. It was cloudy, chilly, and blustery, and she closed her coat as she scanned all directions for a cab. They were everywhere this early on a Sunday morning, and one pulled right up.

"I'm going to 233 East 67th," she told the driver. She tried not to notice whether he was cute or not. She didn't want to know. When she looked a moment later, she saw that he was close to sixty and Irish, the almost lost breed of vintage New York cabbie—and not, she was grateful, one to rouse any thoughts of shenanigans. They drove without chat through the quiet streets, Nick noticing church after church in the process of filling up or emptying. She thought about Kerrigan. She was determined not to rehearse anything. She was going to show up and cooperate and get this over with.

As the cab turned the corner onto Sixty-seventh Street, Nick saw the precinct house. Then she saw something that made her shrink back. Across the street from the entrance was a Channel 5 Action

News van. And, sure enough, there was a woman next to the van: Connie Cuevas.

★   ★   ★   ★

How on earth could she have known that I was coming, Nick thought. Or was it a coincidence? Was Connie Cuevas simply trying to get some information out of the cops?

"Stop the car, please," Nick said simply but with enough urgency to bring about the desired result. The cabbie turned his head to her.

"You getting out here?"

Nick saw a phone booth on the corner. "Yes," she said, handing him the borrowed fifty. The meter read $3.75. She knew that most New York cabbies would as soon shoot her as change a bill that large. "I'm sorry. That's all I have. Make it five even." The cabbie, to her relief, pulled out a wad of bills without missing a beat. Nick pocketed the forty-five dollars, got out, and crossed the street fast, in a beeline for the phone. As she lifted its receiver she was relieved to hear a dial tone. She dialed 411 and got right through.

"New York Telephone. What borough please?"

"Manhattan. I need the number for the Nineteenth Precinct." She waited as the background sound changed and a robotlike voice spat out prerecorded digits. Repeating them over and over to herself, Nick deposited a quarter and dialed.

"Nineteenth," said a falsely enthusiastic voice.

"Detective Kerrigan, please." She waited a few seconds as the phone clicked and rang again.

"Kerrigan."

"Detective. This is Nicolette Stallings."

"Hiya. Where are you? Anything wrong?"

"No. Well—yes. I'm on the corner. There's . . . a news van out-side your entrance."

"Shit. Excuse my French. That little Cuevas bitch—excuse my

French. Uh, okay. You know what? There's a back entrance, on 68th Street. You mind going around there?"

"I'd be almost delighted."

"It's unmarked. What are you, on Second Avenue?"

"Yes."

"Okay. Go to 68th, and you'll see a door right after the Chinese laundry on your . . . left. Ah Fong, or Ma Fong, or some goddamn Fong, and you'll see a metal door with a lot of grafitti all over it. That's the one. Just tell whoever's at the door that you're looking for me. Better still, I'll meet you there. I don't want some weisenheimer not letting you in."

"Thanks. I'll see you in a minute."

As Nick walked around the corner and across 68th Street, she wondered if her mother had heard anything yet. She must have. The thought made her stomach stir. And what about Todd? Or Sam? Had news spread out to the coast? No, she told herself. It wasn't even in the papers yet. But maybe that was, as Frankie had said, only because the papers had gone to press just as Connie Cuevas was breaking the story. Channel 5, at least, was apparently trying to run with this. She got halfway up the block. There, with a little rectangular painted wooden sign out of the fifties, was T. Fong's laundry. Beyond it was The Door.

She didn't want to pause, think, or consider. She just wanted to get this over with. She reached for the weathered, often-jimmied metal door handle. It turned, the grafittied door opened, and there was Detective Kerrigan. He was wearing a virtually identical, yet different, nondescript suit. She wondered if every suit he had was a variation on a theme. Even in the dank, linoleumed back stairway, she could see that his shoes were phenomenally well shined.

"Hiya," he said, opening the door wider for her and checking outside as if something or someone dangerous was likely to be there. "Sorry you had to come in this way. I talked to that Latino bitch two hours ago. I figured she left. I told her 'no comment,' that we had nothing for them. I swear to God, they all think they're Geraldo fucking Rivera, you should pardon my French. Come right this way." He led her up a flight of stairs.

"So you talked to her?" Nick asked warily.

"Sometimes you gotta move your lips or they'll *never* go away. But she knows I'm not gonna comment on something like this. It's right down here," he said, wending his way through a large outer office that looked to Nick as if it had been modeled after a TV cop show's set.

"Donnie," Kerrigan called out to a burly, uniformed cop across the room, "take my calls, okay?"

"You got it," said Donnie without looking up.

Kerrigan pushed open a door with frosted glass on its upper half and motioned for Nick to go in. "You remember Sergeant Whelan," he said.

Whelan, who'd been reading notes from a pad, smiled and stood. "Hi, Miss Stallings. Thanks for coming in."

"I was just telling Miss Stallings that I thought we could make that Cuevas lady go away, but no such luck."

"Dogs looking for dog meat," said Whelan with disgust.

Kerrigan pulled out a straight-backed chair of old green leatherette with an aluminum frame. "Please. Make yourself comfortable."

"Thank you," Nick said quietly as she sat.

"Can we hang up your coat?" asked Kerrigan.

"I'm fine. Thanks," said Nick, who couldn't shake the chill brought on by the sight of Connie Cuevas.

"You know what I think?" said Kerrigan to Whelan. "I think it's our little whiz-kid medical examiner." He looked at Nick. "That Cuevas lady must've gone down to the goddamn morgue. That's what I think. She must've waited for the M.E.'s report and finagled it outta somebody—maybe that little worm himself." He shook his head and shuffled some papers in a folder that had been sitting at the head of a rectangular, standard-issue oak table. "I'm sorry, Miss Stallings. There's nothing we can do about that. Who knows? The little bastard might have let somebody leak it onto the news to show the mayor he's helping solve every goddamn murder in this city."

Nick noted Kerrigan's use of the word "murder."

"So. Anyway," said Kerrigan. "Thanks for coming down. Really. I appreciate it. How you feelin'?" He looked genuinely concerned.

"I'm . . . I don't know," Nick began.

"You sleep?"

"I think so. I guess so." Nick had the thought that a good night's sleep was a sign of a clear conscience. "Yes," she added, "like a log."

"Good. That's good," said Kerrigan, nodding and looking at Nick as though he had no further agenda. She shifted her weight on the chair. Kerrigan looked at his notes.

Wait for him *to ask something.*

"What exactly . . . do you think the medical examiner might have leaked?" asked Nick, unable to help herself.

"Well, unfortunately, probably the same goddamn thing he told me. The little rat bastard son of a bitch."

"And what was it . . . that he told you?" asked Nick, trying to make it sound as though it were *not* the 64,000 dollar question.

"Lemme ask you one thing before I get to that, Miss Stallings. Are you a *close* friend of Judge Costantino's?"

"Not exactly close, I guess," said Nick. "Why?"

"But you've known each other for a long time?"

"Well, actually, no. I . . . just met him the other night."

Kerrigan looked up from his notes. "What night was that?" Certainly Uncle Edward had already told them, so there was no harm in telling the truth.

"Friday."

"Night before last?"

"Yes."

He raised his eyebrows a little. "So, when Jeffrey White, as you've said, killed himself, you went to the apartment of someone you'd met *the day before?*"

Nick was determined not to get defensive. "It was just an instinct.

I . . . needed help. I wanted to make sure I was doing the right thing. He seemed like someone who would, you know, be there for me." She was holding her own.

"Be there for you better than, say—your shrink?"

Nick's eyes popped open. Kerrigan looked at his pad. "You placed a call to a Martine Gersch before you dialed 911. She's your shrink, am I right?"

"Yes," said Nick, startled that he'd checked her phone calls. "But I didn't speak to her. I got her machine." Kerrigan was looking at her, seemingly unjudgmental. "I was distraught, Detective. I knew I hadn't done anything wrong, but I also knew it might, well, look . . . bad. I wanted advice."

"Uh-huh. Okay. I understand," said Kerrigan. He seemed on her side. Nick's breathing returned to something approaching normal.

See. Just tell the truth.

"Now," he said, picking up a different set of notes. "Okay. The autopsy." He looked into her eyes. "You know what we got here, Miss Stallings? We got something which is, I gotta tell you, the goddamn bane of any cop's existence. Am I right, Joey?"

"Oh, yeah," agreed Whelan.

"We got . . . cuppy." He looked at her and nodded conclusively.

"Cuppy?" asked Nick, her eyes moving from Kerrigan to Whelan and back. "I'm sorry . . . what's . . ."

"Cuppy," said Kerrigan again. "Circumstances undetermined pending police investigation. C-U-P-P-I. We call it cuppy. And can I tell you something? We hate cuppy. Cuppy is a pain, a royal pain in our individual and collective butts, and that's why we're here and that's why we asked you to come down, because I'm sure you can straighten this whole thing out and we can put it to rest."

Nick tried to breathe deeply to keep her by-now familiar nausea from reasserting itself.

"Listen," said Thomas Kerrigan, taking Nick into his confidence. "I got cases enough to keep me busy from now till I'm ninety-seven. I don't need a cuppy here. Cuppy is purgatory as far as I'm concerned. I mean, I think this guy White did just what you said. I think he Toshiro Mifuned himself—which I don't mean to make light of for a minute, because I know how awful this must have been for you. And I think it was just like you said: a suicide. As far as I'm concerned, bingo, it's a suicide. But the *M.E.,* I think he wants to run for president or something, so I just gotta ask you a couple of questions, and we'll get this thing out of cuppy, close the books on it, and we'll all go home and do whatever we do on Sunday afternoons. So. You sure you don't want a glass of water? Some coffee? Our coffee here gives coffee a bad name, but . . . Joey—did somebody plug in the new Mr. Coffee?"

"Not yet."

"Not yet? Jesus." Then, to Nick: "I buy a new Mr. Coffee but nobody—forget it. So. A couple of questions and we're out of here. These are not *my* questions, you understand. These are young Perry Mason's questions I gotta ask you. And can I tell you something? We really appreciate you coming down here this morning."

Despite her chill, Nick could feel sweat like a running faucet under her arms. She was glad she hadn't removed her coat.

"First question." Kerrigan looked at what must have been the M.E.'s report, and read. "How did the knife, with Miss Stallings's prints on it, end up on the floor three feet from Mr. White's body?" He looked at Nick. "I answered that one for him. I told him you took it out. Correct?"

"Yes. I told you."

"Right. Bear with me here. You wanted to try to help him, but you were afraid he might lash out at you, so first you wanted to get the knife out of his hands. Right?"

"Right."

Kerrigan looked at Whelan. "I told him that. Did I tell him that?"

"You told him that," said Whelan, who seemed permanently disgusted at the thought of the medical examiner.

"That would explain your prints over the blood on the knife. You see, I got no problem with this, Miss Stallings, but the M.E., he's gotta know why your hand was on the knife after it got bloodied, blah-blah-blah. He's gotta make sure you weren't using the knife."

"Is that what he thinks?" asked Nick, her voice rising a little, betraying the alarm she was sure she had hitherto concealed quite well.

"It might have crossed his mind. But we set him straight on that. Okay. That takes care of the knife. So. Question number two from our little friend. He's doing the autopsy, see, and everything is just like you told us. But then, when they clean the blood off the body, he finds this bruise."

"Bruise?" said Nick, as though merely curious.

"Well, in fact, there's a bunch of bruises, and a cast on his arm, and some cuts on his face. Now. You didn't say anything about that. And I'll get to that in a minute. But this one bruise, it's on his rib, and it's *fresher* than the others, which are around a day old. So, in addition to these cuts on his face and this cast—which you said nothing about—he's got this very *fresh* bruise, it seems, on his rib." He looked at her. "Where do we start?"

She cursed herself for coming without a lawyer. But she knew nothing about a bruise. She didn't speak.

"Well, I'm sorry, Miss Stallings, but, you know, presumably you *have* seen the deceased fairly recently . . . without his clothes on. Now. The M.E. says these cuts and other bruises all pre-date his death by maybe twenty-four hours, so for now we'll skip over why you didn't mention any of that."

She tried to think how to finesse this and get out of there so she could wait for a lawyer. "I figured that those cuts were all so obvious," said Nick, feeling vaguely sure of where she was headed. Kerrigan, it seemed, was thorough. There was a good chance he'd found out that Jeffrey had been admitted to a city hospital night before last.

Tell the truth.

"I mean, he'd had a fall . . ."

"Whoa. Whoa," said Kerrigan. "*Excuse me? What fall?*"

Shit.

"What fall? Miss Stallings. We spoke to his wife. She said nothing about a fall. She saw him the morning after he was with you. She threw him out, she spent the day with lawyers starting divorce proceedings, and she says she didn't see him after that. So, this fall— which I frankly am dying to hear about—had to take place *after* he saw his wife. So. What about this fall?"

"He jumped . . ." Nick started to say, then faltered.

"Excuse me? Come again? He jumped, Miss Stallings? When? Where?"

Nick rubbed her temples. "Anything I say here can and will be used against me in a court of law, won't it?"

"Oh, hey, come on," said Kerrigan warmly, as if they were old friends. "You're not under arrest, Miss Stallings. You're not even a *suspect*. There's been no crime declared. You know what I mean? Hey. I get a little impatient because maybe you didn't tell me the whole story yesterday, but, jeez. I'm sorry. That's the way I am. I got a lot of things on my mind. But this is just a cuppy." Nick was quiet. "However. There's a fairly big, fresh bruise on his rib, and now you tell me about a jump, which, frankly, Miss Stallings, I can't wait to hear more about, because I'm trying, you know, I'm trying to stay in your corner here, I really am. I do *not* want a big investigation here. I hate cuppy like I hate my mother-in-law, Miss Stallings. So. What jump?"

"I shouldn't say any more without talking to a lawyer."

Kerrigan glanced at Whelan, then back at Nick. "That's your right, Miss Stallings. Sure. I just thought, you know, maybe we could put this whole thing to rest today without a lot of fuss and expense to you. Otherwise, hey, I would never have asked you to come in. Frankly, I'd rather be home watching the Knicks' pregame show. You don't want to talk about the jump because you're afraid it might incriminate you—I understand. I wish to God I knew how to make that fear go away. Joey and I were just hoping to avoid a, you know, a full-blown investigation."

Nick felt the coffee's acid gnawing at her stomach lining. "Jeffrey

White came to see me the afternoon after I had . . . been with him. I didn't think he was actually dangerous, so I let him come up. And then these friends of mine—the judge's nephew and his wife—came up too. They had just given me a ride home. . . ."

She paused, wishing she could leave Joanne and Frankie out of this, but realizing that she couldn't.

"They saw Jeffrey there when they dropped me off, and he looked . . . just very weird. So they came up a few minutes later— to check on me. Jeffrey didn't want me to let them up. But he was starting to act a little crazy."

"Did he threaten you?"

"He took off his clothes. He wanted, I think, some kind of . . . replay of the night before."

"Go on."

"Well, I was thrilled that my friends came up, 'cause I really didn't want to be alone with him. He calmed down and got dressed after they arrived, and asked to talk to me in private. He seemed so pathetic, and I felt bad for him, so I asked my friends to go into the bedroom. Jeffrey said he wanted to see me again. I told him I didn't think that was a good idea. And then"—she took a breath—"he jumped out the window."

"He—jumped out the *window*?" said Kerrigan. "Then what? His parachute opened and he wafted gracefully down to the street?"

"I'm pretty sure he was trying to kill himself. But there's a balcony one flight down." In another context, the memory of Jeffrey splayed out on the barbecue might have made her laugh. "That's how he got those cuts, and the broken hand, and maybe even the bruise you're talking about. That's also how he got the Demerol he took before he died."

"You never mentioned this before," said Kerrigan, a soupçon of anger creeping through.

Nick paused. "I didn't want to get my friends involved. Which was stupid of me."

"You could say that, yes." Kerrigan got up and walked around the table, then came back. "But your friends didn't actually see him jump?"

"No. They were in the bedroom."

"Uh-huh. Then what?"

Nick continued, knowing that this was information Kerrigan could get from Joanne or Frankie. "The doorman let us into the apartment below to help Jeffrey out. We called EMS and they came and took him to a hospital. You can check this all out with Fernando —that's the doorman's name."

"He already told us."

Nick's eyes widened.

Kerrigan went on. "He told us that White said he fell out the window."

"Why didn't you tell me?" said Nick, flabbergasted.

"Hey, Miss Stallings. Why didn't you tell *me*?"

She couldn't collect her thoughts. "I'm sorry. I—I just . . . I didn't want to involve the people who work in my building, or my friends. I haven't known them very long."

"How long?"

"I just met them, actually. I couldn't find a cab the other night because of the rain, and they gave me a ride home."

"Friends . . . who you just met. This gets better and better." He turned to Whelan. "Cuppy hell, Joey." Then back to Nick. "Okay. I want their full names before you go."

"All right," said Nick. She knew she mustn't answer any more questions.

Whelan scribbled and Kerrigan looked at his notes as if they might provide something helpful. "You know," he said, "if this guy jumped, it strengthens the idea that he might kill himself eventually. Why didn't you mention that yesterday? I mean, he jumps, and it makes your story look good, Miss Stallings—that he would kill himself later. It makes him seem very unstable. But I guess, unfortunately, nobody actually saw him jump—except you. Boy-oh-boy-oh-boy. You make it hard."

"I was in a panic yesterday. I wasn't thinking logically. I'm flying by the seat of my pants here. I came in good faith, without a lawyer, and I was depending on you not to take advantage of me."

"And I'm depending on you, Miss Stallings, not to bullshit me anymore! Because I got cuppy here, and it's not getting any better, and I got Action fucking News out there—and you got them too!"

Nick felt tears rising and summoned everything she had to force them back. She refused to be any more pathetic in his eyes.

"Okay," said Kerrigan, "he goes to the hospital. He gets the Demerol—which, at least, checks out. The M.E. said if the knife hadn'ta killed him, the Demerol probably would've."

So—if I'd gone to the beach with my cab driver, Jeffrey might have been dead by the time I got home.

Kerrigan jerked his head from one side to the other, making little popping sounds in his neck. He sat back down, smoothed his papers, and looked at her.

"Last question. Repeat question: Do you remember a bruise on his rib?"

She felt as though she were watching all this in an out-of-focus movie. She knew it would be best not to let too much time pass without answering. She had no recollection of a bruise on Jeffrey White's ribs. Should she lie and say she *had* seen the bruise? She recalled her face in Joanne's bathroom mirror. It was the face of a person who simply could not tolerate any more lies, big or little. It had nothing to do with honor. She decided to terminate this interview and resume when she'd found a lawyer.

"Does that ring a bell, Miss Stallings? A bruise on his rib?"

Say: Yes, I remember the bruise, it was there all along.

"I better talk to a lawyer," said Nick with a sad finality.

"Of course," said Kerrigan, making it a forlorn statement. He looked at Whelan, whose heavy, puffy eyes darkened.

"You sure?" asked Whelan as though she still had a chance to save herself.

"I'm afraid I'm sure."

"A pretty good one on his left side, about three ribs up?" said Kerrigan, taking one last stab. "Not related to the fall off the balcony. Fresher. Did he, maybe, hit against something when he went down to the ground? Does that maybe ring a bell?"

She saw that Kerrigan was actually trying to help her. It probably had more to do with not wanting to add to his caseload than with getting her out of a jam, but at least he hadn't turned on her completely. She stood up to leave. Kerrigan moved between her and the door.

"See, the M.E. didn't say it in so many words," he went on, "but he's thinking maybe there was a struggle. A fight. But couldn't White have just banged against a chair? Or, you know, hit the corner of a table when he fell down? Isn't that possible?"

Nick was about to say that, yes, anything was possible, when she heard the sound of a woman's voice outside, yelling at Donnie, the cop at the desk.

"Lady," Donnie was insisting, "nobody goes in there."

"Perfect! I'm nobody," Nick heard Joanne's voice insist, "so I'm going in."

"Sergeant," said a clear, strong, unfamiliar voice that reminded Nick of Jack Webb on *Dragnet,* "you know as well as I do that you've got to let us in there."

"Susan!" yelled Joanne.

"That's my friend," Nick said, rising.

"If she's your friend, why is she calling you Susan?" asked Kerrigan, also rising and reaching for the doorknob.

"Long story," said Nick.

"You're just full of long stories," said Kerrigan as he opened the door. Joanne walked in, followed closely by a fierce-looking man in a more expensive sharkskin suit than Kerrigan could ever have dreamed of. He was completely bald, with an odd purplish do-rag tied around his head, giving him the appearance of a recovering pirate.

"Who're you?" asked Kerrigan brusquely.

"Ernie Moran," said The Wizard, offering his hand. "Representing Miss Stallings."

CHAPTER 18

Didn't we meet on the Jackie Torrino case, five years ago?" Ernie Moran asked Kerrigan. Kerrigan nodded unhappily.

"I tracked him down after you left," Joanne whispered in an aside to Nick. "I thought we better come over and see how everything's going."

"It was *six* years ago," said Kerrigan to Moran, doing his best to smile. "And we never actually met. I'd remember. But you pulled a few rabbits out of a few hats. And Jackie Torrino is a free man."

"Thanks," said Ernie Moran.

"I didn't really mean it as a compliment," said Kerrigan. "You know Joey Whelan?"

"Nice, uh, hat," said Whelan, sarcastically referring to the purple bandanna.

Ernie Moran shook Whelan's hand like a candidate doing his best to make a campaign worker feel important. He turned to Nick. "Sorry I couldn't be here earlier, Miss Stallings. Everything all right?" Before Nick could answer, he went on. "You don't mind if I take a few minutes to talk to my client, do you, Detective?"

Nick figured she shouldn't let on that she'd never seen Ernie Moran before in her life. She couldn't believe that Joanne had made him materialize.

"You two want to talk?" asked Kerrigan, recovering gracefully. "Hey, no problemo. Make yourself comfortable. Joey, let's put Mr. Coffee to work." As they moved out of the room, Whelan did his best not to reveal his displeasure at the arrival of counsel. Kerrigan added, "Take a few minutes, Mr. Moran."

"Thanks, gentlemen," said Ernie Moran. He was about forty-five, with dark gray circles around deep-set eyes, and a slightly ashen complexion. He looked as though he were fighting off the flu. With hair, he might have been handsome, and he seemed self-assured but distracted. There was something magnetic about him, but his cockiness irked Nick. He closed the door behind the retreating detectives and extended his hand. She shook it. It was cold and dry.

"Joanne told me you could use some help. I learned a long time ago never to argue with Joanne when she insists on something."

"He and I were . . . close for a while," said Joanne. "Pre-Frankie. Don't tell Frankie. Oh, fuck it, never mind. I'll tell him. I can't keep a secret from him anyway."

Nick wondered if Uncle Edward knew that his new niece-in-law had had an affair with Ernie Moran.

"Anyway," said Joanne, "I found his car phone number in an old address book. There's an early Knicks game today. He was on his way to this brunch place across the street from the Garden. Part of his Knicks weekend routine. Still have the season tickets, Ern? I should've remembered."

"Joanne," said The Wizard, "we don't have much time."

"So I called in a marker, so to speak. Now, I'll just shut my trap for one brief motherfucking second—in fact, I'll wait outside. Right?"

"Please," said Ernie Moran.

"*Sayonara,*" said Joanne with a step toward the door. "Frankie's outside with the car, Susan."

"I love you," said Nick simply.

"Okay," said Joanne. "Je swee hiss-toire." She went out and Ernie Moran closed the door. He turned to Nick and spoke quickly.

"We probably have about five minutes, Miss Stallings. These guys don't know we've never met, and I have no problem with that, but we'll have to dispense with niceties. I need you to tell me, without embellishment, what's going on. Joanne filled me in on what she could, but it's pretty sketchy."

Nick wondered how long a body could go on producing adrenaline, on which she was sure she'd been running for what felt like forever. But there was more kicking in now.

"I had a one-night stand with Jeffrey White two nights ago, at the Pierre Hotel . . ."

She went on, fighting for coherence, through the events leading to Jeffrey's self-mutilation.

". . . there was nothing anybody could do for him, and I was completely freaked. I just left."

"Without notifying the authorities?"

"I'm afraid so. I'm sorry. You're gonna earn your money here, Mr. Moran. I left. I didn't have a plan. I took a cab to Edward Costantino's apartment. For advice. He said to call the police. He also recommended two lawyers, but I haven't been able to see either one yet. The police picked me up and took me to my building, Kerrigan questioned me, and I called Joanne to see if I could stay with her. Unfortunately, Action News was outside—"

"I saw it last night."

"You did? Well, they edited it—a lot. It was pretty bad, wasn't it?"

"It wasn't good."

"So I went to Joanne's, tried to reach the lawyers, and slept."

"And they called with the medical examiner's report this morning?"

"Yes. Kerrigan said he had some questions about it and asked me to come in. He made it sound like no big deal."

"Did he *say* it was no big deal?"

"No. It was just his tone of voice."

"Don't ever go to a police station for questioning without a law-yer again."

"I won't."

"So you came in—how long've you been here?"

"I don't know. An hour?"

"And . . . ?"

"Apparently, there's a bruise on the body from close to the time of his death, and I guess the M.E. thinks we might have struggled while Jeffrey was dying. And that I might have stabbed him."

"*Did* you struggle?"

"No. But my prints were on the knife."

"Because you took it while trying to save the man's life."

"Well. Yes. They were just asking me about the bruise when you came in. Thank you for coming. I don't know if I can afford you."

"We'll talk about that later. What did you say about the bruise?"

"Nothing."

"Good."

"He didn't have the bruise the night before. If I say the bruise was there all along, maybe his wife will say that it *wasn't* there. No. I didn't see it. I wasn't going to start lying."

There was a knock at the door, followed by Kerrigan and Whelan reentering. "Sorry, Mr. Moran. We gotta get on with this."

Moran walked over to the door and closed it quietly, as if he were in his own home. He crossed his arms and looked at the floor for a few seconds.

Kerrigan said, "Mr. Moran, can we go on? I really only had one more question."

Moran looked up at Kerrigan slowly. "Detective, my client has cooperated with you to the fullest extent *imaginable,* and she is simply not in any condition to go through any more of this today."

"Mr. Moran," Nick said, protesting slightly. Moran turned and gave her a look that silenced her.

"My client will be happy to cooperate with you in any way, but she's had an unspeakable tragedy in her life, and she needs rest. I'm going to take her to a doctor myself, since no one else seems to have thought of it." He gave them a withering glance. "I want to make sure she isn't suffering from stress-related shock."

"I gotta tell you," said Kerrigan, doing his best not to sound uppity, "she seems quite lucid to me."

"She's very brave," said Moran matter-of-factly. "And eager to cooperate."

"Okay, great," said Kerrigan quickly. "Because I just have one more question . . ."

"Sorry, Detective," said Ernie Moran.

"No, *I'm* sorry, Mr. Moran," said Kerrigan in a new and un-friendly way. He reached into his pocket and pulled out a plastic bag with a weathered, tagged gold bracelet inside. He held it up near Nick's face. "You recognize this, Miss Stallings?"

Nick studied it for a moment.

"No," she said simply.

"Really," said Kerrigan. "See, Mr. Moran, they just brought this in from Miss Stallings's apartment while you two were talking. I asked my boys to go through the place again. Sometimes when there's a corpse, it's a little hectic the first go-round. This was on the floor behind your bureau, Miss Stallings."

"That's . . . impossible," said Nick.

"I suppose it's also impossible that there's an inscription on the inside of the clasp. Wanna know what it says? It says, 'We'll always have last summer—Jeffrey.' "

"What?" said Nick, fighting for air. Ernie Moran looked bewil-dered. Nick looked at the bracelet hanging in the bag in Kerrigan's hand. It was scratched, worn, and very real.

Nick just shook her head.

"Enough is enough!" Ernie Moran broke in. "With what this woman has been through, I don't know how you can honestly ex-pect to subject her to any more of this."

"Mr. Moran," said Nick finally. "I'll answer any questions they've got." She turned to Kerrigan. "What do you want to know? Really. The capital of Idaho? Boise. Capital of North Dakota? Bismarck. Not Fargo, mind you—Bismarck." She tapped her nails on the table nervously. "What else?"

"There's a lot of things I'd like to ask you, Miss Stallings," said Kerrigan roughly. "Like why your good friend—who you've only known for two days—calls you Susan."

"I think you can see that the time has come to call it quits for the day, gentlemen," said Ernie Moran, taking a step toward Nick.

"Jesus, Mr. Moran," said Kerrigan. "I'm not even sure we know her goddamned *name*."

"Susan is my real name!" yelled Nick suddenly. "Nicolette is a stage name."

Kerrigan looked at Whelan. "I love actresses, don't you, Joey? They love to act."

There was a knock at the door. "What?" snapped Kerrigan.

"Sorry, Tom," said Donnie, the desk cop, through the door. "But there's a call I think you might wanna take. That insurance check."

"Don't go anywhere," said Kerrigan, pointing at Ernie Moran and Nick. Moran made a show of buttoning his coat, wearily.

"Detective," Moran said, corralling Nick to stand up and join him. "I'm taking my client to see a doctor. Any questions you have regarding this, I trust you'll call me first." He offered his card, but Kerrigan was already past him, three steps out the door, heading for the phone.

Moran gave the card to Whelan. Joanne, who'd been seated on a bench thumbing through wanted posters, looked up.

"Let's go," Moran said abruptly to Nick.

Nick didn't like him. His protectiveness felt patronizing. She knew she was exhausted and frazzled, but she couldn't believe the whole thing wasn't wrapped up. She was utterly thrown by the bracelet. And the great Wizard of Ern was helplessly stalling. She watched Kerrigan, who was listening intently on the phone. He nodded, and then his eyes darted across the room to her.

"Don't go anywhere, please, Miss Stallings." He listened. Joanne froze. Ernie Moran kept attempting to steer Nick toward the door. She turned to him and spoke quietly, her lips barely moving.

"Mr. Moran. I may be in shock—I don't know. I'm grateful that you're here, but I want this finished. I'm telling the truth. I want to answer their questions."

"No, you don't," said Ernie Moran.

Kerrigan hung up the phone, never having taken his eyes off Nick. He clapped his hands unenthusiastically, and walked over to Nick and Moran.

"Cuppy, cuppy, cuppy," said Kerrigan, his mouth tight. "We ran a check on Jeffrey White's insurance. Standard procedure. You wanna maybe go back inside?" he asked, nodding toward the room they'd just left.

"We're all friends here," said Nick. "What is it?"

"Jeffrey White was heavily insured. Heavily. I mean, we're talking *heavily* insured. Metropolitan Life. Coupla million. And get this—he just adjusted his policy ten days ago. Changed his beneficiary. Can you believe that?" Nobody answered. "Ten days ago. So—guess who the new beneficiary is." No one spoke. "Lemme give you a hint. It's not his wife. It's not his kids. It's not his parents. Nope. Nosiree. Give up? Okay: Everybody in this room who is *not* Jeffrey White's beneficiary, take one step forward. Not so fast, Miss Stallings."

"What the hell . . ." said Ernie Moran.

"Old joke. Bad joke," said Kerrigan. "I apologize." He took a short breath. "It's you, Miss Stallings. You're the beneficiary."

Nick went to the bench and sat down near Joanne.

"Miss Stallings," Kerrigan continued, "the policy was signed ten days ago."

"That's . . . impossible," said Nick, taking Joanne's hand. "I didn't know Jeffrey White ten days ago."

"Or last summer, I suppose," said Kerrigan.

"If I wanted to kill Jeffrey White—" said Nick. She was cut off by Moran.

"You're tired, Miss Stallings, let's get out of here."

"If I wanted to kill someone for the insurance, Detective, would I do it in my own apartment?"

"I don't know, Miss Stallings," said Kerrigan. "Would you?"

Nick started to laugh. "No matter what I say, it sounds wrong. I'm too tired to think." Ernie Moran started to say something, but Kerrigan spoke first.

"Why'd you leave your apartment after he died, Miss Stallings?" he said, pressing.

"That's all for today, guys," said Ernie Moran. "I mean it. Come on, Miss Stallings."

"Are you saying I killed him for the insurance and left him dead in my own apartment?" Nick said, her voice rising a little. Joanne squeezed her hand, and Nick shook it away.

"Maybe something went wrong," said Kerrigan, looking at her hard. "Maybe you two had a fight, maybe you panicked. Maybe you had a whole plan and it blew up. Maybe you left the scene in order to buy time and make up a good story."

"Miss Stallings," said Ernie Moran angrily. "Do *not* engage in this."

"You don't strike me as a stupid woman, Miss Stallings," said Kerrigan. "We found this bracelet. Okay? And I'm, shall we say, *troubled* that this policy was dated ten days ago. 'Cause you've been saying all along that you just met this guy. I would have to be retarded not to wonder if maybe you're not being entirely truthful with us. Which makes me rethink everything, Miss Stallings. The bruise, everything. Because that's my job."

Nick felt as though she were falling. She spoke very evenly to compensate. "I met him Thursday night—three days ago."

Ernie Moran spoke up. "You just heard about this policy over the telephone. With all due respect, when you get a copy of the policy itself, and not just some report *about* this alleged policy, then we'll all talk."

"Ern," said Kerrigan with nonchalance, "I do believe you're stalling."

"My client swears that she met the deceased on Thursday night."

"She's not under oath," said Kerrigan.

"Fuck you," said Nick simply. Kerrigan and Whelan looked stunned, as though no woman had ever before said such a thing in their presence. "How dare you imply that I'm lying?"

"Oh. I beg your pardon," said Kerrigan, teeth clenched.

"Okay," said Ernie Moran, "we can discuss this, say tomorrow, after she's had some rest and you've substantiated these reports with some hard evidence."

"I met Jeffrey White three days ago—not even three full days," said Nick a little too loudly. "That's all there is to it."

"Except," said Kerrigan, reading from the bracelet, *"we'll always have last summer.* And I gotta tell you, this insurance thing is from a very reliable source."

"Your disrespect is beneath contempt, Detective," said Ernie Moran, who seemed less and less to Nick like a wizard. "Come on, Miss Stallings. Joanne . . ."

"Wait a second, please," said Kerrigan. "I need the names of your friends."

"Joanne and Francis Triziani," said Joanne, who then spelled *Triziani* proudly.

"You already have their phone number," said Nick. "It's where I was last night." Whelan made a note.

"You better use the back door again," grumbled Kerrigan. "Just in case Connie Whatsit and her pals are outside." He led them a few feet in the direction of the stairway. Nick stopped and turned to Kerrigan.

"Please excuse me," said Nick. "This has been . . . very hard."

"I understand," said Kerrigan unconvincingly.

As they went down the back stairs, Nick heard Kerrigan say to Whelan, "Cuppy, Joey. Motherfucking, dick-licking cuppy." When they were out of earshot, near the bottom of the stairs, Ernie Moran stopped and looked at Nick.

"From now on, when I ask you to be quiet, you damn well be quiet. Or get yourself another lawyer."

"Hey, hey, hey. Come on, you two," said Joanne.

"In a courtroom," continued Ernie Moran, "they can make you look like shit for having sworn at them like that."

"Oh, that's very comforting," said Nick, "talking about a court-room. Are you saying that's even possible?"

"Did you know Jeffrey White last summer?" asked Moran.

"Fuck you too," said Nick, and she pushed the door open. She took two steps and was stopped by a bright light across her face and the flashing of cameras. The flashbulbs blinded her momentarily, but she heard voices, men's and women's, overlapping.

★   ★   ★   ★

"Miss Stallings! Look this way, please . . ."

"Nicolette! Why are you here today . . . ?"

"Did you kill Jeffrey White . . . ?"

"Keep moving," said Ernie Moran. Nick squinted and was able to make out the forms of at least two photographers and a video crew. The video camera said ACTION NEWS on it, and was following them.

"Frankie's waiting on Third Avenue," said Joanne. "Just keep going, Susan."

"Why did you call her Susan, miss?" said Connie Cuevas, now emerging from behind the video camera. "Isn't her name Nico-lette?"

"My friends call me Susan," said Nick, on the move, attempting to put it to rest and give them something harmless.

"Miss Stallings, what did the police ask you?" said a morose-looking young guy in black with extremely short hair and tiny, puffy eyes. He moved the stub of a pencil across a little pad as he walked backward, scribbling Nick's last answer, poised for more.

Ernie Moran stopped. He did it so suddenly that without thinking Nick and Joanne stopped with him. He straightened his do-rag and raised his hand. There were two photographers, two reporters, and the camera crew of three. They had seemed to Nick like a crowd of fifty. Moran put his arm around her.

"We're just here to answer a few routine questions and cooperate in any way we can with the police. There've been no charges or allegations."

"It's my understanding," said Connie Cuevas, "that the medical examiner did *not* make a ruling of suicide. Does that mean that you're a suspect, Miss Stallings?"

Now that she was being fed to the lions, Nick let Ernie Moran talk. "No one is a suspect, Connie," said Moran as though they were old friends. "Miss Stallings came in of her own accord today to help in any way she could. The police just had a couple of questions. She's very tired. She's very upset. I'm sure you understand." He edged Nick and Joanne along the sidewalk. Nick could see Frankie waiting by his car at the corner.

"Miss Stallings," said Connie Cuevas, following closely, "do *you* have anything to say?" Nick started to open her mouth, but Joanne dug her nails into Nick's palm and looked at her with a poker face as though to say *Shut up.*

Nick, furious at the police, who, she figured, must have tipped off somebody about the back door, had a reckless desire to vent her anger. But she kept walking. They reached the corner. Frankie had the back door open. Ernie Moran said quietly to Nick, "I'm coming with you." Nick didn't protest. The reporters kept shouting the same questions and taking pictures. Joanne got in first, Ernie Moran held the door for Nick, and Joanne reached out to pull her in. Just as she was about to disappear into the relative sanctuary of the back seat, she stopped and turned to Connie Cuevas's camera.

"Mrs. White?" said Nick, looking directly into the camera's lens, "Mrs. White—I'm sorry."

Ernie Moran looked startled, shoved Nick inside, threw himself in, and slammed the door. Frankie was already in the front seat, and he gunned up Third Avenue. Unfortunately, the Action News van was ready, and Nick turned her head to see Connie Cuevas and her little crew pile in. Just as Frankie approached the first corner, the light turned red.

"Run it, Frankie," yelled Joanne. "Run the motherfucker!"

"No, don't!" said Ernie Moran. "There's a police car on the corner." They watched helplessly as the Action News van pulled right behind them.

"Maybe I should just get out and ride with them," said Nick.

"I wish you hadn't said that, Miss Stallings," said Ernie Moran.

"I was kidding," said Nick flatly.

"I meant your little . . . apology to Jeffrey White's widow," said Moran. "What was that?"

"I wanted to talk to her. I figured I might never get the chance again," said Nick.

"Did it occur to you that it might possibly have sounded like a confession?"

"No," said Nick angrily. "I figured I might as well use the goddamn cameras to say something I wanted to say."

"I just don't think you're going to like how it plays on the news, Miss Stallings," said Ernie Moran.

The light had changed and they were headed up Third Avenue, the van a discreet distance behind.

"Where to?" said Frankie. "You want me to lose 'em? I don't see no cops right now."

"Can you do it without breaking the law?" asked Nick. "I don't think I want to get stopped by the police."

"We have to go to Ninetieth and Park," said Ernie Moran. "Dr. Klein."

"Why? I don't need a doctor," said Nick.

"It's essential that I take you to Dr. Klein," said Moran. "He can establish that you've been under a lot of stress, maybe even a delayed kind of shock, and that might help explain things like swearing at police, and so forth." Nick started to protest. "Trust me, Miss Stallings. It's very important. Please do this for me. It won't take long."

"He works on Sunday?" asked Nick.

"He'll be there," said Ernie Moran. "He's a friend."

"Sounds like a good idea, Susan," said Joanne. Frankie looked at Nick in the rearview for an okay, and she nodded to him. He took a sudden left on Eighty-third Street, but Action News reacted quickly and the van was right with them. Frankie zigzagged his way across to Park Avenue, making sudden last-minute turns, but the van driver was equally expert. As they pulled up to the address on Park, Action News rolled in behind.

"Come on! Come on!" urged Ernie Moran, "Before they get out! Wait for us," he said to Frankie as he pulled Nick out and shoved her across the sidewalk and into an entryway with a polished brass sign reading STEVEN J. KLEIN, M.D. They were buzzed in, and Ernie Moran shouted to a receptionist, "Don't let anybody else in!" The receptionist, a heavyset woman in her fifties seated at a computer surrounded by manuals and just-opened boxes, looked bewildered. But when the buzzer sounded again almost immediately, she ignored it.

"Sorry, Bev," said Ernie Moran. "I'll explain later."

"Is that you, Mr. Moran? I didn't recognize you. Dr. Klein is waiting."

"He's waiting?" said Nick. "How did he know we were coming?"

"I called on my way over to meet you," said Ernie Moran. "Look. It's very important. Just in case."

"You had no idea if I needed a doctor or not."

"I saw you on the news. I figured it couldn't hurt. Really, Miss Stallings. It's for your own protection. Let me do my job. I've done this before."

The door buzzed again. Ignoring it, Bev handed Nick a clipboard with a lengthy form on it. "Fill this out," she said. Nick somewhat absently wrote her name and phone number.

"We're in kind of a hurry, Bev," said Ernie Moran. "She can do this later. And sorry to bring you in on a Sunday."

"I had to come in anyway," said Bev. "New computers. Sunday's the only day I can learn the goddamn software." She looked at Nick and said, "Come with me." She led Nick down and around an L-shaped hallway and into an examining room. It had a small sink, a cushioned examining bed with paper covering it, and a window with wooden venetian blinds offering a slatted glimpse of an un-healthy-looking tree out on Ninetieth Street.

"Dr. Klein," called Bev, "patient is ready in 2." Nick sat on an aluminum rolling stool and almost immediately Steven Klein walked in. He was tall, and younger than Nick expected. He had scruffy, receding reddish hair, steel-rimmed glasses, and a slightly apologetic air. Nick realized that she'd expected a rubber-stamp patsy in the twilight of a long, tired practice, who would give any diagnosis Ernie Moran might request.

"Hi," he said cheerfully.

"Hi," said Nick.

"You're, uh, sitting in my seat," he said. Nick started to stand up. "No, no. That's okay. You look . . . better than I do in it." Nick found herself involuntarily glancing at the ring finger on his left hand. It was empty.

"Well," he said. "I guess you've been through quite an ordeal."

"You could say that."

"I'm just gonna have a quick look, make sure everything's okay, and we'll have you out of here. I'll give you a minute, if you don't mind changing down to your underwear. There's a gown on the back of the door. You can hang your stuff on the hanger.

To her astonishment, the junkie in Nick lurched uncontrollably to life. As always in sensing a chance for a fix, the urge had no respect for the inappropriateness of the moment. As Dr. Klein turned to go out the door, Nick suddenly spoke, arresting his exit. "I think I'm okay," she said, lifting the muslin dress over her head. "Except for a killer headache—right here." Indicating her temple with one hand, she tossed the dress on the stool with the other. She was now in her slip. The doctor turned to look.

Stop. Stop.

"Do you think you could give me something for that?" she asked.

"Uh . . . sure," he said, turning away suddenly and leaving. "I'll . . . be right back."

She quickly kicked off her sneakers, removed her slip, bra, socks, and underpants, and took the hospital gown off the hook. Partly excited, partly disgusted, she couldn't control her longing to toss the gown to the floor and greet Dr. Klein nude when he returned. The sheer pleasure derived would surely blot out all her anxieties. As always when she was in the thrall of a potential fix, she couldn't reason it through. She tried to remind herself of the situation she was in. Her junkie whispered back that it would feel wonderful, it was okay, this was a nice doctor who would never tell anyone. Her junkie spoke not with words but rather stirrings at the base of her spine that promised the familiar high of highs.

He rapped at the door. She found herself tying the gown in back. She sat, crossed her legs, and said, "Come in." He opened the door a little and poked his head through, as though to be sure he wasn't intruding.

"All set?" he asked a little nervously.

"All set," she said.

He put his clipboard down near the sink and washed his hands. "How's the headache?"

"A little better, actually," she said, surprised.

"Ernie felt that you might be still suffering from shock."

"Did he?" said Nick flatly.

"It wouldn't be unusual. You've been through something pretty traumatic, and—"

"Did he tell you?"

"Just that you'd witnessed a . . . uh, suicide."

"Yeah," she said, not wanting to take it further.

"I'm sorry. Well, let's make sure your ticker is okay," he said as he put on his stethoscope. He placed it an inch above her heart. As he moved it from spot to spot, Nick could tell that he was being careful not to touch her breasts.

When he put the stethoscope to her back, she reached around and untied the tie string. The gown opened just a little.

Junkie behavior . . .

He turned away for something, put down the stethoscope, and picked out a tongue depressor from a mug filled with them.

Seemingly absorbed, he asked her to say "ahh." She stuck out her tongue. He peered down her throat, then picked up a black flashlight for examining nose and ears, turning again to her. This time their eyes met. He shifted his weight and lifted the instrument to her face.

"Look left," he said, shining it into her left eye. "Now to the right." Nick admired his simple, fierce concentration. He moved the light onto her right eye. "Okay." He put down the light. "I'm just going to take your blood pressure, and that'll be it." He applied the blood pressure cuff, pumped it up, and took a reading.

"You obviously exercise," he said. "Your blood pressure's terrific." She smiled. It was her last chance to let the gown drop.

Go ahead.

It would be so easy.

You'll never see him again. . . .

He pushed away the blood pressure device, stood, and took up the clipboard. "All the measurable things look . . . fine," he said, blushing a little. "If you don't mind my saying so though, you seem a little jumpy—which is totally understandable. I can give you something that'll help you sleep. You think you might need something tonight?"

"I'll just tough it out," said Nick, amazed to notice that her headache had stopped.

"Well," he said, taking a card out of his pocket. "I'm on rounds tonight at the hospital, so I'm not that hard to reach. Call me if you need anything." She rose, facing him, the gown open in back.

"That's very kind," said Nick, taking the card. She flashed on the last calling card that had been offered to her—Jeffrey White's, in the restaurant not three full days ago.

She did not let her gown drop.

"Thanks," she said simply.

"No trouble. No trouble at all," he said, starting out the door. He stopped and turned to her awkwardly—"Uhh. Nice meeting you" —and then was out the door. She stood for a few seconds, digesting what had just happened.

All I did was behave like a normal human being.

Not much of a victory, she thought.

If that was the right thing to do, why doesn't it feel better?

She let the gown slip off, started putting on the borrowed underwear, then, remembering that her interviews were finished, she stuffed the bra, slip, and underpants into her purse and reached for the dress. As she raised it over her head, she heard a muffled clicking sound. The sound was familiar, but she couldn't put her finger on it. She turned around, her dress still over her head. There, between the slats of the venetian blinds, Nick saw the lens of a camera, behind which the guy in black was snapping away, his motor drive whirring. She stood frozen for an instant, then reached for the venetian blind cord and pulled it hard. Instead of dropping, the blinds rose halfway up. She sank to her knees to cover herself, yanking the cord the other way. The blinds fell with a lopsided clatter, and she reached over and grabbed the cord on the other side of the window, snapping the shades shut.

Squatting on the pasty-cool linoleum, she felt herself come apart. She opened her mouth to scream, but nothing came out. She pulled on the dress and her sneakers, grabbed her bag, and flew out of the room, leaving Joanne's socks behind. She ran the wrong way down the maze of Dr. Klein's inner office. Yanking open a door, she found it full of medical supplies. She yanked another which opened into a tiny bathroom. She pivoted and changed direction. Rounding a corner, she heard the voice of Ernie Moran conferring with Dr. Klein. They stopped and turned as they heard her approach.

She picked up speed and moved past them without a word, pushing through the doors and out onto the street. Connie Cuevas was still there, but her crew wasn't quite ready. Nick saw the sound guy spring to life, reaching for his equipment, while the cameraman hurriedly slung his camera over his shoulder and groped its buttons while keeping one eye on Nick. Nick, seething, looked at Connie Cuevas and, realizing she had a few seconds before the camera would be on, demanded, "Where is he? *Where is he?*"

"Who?" asked Connie Cuevas, seemingly in the dark.

"That guy with the camera. Did you give him a goddamn ride over here?" Connie Cuevas did not reply. Nick looked in one direction, and then the other, trying to figure which way to turn to find the man in black. She started to head in what she thought was the right direction, when she saw him turn the corner, moving toward her and looking down at his camera as he wound down a roll of film. She ran up to him. Connie Cuevas silently signaled her crew to follow. Before he looked up, Nick grabbed for his camera.

"Hey!" said the photographer, unprepared to meet his subject. "What the fuck?" Nick got her hand on the camera, but it was held by a strap around his neck. She jerked and tugged on it, almost pulling him down to the street.

"Son of a bitch!" Nick screamed, losing it. The lanky reporter, apparently not too strong and having been taken by surprise, had his hands full. "Son of a bitch! Son of a bitch!" Nick repeated. The doors to Dr. Klein's office were flung open, and Joanne ran out, followed closely by Ernie Moran. What they saw was the Action News team shooting something akin to a school-yard brawl.

"Give me that!" Nick went on in a tug-of-war with the camera.

"First Amendment! First Amendment!" the reporter shot back, playing for the news crew. "I'm a journalist covering a story!"

"You gutless little slime!" said Nick as they wrestled awkwardly down to the pavement. "A real journalist would spit on you." Joanne moved in a beeline to Nick, wresting the camera from what was left of the photographer's grip. She pulled the strap over his head while Nick engaged his arms.

Ernie Moran moved in to break them apart. Seeing that Nick was safe, he turned around to the news crew and held up his hand, imploring Connie Cuevas to stop shooting. When she didn't, he looked right at the camera and said, "This kind of so-called reporting demeans journalism and insults viewers. If you have any self-respect, Miss Cuevas, or any respect for privacy or decency, you'll turn off your camera." Nick glanced over and saw the cameraman look to Connie Cuevas for orders. She made a whirring motion with her finger to indicate that he should keep rolling. Ernie Moran moved to the camera and blocked it with his body, his do-rag flapping in the breeze. Joanne took that opportunity to elbow the man in black in the groin. As he rolled over in pain, Joanne helped Nick up and away from the reporter, who reached around and made one last futile stab for his camera.

In as even a tone as possible, Ernie Moran said to Nick, "Miss Stallings, Joanne—into the car!" Nick hadn't seen Frankie until now, but the Cadillac had just pulled up, and he emerged from the driver's side, ready for action.

"Cop made me move. I was double-parked," said Frankie breathlessly, moving toward them in confusion. "I had to circle the block."

Ernie Moran managed to keep his body in front of the video camera while the cameraman danced around, trying to clear his lens. "Into the car, everybody," said Ernie Moran, jerking his head at Frankie to get back in. Frankie, looking bewildered, nonetheless opened the rear door for them and ran back to the driver's side. Still blocking the lens of the Action News camera, Ernie Moran bought Nick and Joanne enough time for them to hurtle into the back seat, Joanne holding the camera she'd taken from the guy in black, who had recovered. Joanne looked up in time to lock her door as he reached for its handle. He pounded on the window.

"Thieves!" he shrieked. "Felons! That camera is private property!" He pounded on the window some more, while Frankie started to pull away slowly, so as not to run over him or knock him down. Ernie Moran was in the front seat now, and Connie Cuevas's camera had a clear shot of the proceedings. The reporter in black yelled, "You're obstructing the First Amendment!"

"Obstruct on this!" Joanne yelled back at him as she rolled down the window just enough to toss the now-opened and exposed roll of film at him as they picked up speed and moved away.

"Wait a minute," said Ernie Moran. "We can't take his camera. Stop the car, Frankie." Frankie jerked on the brakes and Ernie Moran quickly opened his door and delicately placed the camera on the pavement. "There you are," he called to the reporter, who was running toward them. "The First Amendment is safe again."

They sped away, leaving the reporter kneeling with his camera while Action News recorded their departure. This time the light at the nearest corner was green. Frankie picked up speed and they were out of sight before the news team could get back into their van. Joanne let out a whoop.

"Jesus," said Frankie with a grin. "I hope they got my good side. What the fuck was all that?"

"I don't think we're going to have much fun watching the news tonight, boys and girls," said Ernie Moran, wiping his forehead and the back of his bald pate with a pristine handkerchief.

"What was that sleazebucket doing?" asked Joanne.

Nick felt oddly calm. She was now fairly sure that she *was* in shock. "He was taking pictures through the window. Real *Penthouse* stuff."

"Son of a bitch," muttered Frankie.

"There are eight million stories in the Naked City," said Nick calmly, "and seven million of them are naked."

"Come again?" said Frankie.

"Thank you, my little SWAT team," said Nick, giving Joanne a pat on the knee. "There's a TV series in this, I just know there is."

Frankie kept turning corners quickly, making sure in his rearview mirror that he'd lost the news van.

"Where to?" he asked.

"May I please go home now?" Nick asked Ernie Moran. Then she corrected herself. "I don't mean 'home.' No. Home is where the police tape is. Home is where the blood is. How silly of me." She felt tears on her cheeks but didn't otherwise experience any of the convulsions of crying. "Or maybe," she said, wiping her eyes with her sleeve, "maybe I should just check into a hotel."

"Forget about it," said Joanne. "Take us home, Frankie. Where can we drop you, Ern?"

"Why don't you just leave me at the Bar Association," said Ernie Moran lightly, "and I'll drop off my license so they don't have to come after me and force it from me. Joanne," he said with a faint smile, "I think you and I are even in the favor department." Joanne nodded. "Take me to my office, please. Fifty-sixth and Park."

"You got it," said Frankie.

"Joanne, Frankie," said Ernie Moran, adopting a new tone, "did either of you see Jeffrey White jump out the window?"

"We were in the bedroom," said Frankie. He turned to Joanne. "You peeked a little. Did you see anything?"

"No," said Joanne. "I heard Susan scream, and that was it."

They rode for a moment in silence. "The man is dead, you know," said Ernie Moran. "We can't bring him back." More silence. "If one of you were to say you saw him jump . . ."

"Are you suggesting perjury, Ern?" said Joanne.

"You know me better than that, Joanne."

"No comment," said Joanne. They rode in silence, pulling up to Park Avenue and Fifty-sixth Street.

"Miss Stallings," said The Wizard. "We need to talk. How about coming up to the office for a few minutes?"

"Oh, God," said Nick. She looked to Joanne.

"Might be a good idea," said Joanne. "You two could use a little strategy."

"How long, Ern?" said Frankie.

"Half hour?" said Ernie Moran, looking to Nick. She nodded.

"We'll wait," said Frankie.

"Oh, no, you guys—go ahead," said Nick. "I've ruined your Sunday enough."

"We'll wait," said Joanne. She looked at Ernie Moran. "Thanks."

"Don't thank me yet," he said, holding the door open for Nick. The temperature had dropped a couple of degrees, and the wind was kicking up. "I'll have her down here in half an hour. You've had a long day, Miss Stallings."

Joanne reached out the window and took Nick's arm. "He's the best, Susan," she said. "Really."

"And congratulations, you two," said Ernie Moran. "It's about time."

"See ya, Ern," said Frankie, who did not seem to care much for The Wizard.

They dashed across the sidewalk and through heavy glass double doors.

★   ★   ★   ★

He signed them in at a security desk and led her to a bank of elevators.

"I like weekends," said Ernie Moran, as they rode to the fourteenth floor. "Quiet. Nobody here."

When the doors opened, a prominent brass sign proclaimed ER-NEST MORAN, ATTORNEY. The sign had an arrow directing them down a long hallway.

"You'll have to forgive me. Things are a bit of a mess." Everything looked quite orderly to Nick. Ernie Moran led her through a modest foyer, down a short corridor of four or five offices, each with secretarial cubicles, and finally into his. Another, smaller brass sign on the door read MR. MORAN. The brass, thin with a florid engraving, didn't quite accomplish what Nick felt was the desired effect of old-world respectability, but there was nothing tacky about the place, which was a relief.

His office was neither showy-large nor small. There were two leather couches in the corner, and a matching chair. There were phones everywhere: three on an imposing classic desk, the leather top of which almost complemented the couches, and Oriental rugs over worn, but clean, wall-to-wall carpet.

Nick found herself wondering about the color of her own carpeting at home.

Two undraped windows looked out onto Park Avenue, and there was a false fireplace in the center of the far wall, its mantel cluttered with papers and books. He reached into a desk drawer, pulled out a small, ancient black transistor radio, and flipped it on. An announcer was yelling at the top of his lungs, "That has to be the most exciting quarter of basketball the Knicks have put together this season! I don't believe it! I do not *believe* it! Wow!" With a sigh, Ernie Moran turned it off and put it back in the drawer.

"Sorry," said Nick.

"It's a kind of punishment," he said wearily. "They only play well when I'm not there."

Behind his desk were several diplomas. Nick tried not to be too obvious about checking the Wizard's college credentials. He had apparently been both an undergraduate and law student at the University of Mississippi. Nick remembered from her football-watching days with Hal that its teams were called the Rebels. She would have preferred Harvard or Yale.

"Can I take your coat?" The office, like all of New York City in the winter, was overheated, and Nick gladly surrendered the coat. She felt his eyes on her. Was he checking her out?

Irrelevant.

"Sit down," he said. Nick sat on one of the little couches, and Ernie Moran took the leather chair opposite her. He picked up a legal pad.

"How do you usually dress?"

"Depends on the occasion," said Nick archly, wondering why he'd asked.

"I'm not kidding. I want to suggest that you dress . . . down, as it were, for the immediate future. There'll be a lot of attention focused on you. So—no short dresses or skirts, nothing that could be construed as sexy or suggestive." It sounded like an order.

"I'll have to borrow some clothes, I guess," she said, a little irritated. He smiled, but the tightness in his face betrayed disapproval.

He thinks I'm attractive.

Shut up.

"I need to ask you a few questions, Miss Stallings."

"Call me Nick."

"Not . . . Susan?" he asked.

"Come to think of it, call me Miss Stallings," she said curtly. She saw a look of annoyance cross his face, but he squelched it as quickly as it had come.

She was finding that she couldn't get comfortable.

"Do you smoke?" she asked.

"I . . . gave it up recently," he said, making a note on the pad. "Sorry. I more or less banished cigarettes from this place."

"Just as well," said Nick. She tried to see what he was writing.

His eyes on the pad, he went on. "It's, ah, too bad you're the only one who saw Jeffrey White jump out that window."

"Why?" asked Nick, standing and moving to the window, then facing him. "Do you think I pushed him?" He didn't answer.

He hasn't ruled out the possibility.

He spoke carefully. "It would just make his eventual suicide more plausible if someone other than you had seen him jump."

"So you think I might be a liar?" she asked, cocking an eyebrow. "Is that it?"

"I was simply making an observation."

"Were you and Joanne lovers, Mr. Moran?"

"Miss Stallings. We're talking about you."

"I know, I know." She craved nicotine. Her cells were screaming for it. "You'll have to forgive me, Mr. Moran, but I don't know anything about you, and I'm sort of placing my life in your hands, so to speak."

"I'm doing my best, Miss Stallings."

"Thank you. I'm sorry," she said, turning away from him because she didn't want him to see whatever it was that was suddenly bringing tears to her eyes. The tears had taken her by surprise. She didn't know what they were for, specifically.

"Pay no attention to me," she said. "These are just . . . general tears." She felt her shoulders heave a little despite her best efforts to keep them still.

Then there was a Kleenex next to her face, offered by Ernie Moran, who was suddenly next to her.

"You've never been in legal trouble before, have you, Miss Stallings?" There was no emotion in his voice. She wasn't sure if it infuriated or calmed her.

She took the tissue. They stood, side by side in front of the window, looking out at mostly unlit office buildings under the increasingly murky sky.

He pressed on. "Do you have anything in your past that the press could embarrass you with?"

Oh, Jesus . . .

"Like what?"

"You're an actress. They're already trying to paint you as dangerous and sexy—it keeps their story going. They'll do their best to make you look irresponsible and—" He stopped.

"And what?" she said, almost daring him.

"Just . . . let's face it . . . you're very attractive, Miss Stallings."

"Okay. Now we've said that." She moved back to what had been his chair and sat.

"I wasn't trying to—"

Her eyes scanned the room. "Do you have anything to drink, Mr. Moran?"

"Uh—let's see," he said, caught off guard. "There's some scotch."

"Scotch?" she repeated, as though it reminded her of a trip to the dentist.

"It's single malt, if that helps. I don't drink anymore, but I keep some around." As though it were an unwelcome interruption, he moved across the room and opened a closet, pulling a dusty bottle from a shelf crowded with overstuffed folders. "Glenfiddich?" he offered, holding it out to her. "Pretty decent stuff."

Not such a great idea.

"Just a little to steady my nerves, thanks," she said. She was trying to like him, trying to get comfortable in some way, trying, as she had been since yesterday, to bring herself to a semblance of solid ground. He went out to the hallway for a few seconds, returning almost immediately with a cone-shaped paper cup. He poured some scotch and held it out to her.

"Sorry there's no ice," he said. She took it from him.

Maybe not such a great idea . . .

She drained it, trying not to breathe through her nose to avoid the aroma, and handed it back to him, empty. "Thanks," she said, not sure she meant it. He crumpled the cup and tossed it basketball-style toward a faraway oval wastebasket. He missed. Nick, with a shudder from the sudden and surprisingly pleasant taste of the scotch, couldn't help thinking that his missed shot was a bad omen. She looked up at the ceiling. "If the press starts poking around in my life, there are a lot of things, plenty of things, they could run with."

He moved back and sat on the couch. "Like what?" he asked.

"Shouldn't we be talking about how to defend me?"

"We are."

"Oh, good," she said, mock-relieved. "So it's okay to tell you about my sex life. I mean, you won't take it, you know, personally?" She slipped out of one of her sneakers, which had been working up a blister on her heel.

"Miss Stallings, I know you may find this difficult to believe, but

I'm trying to help you." He reached over to pick up his pad. At the same time, she put her shoeless foot up on the table and brushed his hand with it. It was an accident, but she was taken aback by the jolt she felt from it. He caught her eye for a split second before slowly taking the pad and moving back into his seat.

The scotch was landing.

"Maybe you should talk to my shrink," said Nick. "The police did. She knows a lot of good stuff. The kind of stuff the papers would love."

He stared at her.

"What are you trying to do, Miss Stallings?"

"Me? I'm answering your questions, Mr. Moran," she said right back at him, "and my foot seemed to graze your hand. Why? Have we . . . violated lawyer-client decorum?" He didn't answer. "You want me to talk about sex? Is that why you brought me up here?"

"Is that what you think, Miss Stallings?" Nick thought he seemed aggressively polite, like an over-earnest psychiatrist. It irked her.

"Because now that this whole case *isn't* wrapped up," she went on, trying to keep her voice from rising, "there's no reason why I can't just meet with one of those other lawyers first thing in the morning, and then you'd be off the hook."

"Suits me, Miss Stallings," he said, tapping his fingers on the arm of the chair.

He doesn't trust me. He doesn't like me.

There was a buzz arriving from the scotch. Far from delivering the hoped-for mood-enhancement, the booze was shoring up the edgy feeling that perhaps she *should* find another lawyer. She glanced at his clock, digging both sets of fingernails into the fleshy part of her thumbs.

"Joanne and Frankie are expecting me in sixteen minutes."

"It's actually more like twenty. I set all my clocks a few minutes ahead."

"Well," she said, looking around the room, "how do you suggest we pass the time?"

"What do you *want,* Miss Stallings?" he said sharply, giving up any pretense of patience.

"What do I want?" She turned, as though addressing a small, imaginary crowd. "He asks me what I want." She faced him again, struggling for composure. "I want someone, Mr. Moran, to get me out of this! Can you do it?"

"I don't know," he said evenly. "You haven't told me enough yet."

"Because if you can't, and there's nothing I can do about this until tomorrow—well, in that case I'd like to—"

Every single item in the room felt suddenly familiar to her. The impression hung there, suspended for a few seconds, as her senses observed everything—the light, the dust, the smoky tendrils of scotch invading her sinuses, the narrowed eyebrows of Ernie Moran —all precisely as if she had experienced them that way once before.

"Do you have any water?" she asked suddenly. She knew she was stalling, looking for terra firma. Then she laughed.

"Is something funny?" he asked, trying to stay with her.

"No, nothing," she said. "Just the idea that water might . . . ground me." He looked confused. "Get it?" she asked. "Water— ground?"

He shifted his weight. "Miss Stallings, we have work to do. I need some answers."

"Do you have any water?" she repeated, annoyed at his impatience.

"Sorry," he said. "Someone forgot to put a new bottle in the cooler. I could give you some out of the tap. . . ."

"Ughh," said Nick with a shudder. "New York used to have such great water."

"I'd like to go on now," he said, ultra-calm, as if speaking to an overexcited six-year-old. "Okay?"

"Okay?" she repeated, imitating him. "Okay, okay, okay—God, you're patronizing!"

"Well," he said, "you make it so easy, Miss Stallings."

"Fuck you."

"Oh, Christ, no," said Ernie Moran, standing and almost shouting, "fuck *you*. Fuck you, Miss Stallings, and the horse you rode in on. I mean, what the fuck do you want? Water, scotch, hand-holding, bullshit, what?"

"*This* is what I want," said Nick. She stood up and pulled Joanne's dress over her head and let it drop to the floor. "If you talk to my shrink, you'll find out that I'm a junkie. That's what she says." She was naked except for her other sneaker. "And my junk is . . . this. This is what I like to do, Mr. Moran," she declared. She looked from his eyes down to her one sneakered foot. "Although I would like to point out, for the record, that I am *partially* dressed."

He looked away, as if he'd had a delayed reaction to the fact that she was nude.

"I think, Mr. Moran, that this may be what people of the medical persuasion refer to as a nervous breakdown. Do you think that's possible?" Another tear ran down her face and onto her shoulder. "By the way," she said with a sudden ferocity, "I don't want to have sex with you. I just want to . . . get . . . comfortable. Okay?"

He seemed to Nick like a coach in a Super Bowl she had watched with Hal. He moved back and forth, as if on the sidelines, considering all the possibilities. He started to walk out of the office. Then, perhaps thinking better of leaving a naked woman there, he stopped and closed the door. He stood with his back to Nick.

She looked down at herself. "I guess I should get dressed. Yes?"

"Unquestionably, Miss Stallings."

"As my attorney, what do you advise?" she asked, deadpan. She felt ridiculous yet almost comfortable.

"*Am* I your attorney?"

"Do you want the job? Or is this just an errand of mercy for Joanne?"

He put his head in his hands for a minute, then turned and looked right at her. He wasn't gawking, but he wasn't avoiding her either.

"I've had a lot of conflicts of interest in my time, Miss Stallings.

I've defended a lot of people who . . . let's just say I've had to ask myself from time to time if I was doing the right thing. Somebody's got to defend them, so I figured it might as well be me. But this is . . . I mean, if you're having a breakdown, I should be getting you to a doctor."

"But if I'm *not* having a breakdown," said Nick, "then maybe I'm enjoying this."

"Are you?"

"Oh, God, I don't know. Are *you*?"

"That's not really important. Though I must say, Miss Stallings, I doubt that any man alive would complain."

"Are you married?" she asked, as if merely curious.

"Long divorced."

"Good. Good," she said, "I couldn't stand the stress of any more adultery. Is this adultery? Never mind. I don't know. Is our time up, Mr. Moran? I mean, we wouldn't want Joanne and Frankie to come looking for me, would we?"

"Appearances to the contrary, I don't think I've done anything unseemly."

"Unseemly." She almost smiled. "Do people talk like that at Ole Miss?"

"We've got nine minutes now, Miss Stallings," he said with a glance at the clock, "before Joanne and Frankie are expecting you." She looked away from him and out the window. "You really should get dressed."

"Okay, okay," she said, moving toward the dress, picking it up and holding it loosely against herself. "This . . . thing on my thigh," she added, looking down at her leg almost matter-of-factly, "is where Jeffrey White burned me with his cigarette while we were having sex." He didn't respond. "Just want to make sure you know everything, Mr. Moran. Let's see. I had sex with three men that night. The burn hurts a lot now, but at the time it actually felt good. What else, what else . . ." More tears came. She dabbed at her face with the now-wadded tissue and looked at him.

"Are you . . . very ill, Mr. Moran?"

"You could say that."

"Are you in pain?"

"No more, I'm sure, than you."

"I can't figure out where I hurt. What about you? Where do you hurt?"

He pointed to his head. "It's the radiation, actually," he said. "It didn't hurt that much before."

She walked behind the couch and slid the do-rag off his head. She leaned over him from behind, her breasts lightly grazing his shoulders, and gently kissed the top of his bald head.

"This isn't sex, Mr. Moran."

"Ah," he said, nodding. "Thanks for telling me."

He untied the little knot on his do-rag, replaced it around his head, and re-tied it quickly.

"I guess if you're getting dressed, I should too," she said. She sighed and pulled the dress back on.

He stood up, averting his eyes. "You're an actress," he said. "You know the secret of comedy?" Nick started to say "what," but before the word was out of her mouth, he interrupted loudly, "Timing!"

She didn't laugh.

"Sorry," he said, shaking his head at himself. "Lousy joke."

"No," she assured him thoughtfully, pulling the other sneaker back on, "it's funny." She faced him. "It's just that my laughing muscles aren't working."

Now that she was dressed, he stared at her unabashedly for a few seconds. "A couple of months ago," he said, "this little episode would have made me throw caution and professional ethics to the wind. But I don't have a whole lot of sex drive these days. Which is ironic, since my wife divorced me for sleeping around. So, once and for all: Do you want me to represent you?"

Nick, who hadn't felt embarrassed when she was naked, now felt ashamed. "You mean I haven't completely discredited myself?"

"I like a good challenge, Miss Stallings, and this one looks about as good as they get. I certainly don't think I'll be bored. So—I'll work with you. But you'd better keep your clothes on, at least around me, because I might just get my sex drive back, and then God knows where we'll be."

"Are you dying?"

He fixed her with his eyes. "Have you ever seen that bracelet before?"

"No."

"Any idea how it got in your apartment?"

"No."

"Why did you leave your apartment after Jeffrey White's death?"

"Because I have lousy instincts. I was afraid if the cops came, it would look like maybe I *had* done it."

"You didn't stop to think how it would look if you *didn't* call the police?"

"He went to a lot of trouble to make it look like I killed him." The tears came again, and she sank to the floor. "And I think he succeeded."

He stepped over and put a hand on her shoulder. She reached for it and pulled herself back up, rising into an awkward hug.

He moved his face closer to hers. Then closer. Their lips almost touched. They stood like that, not moving. She felt him stirring below the belt.

"Well, I'll be damned," he whispered.

"I'll probably be damned first," she said.

She felt his breath on her lips.

"Joanne and Frankie'll be waiting," he said finally, backing off a step.

"Yes," said Nick, hugely relieved. She wanted to look away, but couldn't.

"Please, please, please," said Ernie Moran quietly, "don't talk to the press if they find you. Promise me that. Not a word. Please."

"Didn't we just establish that I'm 'stressed out'?" asked Nick, suddenly irritated. "I mean, wasn't that the point of our little trip to the good doctor's office? Aren't all my sins forgiven because I'm so goddamned 'stressed out'?"

"I need you to be superhuman. You've got to be the picture of restraint, Miss Stallings. I can't represent you if you talk in front of cameras again like you did."

"So you *do* trust me," said Nick.

"Trust is a feeling," said Ernie Moran, "and I don't like to go on feelings. You never saw that bracelet before?"

"No."

"Is there any way the police could come up with an insurance policy that would show that you knew Jeffrey White ten days ago?"

"Impossible," said Nick.

"So you met Jeffrey White Thursday evening?"

"Yes."

"Good," said Ernie Moran, who didn't seem soothed. "What about your fee?"

"Joanne gave me a retainer check. In return for which, you have my presumption of innocence."

Nick shook her head quickly. "So, you have your check—and I'm innocent? Is that it, Mr. Moran?"

"Yeah," he said tiredly. "I also beat my wife and abuse helpless children."

She turned and started out. He grabbed her arm.

"So help me God, I'm going to make it over to the Garden for the fourth quarter—so just listen. Don't take any calls from the police or the press without talking to me. I'll be in touch as soon as I know anything. Don't watch the news tonight if you don't want to get depressed. Don't go out, or be seen in flashy, dressy clothes. Or out of them, God forbid. Get some rest. I don't think we'll hear anything till tomorrow. You sure you can't explain that bruise?"

"Sorry."

"I'm not a doctor, but I don't think you're having a nervous breakdown." He stared at her for a few seconds. "I can't say this hasn't been as interesting a half hour as I've ever spent, Miss Stallings.

If Joanne weren't your friend, I'd be off this case so fast it'd make your inscrutably attractive head spin. Here. Take my card." He handed her one. "You're more trouble than I can shake a stick at. Now, please get out of here."

She searched for words, found none, turned, and walked out. She made her way back down to the lobby, and sure enough, there was Frankie's car, idling at the curb. She got in.

"So?" said Joanne.

"I guess I have a lawyer."

"Ern," said Joanne with finality, as though putting a period at the end of a sentence. "I gotta tell you, Susan, he's the best."

"You ever hear of Dan Giometti?" said Frankie. "Danny the Hat, they called him?" Nick looked blank. "D.A. had an open and shut case. Ernie Moran got him off. My uncle told me. I don't think my uncle likes him, but he said he'd never seen a lawyer bop like that in court. Said he had to admire the guy."

"He used to have this wavy, thick black hair," said Joanne, a little lost in thought.

"Why does he owe you?" Nick asked as the car turned up Third Avenue.

"You don't wanna know," said Joanne.

"*I* sure as hell wanna know, O wife-of-mine," said Frankie, shooting Joanne a look in the rearview mirror which Nick caught.

"Probably the all-time-greatest blow job of this or any other century," said Joanne. Frankie jumped on the brakes, hurtling them all forward.

"Kidding!" said Joanne, laughing. Seeing the murderous look in Frankie's eye, she added, "Jesus. A little levity, for chrissakes."

"Don't fuck with me, Joanne," yelled Frankie. "We're married now. . . ."

"Sorry," said Joanne, meaning it. "I'm sorry, honey. Start the car again, please." Frankie turned the key in the ignition, but the engine was still running and made a horrible grinding sound. He threw the car into gear, and they continued up Third.

"I was a secretary at his firm," said Joanne. "There was . . . some trouble. I never knew who it was, but one of the partners—there's Ernie and two others—screwed up pretty royally on some billings. The only way they could save face with their clients and the IRS was for someone to have made a clerical mistake. They came to me. I said it was a computer thing, and everybody was more or less happy. Except somebody had to get fired, and that was me."

"Why didn't you ever tell me that?" said Frankie.

"Because I'm not proud of it, Mr. John Q. Inquisitor. But," said Joanne, pulling on Nick's arm a little, "he's good. I thought you needed somebody good."

"I did," said Nick. "I do."

"Did you ever make it with this guy?" asked Frankie, slamming on the brakes again.

"No," said Joanne, meeting Frankie's eyes in the mirror. "N-O."

Nick looked at Joanne. "So you quit his firm, and that was that?"

"There was a little cash," said Joanne. "Enough for a down payment on what is now our apartment."

"What are you sayin'?" asked Frankie unhappily. "I thought that was your money."

"It *was* my money," said Joanne. "I earned it."

Frankie swallowed. "You *Erned* it," he said quietly. "E-r-n-e-d."

"Yeah," said Joanne with a mirthless laugh. "I guess."

They pulled up to a light. Nick watched as Sunday strollers crossed in front of the car, their heads pushed down against gusts of wind from the quickly blackening sky. She saw the rest of this Sunday stretch out before her—one long, awkward wait at Joanne and Frankie's. She knew that Joanne's invitation to stay "forever" was from the heart, but she didn't think she could make it through the afternoon. Her apartment was still sealed off, a possible crime scene. The thought of facing her mother with all this was intolerable, and her father was stuck on St. Maarten in the aftermath of a hurricane which, by the look of the wind that was starting to hurl litter every which way, might, indeed, be on its way. She saw a cab just to her right, in the process of letting someone off. She spoke quickly to her new friends.

"I love you guys. You know that. I'm going to get in that cab now, Frankie. Please don't follow me—which I know you could if you wanted to."

"Susan," said Joanne, who looked stricken. "What—"

"I'm sorry. I'll call," said Nick, opening the door and getting out. "I'll call. I will."

"Susan!" Joanne shouted through the closed window. Nick turned as the window came down and Joanne pushed her raincoat out to Nick, who took it automatically, tossing her overcoat through the window. "Be careful, you," said Joanne. Frankie had a quizzical look on his face.

"I will. Thank you. Thank you." Nick slammed the door and ran toward the taxi, her head bowed against the gathering wind. A gust knocked her sideways, but she recovered in time to slap the side of the just-vacated cab before it set off down the street. Its brake lights went on, and Nick opened the door.

"Grand Central Station," she said.

CHAPTER 19

As she headed into the towering train station, the wind was blowing whole sections of the Sunday *Times* around the street like so much ticker tape. Nick pushed through the doors, down the ramp, and around to where she could see the big information board. She scanned DEPARTURES for the Croton local, the train she knew would take her to Hastings-on-Hudson, home of Jeffrey White. Having grown up in Dobbs Ferry, the stop after Hastings, she knew the route as well as she knew the Lord's Prayer. Her father, on his daily commute, had usually gotten off at Hastings, since that station was more convenient to their house than the one in Dobbs Ferry.

The next Croton local was leaving Track thirty-five at twenty minutes past the hour. She looked up at the huge clock on the wall. She had two minutes. Nick ran across the marble floor, through the gateway to Track thirty-five, sprinting toward the waiting train as the last conductor was getting ready to board.

"Hastings?" she gasped just to be sure.

"Hastings," he nodded, then called, "All aboard!"

She entered the crowded car and saw a spot on the side she knew would face the Hudson River. It sat three across, with a large, fat, friendly-looking Caribbean woman and a sleeping baby already settled in. A quick scan of the rest of the car revealed no other empty seats, so Nick joined them, careful not to disturb the baby. The woman gave her a look that made it clear she'd been hoping no one would sit there.

"Sorry," said Nick automatically, squeezing in as the train pulled out.

"Last time I looked, it was still a free country," said the lady matter-of-factly. Then she snorted, as if she doubted what she'd just said. Nick tried in vain to get comfortable. The lady's girth, together with her sleeping baby, took up more than two-thirds of the seat. Nick closed her eyes and let her head fall back. She knew she should think, plan, but wasn't sure she could resist the urge to sleep.

"Tickets, please," the piercing voice of a too-near conductor said. Nick, asleep perhaps three minutes, struggled back to consciousness, noticing a faraway ache that promised a migraine if she didn't get her eyes closed again soon. The conductor was looking at her with weary impatience. The woman with the baby shoved a ticket across Nick, who remembered that she had some cash for the first time in a couple of days.

"Round trip to Hastings," said Nick.

It's a small town. Jeffrey's number must be in the book. I'll take a cab.

"Ten dollars," said the man automatically, already punching tiny holes into innumerable copies of Nick's ticket. Nick handed over a twenty, and, as she took the change, the conductor plugged two receipt stubs into the slot above their seat, then moved on.

The train came above ground, and Nick, zombielike, eyes open, heart still racing, found curious comfort in the oft-seen view of the sorriest portions of Harlem and the no-longer-Grand Concourse. This had been her train ride home as a kid and teenager. In times past, this ride had always marked the end of a special journey: returning late on Christmas Eve after last-minute city shopping; necking with her senior year boyfriend on the way back from a Broadway show; riding home with Daddy after visiting him at the office. And now this. Derelict buildings swept by like once-familiar wallpaper. Her eyes fell shut, and she drifted back toward that nap.

"You on one of my stories?" the fat woman asked suddenly, as though Nick had been holding out on her. Nick's eyes shot open. Now the headache was palpable, hard behind her right eye.

"I'm sorry?" said Nick, the eye throbbing.

"Which one you on? You on one of 'em. Which one?"

"I'm not an actress," said Nick, closing her eyes too tightly. She felt a trace of self-loathing in noticing that she was trying to be polite.

"Well, then you got a double running around this city, if you ax me. You a dead ringer for that girl used to be on . . . what was it? *Eagle Squadron*. That's the one."

"Sorry," said Nick, trying to dismiss it.

"I always wanted to be an actress, but that *Eagle Squadron* bitch is one bitch I would not—repeat—would not—want to change places with. She in big trouble. You see the news last night? Oo-ee."

Nick was feeling increasingly narcoleptic. "Listen," she said, trying another tack, "could you wake me just before Hastings? I think I'm going to fall asleep now."

"Can't do that. Nope."

"Okay. Fine. Whatever," said Nick, eyes closed.

"We're gettin' off at Greystone, so we won't exactly be here when Hastings comes along." Greystone, Nick knew as well as she knew her name, was the stop before Hastings.

"Well, just wake me before you get off, okay?"

"Sleep, baby, sleep," said the woman, abruptly quiet. Nick wanted to thank her, but she was too busy dreaming.

Against harsh paisleys of blurry red and purple, Jeffrey White grinned at Nick. He laughed and laughed and laughed until she was wakened by a nudge from the woman. Simultaneously the conductor bellowed, "Greystone. This stop is Greystone. Hastings-on-the-Hudson next."

The woman and baby made their way into the aisle. She turned to Nick as they headed to the exit. "I was wrong. I been watching you. You don't look so much like her, Miss *Eagle Squadron*. She pretty. You pretty too, but she prettier. No offense, honey," she said, giggling as she walked away, lugging her still-sleeping child and battered stroller.

Nick looked out at the Hudson. The storm was huge, impressive. There were whitecaps, tall ones, everywhere, like surf. Fireworks of lightning erupted, revealing the Palisades in brief snapshots. It was raining hard.

Nick rose and moved steadily toward the door. She knew it was only about two miles to the Hastings station, and as she peered out the window at the approaching landmarks of the little village, passing the once-teeming Anaconda Wire and Cable plant, slowing as they breezed by Hastings's few semi-slums, she saw the tall wrought-iron gate that separates the tracks from the parking area where she and her mother had countless times waited for her father's nightly arrival from the city. As the storm threw solid masses of rain against the windows of the train, Nick couldn't help, on top of everything, feeling as though she were heading home.

★　　★　　★　　★

Stepping off the train, she found it was prematurely dark from the storm. Through the rain Nick, under a protective overhang, saw the rear lights of what looked like one of Hastings's run-down station wagon cabs, waiting to pick up the occasional passenger who disembarked unmet. The rain was relentless. There was no hope of even a short dash without getting soaked. The temperature, Nick thought, must be hovering just above freezing. She raced up the few steps to the parking lot, the icy drops slicing into her face, and knocked on the cab's window. Its driver rolled it down an inch or two with an impatient look.

"I'm going to need a ride," she shouted above the wind, "but I

have to look up the address. I'll be right back." The driver shrugged
and closed the window quickly. Nick ran back down the stairs under
the overhang, then up a long flight of steps to the locked station
house. A few feet away was a phone booth. Its sliding door, long
torn from its runners, was dangling open, slapping the sides of the
booth in the wind. Hanging below the phone was a tattered copy of
the Westchester directory, missing its cover and assorted pages. Nick
grabbed it. Much of Y and most of Z were missing, but W was
intact. She ran a cold, wet index finger down and up columns of
WHs until she came to the Whites. Sure enough, there was Jeffrey:
91 Scenic Drive.

She sprinted down the stairs and back to the parking lot and saw
the cab starting to pull away. She leapt out into the rain and whacked
it on its taillight, her feet submerged to the ankles in frigid, swirling
rainwater. The cab stopped and Nick got in, soaked.

"I told you I'd be right back," she said angrily.

"Hey, lady—I don't know you. How do I know you're coming
back?"

"I was gone maybe two minutes," said Nick. "You were gonna
leave me here?"

"Relax," said the driver with a dismissing wave. He hit the accelerator too hard, and the cab skidded and swerved as it climbed up
the steep hill toward the town. "Where to?"

"Ninety-one Scenic Drive," said Nick, running a hand through
her flattened wet hair. She looked out. Even with the blur of the rain
on the window, she could make out the library, police station, and
liquor store. There was the old movie theater, home of her first kiss
and now the miniest of mini-malls. They swept by the big Catholic
church and up another steep hill, moving along the same route she
once used to get home.

Exhausted, hungry, wet, and cold, Nick thought of turning
around and heading back to the city.

No.

The car slugged on through the storm, which, if anything, was gathering force. She saw a familiar sign at the bottom of another hill, proclaiming RIVERVIEW MANOR, the nicest part of town. As they headed up, a large tree branch fell into the street less than fifty feet in front of them. The driver swerved around it.

"Some fuckin' storm," he said. "Fuckin' hurricane. They name 'em after guys now, you believe it?"

"I believe everything," said Nick.

"Wish it'd stayed in the goddamn Caribbean. I hate that Caribbean. They can have their fuckin' hurricanes." Nick decided not to pursue this with him, but couldn't help wondering how her father was doing in St. Maarten.

The car plowed uphill, then turned left onto an unfamiliar street. Rivers of rainwater charged down the gutters, the drains already overchallenged by the storm. The cab took a right, then slowed almost immediately and pulled over.

"That'll be three-fifty," said the driver. Nick gave him four, opened the door, stepped out, and hopped immediately up onto the sidewalk to get her feet out of the water. The cab drove off, and Nick took a step toward the house, a gabled Tudor, its brick glistening from the rain. Joanne's coat, it turned out, wasn't terribly waterproof, and the cold had started to invade her body. She moved slowly up the short walk to the front door, her neck craned to get a better look at the people she could slightly make out through what was apparently the dining room window.

The drapes had been shut, but Nick was able to see through a space on one side where they failed to cover the opening. There were several people standing around with coffee cups or tumblers in their hands, looking uncomfortable, barely talking. Nick recognized Barbara, sitting with a drink, sifting through papers, while two children, a boy of perhaps twelve and a girl of roughly kindergarten age, sat listlessly pushing food around dinner plates. There were too many people in the room, as though no one wanted to be alone. Nick watched. A wet gust nearly knocked her over. The girl took a bite. The boy said something to Barbara, who seemed not to hear him.

Then she nudged her reading glasses up to her hairline, took a long sip from her drink, and nodded. An older woman came in, spoke with a strained smile, collected the plates, and went out. The children hardly moved.

Nick continued to the front door, searching for a doorbell. Not finding one, she grabbed the heavy horseshoe knocker, then lost her nerve and pulled her hand away. She stared at the door. The next thing she knew she was banging the knocker loudly. She stood up as straight as she could, almost at attention.

The door opened, and there was Jeffrey White's son, pale, slim, with sandy, short hair, in a rugby shirt and pressed khakis. He looked tired but alert.

Jeffrey's eyes.

A tall, thin man appeared with a weathered maroon crew-neck sweater over corduroys. "I'll do this, Devon," he said to the boy. "Your mother doesn't want you talking to people."

"Yes?" said the boy, ignoring him. He seemed confused that Nick hadn't yet spoken.

"I'd . . . like to speak to your mother," said Nick.

"This isn't a good time," said the man, impatient.

"I'm sorry," said Nick.

"Who may I say is calling?" the boy asked by rote.

Did he know the name of his father's nearly-alleged murderess? He didn't seem to recognize her, nor did the man. But they would have heard her name by now. She cleared her throat, stalling, studying the boy's face. The silence was broken by Barbara's voice, moving toward them from the dining room.

"Devon, I told you not to go to the door! Who is it?"

"I, uh, don't know, Mom."

"For God's sake, Bob. Can't anyone keep the children away from the *door*?" With that, Bob, whose patience had apparently been overtaxed today, muttered something and headed upstairs.

Barbara appeared. She looked almost exactly to Nick as she had at the restaurant less than three days ago. Tall, too thin, black hair, with

a beauty-contest face that was starting to tighten from a life of unexpressed feelings. Her features were brittle, in danger of losing the
composure Nick felt sure was her trademark. She didn't seem to
have been crying. Her makeup—simple, immaculate—showed no
signs of wear.

"We don't want to speak with anyone just now," said Barbara,
sizing Nick up as a reporter.

"Oh," said Nick, fumbling, losing her courage. "No. I'm not
from the press, Mrs. White. . . ." There was a lightning flash and
quickly following thunder.

Barbara moved her glasses back down to her nose and focused on
Nick.

"Mrs. White . . ." Nick began to say.

Barbara's eyes narrowed suddenly in recognition. "Devon," she
said evenly, "go back and finish eating."

"I finished, Mom."

"Do as I say, Devon. Now!"

Devon's lips tightened. He turned and obeyed. Barbara watched
him go, and then looked to Nick, on whom rain was pouring.

"You know who I am . . . don't you, Mrs. White."

"You looked better in the restaurant," said Barbara White, as if
she were recounting a distant dream. "But then, so did I."

"I had to . . . talk to you. No one knows what's going on . . .
and it's all . . . I just thought if we—"

"Get out," shrieked Barbara White, her composure annihilated.
The sound of her own voice seemed to shock her, but she went
on. "How dare you come here? *How dare you?* I'm calling the police.
Devon! Call 911. Do it!" She slammed the door.

Nick turned and ran down the walkway into the street, the wind
plowing against her, her body drenched. She ran downhill, her tears
camouflaged by the rain, her feet almost numb from the icy water,
down and down. There was no traffic. The street was unfamiliar, but
she knew if she kept going downhill, she'd find her way to town and
the station.

She also knew that she'd just made a stupid, perhaps fatal mistake. She knew that Ernie Moran would probably give up on her now. She also knew that the Hastings police might show up at any minute and arrest or detain her. She kept running downhill, pushing hard to maintain some body heat.

She sensed car lights behind her and trotted onto the sidewalk. The lights swept by, illuminating the road ahead. It was a police car, now alongside her. Nick slowed to a fast walk. The car emitted a shrill, blipping sound, and a miked voice said, "You shouldn't be out in this storm, miss."

"I know," called Nick. Had Barbara phoned the police? "My car's broken down, and I have to get to the station."

"It's your lucky day," said the voice, friendly. "I'll give you a police escort." Nick knew it would be insane not to comply, so she walked around, opened the door, and sat in the shotgun seat. The cop was alone. He looked at her and laughed sympathetically.

"Ever hear of this new invention—the taxi?" asked the cop. He appeared near retirement age, with silver hair and a patrician, handsome face.

"I always walk," Nick said. "I didn't realize it was raining this hard. Once I started, I figured I couldn't get any wetter."

"Hope you're not going to a fancy party or anything," he said with a smile. They were almost in the center of the village, just up from the station.

"Not tonight," said Nick, who was wondering if a police call was about to burst onto his radio ordering him to pick up a murder suspect in the vicinity of 91 Scenic Drive. She wondered, too, if anything she'd just said to this cop could be used against her in court. Had she lied? She couldn't think. She just wanted to get out of the car. A lightning bolt lit up the train station below as they moved slowly down the hill.

"What takes you into the city on a night like this?"

"I live in the city. I was just visiting someone here."

"The way you were running, I figured you were on the lam."

Nick looked at him, startled. "No, but seriously," he went on, "they should've asked you to spend the night, with your car broken down and all." Nick didn't reply. They reached the station. She started to get out.

"You're welcome to wait with me till the train comes. I've got a good heater." Nick searched his eyes for sexual subtext. She was shivering and wanted desperately to take him up on it, but thought better of it.

"You're awfully kind," she said, "but I'm fine."

"You certainly are," he said like Stan Laurel. "Even all wet."

"Thanks for the lift."

He gave a quick salute. Nick slammed the door, and he shot off in another direction, attempting, it seemed, to leave rubber. She reoriented herself and headed around to the platform just as another car came screeching down the hill toward her, spewing water from both sides like a speedboat. It fixed Nick in its headlights. She backed away from it, nearly falling as she slipped on the wet cobblestones. The car headed straight for her. She kept backing up. She couldn't tell if it was going to stop, and there wasn't time to move in either direction or jump away. The brakes screamed, the car swerved to one side, then straightened out and stopped inches from Nick, who was blinded by its high beams. The driver rolled down the window. A woman stuck her head out and yelled, "Get in!" It was Barbara White.

CHAPTER 20

Rattled and queasy, Nick moved around and reached for the door handle of what appeared to be a late model Lincoln Town Car. The door wouldn't open. She heard electric locks jerk up and down while she kept trying to open it. Barbara yelled from inside, "Take your goddamn hand off the handle for one goddamn second!" Nick did so. It was impossible to get any wetter. She heard one final lurch of the locks. Afraid to make a move now, she waited until Barbara screamed again, "Open the goddamn door!" She did, then leaned over and peered in, as though awaiting further orders. Barbara was amazingly unwet.

"Get in, for Christ's sake," she said. Nick obeyed, closed the door, and turned to Barbara, who looked straight ahead and didn't speak for a moment.

"He would have had a fit if anyone got his precious leather seats wet," muttered Barbara, shaking her head and still not looking at Nick. Nick didn't speak.

"The news was on right before you showed up," Barbara finally said. "I wouldn't let the children watch, but I couldn't help myself. You . . . said something. To me. You spoke—right into the camera

—to me. You said . . . you were sorry." Fixing Nick with her eyes, she sucked on her teeth. "What was that?"

"I just wanted you to know how I felt," Nick said carefully. "I wanted you to know that I didn't—"

"You think I care how you feel?" snapped Barbara. "Look. I'm not as bent out of shape as you think. Things were . . . there was a lot of trouble in paradise . . . I mean, it's just . . . the kids." She fought back tears with a shake of her head. "I don't know what happened between you and my husband . . ."

"I didn't—"

"Shut up. I don't really care. How about *that*? I don't. But when you spoke to me that way, on TV, it . . . startled me." She took a deep breath. "It made you real."

Nick began to say something, but Barbara interrupted. "Look. I don't know you. You may just be some slut, and I don't want to *chat* with you! Okay? Are we straight on that? I just want to get through the next two days, the memorial service, and get on with things." Nick stared and nodded slightly.

Barbara went on. "There's just . . . something you should know, and then I hope you'll kindly fuck off. Okay?" Nick's eyes agreed. "He took me to dinner the other night to patch things up." She paused, looking away from Nick and out the driver's window. "Let's just say . . . you weren't the first. He hit the kids. And me. He never slept. Drank. Lost his job." She exhaled. "He turned into such a . . . loser. The thought of . . . sleeping with . . . I had to get drunk. Jesus—you weren't in love with him or anything, were you?"

"No," said Nick, her teeth chattering. She craved some heat, but didn't dare make a move or ask for anything.

"So," Barbara went on. "The bruise." Nick's eyes widened. "I see I have your attention. They called me this morning to double-check about this . . . bruise. Okay. See, he came back to the house yesterday morning." She shook her head. "Jesus—it was really yesterday." She drew a breath. "I had a restraining order on him, and the son of a bitch shows up like nothing's happened. Well, I just lost it. I threw—" She laughed sadly. "It was so *pathetic!* I threw this big crystal ashtray at him. God. It was an awful wedding present from his parents. I kept hiding it, he kept finding it, and he'd leave it somewhere just to—anyway, it hit him. Hard. On his side. I thought he was going to throw it back at me. But he just . . . left. I didn't tell the police about it. I was embarrassed. It was in front of the kids and . . . I just felt . . . humiliated that I'd done something like that. I figured he was gone, what did it matter? So when they called again today, I told them I'd thrown Jeffrey out on Friday morning and hadn't seen him since. I was afraid they'd think if I had thrown something like that at him, then maybe *I* was capable of killing him too. I was paranoid. I didn't know it would create a problem for anybody. They seemed to believe me. I asked them if there was a suspect. I got the impression there might be, and after I hung up, it occurred to me it might have to do with that bruise."

Nick didn't move.

"So, anyway." She looked straight ahead. "I'll tell them that. I'll call the police and tell them. Now that I've had a chance to calm down, well, there's no way I could be a suspect, and—whatever you did, you don't deserve to go to jail because of that bruise. I could use a clear conscience. So. I just wanted you to know that."

"Thank you," said Nick. She saw the light of the next New York train approaching, a mile or so down the track. "Thank you."

"Yeah. Well."

Nick started to get out. Barbara stopped her. "By the way. One other thing. Did you? Kill him?" Nick stared. Barbara added, "Just curious."

"Mrs. White. He . . . did it himself."

"Well," she laughed brusquely, "I suppose you have to say that." She turned on the ignition. "You'll never get any money, you know."

"What?" asked Nick, half outside the car, leaning her head back in.

"He's either a suicide, or you murdered him. Either way, you don't collect." She looked away from Nick again. "He must have been nuts over you to make you his beneficiary."

"Mrs. White. I met your husband last Thursday night. This whole thing about the insurance policy . . . I have no idea—"

"Bitch! Lying *bitch*! How dare you!"

"Mrs. White, I swear to you—"

"Save it for your trial! I hope they get you for this. Maybe I *won't* call the police and tell them about the bruise. Maybe I'll just tell them you came out here and tried to get into my house—and maybe this conversation never took place. Christ. I hope the two of you meet somewhere in hell." She started the engine and pulled away with Nick's door still open. It slammed shut as she whipped around a curve. Nick turned and ran for the southbound train.

CHAPTER 21

On the ride back she barely moved, sometimes dozing, sometimes staring out at the storm, which still danced through the darkness, making treetops sway and waking her with shots of thunder. She was grateful for a seat to herself. Not much traffic into the city on a Sunday night. She'd been shocked to learn from a woman conductor that she was on the 6:46 local back to Grand Central. It felt like midnight. The conductor had offered Nick her coat to cover her. Nick had quickly accepted. She was a little warmer, but couldn't quite bring her chills under control.

Her eyes opened with the sudden realization that April and Mae hadn't been fed for several days. She'd never forgotten before. She had no idea if they could survive. The thought of more death in her apartment made her eyes throb. A clap of lightning struck so near that it seemed a giant flashbulb had gone off in her face. She thought of reporters, the news. What would it be like tonight? Would the morning papers be running with the story? Connie Cuevas's report at ten would, no doubt, send her mother to her grave.

The train stopped.

"Ladies and gentlemen," intoned an officious, lackadaisical voice on the P.A. system, "we are experiencing a loss of power due to an electrical storm. Please bear with us. We will do our best to have you under way and into New York on schedule or close to it." Then the lights went out.

Nick dreamed she was in jail. It was visiting hour. Her mother was yakking incessantly about the importance of preheating an oven. Sam was waiting patiently, next in line to see her. But her mother wouldn't stop talking, and Nick couldn't make her own mouth work because her teeth were chattering. Sam looked at her expectantly, but Nick found she couldn't work her face into an encouraging smile. Sam got up and left.

When she woke up, the train was easing into Grand Central. She was clammy and Joanne's dress itched. Her head ached and her stomach growled with hunger. She had no idea how long she'd slept. She put the soggy sneakers back on and handed the conductor's coat to her as she walked by.

"Thank you," said Nick. "I think you saved my life."

"De nada," said the conductor tiredly. Then suddenly he perked up. "Have we met before?"

"I'd remember," said Nick, moving down the aisle and out the door before the conductor figured out who she was. She took in the familiar pleasant-stale aroma of Grand Central's platforms. As she made her way into the huge interior of the main station, the clock read 10:56. She trudged up the stairs to the Vanderbilt Avenue exit and got into a waiting cab. It was still raining, but the storm was quieting.

"East End and Eighty-fourth," she said. "And step on it." She had to get some food into April and Mae's bowl. That was all there was to it. Then back to Frankie and Joanne's.

"I love a good storm," said the cabbie, his eyes darting. "Keeps the fuckers off the streets, you know what I mean?"

"I know what you mean," said Nick, as if she did. There was no traffic, and the cab zipped over to First Avenue and then up to and across Eighty-fourth in no time. As they approached her building, Nick spotted the Action News van, and a handful of reporters huddled under the awning of the building next door.

"Drop me off right here," she said, still a half block away from her building. The cab stopped. Nick paid, and, while waiting for her change, noticed a copy of *Newsday* on the front seat. "Are you done with that paper, by any chance?"

"Actually, no," he answered. "Sorry."

"Well, hmm," said Nick, sizing up the distance between the reporters and her building's entrance. "How about selling it to me?"

"You want to *buy* my paper?"

"I actually just need a few pages of it."

"Five dollars."

"Five dollars?" said Nick. "Are you nuts? For a paper? For *part* of a paper?"

"Hey." He shrugged. "Supply and demand." He looked at her like a poker player who's just raised. Nick shook her head.

"Two bucks," said Nick. "I'll give you two bucks. Just give me some of the want ads or something."

"Four bucks."

"Do we have a deal at three?" asked Nick, dangling a five toward him. He pulled two dollars out of a wad from his pocket, took the five, and handed her part of the paper with her change.

"I don't understand, lady. You're already soaked. I don't get it."

"Watch," said Nick. She opened the cab's door, started to get out, arranged the newspaper over her head like a shawl, and made directly for the entrance to her building. As she got to within ten feet of it, the reporters came to life.

"Somebody's coming in!"

"Is that her?"

"Incoming! Incoming!" another yelled, and they all swarmed toward Nick, who kept her face covered and made it up and into her building a few steps ahead of them.

Fernando greeted Nick with a surprised nod, closing the door behind her in the reporters' faces. Nick could still hear muffled shouts. "Miss Stallings? Just one question? How do you feel? Did you do it?"

"Hi, Fernando." He smiled woodenly. He was holding the early Monday edition of the *Post*. The headline read "Love Nest Actress on Rampage." Nick was desperate to read it but had to rescue April and Mae. Fernando glanced down the hallway, and Nick's eye followed. A policeman jumped up off the sofa. It was the young one who'd driven her to Frankie and Joanne's.

"Miss Stallings!" he said, glad to see her and not too good at covering it.

"Oh. Hi," said Nick as friendly as possible. She was embarrassed at how appalling she must look.

"I'm sorry," he said, meaning it, "but I can't let you up there."

Nick couldn't remember his name. She knew it was a simple one —John or Jim. She searched her brain, knowing it might help with the favor she was about to ask, but nothing came.

"Officer," she said, taking him by the arm and moving a few steps away from Fernando.

"You can call me Billy," he said.

"Okay. Billy . . ."

"Are you, like, all right?" he asked, concerned.

"Oh, God," said Nick, "I don't know how I am. Don't ask me—"

"Sorry," said Billy, putting a hand up immediately as if to acknowledge a lack of professionalism. "Is there anything I can do for you? Other than let you up to your place? I guess you know I can't do that."

"Of course. Sure. There is something I need you to do though."

"Sure. Sure."

"I have to feed my fish."

"Uh-huh. Uh-huh," said Billy, nodding intently.

"I just need you to go in and I'll tell you where the fish food is and then I need you to sprinkle a little—not too much—just, like, I don't know, a few pinches. Can you manage that?''

"Uh. Yeah. Sure," he said, eager for the assignment. "Where's the food?''

"Okay," said Nick, forcing herself to concentrate. She imagined April and Mae listlessly floating to the top of the aquarium, dying slow deaths. Then she remembered that she was out of fish food. It was Sunday night. Not a good time for running out and picking up a little fish food. She bent over and started to cry.

"What?" said Billy. "What is it?"

"Oh, God," she said, sniffing. "Oh, God. What time is it?"

"Ten after eleven."

"Fernando," she called suddenly. "I have to use the intercom."

"Okay," said Fernando. "I guess. It's okay?" he asked Billy.

"Hey, she can call whoever she wants," said Billy. "Her apartment is sealed off, that's all."

"Who you call?" asked Fernando.

"Mr. Kazura," said Nick, straightening up and wiping her eyes. She looked at Billy. "He has fish too." Fernando lifted the receiver, pushed a button, and handed the phone to Nick. It rang with a distant bleating sound several times.

He's asleep.

A voice finally came on. "Yes?"

"Mr. Kazura! Oh, Mr. Kazura, is that you?"

"I can't imagine who else it could be. Do we have door*women* now? Who is this?"

"Mr. Kazura. It's Nick."

"Nick! Are you all right?"

"Did I wake you, Mr. Kazura?"

"I was just watching you on the news. And now you call. What? What is it?"

"Oh, God, the news. Oh, God . . ."

"Is it true, Nick, what they say?"

"No, Mr. Kazura."

"Good! I knew it."

"Mr. Kazura?"

"I'm still here."

"Can I borrow some fish food?"

"Fish food? That's what you want?"

"Yes."

"For little March and April?"

"Yes. April and Mae. Yes."

"Of course. Come on up."

"I'll be right there." She turned to Billy. "I need to go up to Mr. Kazura's. Right away."

"Eight D," said Fernando.

"I have to go with you," said Billy. "Orders."

"Come on!" said Nick, already in the elevator. Billy rushed to follow. She pressed 8. They rode up in silence. Nick knew that Billy was looking at her, but she kept her eyes on the lighted floor numbers. She practically pushed the door open at the eighth floor. Mr. Kazura was waiting in his doorway in an old sweatshirt and pajama bottoms. He held a little can of fish food.

"Who's this?" he said, referring to Billy, who stayed by the elevator.

"My apartment is sealed off, Mr. Kazura. I'm not allowed to come up without an escort."

"Here. For April and Mae. When did you feed them last?"

"Three days ago."

"Oh, dear. Well. They may be all right." Nick took the can.

"Thank you, Mr. Kazura."

"Did I thank *you* for those flowers?"

"Yes, you did."

"Ellie would have loved them. You're the only one who sent anything. Almost all our friends, they're gone, or too busy, I suppose. So. I see you on the TV, and I'm worrying. But you're all right, Nick?" He took her hands and looked into her eyes.

"Well," said Nick, attempting a laugh. "I've been better."

"The stronger the roots, the stronger the wind that blows the tree," said Mr. Kazura. "You know who said that?"

"Who?"

"Ellie said that. Right before the end. I was a little, you know, upset. And she said, 'The stronger the roots, the stronger the wind . . .' I don't know where she got that. So you, my dear, must have some very strong roots."

"The news," Nick started to ask, "was it really awful?"

"A lot of noise. That's all. Feed your fish."

"Yes. Yes, I will. Thank you." She hugged him quickly and tightly.

"I knew there was a reason I got up today," he said. "Feed your fish." And he turned and went inside. Nick walked back to Billy, who'd been holding the elevator door open. He pushed the button for the main floor.

"Can't let you go to your place, Miss Stallings. My partner's guarding your door. No one's supposed to be on the floor except the other people who live there. You'll have to wait in the lobby." He let her off and she handed him the fish food.

"Just sprinkle a little on the top, not even a teaspoonful," she said, controlling her anxiety. "You know how much a teaspoonful is?"

"Hey," said Billy. "I'm a cook." And he went back up. She paced around the lobby near Fernando's desk, wondering what it was like in her apartment. What did it smell like? Would she go to jail and forfeit the apartment and never set foot in it again? Would government movers come in and throw everything willy-nilly into storage, dumping out April and Mae?

Fernando was reading the *Post*. She could see that the cover picture was from the scuffle outside the doctor's office. The sub-headline proclaimed "Victim's Alleged Mistress Attacks *Post* Reporter." It was a shot of Nick lunging at the photographer who'd attempted the nude pictures through the window. Ernie Moran was in the foreground, his mouth open unattractively wide and his arm pointing at the action, like a basketball referee calling a foul. Fernando snapped the paper behind his back before Nick could read the accompanying text.

Don't read it.

"May I see that, please, Fernando?" Nick asked. She felt an odd detachment, as though she were going to read about someone else. Fernando looked sheepish, but shrugged and handed it over.

"This was the scene outside Nicolette Stallings's doctor's office, where Ms. Stallings was treated for shock and exhaustion today following her grilling by New York detectives in the death of Jeffrey White, the Westchester philanthropist. . . ."

Philanthropist?

"Sources close to the police say that an investigation is ongoing, centering around possible inconsistencies between the medical examiner's findings and the testimony of at least one key figure, possibly Ms. Stallings. Detective Thomas Kerrigan, N.Y.P.D., was quick to say that no charges have been made. 'We're checking everything out,' said Detective Kerrigan. 'That's what we do.' Pressed about the possible involvement of Ms. Stallings, who sources say was present at the death of Mr. White, Detective Kerrigan offered no comment, but added, 'We'll have something for you soon.' (More on White case, pages 4–5.)"

Two more pages?

Nick riffled through to page four. There, after some condensed national news, was Nick's old headshot, the same one Action News had carried. There were little articles peppered throughout the two pages. One was basically her résumé. There was no mention of any of her theater work. They seemed to be painting her as a third-rate TV actress.

There was even a quote from one of her *Eagle Squadron* co-stars, George Block, with whom she'd once necked when he happened to walk into her trailer dressing room one day by mistake. The trailers had all been identical, lined up in a row on the Universal back lot. Nick had been changing, and was wearing only cutoff jeans. George had blushed and apologized. Nick made a halfhearted attempt to cover herself, invited him in, and soon found herself kissing him. He wasn't much of a kisser and proved to be a worse actor. It never went any further. Nick always felt that if the kissing wasn't good, nothing would be.

And now here was George Block, tracked down by the *Post* on the set of his daytime soap, offering this bit of wisdom: "I like Nicolette. It's hard not to like her. Is she capable of murder? Hey. Anybody's capable of anything. I don't know. Ask her." And below that, the pièce de résistance, a sidebar with a picture of Todd Morgan, her date the night she met Jeffrey White. He was smiling, squeaky clean, and toothy. The caption read, "Todd Morgan, star of the daytime hit *Gathering Storm* and seen lately on the arm of Nicolette Stallings, most recently at the exclusive restaurant Bouley, where they were spotted last Thursday night intimately enjoying a candlelight dinner, was shocked to hear the news about his girlfriend. 'It just goes to show you,' he said, 'you think you know somebody really well—but you just don't. I'll pray for her.'"

Nick tossed the paper back to Fernando as Billy returned with the fish food. He looked pale.

"My partner won't let me in there, Miss Stallings. No one's to go in without permission from above, under any circumstances." Nick felt the blood drain from her face. "I'm really sorry. I tried arguing with him," Billy said, giving the can back to Nick, who in turn handed it to Fernando.

"Can you put this somewhere where it won't get lost and I can get it quickly? Can you? It's very important."

"*Si, si.*" Fernando nodded, holding the little can as if it were nitroglycerin.

"Now," said Nick, "I need to use the phone." Fernando raised his eyebrows a little disapprovingly, but beckoned to her that it was okay. Nick pulled her beeper out of a pocket and called her machine. She hadn't checked messages since before Jeffrey died. It took forever for the machine to rewind. She listened.

"Nick? It's me. Todd. Are you, like, avoiding me? Just kidding. But hey, where are you? This gorgeous Saturday is running out and I was hoping to fill some of it with you. Call me. Irresponsible. Oh, God, did I say that? Anyway—call. Okay?" Beep.

"It's your old friend Todd again to see if you might be free for dinner, or just a bite. To eat. I mean . . . oh, God. Did that sound . . . ? Sorry, sorry. I, ah, sure would like to see your face. And any other part of your anatomy that you so choose." Beep.

"Nick? It's Linda, your faithful agent. It's Sunday morning, or is it afternoon—I don't know what time it is—I'm never up on Sunday morning—and I know this is crazy, but I got the weirdest call from Natalie LeVine, and she said—quote—don't take another job without calling them first. She said she was also calling to see if you're okay. She said she saw something on the news. I don't know, I haven't seen it. She was talking as if you two were old friends and she seemed sure I knew what she was talking about, so I just played along. Anyway, it turns out Sidney Halpern *didn't* fly back to L.A., apparently, and *he* saw the news too, and I don't know, it's crazy, but they might want to talk to you about a different part completely than the one you went in on. Do you *believe* this business? Anyway, call me. And, hey—*what* thing on the news? Why am I always the last one to know anything? Call me at home." Beep.

"It's the Toddster again. You and I, uh, had dinner the other night? Ring a bell? We, uh, had dessert at your place? Have you lost my number? If so, dial 847-3826. For a good time." Beep.

"It's your mother. Please call." Beep.

"Dear? It's your mother. What in God's name is going on? Jeanne Shea just called and told me about the ten o'clock news? What in God's *name*, Susan? Please." Beep.

"Susan. For God's sake. I'm wild. Do I have to call the police to find you? And I'm very, very worried about your father. Something terrible has happened to our condominium in St. Maarten. The hurricane has just about flattened it, I'm told. I got through to the airport this morning, and they said everything is just leveled. I haven't heard from your father, and that's not like him. He would get himself to wherever a telephone was working and he would call. I'm just so afraid. Please, please, please call me. No matter what I may have done to you in your life, Susan, please don't *torture* me this way. I'm sorry. I'm frantic. I'm all right." Beep.

"This is the police, checking to make sure this line is working properly." Beep. It was Kerrigan's voice. That was the end of the messages. Nick dialed her mother. It rang and rang. There was no answer, and no machine picked up. She turned to Billy.

"I have to get out of here without them seeing me," she said, referring to the reporters outside.

"Service entrance?" asked Fernando.

"Nope," said Billy. "They had that covered last I looked."

"Super, super," said Fernando brightly, moving down the entrance hallway toward a door.

"What?" said Nick.

"Super gone till tomorrow." Nick looked blank. "Go out his window." Fernando was opening the super's apartment.

"Yes, yes. Great. Thank you, Fernando." She looked over her shoulder to Billy. "Thanks, Billy," she said. "All I do lately is thank people." Through the tiny living room she could see a window facing the street, about twenty feet off to the side of the building's entrance. Fernando opened it slowly and noiselessly, evidently enjoying the role of co-conspirator. Nick looked at him.

"You famous," said Fernando, grinning. Nick climbed up carefully, carrying Joanne's raincoat now over her arm, being careful not to let it snag as she jumped the few feet to the pavement. Her wet sneakers made a small smacking sound as she landed, and she turned away from the reporters and walked as fast as she could.

"Hey, there's somebody!" said one. Nick heard footsteps behind her. She started to run.

"It's her!" called another. Nick pushed her cold, wet feet as fast as she could, turning the corner onto First Avenue. This would be a true test of her cab karma. She ran up to Eighty-fifth Street. Sure enough. A vacant cab. But the driver, facing away from her, didn't see her. From the blinking of the DON'T WALK signs, she knew the light was about to change and he'd take off. There were no other cabs in sight. The footsteps were close behind. She didn't want to turn around to see how close. One of them might snap her picture in desperate flight. She screamed, "Taxi!" as the light changed, and saw the driver look back to see where the sound was coming from. She thumped the rear door with her fist, and he sprung the lock. Nick threw the coat inside, then herself, slammed the door, and put her head down just before a reporter stuck a camera to the window and flashed. "Go!" she yelled, and the driver took off.

"Hey," he said as they picked up speed. "That was great! Now I 'spose you're gonna tell me 'Follow that car!' Right?"

"Listen—I'm temporarily without a sense of humor," Nick said, sitting up and looking behind her at the receding image of the photographers. "Would you please not ask any more questions and take me to Beekman Place?"

CHAPTER 22

The cab pulled up to her parents' building. Nick paid, noticing she now had less than twenty dollars left from the fifty Joanne had lent her. As she stepped toward the immaculate thick glass doors, she saw the daytime doorman, Jerry. Or was it Terry?

"Working the night shift?" she asked as he opened the door for her.

"Yeah, double shift today, Miss Stallings. Still raining, hah?"

"It's a beaut," said Nick, feigning normalcy. She noticed an open copy of the *Post* on his seat. She couldn't tell if it was the latest edition. Jerry/Terry's behavior toward her seemed to be the same as always. Maybe he hadn't read or seen the news. "Could you please ring my mother?"

"You got it."

He picked up the intercom, buzzed, and waited. There was no answer.

"Jeez, Miss Stallings," he said with a facial shrug, "I'm pretty sure she's up there." They waited several more rings. Her mother was a light sleeper. She seldom went to bed before midnight. Why wasn't she answering? Nick felt a surge of perspiration. Then she remembered she had the key her mother had given her on Friday.

"It's okay," she said, doing her best not to sound edgy, rummaging through her bag. "I've got my own key now. I'll just go up."

"Oh," said Jerry/Terry. "Uhh, okay. Sure." He beckoned toward the elevator. "Maybe I should go with you?"

"That's all right," said Nick, her mind churning. "I'll call down if there's a problem." She moved into the elevator. He was now looking at her as though she were armed and dangerous.

He's heard.

Or maybe he's just concerned.

"You sure?" he called as she pushed the button.

"Yes, yes," said Nick, letting the doors close. She readied the key, tapping her nails on the elevator walls as it moved quickly to the fifth floor. In the hallway she wrestled with the lock for a minute, turning the bolt back and forth several times before the door would open.

The lights were on, but it was silent. Suddenly a loud whirring sounded from the kitchen. Nick jumped, startled. She moved quickly toward it.

There was her mother, holding the top onto the blender with one hand as it swirled, turning away from it to check something in an open cookbook. It was the same blender her parents had owned since people first had blenders. Nick watched for a moment, relieved. This, she thought, is my mother's natural habitat.

The intercom phone rang. It would be Jerry/Terry calling, Nick thought, to make sure everything was all right. But Nick's mother seemed oblivious to it, as well as to Nick's presence in the kitchen doorway. The intercom rang a few more times, loud enough to be heard, even over the blender. Nick stepped all the way into the kitchen and reached for the receiver.

"Hi, Mom," she said before speaking into the phone. Her mother turned, as startled as if Nick were a ghost.

"Susan! Good Lord! What are you doing here! Oh, God. Are you all right?" She turned off the blender. "How dare you march in here like this, without any warning? Oh. Oh." She held her heart. "What are you doing with the phone?"

"What's the doorman's name, Mom?" Nick whispered, cupping her hand over the intercom.

"Terry. He doesn't usually work at night."

"Everything's okay, Terry. Thank you," Nick said quickly, and hung up.

Her mother was totally absorbed again in her recipe.

"I'm making soup," she said, thrusting an ancient wooden spoon into the blender and tasting a little. Nick stood, watching.

What's wrong with this picture?

There was a glass of red wine, a quarter full, on the counter near the cookbook, and a half-empty Bordeaux bottle nearby. Her mother, she knew, hadn't had a drink for—what was it now? —four or five years.

"Mom?" Her mother looked up and smiled. "Wine?" Nick asked.

"It's wine, yes," she said, taking a sip, then another, seemingly lost in the recipe. Then she slammed the book shut. "I could make this soup in my sleep," she said with apparent disgust. "Why haven't you called me? Do you have any idea, *any idea,* how worried I've been?" She looked at Nick, then seemed to snap out of something. "*What* are you doing here?"

"You didn't answer the phone," Nick said carefully. "And the machine wasn't on."

"I'll never know how that thing works—"

"You sounded so bad on your last message—"

"Help me chop this parsley." She slid some over toward Nick, then retrieved a wooden cutting board Nick had given her for Christmas years ago. Nick placed the parsley on the board, and her mother handed her a knife. "Not too much," she said as Nick began chopping. Her mother took a pot of bouillon that had been heating on the stove, and half filled a Pyrex measuring cup. While Nick chopped, her mother turned the blender on low, slowly adding the bouillon. No one spoke for a minute. Nick almost wanted it to stay like this. Everything felt, in a way, quite nice. When Nick was a kid and her mother had been depressed, drunk, or in a crisis, she would call Nick into the kitchen and they'd cook together, measuring, chopping, tasting, assisting each other in a smooth, comforting dance of denial.

"What do you mean, I didn't answer the phone?" her mother asked suddenly, turning off the blender. "I most certainly would have answered the phone. If you had only called. Do you have any idea? No, you obviously don't." She finished the glass of wine, and poured herself another, looking pointedly at Nick. "Yes. Five years of sobriety down the drain. Thank you very much."

"Mom," said Nick, reaching for the glass, "why don't we just pour this back into the bottle and—"

"Why don't we just pour this back . . . ?" her mother mimicked her rudely. "Why don't we just *call* . . . ?"

"I *did* call—"

"Why don't we just explain what—*in God's name*—is going on? *What?* I had to turn off the television. It's all about hurricanes, wreckage, and you. I'm sorry, dear. I can't watch it. But Jeanne, bless her heart, has been calling in reports. I've been frantic. Frantic! Between you and your father. No one seems to know where he is. It's the worst hurricane in thirty-five years. The lines are down. The condominium is gone. Gone!"

"I'm sure he's all right, Mom."

"You are? You *are?* I'm glad for you." She tossed a pinch of salt into the blender. "I'm sixty years old and I have never managed any of our finances. I don't even know how to turn on that computer in there, and I have this feeling that your father is dead."

"Oh, Mom. No. I'm sure, you know, he's just, you know—"

"Stop saying 'you know'!" she yelled. "I *don't* know!" She started to mock Nick angrily. "Y'know. Y'know. It's like—y'know? Good

Lord. Who taught your generation to speak like that? Certainly not me."

"Certainly not *I,*" Nick corrected her mother.

Her mother looked dazed, and reran the sentence in her head.

"You're absolutely right," she said, calming suddenly. "There's hope for the world." She grabbed a handful of the newly chopped parsley, tossed it into the blender, and turned it on again, then readied an antique Tupperware container for the finished soup. She turned off the blender and poured the smooth stuff into the plastic, pulled out a roll of masking tape, stripped off enough for a label, stuck it onto the container top, and quickly wrote VEG. SOUP and the date with a felt-tip pen. Then she opened the freezer and slid the container in amid a perfectly sorted arrangement of frozen food.

"I'm going to bed," said Nick's mother. "I'm drunk and I'm ashamed, but I'm also a little drowsy and I'm going to take advantage of it." Uncharacteristically, she did not clean up the kitchen, but tossed her apron to Nick and walked out.

Nick wiped the counter until it was spotless, rinsed the pots and the blender, and put them in the dishwasher. She realized she was starving, opened the freezer, and withdrew the soup her mother had just finished. Removing the plastic top, she stuck in a spoon and took a sip. It was warm-cool from its brief sojourn in the freezer, but, as always, it hit the spot. Nick took four or five hearty spoonfuls before she remembered.

Kerrigan.

She had to tell him about Jeffrey White's bruise. She replaced the soup, rinsed the spoon, and put it in her mother's dish rack. She found Kerrigan's card in her purse and dialed from the kitchen phone. A machine answered and someone announced stiffly and loudly that this was Detective Kerrigan's line. It beeped.

"Mr. Kerrigan? It's Nicolette Stallings. It's around midnight. We . . . need to talk. Oh. I'm not where I said I'd be." She remembered April and Mae. "Oh, God. Listen. Do you think you could tell one of your men to feed the fish in my apartment? I left some food with the doorman, Fernando. Is that possible? I mean, would it void the investigation? Because, see, I'm not sure they can make it much longer. If you could just take care of that and . . . if you get this, call me at 805-3834 so I know they're all right. Otherwise, I'll call first thing in the morning. There's something else we have to talk about too." She hung up and dialed Frankie and Joanne. Someone picked up on the first ring.

"Yeah," said Joanne eagerly.

"It's me," said Nick.

"Susan! Oh, Mother of God. Are you okay? Where are you? Frankie!" she called to him, "It's her. Susan. God. What? Tell me."

"I'm okay. Listen, I'm at my mother's. I'm fine."

"We've been frantic. Ernie called and he's, like, unbelievably pissed, Susan. Did you see the news?"

"No."

"Good. Good. Don't watch the news, Susan. You hear me? Don't —watch—the news. Are you really okay?"

"I'm fine. Are you sure he's really such a wonderful lawyer?"

"Yes. Really. But he's, like, frantic."

"Would you call him and tell him I'm okay, and that I'll talk to him first thing in the morning?"

"What's your number over there?"

"Joanne, I love you, but if I give you the number here, you'll give it to The Wizard, and he'll call here, and my mother needs to sleep. They have these prehistoric phones here, and there's no way to turn hers off, or unplug it. I can't talk to him now anyway. I'm too fried."

"I'll tell him you're at your mother's."

"No. The cops may be calling, and I don't want my mother woken up all night. She has to sleep. Listen. I'll call him in the morning. I'll call you too. If you need me, leave a message on my machine at home. I love you. If I ever get out of this, I'm buying you a new raincoat."

"Susan, just tell me—"

"Give my love to Frankie. I'll call you in the morning."

She hung up, moved through the apartment turning out lights, and entered her parents' bedroom. Her mother was lying on her father's side of the bed, curled up, still in her clothes. The blinds were open. The storm seemed to be clearing. There was even some moonlight, hidden now and again by huge, fluffy, racing cumulous clouds. Nick pulled down the quilt on the other side of the king-size bed. She removed, at last, the clammy, still-wet dress and sneakers. She tiptoed to the bathroom, found one of her mother's nightgowns on the door hook, and put it on, feeling warmed at once by the flannel, cozily redolent of her mother's Ma Griffe perfume. Fighting off a chill, she got into bed and hunched under the covers. Her mother was turned away from her. Nick stared at the ceiling, then out the window. A cloud moved by, exposing a star. She made a wish.

Let Daddy be all right. And . . . help me.

She opened her eyes and found the star again. Her wish registered, she let her eyes fall shut.

"It's an act of faith, you know," her mother said out of nowhere.

Nick's body jumped. "I thought you were asleep."

"Oh, sure."

"What's an act of faith?"

"Soup," said her mother. "I figure if it's here for him, he'll come home."

"I call that superstition."

"No. Soup . . . is faith. Do you have a good lawyer?"

"I'm . . . told I do."

"Is that why you called last night?"

"Uh-huh."

Nick's mother sat up suddenly. "Is it as bad as they've been saying on television?"

"What are they saying on television today?" Nick asked.

"You haven't *seen* it?"

"What about you?" said Nick equally exasperated. *"You* haven't seen it?"

"Someday—perhaps—you'll have children. And you'll understand that you simply don't watch things like that—about your children. Now, will you tell me what in God's name is happening? I feel as if I'm losing my mind. Just tell me."

"Well, I walk in here, and you're making soup, for Christ's sake. At midnight. You don't answer the phone because you're drunk. You're impossible to talk to when you're drunk. I thought you figured that out years ago. I thought that's why you stopped. Oh, hell. I can't take care of you right now. Just don't ask any questions."

"They're on television talking as though you killed somebody, and I'm not supposed to ask *questions?"*

"Then ask! Ask! You talk about soup and Dad. Soup and Dad. That's your whole life. You're drunk. No. I did not kill anybody. Just . . . go to sleep."

"It seems to me that if there were ever an acceptable time to fall off the wagon, this would be it."

"Oh, Christ, Mom. This is about *me!"*

"Your father may be dead, Susan."

"And I might go to jail. And it wouldn't be about me. And if Dad is dead, it wouldn't be about him. Somehow, *somehow,* it would all be about you."

"Well, you're not going to jail—unless you killed somebody. Did you kill somebody?"

"What did I just say? What did I just say?" Nick was yelling.

"Silence!" her mother hissed with a ferocity Nick hadn't heard in years.

"No! Not silence! Not silence, Mom," Nick wailed.

"The neighbors, for pity's sake, Susan. . . ."

"The hell with the neighbors! Daddy may be dead. I may be a killer."

"Susan!"

"Come on, Mom!" yelled Nick, standing now on the bed, her arms out like a boxer's. "Let's duke it out. My tragedy or yours? Who's got it worse?"

"I've just been so upset about your father," her mother said, starting to cry. "I'm sorry. I'm sorry. Oh, Lord. Please don't hate me."

Nick realized with a sudden lucidity that she had more comfort to give her mother than her mother could give her. She surrendered to that and lay down, cradling her mother in her arms. Nick had another moment of déjà vu. Or was it memory? This had happened before, many times, when she'd been in need as a child. Her mother had always seemed to be in greater need. And Nick, to make things all right and safe for herself, became the comforter.

Her mother soon slept soundly. The only part of Nick that did so was her right arm, cramped most of the night by the dull force of her mother's shoulder. Whenever Nick attempted to free herself, her sleeping mother found Nick's arms and pulled them back around herself, like covers.

★   ★   ★   ★

Maybe I did sleep, thought Nick. There was daylight behind the blinds. She didn't remember dreaming. Her mother's elegant old Tiffany traveling alarm proclaimed it almost 8:30. Lying still, Nick looked at the clock's beveled glass, and maroon leather back. It had been stationed at her mother's bedside, in one residence or another, all of Nick's life. One arm still around her mother, she pulled the clock slowly to her face with her free hand, taking in the familiar musky smell of the clock's leather. It ticked its no-battery tick. Her mother wound it every day. Nick, who had lived in her present apartment for about four years, had had at least as many alarm clocks —sleek, silent, black Brauns built to last a lifetime, but which always seemed to get lost, tossed into an overnight bag, left at some bed-and-breakfast or in a trailer dressing room.

She didn't remember ever in her life waking up before her mother. She wasn't sure she had ever seen her sleep. She slipped out of bed and moved into the living room.

Ignoring Joanne's advice, she turned on the television. It was set to Channel 5. A local New York morning show was in progress.

"We'll be back, recapping this morning's big stories right after these words," said a capped-toothed anchorman affecting a no-nonsense, all-business tone. Nick's stomach burned with either hunger or nausea. She took a chance on the former, and tiptoed into the kitchen. In her mother's ever-filled fruit bowl was a bunch of bright yellow, unripe bananas. She took one, peeled it, and munched a bite of the not quite sweet pulp. She went a few steps into the hallway toward her mother's room, checking to make sure she was still asleep. Then she moved back to the living room and sat on the floor by the TV set, turning the volume down on a network promo featuring phenomenally gorgeous model-actors in their early twenties who were apparently all playing undercover police with ultra-hip haircuts, the men in distressed leather jackets, the women in bra-less halters and perfectly faded, perfectly fitting jeans.

"We're back," said the anchor, "and Sally has these updates for you, including dramatic footage from our Action News team, as events unraveled further yesterday in the possible murder of a Westchester man." Nick felt an agitation in her bowels. The banana hadn't been a good idea.

"Sally?"

"Thanks, John. Well, this was the scene yesterday on Park Avenue as actress Nicolette Stallings had herself a bit of a run-in with a *New York Post* reporter. Our Action News team was on the scene, trying to get Stallings to answer questions relating to the death of Jeffrey White, a Westchester philanthropist and father of two. There's some unseemly language here, so, parents, you may want to exercise discretion if children are watching."

They cut to a shot of Nick as she tackled and wrestled the *Post* photographer. It was jerky, hand-held footage.

"Son of a bitch! Son of a bitch!" she saw herself yell.

"First Amendment! First Amendment!" the photographer was screaming back. Nick had the better of him. He appeared helpless. She looked like a witch-aggressor.

"We have Connie Cuevas standing by in our studio. Connie has been covering this story since she broke it Saturday night. Connie?"

"Thank you, Sally," said Connie Cuevas, who appeared upset and tired. As always, she stressed words in seemingly arbitrary ways as she spoke. "Nicolette Stallings, whom close friends apparently call 'Susan,' is something of a mystery woman. Yesterday, Action News tried to get her to answer a few simple questions about what happened in her apartment two days ago. Jeffrey White, a family man from Hastings-on-Hudson, died in that apartment on Saturday. The medical examiner, our source tells us, has not ruled out foul play. The police have made no charges, but have reason to believe that no one except Miss Stallings was with Jeffrey White when he died. We caught up with her outside this upscale Park Avenue doctor's office where, apparently, Miss Stallings was treated for shock." They cut to a shot of Dr. Klein's receptionist in the street outside the office.

"As far as I know, she was involved in some kind of personal trauma, and was seeing Dr. Klein for treatment. I, ah, really don't think I should say anything else." Back to Connie Cuevas in the studio.

"Trauma," Connie repeated, looking disgusted. They ran the footage again, Nick taking down the photographer and yelling "son of a bitch." The photographer looked vulnerable, defenseless.

"All we were trying to do," said Connie Cuevas, "was ascertain a few simple facts about what happened in Miss Stallings's posh Upper East Side co-op. This is how Miss Stallings reacted to a member of the press who, as far as this reporter could see, was merely doing his job. Stallings's lawyer, the reportedly *very* pricey Ernest Moran, known for his successful defense of alleged mob figure Jackie Torrino, had this to say." They cut to Ernie Moran as he faced the camera. He had been so close to the lens that his face looked bloated and distorted.

"If you have any self-respect, Miss Cuevas, or any respect for privacy or decency, you'll turn off your camera." Then they cut back to Connie, lips tight, struggling with her emotions.

"Let me say this to our viewers. I have the utmost respect for the truth, for journalists' rights to perform their duty to the public, and for the public's right to be informed, however much it may displease a high-priced lawyer and his celebrity client. I'm doing my job, and I'll continue to do it. The police have not filed any formal charges against Nicolette Stallings, but there *are* unanswered questions about what happened in her apartment the day before yesterday, and the police have questioned Miss Stallings several times. Jeffrey White, who recently contributed a wing to the children's library at the elementary school in Hastings and coached his son's track team, is mourned by friends. John?"

The anchorman reappeared. "We take you now to Lisa Badger, live on the Hastings street where Jeffrey White lived." They cut to a somber-looking young woman in a perfect Bogart trench coat.

"Thank you, John. I've just been speaking with Edward Morrison, who lives here, next door to the house where Jeffrey White will never again come home to his children. Mr. Morrison. You *knew* Jeffrey White."

"Yes," said a man of thirty-five or so with thin hair, glasses, a crisp business suit, and striped tie. "It's . . . a tragedy. Our kids played together. What can I say?"

"Jeffrey White," she said heavily, as though his name carried the weight of history. "What *personal* thoughts come to you? Memories."

"Oh, boy," said Ed Morrison. "Just . . . what can I say? You know? A heck of a guy. A *heck* of a guy. Always had a smile for you."

"A good . . . friend?" asked Lisa earnestly.

"Well, you know . . . I've only lived here for a little over a month, but he, you know, you just had the feeling you could depend on the guy if you needed to. He had that. He inspired confidence. It's just . . . he . . . what can I say, you know? It's such a loss. For his family, for the community."

Lisa Badger pulled her microphone away, and the camera tightened onto her face, excluding Ed Morrison.

"A blow to the neighborhood, in the words of a close friend. Not, I'm sure, as big as the blow to Jeffrey White's family. Back to you, John."

The anchorman nodded solemnly. "Any last thoughts, Connie?"

"John," said Connie Cuevas sadly. "Yesterday afternoon I was outside the Nineteenth Precinct with Detective Thomas Kerrigan of New York's finest, who is handling this case. I asked him something point-blank."

"Are you going to arrest Nicolette Stallings?" asked Connie Cuevas. Kerrigan paused and exhaled. His breath was visible in the cold.

"You know I can't comment on that," he said, and disappeared inside the building. They cut back to Connie in the studio.

"Action News viewers can be sure we'll be updating this story throughout the day, and the days ahead. Back to you, John."

Nick turned off the TV, went into the guest bathroom, and took a quick hot shower, trying to decide how to proceed. She toweled off, walked across the hall to her mother's room, noticed gratefully that she was still asleep, and quietly made her way to the closet. Her clothes from the night before were still too damp to wear. Nick opened the closet door carefully. Apart from the nightgown she'd slept in, she hadn't dressed in anything of her mother's since she was four years old. She quickly found a plain white turtleneck and denim jumper that didn't look too absurd, and added the sloshy sneakers, knowing her mother's shoes would be too small. She went quietly back into the kitchen, retrieved her answering machine beeper from her purse, and called again for messages. Her machine rewound more quickly today.

"Miss, uh, Stallings? This is Dr. Klein. I, uh, just wanted to see how you were doing, and, uh . . . you know, I was just thinking that if you need anything at all, I could, uh, you know . . . drop by. I've been . . . known to make house calls. I, you know, hope you're feeling better. And . . . I . . . it was nice . . . meeting you. I don't think I gave you my home number, but if you need anything, I'm at 358-4734." The machine beeped.

"Hello? This is Ferris Fanning." His voice sounded friendly, not at all the evasive tone of yesterday. "It's early Monday morning, but I thought I might find you in. I just wanted to make sure you were all right. I believe we, ah, have an appointment this morning? I certainly would like to be of whatever assistance I can to you. I've been following the events over the weekend . . . *so*—I assume I'll see you at ten. Oh, and look. I'm awfully sorry about yesterday. Family and all."

Her stock had apparently gone up with Fanning in the last twenty-four hours. There was another beep.

"Miss Stallings. Detective Kerrigan here. It's 8:10 Monday morning. I wish you'da told me you were gonna go out and . . . visit Mrs. White. I think you better call me, or get down here as soon as you can. I'll leave the same message with Mr. Moran." Beep.

"It's Ernie Moran. Where the hell are you? Goddammit. Call me. 876-8852." That was the last message. She beeped to reset her machine, disconnected, then dialed again. After a few rings a secretary answered.

"Mr. Moran's line."

"This is Nicolette Stallings—"

"Oh, *hello*. He left a message for you. He'll be at the Nineteenth Precinct at ten o'clock." Nick's heart jumped.

"What for?"

"He just said to give you that message if you called in."

"Am I supposed to meet him there?"

"All he said was he'd be there at ten."

"Christ," said Nick, confused. "Thank you." She then dialed Ferris Fanning's office. He answered the phone himself.

"Fanning."

"Oh," said Nick. "I was expecting a secretary or something. It's Nicolette Stallings."

"I'm here alone. Like to get a couple of hours in by myself on Mondays. What can I do for you—and please accept my apologies for yesterday."

"Listen, Mr. Fanning, you said you've been watching this stuff on TV—"

"Afraid I have. You've got Mr. Moran working with you, is that correct?"

"Well, that's just it, Mr. Fanning. This has all happened so quickly, and I guess I'm not entirely sure he . . . should represent me."

"Well, as I said in my message—"

"But I just called his office and he's evidently going to be at the Nineteenth Precinct at ten. I *think* I'm supposed to meet him there, but I don't know what he has up his sleeve, and I don't want him doing anything without consulting me."

"Let's see," said Ferris Fanning, "Would you like *me* to join you over there?"

"Well, I guess, maybe—yeah. I know it's awfully last-minute."

"Miss Stalling, you need help, and you need to have every confidence in the way your situation is being handled. It's your call. You tell me I'm on the case, and I'm on the case."

Nick thought about what had happened in Ernie Moran's office yesterday. She felt horrified by what she had done, and sure that it must have hurt her credibility with Moran. On the other hand, why hadn't he been more adamant about her putting her clothes back on?

He was *adamant*.

She didn't know what to think. She heard Fanning exhale loudly.

"Okay," said Nick, who had never felt less suited to decision-making. "You're on the case."

"All right, then. It's a little after nine. How soon can you get over to the precinct?"

"We should probably get there before Mr. Moran."

"Exactly," said Fanning.

"I can be there in fifteen minutes."

"I'll meet you in the lobby, then. We can chat for a few minutes anyway. I need to ask you a bunch of questions, just a *bunch* of questions, but we don't have any time, so let's get over there and do the best we can. Don't make any kind of statement to anybody or answer anybody's questions until you see me. Okay?"

"You know where the precinct is?"

"Yes, Nicolette. I believe I do," he said with a little laugh.

"How'll I know you?"

"I just watched you on TV, Miss Stalling. I'll know *you*."

"Okay." She hung up. It had sounded like he'd been leaving the final "s" off her last name, but she wasn't sure and hadn't wanted to correct him. She removed the grocery list pad from its magnetized spot on the refrigerator and scribbled a note to her mother.

Don't watch TV. Avoid the Post. Don't eat the bananas yet. I love your soup, your faith, you. Praying for Dad. Kindly do same for me. Susan.

She went out, closed the front door quietly, and took the elevator down. There was a new doorman, one she hadn't seen before. He looked at her as if he might know her. She breezed by him, moving quickly through the door before he had a chance to explore his memory further, and hailed a cab that had just dropped off a passenger next door. It was a little below freezing, but the storm had passed, leaving the morning clear and bright. The cab stopped, and Nick got in.

"Two-thirty-three East 67th," she said, amazed that she remembered the precinct address when she felt as though she hadn't slept, ever.

CHAPTER 23

The driver, a young Haitian, was of the race-car variety of cabbies. He gunned the accelerator every chance he had, if only to hurtle to the next red light, where he'd jam on his brakes again. They lurched like this all the way to the precinct station, the banana now haunting Nick as it tried to make its way through her intestines. She knew that she should be practicing something: how to explain why she had gone to Hastings. How to tell Ernie Moran she was bringing in Fanning. How to handle the press if they were there.

The cab turned left onto Sixty-seventh. As they passed Third Avenue, Nick saw the Action News van in the distance. She thought about getting out and walking the last half block. Or maybe she could use the back entrance again. But where was it? Hurried as she was, and approaching the station from a different direction, she couldn't picture it. She decided to drive right up to the main door, stonewalling Connie Cuevas or whoever was waiting. As the cab got closer, she saw her friend the *Post* photographer amid a slightly larger group of reporters than yesterday's. They were all bobbing and shifting their weight in the cold, looking in every direction in hope of sighting someone relevant to their vigil. As the cab slowed and Nick paid the driver, they all started moving toward the car. Nick straightened her hair reflexively. She remembered she had no makeup on and figured she must look like hell.

She opened the door and saw them look up expectantly. Their faces became animated—radiant—when they saw it was Nick. They closed in around her, twenty or so, thrusting microphones and tiny tape recorders in the air toward her, their cameras' motor drives eating up whole rolls of film in seconds. There were two minicams, their red lights flashing. Sure enough, Connie Cuevas was there, in the lead, right in Nick's face.

"Are you turning yourself in, Miss Stallings?" Connie Cuevas asked thoughtfully. Nick kept moving. It was slow going. She told herself not to shove, not to let her temper go.

"Would you describe yourself as violent, Nicolette?" Connie Cuevas continued, following, as though they were alone together and Nick had answered the first question.

"Does it bother you that your lawyer defends mob figures?" yelled another over the din.

Nick pressed forward, keeping her eyes fixed on the door above. A couple of cops came out and began to elbow a little path for her. She was determined not to speak.

"Why did you say you were sorry to Jeffrey White's widow?" Connie Cuevas asked pleasantly, as if they were chatting about politics.

"Who you going out with these days, Nicolette? Or should we call you Susan?"

"When are you gonna pose nude for me again, Miss Stallings?" Nick's head whipped around against her will. It was the *Post* photographer, grinning, and now snapping her picture one, two, five times, capturing Nick's shock and her narrowed, angry eyes. She started to speak, but stopped herself, looked forward, and pushed on. She was almost there.

"Anytime, Nicolette," taunted the *Post* guy. "We could make a few bucks, I can tell you that." A few around him laughed.

"Nicolette—do you have something to hide?" asked Connie Cuevas as if posing an interesting theory to a student in a classroom.

"Come *on*, Nicolette. Give us *something*. It's cold!" a voice called. There was a little giggling. Nick started through the doors.

"Hey—how about an *Eagle Squadron* reunion, Nicolette?" one teased. "George Block says he'll do it if you'll do it. . . ."

The lobby was mercifully uncrowded, swept free of press. Nick looked around for some sign of Ferris Fanning. Instead, Kerrigan approached. She had hoped not to see him down here. His face was difficult to read. She didn't want to say anything until she talked to Fanning.

"Morning," he said, avoiding her eyes and looking out at the press as some of them jumped up and down to get a glance through the high window. "Lovely group, aren't they?"

"I think they're actually having a good time," said Nick, grateful he hadn't asked anything more pointed.

"Oh," said Kerrigan. "You think they should be, like, somber?"

"Well, I think they might show people a little respect."

"What planet are you from, Miss Stallings? You're an actress. You see them respect, say, Lady Di? And she's a fucking princess." She noticed he wasn't apologizing for his language this morning. "To Meryl Streep, they might show a little respect. *May*be. I kinda doubt it, if she was in your shoes."

"Have my fish been fed?"

"Come again?" said Kerrigan, annoyed.

"Didn't you get my message?" asked Nick.

"My machine is kinda on the fritz. I just got in. The fucker ate whatever messages came in last night. When did you call?"

Nick fought back tears at the thought of April and Mae. "Late last night."

"Sorry. So—*what* about your fish?"

Nick was so frustrated she couldn't speak for a moment. April and Mae, she thought, must be dead. Not wanting to show him how upset she was, she turned away.

"You're a little early," said Kerrigan. "Want to wait upstairs?"

She cleared her throat. "I'm meeting my lawyer down here," she said, her eyes searching for Fanning.

"I can tell someone to direct Mr. Moran to my office. It's a lot quieter."

"I'm waiting . . . for someone else."

"Oh, yeah? Who?"

"I don't want to talk about it," she said, trying to keep her voice down.

"Okay." He said nothing for a few seconds. "You want to talk about your little visit to Mrs. White last night? That must've been pretty interesting. I for one would sure like to hear about that." Nick had no path of escape. She turned her back to him. He stuck close by, his body language loose, no trace of anger in his face, as though he were exchanging pleasantries with her.

"She tells me you upset her children," he went on, over-smiling. Nick didn't speak. Had Barbara White told him about the bruise?

"Look. I got lotsa other things to worry about," he went on. "And Joey's out sick today. So I'll be upstairs," he said, backing up a couple of steps, still facing her. "Looks like we traded in one cuppy for another." Nick turned her eyes to his. He squinted at her, as if he were trying to see her better. "Yeah. Mrs. White told me about the bruise. I already told Moran when he called. And, hey, the medical examiner is now a happy man." He blinked thoughtfully. "Y'know, if it weren't for a little bracelet and a little life insurance, I'd be happy too."

A tall, extremely thin man appeared at Nick's side and tapped her arm.

"Miss Stalling?" he asked politely, getting her name wrong again. He had a head too small for his body, a long, pointy nose, bright eyes, and an elegant tweed suit with an English collar and striped tie. "Ferris Fanning."

"How do you do," Nick said eagerly. "This . . . is Detective Kerrigan. Mr. Fanning is . . . representing me."

"Ernie Moran is due here any minute," said Kerrigan, irritated. "What's goin' on? You're changing lawyers?"

"I think I'd like to speak with Mr. Fanning in private," said Nick.

"Hey, talk as much as you want. I'm meeting Moran here at ten. He didn't even know for sure if you were coming. You want to stay, stay. You want to take off, take off."

Fanning cleared his throat. "As I'm handling Miss Stalling's affairs now, perhaps we—"

"Oh, like the affair she had with Jeffrey White?" snapped Kerrigan.

"Mr. Kerrigan," said Fanning, "if you think you can talk like that to my client—"

"I was talking to *you*. I just asked a question," said Kerrigan, all innocence. "She *had* an affair. It's common knowledge. She knows it, Mrs. White knows it. It's all over TV. What—are we being polite here?"

"Let's go, Miss Stalling," said Fanning, taking her by the arm. Nick reflexively stiffened, sure now that Fanning didn't have her name right.

"Could we use that back exit to get out of here?" Nick asked Kerrigan.

"Sorry," said Kerrigan unapologetically. "They're . . . working down there today. It's closed." His eyes fixed hers, saying: Go out the front door, where the reporters are, or stay here. "So why don't you two get to know each other—since you obviously don't—and maybe you can figure out a way to make your name disappear from Jeffrey White's insurance policy."

"Morning!" said the voice of Ernie Moran, who had just slipped in from another direction, surprising them both. He looked even more tired than he had in his office.

"Where'd you come from?" said Kerrigan.

"The back entrance, the one you showed us yesterday," said Moran. "Good morning, Miss Stallings." Kerrigan looked away.

"Mr. Moran . . ." said Nick hesitantly.

"I think there's been a coup, Ern," said Kerrigan.

"What's going on?" asked Ernie Moran, who did not seem, as Joanne had indicated, frantic or angry. Aside from his distractedness —as if he were expected to be somewhere else at the same time—he was all business. It was as though nothing untoward had happened yesterday in his office.

"I just feel," said Nick, whose panic was rising, "maybe I—it's just . . . I need . . ."

"Miss Stalling has asked me to come aboard, Mr. Moran," said Fanning politely, extending his hand. "Ferris Fanning. It's an honor," he added deferentially. Nick immediately had the feeling she'd made a mistake—and that there wasn't enough oxygen where she was standing.

"Well, well, well," said Ernie Moran with an irritable look to Nick, "does Mr. Fanning know something I don't know, Miss Stallings?"

"I just don't feel comfortable . . ." Nick tried to continue. Her knees were weakening. The pounding had returned behind her eyes. Her lack of sleep, the tenacity of the press, and Kerrigan's apparent hatred were making it difficult for her to frame her thoughts. She didn't know why she'd wanted to change lawyers. It was a *feeling*. She wanted Fanning to take charge.

"What'd you want to see me about, Ern?" said Kerrigan impatiently, moving a step or two toward the elevators, beckoning Moran to follow.

"Just something I think might be of interest to everybody here," said Moran, staying put. "But I'm not sure I'm even on this case. Maybe Miss Stallings can enlighten me?"

"Well," said Nick, trying to look composed. They waited. She went blank.

"Miss Stalling," said Ferris Fanning softly, "perhaps you and I should caucus for a few minutes—"

"Stallings," said Nick, certain, at least, of that. "Stall-eengs. *Plural.*" Her hands were shaking.

"I *beg* your pardon, Miss Stalling—Stallings! I *am* sorry. But, uh, perhaps you and I should sit down over there, or something."

"Is there . . . a drinking fountain?" asked Nick, taking a few steps backward. She felt as though she were moving underwater.

"Does anybody wonder just the least little bit why I'm here?" said Ernie Moran almost cheerfully.

"Maybe we should go upstairs," said Kerrigan.

"No, thank you," said Moran. "My client—or maybe she's *your* client now, Mr. Fanning—but, anyway, she was up there yesterday and she doesn't like it, and I don't want the press to write that she's being 'grilled' again. Let's talk right here." Nick could see, past Moran's face, a small crowd gathering in the street beyond the reporters.

"Don't fuck with me, Moran," said Kerrigan.

"We don't have to stay, Miss Stalling," said Fanning.

"Stall*ings!* Stall*ings!*" shouted Nick.

"Oh, my," said Fanning, his hand to his forehead.

Nick followed Ernie Moran's eyes to the front door, outside which a breathless, helmeted young black messenger was propping his bike up against a rail and locking it. He took a manila envelope from a basket attached to the bike's seat and made his way through the reporters into the building, searching the lobby with his eyes. Ernie Moran raised his arm, and the young man worked his way quickly to him.

"Here you go, Ern. Am I late?"

"I owe you a hundred bucks, James," said Ernie Moran, taking the envelope from him.

"Payable now," said James with a big smile, holding out his hand.

Ernie Moran reached into his wallet, extracted a hundred-dollar bill, and handed it to James.

"You got anything smaller?"

"Get out of here," said Ernie Moran, checking the envelope's contents. "And . . . thanks."

"Ah—I believe your Thursday Knicks tickets were also part of the package."

"I only said I'd throw in the tickets if you made it here by 10:30, James," said The Wizard, looking up again.

"I got 10:29," said James, checking his watch.

"And I've got 10:33," said Ernie Moran, exposing an antique Rolex for all to see.

"You're fast, Ern," said Kerrigan, checking his own Timex. "Official city time says 10:30, and this is quartz."

"Your watch is always fast, Ern," said James. "Fork over."

Ernie Moran glared at Kerrigan. "You can pick up the tickets at the office, James."

"Yes!" said James, who made his way back outside.

"Pardonnez-moi, but what the fuck is all this, Ern?" asked Kerrigan.

Ernie Moran suddenly, in a barely restrained burst of anger, took Nick's arm. "Excuse us just a second, would you, please?" He pushed her a few feet away and spoke in a measured, low voice that scared her. "You know, Miss Stallings, your faith is touching. If you want this bozo to represent you, take him. I've been racking what's left of my brain for the past fifteen hours, and now you pull this little stunt? You don't trust me? Fine. Why the *hell* should I trust you?"

"I'm sorry," said Nick. "I'm not thinking well. I just thought maybe you'd change your mind after what happened—"

"When I change my mind, I'll be a professional and I'll let you know that, Miss Stallings."

"I'm sorry . . ."

"Stop saying you're sorry. Jesus. There isn't time. I've got something, and I'm going to proceed with it. All right?" She nodded. "You can figure out what to do with Fanning later. If this doesn't

work, you may want him after all. Now, come on." He ushered her
back over to Kerrigan.

"This," Ernie Moran said, holding up a stack of papers, "is a copy
of Jeffrey White's life insurance policy. James just came from the
Metropolitan Life building."

"Is there something about an insurance policy I should know,
Miss Stallings?" said Fanning, careful to pronounce the s at the end
of her name.

"Jesus," Kerrigan said dismissively to Fanning. "Is this guy your
lawyer, or what?" he asked Nick. Nick looked at Kerrigan but didn't
muster an answer.

"I've had more than a few dealings with Met Life," Ernie Moran
went on, "and I was able to contact Jeffrey White's agent this morning. White's policy was indeed altered, naming Miss Stallings as beneficiary, on a form dated two weeks ago."

Nick felt she was going to pass out.

Moran continued. "White, it turns out, delivered the form himself, Friday afternoon. The agent faxed it immediately, at White's
request, to their central office, and they put a notation on their
computer about Miss Stallings being the beneficiary. Here's a copy
of the form White filled out. It's signed and dated two weeks ago—
notarized, one hundred percent official." He showed it to Kerrigan,
who nodded.

Nick's ears started to ring. It was difficult to hear, as though
Moran were in another room. Moran handed the papers to Kerrigan.

"I figured we were hurting, Miss Stallings," said Moran. "But
then I remembered—I just got some new life insurance a couple of
months ago, and I didn't have to get my signature notarized."

"Blah, blah, blah," said Kerrigan.

"So I call my guy over there again and he checks the notary stamp
on White's policy. Every notary has a stamp with his or her name
and number." He showed it to Kerrigan. "I just put in a call to the

secretary of state's record office in Albany and asked them to run a check on this name."

He stopped as though finished.

"*And?*" said Kerrigan, annoyed.

"Well, *excuse me,* Detective, but the secretary's office hasn't been open that long, and I'm waiting for her call now." He reached into his pocket and pulled out a tiny, folded cellular phone.

Suddenly, Nick blurted out, "He was a notary."

"What?" said Kerrigan.

"Who?" said Fanning.

"Please be quiet," said Nick to Fanning as politely as she could. She turned to Kerrigan. "The night we met—*Thursday* night—he made a little joke about it. He said he was a notary public."

"So?" said Kerrigan. "All this is irrelevant, since the form doesn't have to be notarized anyway. I don't see how this makes any difference."

"We were able to explain the bruise, Detective," said Ernie Moran patiently. "I'm trying to explain the insurance."

Kerrigan interrupted. "But we still got a whole mishmash here. And we still got a bracelet which tells us Miss Stallings knew Jeffrey White last summer. So, as far as I'm concerned, Ern, we got a client of yours who doesn't *appear* to be telling the truth—which doesn't exactly astonish me, since it turns out she lied to Judge Costantino about her name." He glared at Nick.

"What?" said Nick, thrown anew.

"The guy you went to for advice after this supposed suicide—we questioned him. You gave him a different name the second time you met him. He was a little troubled that you didn't tell him your real name when you first met." Nick knew she could explain this under normal circumstances, but couldn't form the words right now.

"Miss Stallings?" said Ferris Fanning hesitantly.

Nick started to answer, but was interrupted by the tweeting of Ernie Moran's phone. He unfolded it hurriedly.

"Yes?" he said expectantly. He listened, nodding slowly. "Just a second, Mrs. Perrone. I'm going to give the phone to a Detective Kerrigan. Would you be so kind as to repeat this to him? He needs to hear it from you." He handed the phone to Kerrigan. "This is Mrs. Perrone of the secretary of state's office of records."

Kerrigan listened, his face grim. "All due respect, Mrs. Perrone, how do I know this is really the secretary of state's office?" he said flatly. "Uh-huh, uh-huh. Okay, okay, I believe you." He took out his little pad and jotted down her phone number, listening all the while. "Got it. Thank you." He handed the phone back to Ernie Moran as if it were a piece of rotten fruit. "Okay," he said. "The notary's name on the form is Walter Street and there's no Walter Street registered as a notary in the state of New York. But—the notary number *is* registered. To Jeffrey White."

Walter Street . . .

"So what are we sayin' here?" Kerrigan demanded.

Walter Street . . . Walter Street . . .

Ernie Moran flipped a switch on the tiny phone and pocketed it.

"Educate me, O great Ern," continued Kerrigan. "Why would White notarize the beneficiary form but sign a fake name?"

"So you'd believe the date on it," said Nick with some certainty.

"Come again?" said Kerrigan.

"He said he wanted to make my life miserable."

"I don't understand," said Kerrigan. "And it's kinda starting to piss me off here."

"Detective," said Nick, "check that form. Does Walter Street have a middle name, or initial? The initial W?"

Kerrigan shuffled through the papers, then looked up. "How'd you know?" he asked.

"When we met, I called him Wally Wall Street. I was teasing him." She grabbed the insurance form out of Kerrigan's hand and examined the signature.

"Walter W. Street," she read. Then she looked up at Kerrigan. "Wally Wall Street."

Kerrigan digested this.

Ernie Moran spoke up. "I think the beneficiary form was *written* last Friday—the day before he died. But he *backdated* it—falsely—to ten days before that. And then he notarized the false form so it would look absolutely believable."

"To implicate me," said Nick.

"I'm not an expert," said Ernie Moran, gathering energy, "but look at this. The handwriting checks with the rest of the policy. See?" He flipped a few pages. White's signature and the signature of Walter W. Street appeared to be in an identical hand.

Ernie Moran went on. "I think Jeffrey White committed suicide—exactly as Miss Stallings said—and tried to make it look as if she could have done it. He knew that being the beneficiary would seem to give her a motive. He figured you'd check his life insurance. So he dated it ten days before they actually met. He knew she'd tell us when they'd *really* met, and there'd be a discrepancy. She would then look like a liar in everybody's eyes. We wouldn't believe anything she said after that. And frankly, Miss Stallings, at first I didn't."

Nick felt as though she were watching from a distance. She wondered if this was what was meant by an out of body experience. Kerrigan's eyes studied the notarized signature at the end of the policy. Moran continued.

"Miss Stallings tried to tell you, Detective, that it was ludicrous to leave Jeffrey White dead in her own apartment in order to collect his insurance. But then the medical examiner discovered the bruise, and you found out about the policy. You figured maybe she'd botched a plan—they'd had a fight or something—and she'd stabbed him impulsively. The fact that she left her apartment and sought the advice of a judge she barely knew *before* she called the police didn't help her story." He turned to Nick, whose knees were having spasms. "If you ever *do* murder someone, don't do that." No one spoke. "I think White knew we'd figure it out eventually," he added quietly. "Maybe that's why he didn't disguise his handwriting. I don't think he actually wanted you to go to jail."

Kerrigan broke in. "What about the bracelet?"

"What bracelet?" asked Fanning. Everyone ignored him.

Ernie Moran again pulled Nick away a few feet. His forehead was perspiring, and she could see that he was exhausted. "You told me the bracelet's a fake," he whispered. "You still say that?"

"Yes," she said.

Ernie Moran moved back to Kerrigan with Nick right behind him. He unfolded his phone, fished a scrap of paper from his pocket, and quickly punched an eleven-digit number.

"Who you calling, Ern?" asked Kerrigan.

"We're on a roll here," said Ernie Moran. "As Miss Stallings likes to say—I have a *feeling*." He waited a couple of rings and someone answered. "Mrs. White, please." He paused a second or two. "Tell her it's Detective Kerrigan, N.Y.P.D." He handed the phone to Kerrigan.

"You could blow the whole thing right here, Ern," said Kerrigan.

"Only if my client is a liar," said Ernie Moran, looking at Nick.

"Yes, Mrs. White. I'm sorry to bother you like this," said Kerrigan into the phone. He looked to Ernie Moran questioningly.

"Ask her," said Moran, "if her husband gave her an engraved gold bracelet." Kerrigan's lips tightened and Nick held her breath.

"Mrs. White . . . we'd just like to know—did your husband ever give you a gold bracelet with the words 'We'll always have last summer' engraved on it?" Kerrigan listened. "Really?" He nodded and raised his eyebrows. "Well, actually—it seems to have turned up. Yeah. That's all I needed to know, Mrs. White. We'll get back to you. Thanks." He handed the phone again to Ernie Moran.

"I used to think cellular phones were pretentious," said Ernie Moran. "But I don't know what I'd do without it now." He turned to Nick. "Jeffrey White planted the bracelet in your apartment, Miss Stallings. Made you look like even more of a liar."

"Well, I'll be a blue-nosed gopher," said Kerrigan. He nodded a few times to himself. "You know something? I ain't a judge, but then again, this ain't a trial either. So, fuck it. I'm recommending case dismissed."

Kerrigan, Ernie Moran, and Ferris Fanning each looked at Nick, whose legs buckled as she slid to the marble floor.

CHAPTER 24

They all swept down to help her, each taking an arm or wrist. She looked up at them and smiled wanly.

"What?" said Kerrigan.

She turned to Ernie Moran. "You *are* a Wizard, aren't you?" He shrugged again and helped her to her feet.

"You okay?" Fanning asked. "Need some water?"

"I'm not thirsty anymore, thanks."

"What can I say?" Kerrigan remarked, holding up the policy. "I'll send this over to the zone commander. He'll get it to the chief of detectives and . . . I'm pretty sure this is history."

"Can I count on that?" said Ernie Moran.

"As far as I'm concerned, hey—no more cuppy. I'm a happy man."

"Great, but how long before the zone commander and chief of detectives make their ruling?" asked The Wizard.

"Couple of days, maybe," said Kerrigan.

Moran shook his head. "Detective, my client has been taking a pretty bad beating from the folks outside. How about calling right now?" Kerrigan exhaled a little laugh of disbelief. Moran went on.

"Look, the press has been vicious. I'm wondering how they'll play it when they find out that you guys were making things so hard on an innocent woman. That there were leaks from the medical examiner's office, maybe even from this precinct? Miss Stallings and I might be willing to overlook some of this, but . . . how about expediting things? You can borrow my phone if you like. Please."

Kerrigan shook his head and smiled a half-smile. He looked at the mob of reporters, then at Nick and Moran, and finally said to Fanning. "I love the way this guy says 'Please.' And by the way, Ern, what *is* that?" he asked, throwing his chin up at the headpiece adorning Moran's baldness. "New fashion statement?"

"That's cancer," said Ernie Moran, clipped, holding his phone out to Kerrigan.

"Oh," said Kerrigan, off guard, nodding as his face flushed. He walked over to the phone on the reception desk and dialed four numbers. Nick, Moran, and Fanning waited. No one spoke. They heard Kerrigan say, "Then get me the chief." Kerrigan shifted his weight, shook his head, and cupped his hand over the receiver, talking to someone. His face betrayed nothing. He hung up and walked back to the group.

"You know what?" he said to Nick. "You can go home."

"It's my apartment again?"

"It's a little early, but—Merry Christmas," he said. "I'll have my boys take the tape off. You owe me, Moran. I like that. If she hadn'ta been all over the news, he would never have agreed, but, hey, the chief says he's satisfied and he'll sign the forty-nine." He looked at Nick. "That's the 'who-what-where-why-when.' Chief said it's a done deal. Oh, and Ern, he says you owe *him* too—which I also like." He clapped his hands once. "Now . . . I guess I'll have to get back upstairs and solve some real crimes." He started out, then stopped and turned to Nick. "Nothing personal, you know, Miss Stallings."

"Shut up," said Nick, who was still shaking a little. "I'm starting to like you."

Kerrigan looked at Moran. "Sorry I said that . . . about what you're wearing."

"Well, you never know," said Ernie Moran.

"Me, I never know anything," said Kerrigan, turning and moving quickly outside. The reporters closed in around him. Nick flexed the muscles in her calves to get her circulation going.

"Well," said Fanning. "I seem to be the odd man out here. . . ."

"Oh—I'm so sorry," said Nick, as though suddenly noticing a party guest she'd ignored. "It was very kind of you to come over."

"Well," he said awkwardly, "I'll . . . send you a bill for my time." Nick's jaw dropped, but before she had time to protest, Fanning reached for Ernie Moran's hand and pumped it. "My pleasure, sir." Then he turned around and headed toward the front doors.

"He's worth every penny," said Ernie Moran, deadpan.

Nick could hear a caterwauling outside.

"The natives are restless," she said.

"Per usual," said Ernie Moran.

"How do I thank you?" said Nick.

"I really do owe Joanne. Maybe we're even now."

"The Wizard of Ern," said Nick, shaking her head and looking at her feet. The reporters were starting to shout questions through the glass. "I'm glad I met you."

"It's been a while since I felt like a wizard, so I guess I'm glad too. Even if you did call in Ferris Fanning."

"I figured you didn't trust me, and then I thought you'd be furious that I talked to Mrs. White."

"Well, the trip to Hastings, though incredibly stupid—some might even say self-destructive—turned out well. And to be honest with you, I did something pretty stupid too. Just now."

"What?"

"The bracelet. White could have bought that bracelet on Friday, got a rush engraving job, and then, you know, distressed it—so it'd look old. I didn't think of that till Kerrigan was on the phone with

Mrs. White. If she hadn't known about the bracelet, this might've dragged on. God almighty," he said disgustedly, "I must be tired."

"You were great," she said. "Better than great."

He seemed not to hear her. "And, ah, as for my office—" He stopped.

"What?"

"It may never look quite the same to me." He looked away.

"Sorry," said Nick.

"There you go, apologizing again." He wiped the perspiration from his forehead. "There *is* something you could do for me."

"Name it," said Nick.

He was sizing up the crowd outside. "Come out and stand next to me while I make a statement." Connie Cuevas was first in line at the door.

Nick felt dizzy again. "Oh, God, no. Let's just use the back . . ." She started away.

"Listen," he said, stopping and turning her. "You've got to clear your name. The papers are going to drop this story fast. If you don't say something, everybody's last impression will be what they saw on the news last night and this morning." He was poised, leaning on the door. She dreaded it, but had the feeling he was right.

He opened the doors, and there was a mini-stampede of reporters' heels on the cement steps coming toward them. They shouted her name and pushed their whirring cameras forward, their tape recorders thrust out again. Ernie Moran summoned up a wide smile, put his arm around Nick, and raised a hand, stilling the din.

"Give us a statement, Miss Stallings!"

"Give us *something.*"

"Give me a break," said the *Post* guy, looking greasily at Nick. She turned away as quickly as she could, as if it might be possible to catch the death that was behind his eyes. There were fifty or more people across the street behind a blue wooden police barrier. Nick couldn't believe they had nothing better to do.

"Who are you?" another reporter called bluntly to Moran.

"My name is Ernest Moran," said Ern, ignoring the insulting tone. He was managing to sound almost breezy, like a politician on a whistle stop. "I represent Miss Stallings, and my client and I are happy that the investigation has cleared her of any implication whatsoever of wrongdoing. There are documents which the authorities have in their possession that show conclusively—"

Nick half listened, looking down to avoid the eager, earnest face of the ubiquitous Connie Cuevas. Nick's feet, in her damp sneakers, were starting to get cold. She wanted to call her mother. She closed her eyes.

Now make Daddy all right.

". . . the medical examiner is in complete concurrence. Miss Stallings has been through an unspeakable—"

Nick opened her eyes and looked at the crowd behind the barricade, not really taking in anything, waiting for Ernie Moran to finish. She supposed she'd have to say a few words too. She saw something move in the little crowd, then move again, and again. It was a hand, waving. Nick looked at the hand, then up to its face. The face was smiling—grinning, in fact, directly at Nick. She grinned back. It was refreshing to see a well-wisher. It was a man—familiar?—waving again, an exaggerated kid's wave, around and around in small little circles. It made Nick smile. And then she realized that it was Sam.

CHAPTER 25

She broke from Ernie Moran, leaving him in mid-speech, oblivious to the cameras following her in a straight line toward Sam.

"Miss Stallings, how do you feel?" said a reporter on her flank.

"Miss Stallings. Hi, Connie Cuevas, Action News." Connie seemed cheerful now, sing-songy. Her intonations, as always, sounded robotic to Nick. "I wonder if you could tell our viewers—"

She turned to Connie Cuevas. "No. Go away." She kept moving toward Sam as though she were in the midst of one of her frustration dreams, fearful that she might not get to him.

"Was there ever a *moment* when you were in *doubt,* Miss Stallings?" Connie asked, her head to one side like Barbara Walters.

"Where'd you learn to talk like that?" Nick asked, pushing in Sam's direction, manically matching Connie's friendly tone. "Journalism school? Or were you a flight attendant? Yes!" Nick said, clapping her hands. "That's it! Okay! Say 'Kindly remain seated until the plane *has* come to a complete halt.' Important to accent the word 'has.' Come on! Please?" Connie Cuevas took a few steps away, a quizzical look on her face, and mumbled something to her sound man. Nick turned to Sam.

But it wasn't Sam.

They stood face to face. He was the right height and his hair and complexion were like Sam's, but it wasn't Sam—and he was beaming at Connie as though star-struck.

"Just . . . a remarkably Sam-like presence," Nick muttered, and turned away, looking right into a camera that flashed in her face. People were asking questions, and she wasn't hearing them.

Then Ernie Moran was at her side, straight-arming reporters out of the way.

"Let's go," he said. A few cameras were still on them. She took his elbow and he pulled her under the barricade, steering her quickly down the street. Several reporters followed. Nick saw the *Post* photographer right behind them. She took her hand from Moran's elbow.

"Nothing personal," she said, walking faster. The *Post* guy danced along behind them, snapping away with a vicious smirk on his face.

Nick saw a cab waiting at a red light up ahead. "Come on!" she said, breaking into a run. A few more reporters were on their heels now.

"Where're we going?" said Ernie Moran as they reached the cab. Nick jerked the door open and they got in quickly.

The *Post* guy followed, snapping a few last times. He reached the cab just after them, and banged on the driver's window. He yelled to the startled cabbie, "Five-ten East 84th Street. That's where she's going." Then he peered into the back window and pointed to Nick. "We know where to find you," he added. The light changed.

"Go!" Nick said to the driver.

"Jesus," said The Wizard, looking at the *Post* guy through the window.

"I've gotta feed my fish," said Nick as the car started off. They didn't speak for a moment.

"To feed your fish," repeated Ernie Moran quietly. "Okay."

Nick looked out the window. "I can't . . . talk right now," she said. "Is that all right?"

"Yes," he said. They rode in silence. At Nick's building he offered to pay, but Nick had already thrust a few dollars into the cabbie's hand. A coatless young man was dozing against the wall by the front door. As Nick and Ernie Moran moved up the steps, he came to life.

"Miss Stallings!" he said, pulling out a small tape recorder. His manner was polite. "I'm from the *Post*. I wonder if you could tell me—"

"It's over," said Nick as she and Ernie Moran swept by him.

"I beg your pardon?" he asked, blinking.

"So you guys were double-teaming me, huh?" said Nick, stopping for a second.

"Call your editor or your boss," said Ernie Moran. "They'll tell you. Case dismissed. It's over. You gotta stay on top of these things."

"You mean I can go?" he asked.

Nick and Ernie Moran pressed on. Fernando was on duty, holding the door open for them. "Good morning, Miss Stallings," he said.

"The fish food, Fernando!" said Nick. "Have you got it?"

Fernando quickly reached into the doorman's closet. "You can go up now. They just call. Police all gone." She took the can, thanking him as she preceded Ernie Moran into the elevator.

Nick studied his face. He seemed restive, as though he might be in pain. At her floor she led him down the hall, fumbling for her keys. Someone's hurried removal of the police tape had taken strips of paint off her door. "Wait here, would you?"

"You really want to go in there alone?" said The Wizard.

"I'll be right out." She pushed the door open slowly, as if expecting someone to jump at her. She walked in and made her way toward the aquarium, careful not to look in the direction of the spot where Jeffrey had fallen. April and Mae were frighteningly still. She got up closer and pressed her nose to the glass. They were moving, just a little. She slid open the top of the fish food can and sprinkled some quickly along the top. The fish swam feebly up, then started to nibble eagerly.

"Chow down, girls," whispered Nick, sprinkling a little more. They perked up almost instantly. Nick kissed the glass. She stood up and started out, keeping her eyes fixed on the door to avoid The Spot. There was a faint odor of formaldehyde, or something that conjured up death to Nick's senses. Maybe she was imagining it. She kept walking.

"Everything okay?" Ernie Moran asked as she closed the door.

"Oh, boy," said Nick. "The fish are fed is all I can tell you." She pushed for the elevator. It was still at her floor, and they got in. She started to reach for the button, then turned to him. The doors closed.

"Have you got any time?" she asked.

He looked at his watch. "I have a meeting in about fifteen minutes, but it's only a couple of blocks from here. What's up?"

Instead of pushing the L button, she pushed 8. They rode up, and Nick led the way to Mr. Kazura's door. She knocked, knowing his bell didn't work.

"I'm not supposed to ask any questions, is that it?" Ernie Moran asked. Nick nodded. They waited.

"All visitors must be announced!" Mr. Kazura recited angrily from behind the closed door.

"Mr. Kazura, it's Nick."

Several locks clicked. Mr. Kazura opened the door still in his pajamas.

"Nick," he said, worried. "It's . . . okay?"

"It's okay, Mr. Kazura."

His face brightened. "I'm glad."

"I had a pretty good lawyer."

"Lawyer, schmoyer—I'm talking about June and April. Did they get their supper?"

"April and Mae, Mr. Kazura. Yes. Yes." She laughed a little. "Thanks to you, they're fine."

"Good. The other thing, you don't have to tell me about. It was on the radio. Congratulations."

"Mr. Kazura," said Nick suddenly. "I'd like to introduce you to"—she turned to her attorney—"my friend, Mr. Moran. This is my friend, Mr. Kazura."

"Hi," said The Wizard. They shook hands. Mr. Kazura looked at him.

"The lawyer?" said Mr. Kazura.

"Yes," said Ernie Moran. They both tried to smile, nodding. Nick said nothing.

Mr. Kazura made a stab at conversation. "I never met any friends of hers."

The Wizard nodded again.

Nick watched them for a second. They looked at her. "I just wanted you two to . . . meet," she said. "My two . . . men friends." Then she shook her head as though to clear some cobwebs. "I'm sorry to disturb you, Mr. Kazura."

"I'm grateful for disturbances," he said. Nick smiled. Ernie Moran didn't seem to know what to say.

"We'll see you, Mr. Kazura," said Nick.

"Whatever you say," said Mr. Kazura.

They headed back to the elevator. "I don't know why I did that," said Nick, embarrassed. She punched the down button. "So. Where's your meeting?"

"Not too far from here," he said. "St. Monica's Church, actually. You know it?"

The elevator arrived. They got in.

"What kind of meeting are you having in a church?"

"Uh," said Ernie Moran uncomfortably. "It's, ah . . . oh—what the hell. It's AA."

Oh, God.

"My wife was a drunk. Still is, I guess. She tried to convince me that I'm an alcoholic too. It was something we could do together— go to meetings. I'm not an alcoholic, I know that now. But when my diagnosis came in, I don't know—I started going back."

"I thought you meant, like, a client meeting."

"No."

"My mother goes to AA."

"Yeah?"

"I'm not sure how much good it does her, frankly. I mean, she didn't drink for five years, but she's still a pain in the ass."

"Maybe there's a Mothers' Anonymous," he said.

They left the elevator, moved out through the lobby and onto the street. It was crisp and bright, almost springlike.

"Are there phones there, at the meeting?" asked Nick.

"I think there's one outside the meeting room. Or you can borrow mine."

"I'll walk you. I don't feel like being alone right now," said Nick.

"Okay."

"I don't feel like talking much either. Do you mind? I need to sleep, but I can't go back up to my place yet."

"I know someone you should call before you go back in there," he said. "Check the Yellow Pages. Apex Cleaners. Real magicians. Trust me."

They walked a little in silence, then turned a corner. He led them toward an Italian Renaissance–style stucco and tile church. "It's in the basement," he said, going past the main entrance a few feet and leading her down a short flight of steps, through a dankly lit foyer and a long hallway. People were filing in around them, entering a small auditorium with rows of folding chairs. It looked as though it hadn't been painted in decades.

"There's the phone," he said. "I'll be out in fifty minutes. If you're here . . . I won't complain." As he went in, someone reached around from inside and closed the doors. Nick heard a voice on a tinny microphone.

"Welcome to the St. Monica's Monday noon meeting of AA. We hope you will find in this fellowship—"

Nick moved to the pay phone. She dialed Joanne. She didn't feel strong enough to have a conversation, and was actually hoping their machine would pick up. It did.

"My newlywed friends," Nick began, "Ernie Moran *is* a Wizard. It's over. Your raincoat is history, Joanne. I love you." She hung up and dialed her mother.

"Hello," said her mother, frogs in her throat.

"Hi, Mom."

"Oh, dear. Susie." She had never called Nick Susie. Only her father had ever called her that. "I heard from Jeanne Shea. I'm so . . . relieved. You must be—"

"I'm just tired, Mom. Anything about Dad?"

"No," said her mother. Nick felt her colon flip. "It's my punishment for drinking. Evidently they'll have the phones back on in St. Maarten today. It's all I can do to keep from having another drink."

"Don't do that, Mom," said Nick. "How do you feel? Are you hung over?"

"Yes. I'm just going out to an AA meeting. I can't believe I have to start over again. It's so depressing." Nick felt she was in 12-Step stereo. She could hear little snippets of the meeting going on inside the auditorium.

"Go to your meeting, Mom. And call me as soon as you know *anything*. Okay?"

"Of course. Thank you, dear. I just feel so humiliated about last night. Did I behave terribly?"

"Yup," said Nick.

"Oh, dear."

"You always did when you drank."

"Oh, dear." There was silence. "I have to go, Susan. I don't want to be late. Why don't you come over for dinner tonight? Would you do that?"

"I'll call you later, Mom. If there's no word from Dad, I'll come for dinner and we'll keep each other company until we know what's going on, okay?"

"Thank you."

"Bye, Mom." Nick hung up and flipped through the Yellow Pages attached to the phone until she got to Cleaning Services. She found the number.

"Apex," a loud male answered in a hefty Bronx accent.

"Do you clean apartments?" Nick asked.

"We clean anything and everything, ma'am," said the man impatiently.

"How are you with blood?"

"Anything and everything," the man repeated.

"Do you have emergency service?"

"Lady. This is New York. What do you want?"

"Can you send a team to 510 East 84th Street immediately?"

"How many rooms?"

"Mostly, it's just the living room. There's a large stain."

"We have a three-room minimum."

"What the hell. Do the whole place, then."

"I got a team'll be free at . . . let me see . . . 1:30. Is that too soon?"

"Nope," said Nick.

"Name?"

"Stallings. S-t-a-l-l . . ."

"I-n-g-s. I got it. We take cash or certified checks only. It'll be two hundred and fifty dollars. If the stain is really bad, it'll be three hundred."

"Then it'll be three hundred," said Nick. "Can you remove carpeting?"

"Wall-to-wall?"

"I'm afraid so," she said.

"Cost you extra, lady. But don't worry, we'll get the blood out."

"You haven't seen it."

"Let my men determine that. We'll see you at 1:30."

Nick hung up. From the auditorium she heard a little applause. Then the miked voice said, "Thanks for that share, Phil. It's always a pleasure to hear you. Okay. Any beginners here today?" Nick heard more clapping. She sank down on the bench, not yet aware she was eavesdropping. "Great. Keep coming. There are beginners' packets at the desk in back. We'll open the meeting for sharing now. Show of hands. Yes . . ."

"Hi, my name is Ernest."

Nick sat up. Her body ached so much that she told herself she couldn't move. Ernie Moran wasn't speaking into a mike, but she could just make out what he was saying.

"I was going to share about something else, but . . . I hate that word—share. Anyway, I met somebody. A client. Was. I'm a lawyer. Jesus, I don't even remember the last time I represented a woman. I've never really known how to be with women, except maybe sexually—and that part hasn't been working too well lately. I've been in radiation and chemo for the past couple of months. I started coming back to these rooms to help me cope with the fact that—" He cleared his throat. "The first opinion I got was that I'd probably hang on for a few years. So like a jerk I went for a second opinion, and this one tells me it could be more, it could be less. I mean, nobody knows. And—what am I saying here? I can't really talk about this. So. This woman—" He paused. Nick held her breath and moved a little closer to the door. "Anyway," he said finally, "thanks."

Nick heard someone else begin to talk. Disappointed, she moved back to the phone and dialed Martine. It rang a few times.

Please be there.

The machine answered, played the waterfally music, and beeped.

"Martine, it's Nick. I really need to talk to you. Are you there? No, you're not—"

Martine picked up. "God almighty. How *are* you?"

"Can you talk?"

"I'm in a group session. . . ."

"When can I call you?"

"After five. Can you hold out till then?"

"I, uh, okay. Okay. Thanks."

"You sure? Do you have a good lawyer?"

"Oh—it's all over, Martine. That part anyway."

"Thank God. Call me after five. At home. You have the number, right?"

"Yes. Yes," said Nick, her eyes on the doors. "Bye."

She hung up and moved closer to the doors. A woman was speaking now. Nick put her hand on the doorknob and turned it. It wasn't locked. She hesitated, then tried it again, pushing it open slowly. A few heads turned to look at her, then back to the woman speaking. Ernie Moran stared, shocked, then made a face as if to ask if she wanted him to leave with her. She motioned for him to stay put. Then she sat down in the back row. The woman finished talking. Nick saw people raise their hands, and then felt her own shoot up. The tough-looking man who was running the meeting called on her at once. She felt everyone's gaze. Her heart was pounding harder than it had since she'd opened the door for the room service boy at the Pierre Hotel just a little over three days before.

"Hi," she said. "I'm, um, an actress, and I played an alcoholic once, on a soap opera, so I think I know how this is done." She took a breath. "Okay . . . my name is . . . Susan . . ."

"Hi, Susan," they all said simply.

". . . and I'm . . . a junkie . . ." She wasn't sure if her body could withstand another bout of shaking, but it was going to be put to the test. "That's . . . all I'm going to say right now, today." She rose. As she did, a young man with an eager face reached for a beginners' packet and handed it to her. She took it, and kept walking, out the doors, down the hall, and into the street. She prayed that Ernie Moran wouldn't follow. She didn't think she could take feeling anything more. Her prayer wasn't answered. He was quickly behind her.

"Hey," he called.

Nick stopped and turned. "I'm going home now."

"That took some balls—"

"I don't know," said Nick, her eyes blinking as she tried to find something on which to focus. "I . . . just want it to stop hurting."

"Oh, well, in that case," said Ernie Moran matter-of-factly, "have a drink. Or smoke something. Maybe eat, shop, gamble. A little sex." He rolled some air around in his cheeks for a few seconds. "Unless you want to let it hurt."

"How do you do that?" she asked as if she were in a great hurry. "How do you just let it hurt?"

"Simple," he answered. "I don't have any choice." Nick looked dismayed. "Okay," he said as if to change the subject. "I'm . . . going back in now." He started in toward the church.

She took a step in the opposite direction but turned again to him suddenly. "I called Apex."

He paused, pivoted, and faced her. "May you . . . always have clean carpets." He moved away again.

Let him go.

"You should take off work for a while," she said abruptly. It stopped him. "Lower the stress. If you got a lot of rest—you know? I've heard of miraculous things . . ."

She felt stupid, and didn't finish the sentence.

"I never want to hear another word about stress," he said, unsmiling. "I've fouled out—okay? This stuff spreads like wildfire. Which is what it feels like." He took a step away, then turned back to her. "Don't take it personally. It's just better for me not to be around people when it decides to hurt."

Let him go.

"Do you have . . . women friends, Mr. Moran?" He grimaced at her formality. "Sorry," she continued, "I can't bring myself to call you Ern."

"Women friends? That's an oxymoron."

"I should know what that means," she said impatiently, "but I don't."

"Words that sound right together, but contradict each other.

'Military intelligence.' 'Radiation therapy.' 'Woman friend.' Never got the hang of it."

"Me either. With men, I mean."

"Well, don't start with me, okay?" he said.

They stood for a moment, looking in different directions. Nick peered up the street, squinting at nothing. "I'm sorry about . . . your office."

"Are you kidding? For ten minutes I didn't feel any pain."

A mild gust swirled around them, and a dirty fragment of a straw's wrapper flew by Nick's face. She swatted at it as though it were a fly.

"The garbage is alive in this city," she grumbled. "I swear to God—"

"Look," he interrupted, "if you're starting on the program, you're gonna need—" He closed his eyes, as if from sudden pain. He opened them again, with effort. "Don't be too . . . alone, okay? It's unhealthy. Trust me on this."

She glanced down at the packet in her hand. "Okay," she said, moving away sideways.

"On the other hand," he offered, "alone is not a bad thing."

"Make up your mind," she said.

"I don't have to do anything of the sort," he said. "I've always been a black and white kind of guy, but I'm planning to spend the next couple of months vacationing in ambiguity—so sue me." He moved around until his eyes found hers. "Look, we may not see each other again and I have a feeling there's no hereafter, so let me tell you something. As long as you can't enjoy being alone . . . you're gonna be alone."

"What are you—the Sphinx?" she asked testily.

"The Wizard, The Wizard," he prompted, unoffended.

"I'm sorry," she said, shaking her head, "I'm on overload. I have to go."

"You're always sorry about something," he said, irritated. "Stop doing things that make you sorry. Then you can stop saying 'I'm sorry.' "

"You know," she answered, chafing, "I go to a shrink for that kind of wisdom."

He looked around. "Is somebody *forcing* you to stand here and talk to me?"

"I was trying not to be rude," she said, raising her voice a little.

"Be rude! Be rude, for Christ's sake!"

"I don't know, I don't know," she said with her hands over her ears. "I just want to go home."

"Please—in this city, if you're not rude to me, somebody else will be. I'd rather it be you than a total stranger."

"So," said Nick, still trying to get her bearings, "you like me?"

"What are *you*—Sally Field? Yes. I like you. Now, run along."

She pushed through simultaneous urges to cry or yell. "Then why are you patronizing me?"

"Because I don't know what to do with you! I can't seduce you. My body doesn't work. There isn't time to be friends. Ex-clients disappear as soon as they're out of trouble. I've seen you without your clothes on. Jesus," he muttered to the air, "listen to me, this is a goddamn play-by-play. You want to go to a Knicks game?"

"Maybe," she said without missing a beat.

"I yell a lot. I make a complete ass out of myself. It scares people."

She stared at him, frowning. "Are you going to die on me?"

"Oh, Christ!" he said, exasperated. "What if *you* get run over by the proverbial ice cream truck? Come on. Do you or do you not want to go to a Knicks game?"

"I never really liked basketball—"

"Well, don't do me any goddamn favors—"

"But, yes. Okay."

"Fine," he said, biting off the word. "I'll call you." He started away again.

"Fine," she said after him.

She whipped around and headed toward her apartment, breaking into long strides though everything in her hurt. In minutes she was back at her building, and as she went by Fernando, she noticed it was almost one o'clock.

"Fernando," she said.

"Yes, Miss Stallings."

"Apex Cleaners are coming in a little while. You can send them up."

"Okay, Miss Stallings."

She remembered she had no cash or checkbook with which to pay the cleaners. The thought of going to the bank right now made her tremble. "Fernando. I'm afraid I have another favor to ask."

"Sure, Miss Stallings."

"I've . . . lost my checkbook and my bank card. If I call and tell them you're coming, do you think one of the guys downstairs could watch the door while you run over to the bank and withdraw some money for me? I don't want to go out in public today."

Fernando reached into his pocket and pulled out a tightly rolled wad of bills. "How much you need, Miss Stallings?"

"Oh, that's sweet, Fernando, but I'm afraid I need three or four hundred dollars." He peeled away a few singles and fives, quickly reaching buried twenties and fifties, smoothly extracting four hundred and presenting it to her with a smile.

"I'll . . . write you a check . . . as soon as I get my new checkbook," she said, embarrassed. She started for the elevator, then stopped. "Thank you," she said, meaning, for everything.

"You famous, Miss Stallings. Thank *you*."

Nick rode upstairs and walked into the apartment. She couldn't shake a chill, and kept her coat on. She started to go past The Spot again, but this time she stopped, turned, and made herself look. She began to heave at the sight of the partly crusty, partly glistening oozy redness. She took a deep breath, forcing herself not to look away. She stared for a moment until the urge to vomit eased. Then she sat. She inhaled, noticing a death-smell she'd noticed before. Had the police sprinkled something on the ground—or on the body? She knew she should open a window, but she couldn't make herself get up. She looked again at The Spot. It seemed endless, moving from the rug, seeping up into the couch, and, no doubt, having made its way into the wood below. She wanted to sleep, but knew there would be no sleep here until the cleaners left, if ever. She might have to go to her mother's. Or Joanne and Frankie's. Maybe she'd call Todd. She felt a rather pure yearning for sex, any sex, even as exhausted as she was. To her disgust, she found herself drifting into a garden-variety fantasy of slipping into something provocative to greet the Apex Cleaning team.

No. I've just been on TV. They'll know me. They'll tell someone.

No. They'll be glad. I know how to make them glad. Who would they tell? No one's ever told before.

I'm a junkie. I'm lucky not to be in jail.

It was too early to call Martine. Her doorbell rang. She walked over to let them in. She was appalled to notice that she wasn't sure, as she had never been sure, whether she wanted the men to be attractive so she might feel compelled to do something, or unattractive, so she wouldn't want to. She opened the door. It was two men, one dark, one fair, neither handsome, though the dark one was appealing in a burly, blue-collar way that Nick had all her life found disarming.

Oh, God . . .

She led them in and pointed out the stain. "No questions, please," she said simply. They studied it, chagrined but determined. The fair one, she was sure, recognized her. Nick sat in a chair and watched. The dark one glanced her way occasionally. She glanced back once, but broke off contact, unwilling or unable to summon up the energy behind the eyes. After an hour her mother called with good news about her father. Nick cried. She moved to a chair by the aquarium and watched April and Mae, now moving gamely through their little world.

The phone rang often, but Nick switched off the ringer and turned down the volume on the answering machine, hearing only its occasional barrage of clicks. At her request, the Apex team removed the carpet and scrubbed out the wood beneath The Spot. There were more glances from the dark guy. Nick met his eyes, neither encouraging nor discouraging him. She placed a small area rug from her closet where The Spot had been. She had them take away the couch, covered in plastic and canvas.

It took them three hours to finish, and, to Nick's shame, it took her just as long to decide to do nothing but watch.

It was starting to get dark when they left. She turned on all the lights in the apartment and lay down on top of her bed, too exhausted to move, intending only to nap. When she woke it was past midnight, too late to call Martine. She was afraid to move around the apartment. She stayed on top of the bed, clothes on, lights on. Each time she closed her eyes, sounds, voices, and images of the past three days attacked her into greater wakefulness. She turned over and looked at her answering machine. The green digital message counter read 32. She hit the playback switch and it started to rewind, but then, dreading to hear them all, she suddenly punched the Play button. It started in the middle of a message from her agent, Linda Blake.

". . . so, anyway, just please, please call as *soon* as you get this. Okay? I mean it." The machine beeped.

"Nick? It's Linda again. I'm going totally nuts here. Natalie Le-Vine has been calling me, I swear to God, every fifteen minutes. Sidney Halpern just called *himself*. I kid you not. He said he saw you on the news last night too. He said he hadn't seen it when you were in the office, but he said the camera loves you. Please God, check your fucking machine. Okay. Listen. Sidney's flying back to L.A. tomorrow at noon. *But.* They're not even asking for a meeting now. It's a firm offer. Shoots for three months in North Carolina. He wants to get together with you for breakfast and answer any questions you might have. *How can you not be there?* They're so goddamn nuts, I told them you're thinking about it. I mean, trust me, I had to tell them *something*. Please, *please* call me, assuming I don't have a heart attack and drop dead. Oh, dear, I'm . . . I didn't mean . . . that wasn't a good choice of words. Where in hell *are* you?" It was the last message.

She felt a twitch in her shoulder. It was as though her shoulder were laughing. It twitched and twitched. She wanted to laugh with her whole body, but her fear of whatever was in the living room didn't quite allow it. I must sleep, she thought, lying down and closing her eyes again. She tried deep breathing. She got up and turned off her main reading light so there wasn't quite such a glare in her eyes. The twitch continued. She sat up and tried meditating for the first time in years, but she couldn't remember her mantra.

She reached for her vibrator, as always tucked out of sight under her bed so she could get to it on impulse. It was dusty and had never before seemed so big and unwieldy. The brand name Panasonic in bold letters struck her as absurd. Furthermore, she was surprised to notice, she didn't feel like sex. She put it back. She inserted earplugs, but the sound of her heartbeat rang in her head. Besides, she thought, if there are monsters in the apartment, I want to hear them coming.

Utterly awake, she zapped on the TV, but the cable was apparently out, and reception was almost nonexistent. She tossed the remote control down, slipped off the bed and over to the bathroom, sat on the toilet, and thumbed through a year-old copy of *Architectural Digest* she'd bought when she and Hal had been thinking about buying a house together. On her way back to bed, she decided to try turning out the lights in her bedroom and leaving the door open, so that light from the hallway and living room could still get in. She checked her closet to make sure there was no one in it. She got down and looked under the bed. As she stood up, she faced the window. It gave her an idea. She moved closer to it, pulling up an old wicker rocking chair she kept close by for gazing at the small patch of sky her view afforded her. She sat, looked out, and with mixed feelings came upon a star, distant and barely bright enough to make it through the city's haze.

No wish came immediately to mind.

Dear God. There's a little star up there, twinkling, twinkling, but I don't know what to wish, or pray for. I feel like I've probably used up a lifetime of wishes. Thank you for . . . everything. On the other hand, Jeffrey lied to me about his sex life so I guess I'm holding a ticket to the AIDS lottery. I'm a declared junkie. I don't know anything about sex. Well, I know a lot about sex, but—I feel like I'm in a very nice minimum-security prison, and the walls of the prison are my body and my desires. Apparently I'm in for life, and I'm just afraid that I'll want to break out. I always have. I mean, no slammer has ever been able to hold me. Okay. I guess . . . I pray for enough money to keep seeing Martine. I mean, what does the girl who has everything pray for? Sleep? That'd be nice . . .

Suddenly she started to breathe deeply, heavily, involuntarily. Waves of oxygen began to rush through her. She seemed powerless to stop, becoming charged, tingling with energy. She began to feel as if her body were much, much larger than it was. She wondered how the room could hold her. She seemed to be less afraid. The breathing had a life of its own. It made her laugh. She looked around to see what or who was making this happen. The breathing continued. She started to cry. She looked out at the star. She twitched and laughed and cried and breathed, as if only the breath could fuel the crazy mix of actions her body was taking. There were tears for a life of unintimate sex which had always diverted her energy and attention from grander goals. She laughed at the thought of breakfast with Sidney Halpern and a part in a movie. She wept at the image of Devon White and his little sister and she wondered if God would ever forgive her for that, or if she'd forgive herself. She cried for Ernie Moran, and for Susan, who had only been over- and under-mothered—yet she couldn't help laughing at the thought of the incorrigible woman who had brought her into the world.

The breathing made her stand up, her back arched and her arms at her sides, palms open. She felt as though she were presenting herself —to the star, to God, and to herself for the first time. She turned and looked into the full-length mirror on her closet door. She tossed off her coat and her other clothes, and touched her skin and looked down at her breasts, her stomach, her body. The breathing now had crested into a smooth flow. She swiveled and found the star again.

I'd like to be a mother. And please give me more of a clue than mine had.

She turned back to the mirror, and then, as she hadn't since she was a little child, she moved to the glass and gently kissed herself on the lips. It was a kiss of greeting, and her arms followed, embracing her image in the glass as tears ran down her face, wetting the mirror. She stood back a little and stared. She would always think her face was too long, her eyes too small, her nose all wrong. It made her smile. She reached out a finger, which met its reflection as if re-uniting her with an almost forgotten friend.

"Hi," she whispered.

A C K N O W L E D G M E N T S

I'm grateful to my parents, who read a lot, and whose implicit, easy-going love of books was an example to me. My mother showed me that a book could make me laugh out loud. My father's admiration of clear writing taught me to choose words carefully.

In high school, I was blessed with a great teacher, Charles Aschmann, now deceased. He made his students write and read far more than the norm, and taught me to be wary of mere cleverness. At Amherst College, I was the beneficiary of a core curriculum that forced all incoming students to write more than we thought we wanted to. If I fell back on "I just can't put it in words," I learned I probably didn't know what I was talking about. I was fortunate to study with Prof. Kim Townsend, who taught me that my own response to experience must form the basis of my writing. In retrospect this seems obvious, but it was revolutionary to a freshman who'd made it to Amherst, I thought, by pleasing others and regurgitating their ideas. I'm forever indebted to the late Nikos Psacharopoulos, who produced my play *Super Sunday* at the Williamstown Theatre Festival, and whose appreciation of my writing made me feel that I must keep going.

Thanks: to Jamie Lee Curtis, whose dinner party inadvertently inspired me to begin this novel, and whose encouragement while I was writing was invaluable; to Alice Gerstman, Kenneth I. Starr, Nancy McQuade, and Cyrus Collins, early and reassuring readers; to Tommy Sullivan, N.Y.P.D., for his thoughtfulness, advice, and time; to Peggy Noonan for her criticism and tips; to Barrett J. Clisby and Edwin H. Roberts, Jr., of Roberts & Clisby in Oxford, Mississippi, for their generous loan of office space where a great deal of the book was written; to Marsha Kisner, Kathy Alexander, and Dana Harwell of Roberts & Clisby for Southern hospitality, good cheer, and message-taking; to Arthur Ginsburg of Frankfurt, Garbus for sharing his expertise in criminal law; to Christopher Guest for encouragement through the years; to Ken Page of New York Telephone and Gwen Grandberry of Pacific Telephone for technical advice; to Meg Blackstone for her enthusiasm, skill, and enormously helpful suggestions at a critical time in the life of this book; to Harvey Klinger, a dream of an agent; to Irwyn Applebaum and Bantam, for taking a chance; to Beverly Lewis, my patient, painstaking editor and my ideal reader.

Finally, to my wife, Faye Grant, for above-and-beyond-the-call-of-duty feedback, editing, ideas, and support—needed and requested at all times of the day and night—without which I couldn't have proceeded or finished.